Cara Lockwood is the *USA TODAY* bestselling author of more than twenty-eight books, including *I Do (But I Don't)*, which was made into a Lifetime Original movie. She's written the Bard Academy series for young adults, and has had her work translated into several languages around the world. Born and raised in Dallas, Cara now lives near Chicago with her husband and their blended family. Find out more about her at caralockwood.com, friend her on Facebook, Facebook.com/authorcaralockwood, or follow her on Twitter, @caralockwood, or Instagram, Instagram.com/cara_lockwood.

If you liked
The Last Affair and *The Love Cure*
why not try

The Player by Stefanie London
Our Little Secret by Rachael Stewart

Also by A.C. Arthur

A Private Affair
At Your Service

Also by Cara Lockwood

Masquerade
Cuffs
The Sex Cure
Double Dare You
Hot Mistake
First Class Sin
Look at Me
No Strings

Discover more at millsandboon.co.uk

THE LAST AFFAIR

A.C. ARTHUR

THE LOVE CURE

CARA LOCKWOOD

MILLS & BOON

First Published in Great Britain 2021
by Mills & Boon, an imprint of HarperCollins*Publishers*
1 London Bridge Street, London, SE1 9GF

The Last Affair © 2021 Artist C. Arthur

The Love Cure © 2021 Cara Lockwood

ISBN: 978-0-263-29791-1

MIX
Paper from
responsible sources
FSC® C007454

This book is produced from independently certified FSC™ paper
to ensure responsible forest management.
For more information visit www.harpercollins.co.uk/green.

Printed and bound in Spain
by CPI, Barcelona

THE LAST AFFAIR

A.C. ARTHUR

MILLS & BOON

CHAPTER ONE

Aurora Mountain Ski Resort
Finger Lakes Region, New York

DESTA HENNER WALKED into the main hall of the ski resort like a boss. That is, her shoulders were back, her chin held high, her steps assured, and nothing but confidence radiated from her body. That's how her assistant, Nessa, described the way Desta entered any marketing meeting. Even thousands of miles away from the office, the same energy applied.

Check-in to the Dear Lover weekend retreat had taken fifteen of the longest minutes of her life, possibly because she'd confirmed her attendance and made reservations at the last minute. Now she wore her name badge proudly and walked past all the people she didn't know, giving nods and smiles before coming to a stop at the farthest corner of the room.

This might be a mistake. Some things were better left unchanged. Especially good things, which was precisely what she'd had for the last three months. An online connection with an intelligent thirty-three-year-old man who shared her love of R&B music and foreplay. Who would've thought a virtual relationship could've brought her so much joy and fulfillment? More importantly, after all she'd been through, who would've thought she'd crave any of those things with a man again? Certainly not her, but she'd taken a chance when she'd signed up for the Dear Lover app. Tonight, she'd meet Dear Lover 1687 for the first time face-to-face.

"Hello, beautiful."

She spun around, barely noticing the trip in her pulse at the sound of a deep and alluring male voice.

"Hello." He was taller than her, so she tilted her head to meet his gaze.

"Why're you standing all the way over here by yourself? This is Mix 'n' Mingle time." She supposed he meant to highlight those words with the waggle of his eyebrows, but it just came across as weird. Besides, she knew what time it was. She'd read the agenda that had been emailed with her confirmation a couple times already.

"I just arrived after a very long drive from the city." Not exactly true. She'd gone to her room after checking in, taken a shower and changed for the welcome party. In addition to being tall, the man had an athletic build, sandy-brown hair cut low and neat, sea-green eyes and a charming smile.

Was this Dear Lover 1687?

Dear Lover offered full anonymity; all posts went through their message board so personal email addresses were hidden. User identifications were numbers instead of some variation of the person's name or nickname. And when couples linked up, they were strongly advised not to reveal any personally identifying information. So, she and Dear Lover 1687 hadn't discussed anything outside of world news, favorite foods, dream vacations and, of course, every sexual position, fetish and/or fantasy they'd ever had. None of which were helpful in figuring out if he was the guy standing in front of her.

"Well, it's Friday, and I don't care what my watch says. It's five o'clock somewhere, so we're having a drink." He snagged two champagne flutes from a passing server's tray and offered her one.

Accepting the glass with a slow smile was polite, but she needed to cut to the chase. "What's your user number? Aren't we supposed to wear them so we can meet up with the one we've been talking to?" After all, that was the purpose of being here. While the Dear Lover app was advertised as just a social networking site for adults, private events were held for their members four times a year. Attendance was voluntary.

Before answering her question, the cheerful green-eyed guy put the glass to his lips, emptied the contents and then stuck a hand in his pocket to pull out a badge.

"This is a long weekend, baby. We're not confined to one meetup." Again with the pet names he probably thought were cute and the strange eyebrow waggling. This time, after she'd peeped the number on his badge, both actions were registering as creepy.

Plus, he wasn't Dear Lover 1687.

"I only came to meet one person." In case he didn't understand the words, she shook her head so vehemently it almost caused an instant headache.

"But it's time to mingle." No doubt hunting for another drink or possibly another meetup, he searched the crowd before returning his attention to her. "And you look hot in that dress. We can keep each other company until our matches arrive."

"I'd rather not." She knew it sounded snippy and probably a little uptight, which were words she'd heard used to describe herself before, but it wasn't intentional. "To be honest, I'm kind of nervous about this first meeting, so I'd really like to get it over with."

Had she just admitted to a stranger that she was nervous? She had, and that was unusual, but it didn't stop her from walking away from Mr. Green Eyes. Desta didn't share her emotions or her personal life with people she'd just met. Butterflies did a quick tango in her stomach, and she took a gulp from her glass. It was great champagne; she might need another one very soon.

By the time she finished the drink, she'd walked halfway across the room to another quiet spot near a wall of floor-to-ceiling windows. The breathtaking views immediately calmed her. Straight ahead was a light wood deck that seemed to stretch the length of the building. Farther out were snowcapped mountains, rolling hills covered in more white fluffiness and a series of smaller buildings that resembled this one in wood coloring and modern rustic design.

"Champagne?"

She managed a genuine smile for the server who'd appeared on her left. It took less than a second to tip her head back and empty the current glass. An additional few moments and she'd traded for another drink and took a sip. Yes indeed, they could keep the champagne coming all night and she wouldn't mind. Her high tolerance for alcohol had always been a source of contention with her five older brothers, who met a drunken stupor three to four drinks in, but tonight it might just come in handy.

As she stared out the window it occurred to her that she was hiding, and that wasn't acceptable. Invitations for this event had flooded her inbox, and eventually she'd decided that signing up for the app and chatting online was no longer enough. If she were really going to reclaim all of her life, she had to take the next step. Standing in a corner downing champagne was a far cry from the fun and exciting weekend the Dear Lover meetup had promised.

She took a deep breath and another sip of champagne to restart her boss mode; then she relaxed her face into a welcoming smile and turned to face the crowd. Suddenly, her breath caught. She gripped the stem of the glass and began to choke.

What the hell was *he* doing here?

"You okay, hon?" came a voice nearby.

As Desta struggled to keep from gagging on a combo of shock and champagne, a woman approached and began patting her back.

"I'm…fine. Just—" Desta cleared her throat. "Fine."

"Okay. We wouldn't want you collapsing on the floor before the fun can begin." The woman's hand was still on Desta's back, even though she was no longer coughing.

"Really, I'm fine. Just went down the wrong way, I suppose." Or she'd seen someone she shouldn't have seen. This room was full of people, how was it possible that she'd zeroed in on him immediately? Her heart pounded in her chest as she chanced another glance in his direction. His gaze shifted and she immediately turned away. Dammit! It really was him.

The woman nodded, her big bouncy curls in a fiery shade of red brushing over her shoulder with the action. "I'm Kelli, with an *i*. This is my second Dear Lover event. How 'bout you?"

Second? Had she struck out with her first match?

"I'm Desta." She resisted the urge to add *with an* a. Instead she said, "This is my first event." And in a few minutes it was going to be her last, because if *he* didn't leave, she would.

"Oh, then you're really lucky I stopped by to keep you from choking to death," Kelli said. "I can show you the ropes, and if it's not a good face-to-face matchup for either of us, we can just hang out this weekend and ditch the full agenda."

That would certainly bring Desta great joy. A weekend with a woman she didn't know.

"Actually, I may just head back to the city tonight. I have so much work to catch up on at the office."

Yesterday was Thanksgiving, and the office was closed from Wednesday to Monday. Ronald Gold Fashions might be one of the top fashion houses in the world, but it was also a family business, and its owner and head designer, Ronald Gold Sr., was all about spending time with family. As Desta didn't have any family on the East Coast, holidays were the best time for her to catch up on emails and research.

Admittedly, she probably should've remained focused on work from the start. Then she wouldn't be in this position—torn between meeting her match and being spotted by the one man who'd tease her relentlessly for being here while making it impossible to separate this private weekend from her professional life.

"Nonsense." Kelli waved a hand with silver rings on each finger. "Look, we'll exchange numbers and keep in touch via text throughout the night. If it looks like our meetups are a miss, we'll gather at the bar and drink till we can barely make it up to our rooms. And in the morning, we'll hit the slopes!" Kelli talked while retrieving her phone from her leather purse.

There was no need for a number exchange if she wasn't staying the weekend. But wouldn't that be running, something she'd promised herself not to do again? With her thoughts still in a jumble she dug into her RGold clutch and pulled out her phone.

About a minute later, Kelli was all smiles once more as she dropped her phone back into her purse. "There, now we're all set. Remember, keep in touch, and I'll see ya in a bit."

Desta's response was a nod and another smile before "Okay. See ya in a bit." Those words didn't even sound right coming from her, but Kelli's upbeat personality was easy to follow.

He laughed, and Desta froze. She knew that chuckle, which started in the depths of his gut and eventually burst out so anyone hearing it would fall into laughter as well. He had a very infectious personality. Maybe he was Kelli's match?

It didn't matter who he was here to meet: he couldn't see her here.

Desta started to move, heading for the door. She didn't bother to pinpoint his location in the room now. He had to be close if she could hear him laughing. Kelli would get a text from her when she got in the car, but now she had to get out of here. No way could she be seen by Maurice Gold. Her boss's son, her coworker and the guy she routinely beat in poker when she visited his parents' house. How totally weird would that be? Having Maurice—the consummate practical joker—find out she'd resorted to an app like Dear Lover to have a social life would definitely create awkwardness at work.

Her exit path had been clear at first, but there was suddenly a slew of people in her way, one of which was a server Desta collided with in her attempt to sidestep the crowd. She dropped her empty glass seconds before everything around her shifted into slow motion. The server's wide-eyed shock morphed into dread as his arm shook from the impact and the tray full of champagne flutes wobbled. Mortification lodged in Desta's chest as she watched the golden liquid sloshing over the rim of those glasses. And as if that weren't enough to prove she'd made a mistake coming here, there was Maurice's concerned face as he reached for the tray and easily plucked it from the server's hand.

Slow motion switched to real time, and Maurice's brow furrowed. "Hey, Des. What're you doing here?"

For the first time in the five years he'd known her, Desta didn't have a quick response. In fact, from the way she was blinking repeatedly, with her lips drawn in that straight line, which usually meant she was annoyed about something, he'd say she was either as shocked to see him as he was her or she was pissed that he was here at all.

"I'll take that," the server snapped before repossessing the tray Maurice had rescued.

"Sure, no problem. Glad to be of assistance." The guy's frown was about as much of a thank-you as he figured he was going to get. Maurice wasn't sorry to see him go.

He was, however, still trying to figure out why Desta—the marketing director at his family's fashion house and the most composed woman he knew—was here at a weekend meetup that, despite its advertising, was sure to be full of frolicking and fetishizing.

"You look really great in that dress." Actually, she looked phenomenal in the short, off-the-shoulder design that could've been made to fit her curves specifically.

"Thanks. You look nice, too." She shifted her weight from one foot to the other, holding her purse in front of her body with both hands. "And I could ask what you're doing here as well."

She could, and that would be just like Des—always ready with questions at any meeting or runway show and expecting quick answers. For a moment Maurice wondered how he should respond. Should he just come out and say he was there to meet the woman who'd had him jerking off in his bed too many nights to count in the past few months? Or should he come up with some other entertaining story about why he was at this ski resort, in this room, wearing the same badge…she was wearing.

"Are you registered with Dear Lover?" The surprised chuckle that followed the question barely had a chance to bubble free when he reached out and lifted her badge from where it was clipped to the top pleat of her dress.

Dear Lover 1288. He knew those numbers very well.

When he dragged his gaze back up to her face, she was directing her eyes to where his badge was boldly clipped to the lapel of his smoke-gray sports coat.

"No." The one word came in a whisper as she finally looked up at him. "This is a joke, right? You're playing one of your goofy practical jokes on me, and I swear to you, Maurice Silas Gold, my revenge is gonna be epic!"

She spoke the last through clenched teeth, and a part of him wanted to tell her she was right. He could easily throw his head back and laugh like he was watching a Kevin Hart stand-up, and she'd believe he'd constructed this elaborate hoax as one of the annual pranks he pulled on her and his siblings. That would've gotten him out of the very uncomfortable spot he was experiencing at this moment.

A variety of emotions went through him, and *uncomfortable* was the least of them. First and foremost, there was the physical reaction—lust, pure and simple—as he recalled all the messages they'd exchanged and how aroused he'd become reading them. Connecting each word from those emails to the sexy-as-hell woman he was staring at now was a little jarring and a lot exciting. But he couldn't have been lusting after Des like this for the past few months. Her calm and controlled personality wasn't his usual type, not to mention the whole coworker situation. In fact, she was more than just a coworker, thanks to his parents always inviting her to their family events because she had no family of her own in New York. Eventually, he'd come to see her as another sister.

Well, that certainly was no longer the case. The woman who'd been at Thanksgiving dinner with his family last night now collided with the woman who'd given him an in-depth explanation of why she loved the doggy-style position during sex. No way was he ever going to look at Des the same now. "Maybe we should go someplace private to talk about this."

She closed her eyes at his suggestion, her long, curled lashes dropping. When they lifted again, she stared back at him with resolution.

Her answer was to turn and start walking toward the door. He followed, letting his gaze drop to the easy and very tempting sway of her ass. She had the age-old and much-coveted Coca-Cola-bottle shape, and from this view, it added to his already growing erection. This was something Maurice had long ago noticed. Des was a great-looking woman. She was dangerously smart, fiercely independent and competitive as hell. Any man would be lucky to have her.

This time yesterday, he would've sworn he was not that man. Yet, here he was, wondering how it was possible that she was the sexy vixen who'd coaxed him to jerk off for the first time since high school?

In less than two minutes they were in the lobby of the ski lodge, going to a far corner where couches were positioned in a cozy square facing a huge open fireplace. Des sat on the end of one couch, and Maurice sat at the end of another a couple feet from her.

"You're the one who's been messaging me all this time?"

Leave it to Des to dive right in before anyone else in the room could talk. It's what she did at meetings.

Particularly when someone in a meeting was acting like she didn't exist. He'd always admired her talent in the business arena and counted her as a very valuable asset to their company. Now, he had to consider if also being insanely attracted to the woman behind all the sexy words was worth jeopardizing the company's biggest marketing asset.

"*We've* been messaging *each other*." He wanted to make sure she accepted that they'd both created this scenario.

"Why? You can get a date by snapping your fingers. Why in the world would you go to a dating app?"

"First, it's not technically a dating app—it's a social networking app." At least that's what he liked to remind himself. The app certainly didn't market itself as a dating app.

Her lips turned up in a familiar look that said he should know better. "With definite sexual undertones that begin with the name *Dear Lover*. That's a marketing tactic they're using. If they don't say they're a dating app, they don't have to advertise like one and be lumped in with all the other apps claiming to help people find a happily ever after."

She was right about that. Dear Lover didn't promise clients anything more than an opportunity to socialize in a private setting. The privacy part had been the deciding factor in him joining.

"I signed up because I wanted someone to talk to, not to go out on the town with. Or be photographed with." Or even to sleep with, because—as she'd alluded to—there was no shortage of women willing to fall into bed with him. No, he'd simply wondered if he'd enjoy talking to someone who didn't know who he was or how much money he had. The answer to that was *hell yes*. He'd enjoyed conversing with her immensely.

Desta's hands covered her face as she shook her head. "Okay." A deep inhale followed by a huff of breath, and her hands fell away. "Well, we'll just take off these badges and walk out of this resort. There're a couple hundred people in that room so they won't notice two are gone. We'll go back to the city and act like this never happened."

It was a good suggestion. Efficient, to the point and effective. Probably exactly what they should do. But Maurice wasn't known for doing what he *should* do. He was the most reckless and unruly of the four Gold siblings—the one who was exactly as the media portrayed him when it came to lovin' and leavin' women. Except *lovin'* only meant sex; there were no emotions other than lust involved with him and any of the women he dated. He probably should just agree with Des and get out of here, but nothing they did from this point on was going to erase from his mind the words they'd already shared.

"Or we could stay for the weekend and act like those two adults who've been exchanging their deepest and most coveted sexual cravings. The two people who've been looking forward to this time together to explore each other's bodies in all the ways they'd described." His pulse pounded with the realization that he was totally flying by the seat of his pants right now. How was the transition from friends to lovers going to work here? And was that what he really wanted? Did he want to have sex with Des? And why hadn't he figured that out before tonight?

She offered a bemused smile. "You're kidding, right?"

"No." He touched her knee. "This is the part where I tell you how much I enjoyed our exchanges these last three months. It's where I ask if you enjoyed them, too, and if so, what's stopping us from going further?" Because the reasons he was giving himself to walk away seemed awfully flimsy right now. Why couldn't two consenting adults have sex? Why did having sex have to ruin a business relationship, or a friendship, as long as they both knew what the limits were?

When she didn't immediately respond, he continued. "It's the part where I confess that all week I've been thinking about this woman who I'd never met face-to-face and how good it would feel to experience some of the things she and I had discussed. Never in my wildest dreams would I have thought you'd be that woman. But here we are, and to be honest, I don't think there's any way I can forget what we've shared now." She licked her lips, just a quick swipe of her tongue, and he knew there was no turning back. "I can only admit that finding out that you're Dear Lover 1288 makes me even more interested in spending this weekend with you."

CHAPTER TWO

MAURICE WAS RIGHT. There was no going back now. Her core throbbed at his words, and she closed her eyes with the second punch of lust to hit her since he'd arrived. But what was the right way forward? Was it spending this weekend with him, possibly exploring all the things they'd written about doing? Or was it walking away and, come Monday morning, trying to work together amid the intimate knowledge they now had of each other? Reclaiming her life had suddenly become more complicated.

"How would this weekend even work?" Because her body was sending signals that didn't coincide with her brain's advice to get the hell out of here.

Maurice shrugged. "We can either go back in there and mingle like everyone else. Or we can get dinner and then head to our rooms. Tomorrow's agenda begins at nine with Morning Sex Mania and Make-Up and Mimosas at eleven."

She leaned back on the couch, resisting the urge to sigh. Being frustrated about how things had turned out wasn't going to change a damn thing. This was the hand she'd been dealt, and now she needed to figure out how she was going to manage the situation. "I mean, what happens on Monday morning when we walk into the office together?"

"You get to work way too early in the morning for me, so there's zero chance we'll be walking in together."

Narrowing her eyes at him did nothing to kill the goofy grin he was wearing. "Don't play, you know exactly what I'm talking about."

"I know you're taking this too seriously."

"You're not taking it seriously enough." When it came to any type of interaction with men, she always took things seriously. She had no other choice. She'd been caught off guard before, and she wasn't about to be in the position of having no control again.

Maurice shook his head quizzically. "Why should I? So what, we chatted on some message board for three months. That's our private business, and we don't have to answer to anyone for what we do in private. If we want to take those conversations to another level, same goes. It's our decision."

"I work for your father," she said as if he didn't already know. "And you're just three steps shy of being called a manwhore across all media outlets. If anybody caught wind of the fact that we spent a weekend having freaky sex at a ski resort, we'd both be in for a whole lot of scrutinizing and questions. Is that what you want?"

His smile vanished and was replaced by a pensive look she rarely saw on him. All things considered, Maurice was a really good, down-to-earth guy. He was a fine-ass millionaire with an MBA in business and public relations, who loved his mother—and his whole family—profusely. Laughing was his favorite pastime, and hot 'n' spicy was his favorite food group. They'd worked well together, which was great because a lot of times their roles at RGF in marketing and PR overlapped. Even knowing all that, there'd never been a day or a moment that she'd ever considered sleeping with him.

Until now.

"You know me better than that, Des. I've never moderated my steps to appease anybody, and I'm damn sure not starting now. You're the woman I've been having very intimate conversations with. That makes you the woman I want to spend this weekend getting to know a whole lot better." His tone remained serious, his gaze holding hers. "What we decide to do on Monday morning will be our decision, and that's it. An option that's not on the table is keeping secrets. Now, I'm not saying we take out a front-page ad describing what we're doing, but I'm not going to hide from the world the way Riley and Chaz tried to do."

Riley Gold was the chief executive of market research and product development at RGF and Maurice's younger sister. Chaz Warren was the social-media guru turned brand manager at King Designs,

RGF's biggest competitor and former rival. Earlier this year, they'd hooked up in Milan for a hot weekend and returned to New York intending to keep their affair a secret. Long story short, word got out and drama ensued. Desta would reluctantly have to side with Maurice on this one: a secret affair wasn't the way to go.

"You never stay with a woman past three dates, anyway." The words sounded much saltier than she'd intended and implied that she'd paid more attention to his personal life than she had.

"You're not a woman I would've ever asked on a date."

That was a sharp retort, and for a few seconds she wondered how she should reply. "Because you know I'm not as gullible as the women you date, and I would never fall for that *now is now and later is whatever I say it is* speech you like to give them."

He raised his gloriously thick and well-maintained eyebrows, giving her a barely amused look. "Stating my terms up front is safer for all involved."

This man really was way too handsome and charming for his own good. His tawny-brown complexion was just a shade darker than her own creamy, light brown skin tone. His thick wavy hair was jet black, cut close on the sides, and his walnut eyes had the power to assess with scrutiny or melt with desire. She was somewhere in the middle of those sensations right now as he stared at her.

Her gaze didn't waver even when she leaned forward again. "Then, I'll be the one to state my terms first this time, so there'll be no confusion."

With a smirk he raised open arms and said, "Be my guest."

Smug and sexy was a deadly combination.

"We've paid for this weekend and come all this way, so we might as well stay. Participation in any of the items on that agenda have to be discussed and mutually agreed upon. Before we leave on Sunday, we'll talk about next steps. I don't make it a habit of flaunting my personal business at work, but I've never been one to hide my truth, either."

The latter wasn't totally honest. There'd been a time—way too long ago, now that she thought back on it—that she'd lost herself and hadn't known which way to go to save whatever part of her was left. But that time had passed, and she'd be damned if she'd start down that road ever again. To prove that point she'd decided to spend this weekend with Maurice, but that decision was in no way acquiescence to his wants. She fully planned to call the shots concerning whatever they did for the next two days. If she wasn't feeling it, she wasn't doing it, no matter what Maurice said or did. She wasn't operating under his thumb anymore, doing whatever he said just to keep the peace or to keep him from… With an inner shake she reminded herself that Maurice wasn't her ex-fiancé.

"Sounds good to me." A nod followed his quickly spoken words. "You wanna know what else sounds good? The BBQ ribs and homemade potato salad I saw on the menu for a little restaurant just down the road. We can be there in ten minutes." He stood as if he were about to get his coat and head out, with or without her.

Desta stood, too. "I could eat." She'd worked right up until leaving her house a little after three this afternoon. It was almost seven thirty now.

"Then, let's go, Dear Lover 1288." Offering her a bent elbow, he smiled bright like he'd just won the lottery.

She certainly wasn't worth millions of dollars, nor did she like thinking of herself as any type of prize, but she did hook her arm in his. "I think we know each other well enough to forego those usernames now."

"We probably know each other better than any of those people in that room." He'd started walking toward the coat-check desk.

"I guess you could say that." Maurice moved quickly, turning to face her, cupping a hand to her chin.

His gaze held hers as if they were both searching for something they'd never seen before. A tingle began at the base of her neck, moving quickly throughout her body until she felt alive in a way she never had before.

"I might not know the exact odds of this happening, but I'd say they were definitely in our favor." He moved in slowly, like he wanted to give her time to decide if she wanted what was certainly coming next.

Did she want it? And from him, no less?

Her answer was to remain still, to wait and see how this would play out. It began with a warm brush of his lips over hers, and the desire she'd felt upon first seeing him expanded. It flooded her mind and her body until she couldn't help but lean into him. His eyes remained open and fixated on her as he eased back slightly, then came in again, touching his lips to hers once more. This time there was no retreat. He slipped his tongue inside next, and all thoughts of odds, words and champagne flutes fled her mind.

He'd planned to wait. Tonight was supposed to be for getting to know Dear Lover 1288 better on a face-to-face basis. Did she fidget when she talked? Was she as pleasant in person as she'd been via email? Did she talk while chewing? That kind of stuff. But then, when he'd learned it was Des…well, he was counting that as a win. He already knew she had perfect table manners, almost to the point of being annoying, especially when she dabbed her napkin at her lips so daintily. She was always composed, so no fidgeting. No tripping over her words, just concise statements, eye contact and an air of confidence that he admired. All of that meant there was no need to wait a polite amount of time before getting his hands—and lips—on her.

Especially not when she'd laced her arm in his, standing so close the heady sophisticated scent of her perfume permeated his senses. Coupled with all those words they'd shared via email, it was a wonder he hadn't actually pushed her dress up and buried his face between her legs the way he'd written he was going to do.

For now, the kiss was enough, especially since she'd leaned into him with as much anticipation as he felt swirling around the pit of his stomach. Craving more of her, he let his hands slide until they were at her waist. Then he eased them down to grip her hips and hold her steady against his unabashed erection.

"Well. Well. Well. There goes my bar partner." Rousing laughter accompanied with clapping had Des breaking the kiss.

"Kelli? Hey." She stepped back from Maurice, touching her fingers to her lips before dropping her arms to her sides.

"Hey, girl." The redhead came closer, her giddiness still apparent in the way she looked from Des to him. "Here, rub my hand so I can have the same luck as you." Never taking her gaze off him, the woman reached out so Des could touch her hand.

Des—in a move that was way too similar to what he would've done—ignored her hand. "Yes. This is my meetup, so I won't be joining you at the bar tonight."

Kelli, who obviously didn't mind Des not playing along with her, returned that hand to prop on one hip. Her gaze was hungry and assessing, and Maurice felt uncomfortable only because his dick was hard but not for her.

"I don't blame you at all." Kelli was very open with her appraisal of him, but it was nothing Maurice wasn't used to.

"If you'll excuse us, Kelli, we're going to have dinner," he said. What would happen after the meal was completely up to Des, but he was leaning toward them sharing one room instead of returning to their individual spaces for the evening.

Kelli's smile was agreeable and knowing. "Sure. Dinner. Okay, well, I guess I'll see you two around."

Glancing over her shoulder she winked at Des before giving Maurice one last head-to-toe look of appreciation. "Have fun, y'all."

"You sure made friends fast," he told Des after Kelli was gone.

Still staring after the woman with an incredulous scan, Des shook her head. "She approached me, but I get the impression she's harmless. This is her second Dear Lover meetup."

"So she's experienced."

"That or she's unlucky in the guys she's choosing to socialize with."

They fell into step again, this time without him touching her. Another public display like the one Kelli had just interrupted wasn't a good idea, and while he didn't make a habit of hiding from the media like his siblings—he couldn't in his line of work—he wasn't game for his private life being on display unnecessarily.

Stanley, the guy at the coat-check desk, was quick to accept their tickets and return. He also made no secret of how he hated the moment when Maurice helped ease Des's long wool coat over her shoulders. Normally, Maurice didn't feel any type of way when another guy looked at his date. He was drawn to beautiful and attractive women— that was no secret—and he subscribed to the *look but don't touch* model where other men were concerned. Stanley's look toward Desta was nothing short of lustful, and Maurice felt a little twinge of annoyance at that.

They bundled up in coats and gloves, and Des even pulled on a fur-trimmed hat before they began walking down the road. "Why Dear Lover instead of a traditional dating app?" she asked.

While there was snow all around, the sidewalks were impeccably cleared, which worked out well since Des wasn't wearing boots but instead had on a pair of the sexiest, strappiest black heels he'd ever seen.

"You already said I don't need help finding a date." Agreeing with her knowledge of his dating life had never bothered him before, but now— considering how his reputation might look in her eyes—there was a spark of regret. "Besides, the app promotes the socializing aspect much more than hard-core dating. Just like you pointed out before, there was no jargon about finding your perfect match or testimonials from couples who'd met up and married afterward."

"True. That's part of the reason I signed up. I'm not really into computers playing matchmakers for anything long-term." She crossed her arms over her chest against the bitter chill in the air.

He considered moving closer, putting an arm around her shoulders to offer a little more warmth, but decided against it. Usually he could control himself under any circumstances. He was finding that a little more difficult now. The same woman whose description of giving perfect head had made a mess of his sheets a few short weeks ago had also sat across from him at a poker table just last weekend, wearing a tight sweater and smug smile as she claimed the winning hand.

"You're not really looking for anything long-term, are you?" He didn't think she was, or at least she'd never given that impression before.

The Des he knew was selective in the men she dated, private and a bit noncommittal in his estimation. As far as he knew, there hadn't been anyone serious for her in the time she'd worked for the company.

"Been there, done that." It was a dry statement, one he sensed held a lot more weight than the flippant way it'd rolled off her tongue.

"And you're not willing to do it again." Phrasing

it as a statement instead of a question was his way of not prying.

"I'm not willing to be in the situation I was in before. And don't ask what that was. It's irrelevant to whatever this is that we're doing."

There was the Des he knew so well. The cut-you-off-at-the-knees-when-required woman who also managed to look damn hot while she did it. He chuckled. "Wasn't gonna ask because I know the tactic well." No lies or jokes there. Not wanting to repeat a mistake from the past was his mantra. Everything he'd done and said since his sophomore year in college had been based on an occurrence that both rocked his world and forever changed the trajectory of his personal life.

Upon arriving at the restaurant, Maurice opened one of two doors in the same wood that seemed to have been used on every building in this upscale ski village. The host was pleasant and quick to take their coats, then guide them to a cozy booth near a fireplace.

"Thank goodness. I was about to turn into a popsicle out there." Des rubbed her arms and shivered as she stared happily at the roaring fire.

Easing out of the booth, he removed his sports coat and leaned closer to wrap it around her shoulders. "That dress is serving its purpose of enticing every man who's lucky enough to see it, but I'm not surprised it isn't keeping you warm."

For a second, she looked startled by his action.

Then she shrugged, pushed her arms into the much bigger sleeves of his sports coat and wrapped it tightly around her. "Good thing I packed plenty of warmer serviceable clothes than this little black dress."

Returning to his seat, he mourned the loss of seeing the entrancing cleavage pressed above the top of her dress. A server came offering coffee, tea or hot chocolate, and after taking their drink order he left menus that they read in silence. Minutes later the server returned with a heavy cream-and-sugar coffee for him and green tea for her. They placed their orders—the ribs for him, hearty beef stew and corn bread for her—and settled back to wait for it.

Des broke the silence. "I never would've dreamed it was you." She stared at him over the rim of her mug before placing it back on the table.

He kept his hands around his mug, enjoying the warmth from the liquid inside as it mingled with the heat of arousal currently swirling through his body. "Same. You were the last person I expected."

"And yet here we are." She took another sip of her tea.

"Here we are." Maurice didn't drink again for fear that the hot coffee mixed with desire burning brighter than the fire a few feet away would be explosive. "Are you nervous?"

This time when she set the mug down, she pulled her arms from the table and let them rest in her lap. "Nervous about what? Having dinner with a man

I've treated like a brother for five years, or having wild, passionate sex with that man?"

Again, with her instinctual candor. Normally, he wasn't averse to brash talking, especially when it concerned sex, but coming from Des, he'd have to get used to it. "Well, since we've had dinner together plenty of times before, the latter, of course."

Her tongue eased between her lips, brushing over them in a way he prayed it'd brush over his dick at some point. He sucked in a breath, not even realizing he was holding it until she spoke.

"No. I wouldn't say nervous. I mean you're right, we've had dinner together before. We've shared working lunches and have even spent a good amount of recreational time together. If you count the days during the summer when your parents have cookouts and I sit by the pool watching you and your brothers threaten to toss Riley in." She held his gaze and took a slow breath. "It makes sense that we address the possibility that we may have sex this weekend."

"How do you feel about that possibility?" Because he was feeling mighty anxious about eating this meal as quickly as he could and then getting back to the hotel with her.

"I've had sex before." She tried for a casual shrug, but the intense look in her eyes told him this was anything but routine for her. "Of course, I've never thought of you in a sexual way."

"Wow. Okay, well, don't take any pity on my ego." He tried to laugh it off, but that stung just a bit.

"Did you not hear the comment about me thinking of you as a brother?" She shook her head. "Tell me you thought of me as a date."

He couldn't tell her that. "Touché. I've obviously noticed that you're an attractive woman. I'd have to be blind not to, but yeah, I never really put you in that category."

"Well, that's probably a good thing considering how you treat your dates," she quipped and then looked at him as if she wanted to take back that comment.

There was no need. The truth was the truth. "But now that's all changed. The way I thought of you before realizing you'd written those emails is long gone."

Reaching a hand up to tuck a strand of hair behind her ear, she nodded. "Same. Now I can only see you as a man. A very attractive and alluring man."

His dick took that compliment and throbbed with pride. "A man that you're considering having sex with this weekend." A statement and a question all rolled into one.

She hesitated briefly. "A man I'm *seriously* considering having sex with this weekend."

CHAPTER THREE

"WHAT'S YOUR ROOM NUMBER?" he asked. After finishing dinner, they'd shared a sort of slow walk—but with a hurried mentality—to get back to the resort.

The subject of sex hadn't come up again, but it had been there, hovering over them as they discussed the food, the area and any other thing they could think of while at the restaurant. They stepped into the warmth of the resort and crossed the lobby, walking toward the bank of elevators. He'd decided that he wouldn't ask, guide or try to influence in any way. As he'd told her a while ago, everything had changed. This was no ordinary date for him—he knew that even while his body tried to convince him otherwise. No, tonight, he would let Des lead the show.

"Three twenty-seven." She stepped onto the elevator and stood toward the back of the car.

He followed her inside, standing as close to her as he possibly could without touching her. "I'm in three thirteen." Which meant his room was on the same side of the floor as hers, but they would get to his first.

Neither of them spoke for the next few moments, and when the elevator doors opened, he waited for her to step out first. Taking the few steps to the proverbial fork in the hallway, she hesitated a brief moment, before turning to the left and saying, "We'll go to your room."

He followed her lead, then let them into his room, taking his time to close and lock the door once they were inside. Watching her walk deeper inside after she'd found the light switch were the strangest few moments of his life. Desta Henner was in his suite, where, just through this sitting area and down a narrow hallway, there was a king-size bed.

"Do you want a drink?" It seemed like a normal question to ask as she took off her coat, hat and gloves and laid them on the couch.

"No." A quick and simple answer spoken succinctly when she turned to look at him. "We don't have to go through any pretenses. This is what we came here to do."

He was removing his jacket when her comment stopped him cold. So they were really going to do this? Considering the circumstances—and if he were staring at any other woman but her—he would've asked that question aloud. Making sure he and the women he got involved with were of one accord every step of the way was something he was fanatical about. But Des never said anything she didn't mean.

That's why he didn't speak another word. He simply took her hand and walked them back to the bedroom. She released his hand when they were a few steps from the bed and turned her back to him, lifting her hair from her neck in a signal for him to unzip her dress.

Her hair was all black now. A few months ago, it had been frosted with some type of honey color. Why he was thinking about her hair now, he had no idea.

"There's no going back once we start down this path." She sounded calm, her voice just a little husky.

"We've pretty much started walking the path, anyway. Knowing what I know about you now, even without touching you, is something I'll never forget." It was the truth. He'd barely been able to stop staring at her during dinner because the memories of all their late-night messages continued to roll through his mind. Yet, he didn't reach to unzip her dress.

She loved back rubs that led to kissing down her spine and sex from behind. It was her favorite way to be wakened in the morning. He flexed his fingers and wondered if that'd be the first thing on their personal agenda for tomorrow.

"You're right." She took a deep breath and released it. There was nothing about her stance that said she was nervous, and she'd already admitted she wasn't but turned to face him. He kept his gaze focused on her, a light coat of the pink lip gloss she wore was still visible on her pert lips. "Then, we should discuss safety."

Des would want a full safety discussion first. She wouldn't wait and remind him to put the condom on moments before he entered her. He almost grinned at the fact he'd already known that about her. "My last physical was six months ago in May. Clean bill of health."

Lifting her hands as she spoke, she pushed them through her hair, which fell in waves to her shoulders. "My last physical was in January. I'm clean, too."

A hush fell over the room. "It doesn't have to be tonight. We can just chill for a while and get started with the workshops in the morning. There's no rush," he said.

She sighed. "This shouldn't be difficult. It's what we both planned when we decided to come up here. We were anticipating it. Your last message even said…" Pausing, she looked at him and then toward the window.

He closed the distance between them and cupped his hands on both sides of her neck. "I said I couldn't wait to get my hands on you. To feel your soft skin beneath my fingertips and my tongue."

The pressure of her leaning into him was the best feeling, and his body immediately reacted.

"And I replied I couldn't wait to feel you deep inside me. I wanted my legs wrapped around your waist and your thick length pumping hard in and out of me." Her voice had grown husky as she said those words, like she was transitioning from the woman standing before him into the woman who'd written all those erotic emails. Arousal pumped through his veins at the sound.

As if anticipating his reaction, she moved her hands between their bodies, wrapping his dick in a layer of warmth.

"Thick and long," she whispered. "That's what I wrote, even though I'd never seen it before. I knew you'd be thick and long." She was pleased; he could tell by the tone of her voice and the way she cradled him in her hands as if he were a prized possession.

"And hard as steel for you." If his throat felt raspy with those words, it was fine because his dick felt fuckin' fantastic in her hands. His mind was overwhelmed by the perfection of this moment.

Her eyes closed and opened slowly again. "It is." That beguiling tongue of hers made another appearance, sliding sinuously over her lips, and the urge to have her turned to frantic need.

Dipping his head, he touched her tongue for a moment before sucking it into his mouth. She moaned, her fingers tightening over his erection, her breasts pressing into his chest. Had he told her they could wait for this? He had, but it had been a lie. He'd waited three months for this. Dreaming of her each night after reading her messages, wondering how every act she described would feel, how she would fit beneath him, over him, around him. There was no question that he wanted her...now.

Hungry didn't quite describe this kiss. *Greedy* might be more like it as he took a deep dive, thrusting his tongue against hers now, tilting his head one way while hers went the other until they were both gasping for air. His hands moved from her neck down to her shoulders, which he gripped before turning her around so that her back was now facing the bed.

She unzipped his pants, hurriedly pushing her hand inside the slit of his boxers until she was skin-to-skin with his rock-hard length. He sucked in a breath, and she took that moment to pull her mouth away from his just enough so she could look down at what she now held.

"Delicious." The word tumbled from her mouth, and his dick jumped in her hand. "That's the first thought that came to mind. You look delicious."

Her fingers were steadily stroking him, her thumb and forefinger rolling over the sensitive slit in his tip. The words were like honey gliding over his ego, but nothing surpassed the warm touch of her fingers along his dick.

"Look, touch…do what you want." It was permission and begging all rolled into one, and he didn't give a damn. He wasn't taking it back. Whatever she wanted to do to him at this moment he was certain he'd love. In fact, he might explode if she didn't do something, anything more to bring him pleasure.

"Do you remember the night I wrote about the art of giving good head?"

For the love of every deity ever prayed to, of course he recalled that conversation. He may or may not have printed it out and framed it for future reference.

"Yeah, I remember." Strained words coming from him weren't the norm, but there was nothing normal about this social-media meetup, nothing at all.

"I said the first step was to adore the dick. If there's no adoration, there can be no pleasure."

He clenched his teeth, adoring every damn word that was coming out of her mouth as she began to lower herself in front of him. Closing his eyes, Maurice bit back a curse of pleasure, deciding complete concentration was needed to keep from coming in her hands in the next few seconds. He opened them again when she was on her knees. She unbuttoned his pants and was now pushing them, along with his boxers, down his thighs.

"I like a long, thick, heavy dick. The way it feels in my hands and the way it looks like it's barely holding back every second I'm near it." And she was certainly near it. She'd moved her head closer, until the warmth of her breath whispered over his vulnerable skin each time she spoke. "I like yours very much."

If he never received another compliment, Maurice would be fine with this one emblazoned on his brain. Snapping out of the blissful trance, he pushed his fingers through her hair again, this time grasping tightly so he could tilt her face up and look into her eyes.

"There's no pressure here." He felt the need to reiterate this fact. Part of his policy on being clear about the ground rules. There hadn't been too many misunderstandings with women before, and he highly doubted Des would be one of them. Still, old habits died hard. He loosened his grip on her hair. "None at all. We can just spend a normal weekend on the slopes if that's what you'd prefer."

He sucked in a breath the moment she lowered her face to him and touched her tongue to the tip of his dick before saying, "I'd prefer you not interrupt me."

Marking another first for her, Desta closed her eyes to the stark pleasure of sucking him deep into her mouth. So deep she had to relax her throat muscles and hold him there for a few seconds to adjust. His fingers raked over her scalp, and she moaned, pulling back slightly while her tongue pressed against the underside of his dick.

She'd never given head on a first date. And to be clear, this wasn't even a date. It was a hookup that may have been considered a booty call if Maurice had personally summoned her to this resort. Whatever it was called, she was in it now, and she couldn't say she felt bad about that. On the contrary, she'd decided during dinner while they'd talked that this was going to happen tonight. There was no use in putting it off because it was what they both knew they wanted. As for how she was going to deal with the fact that he was a coworker come Monday morning…she didn't want to think about that right now. Instead, she let herself surrender to the warm and tingly sensations coursing through her as her mouth closed around him again. Bobbing her head up and down over his length had her heart thumping and her pussy pulsating. She was wet, dripping as she felt moisture on her inner thighs. Her breasts were heavy with desire, nipples already puckered.

She pulled back, allowing his dick to plop free of her lips, then sucked in a breath as she used both hands to continue working him. Stroking from his base to his tip, she watched as pearls of pre-cum seeped from his slit before ducking her head to devour them.

"Enough," he whispered. It was more like a strangled moan, but she heard the word and felt his hands going to her shoulders as he guided her up to a standing position.

"You've had enough of me already?" How vulnerable had that sounded? She couldn't take it back no matter how much she wanted to.

His brow furrowed as a completely confused look covered his face. "Never. I'd just like you to experience some pleasure, too, before I make a complete fool of myself and come all over the place."

He grinned so she smiled, even though a slow trickle of insecurity had already dared to creep onto the scene. It was ridiculous. This was a different time and place, and Maurice was unlike any man she'd ever met before. Hell, this situation was unlike anything she'd ever experienced. The past had no business here. She'd remind herself of that whenever necessary.

"I really like your mouth," he said, running a finger over her lip line. "Really, really like it."

Before she could reply, she was being turned around and Maurice unzipped the dress, pushing it past her shoulders and down to the floor. When she stepped free of it, he ran his hands up and down her outer thighs, his breaths coming faster as he was the one kneeling now.

"There was a night we stayed late at the office. When the Golden Bride line first launched. You were wearing these black pants with gold-zipper pockets at your hip. And I wondered, what if those zippers went all the way down your long legs, and would the material fall from your body if they did?" His face was awfully close to her ass, the warmth of his breath fanning over the skin left bare there thanks to the black lace thong she wore.

"You thought about me sexually?" That had never occurred to her before. She and Maurice snipped at each other competitively. Never out of anger, but as friends, or even family. There was definitely a one-upmanship going on between them that most days she found entertaining.

Maurice was funny and totally self-absorbed at times. But he knew his job like no other PR exec she'd ever met. He handled everything that came at RGF, from the scandal with Riley and her first fiancé to just recently when a reporter attempted to undermine the partnership that Major—Maurice's twin brother—had with Nina Fuller, the owner of a fashion app. Maurice was a whiz at crisis management and totally invested in his family's fashion house. Yet, there'd never been a time she thought of him as just a man. Now, before anything else happened between them in this room, she knew she'd never think of him as anything less again.

"It was just that one time, and I cursed myself every second for the rest of that evening, swearing I wasn't some type of sick bastard for thinking of you in that way."

Because they hadn't considered each other that way. Until they'd met anonymously online and got to know each other as man and woman. Dear Lover 1687 was the kind of man she'd longed for; he knew her in ways she'd just begun to know herself.

"And now we're making our relationship awkward." Doubt that hadn't been there moments ago when she'd had him in her mouth now circled her mind like rain clouds.

He stood now, turning her so that she faced him again. "No. We're making it better. Otherwise, all that pent-up desire we were able to release on that message board would remain locked up inside of us. We both deserve better."

With those words he wrapped his arms around her waist, lifting until her feet were off the floor and he could ease them back to the bed and lay her down. His movements from then on were methodical. Long fingers undid the clips holding the garters to her thigh-high black stockings. He unhooked the garter belt and her bra, tossing them both aside. When all she still wore were the thong, nylons and shoes, he stared down at her, passion alight in his dark eyes.

"You're not beautiful."

The walls around her immediately closed in until she had to gasp for breath. Memories came flooding back, and she rose up on her elbows, ready to push him away, get dressed and leave him in that room alone. A featherlight touch of his finger to the line of her jaw held her still.

"That's not enough to describe you. It's too ordinary. Too cliché."

The rich timbre of his voice saying exactly what she needed to hear made her too hot.

"I don't need flattery." Although it was welcome, she'd resigned herself to not accepting it if it wasn't sincere, which oftentimes it wasn't. Really, that excuse had become a security shield to prevent her from the opposite: demeaning criticism.

"You deserve it." He tilted her chin and leaned in to place the softest kiss against her lips. "Now, lie back and let me reminisce on something I wrote."

She did as she was told. "You mean, you're going to kiss me all over, stopping only when I beg."

He'd already eased down until his mouth hovered scant inches over her nipple. The look he gave her—arched brows, mischief in his eyes and a quirk of his lips—was the most devilishly sexy expression she'd ever seen.

Maurice gave no verbal response, but he did suck that nipple into his mouth, gorging on it as if he'd been starving for years. She arched into the pleasure seizing her senses. The assault continued when he palmed her other breast, tweaking her other nipple until pleasure and pain had her gasping. Who would've guessed he'd have such a phenomenal mouth? Every spot of skin his tongue and lips touched they tortured. From the sensitive area beneath her breasts that she'd never considered an erogenous zone down to the spot just above her hip bone where his tongue traced lazy circles until her head thrashed against the bed. She was close to begging, and the wicked grin he gave when he lifted his head and spread her thighs wide said he knew it.

The fire that had been brewing between them for the last three months via email was now an inferno as her body craved every touch from him. Desta knew what was coming next. She'd received good oral before and was poised for Maurice to bring no less passion and desire than he'd already shown her. Nothing could've prepared her for the jolt of delight that shot so quick and hot through her body the second his tongue touched her clit. She almost leaped up off the bed. He'd patiently placed his palm on her lower abdomen, holding her steady as his other hand parted her pussy and he licked her again.

She huffed and grabbed the comforter.

He licked her repeatedly as if she were some new flavor of ice cream, and her thighs quivered. Sucking each lip into his mouth was another sweet torture, and Desta breathed out heavily before biting down on her lower lip. It was the only way to keep from yelling out and insisting he get inside her immediately.

"You can let go, lover." His words were hot and teasing. "Just tell me when you're ready, and I'll lead you there."

In other words, *beg for more*. No. She wasn't begging, at least not yet.

Her nonresponse led to an arrogant chuckle from him, and she continued to hold onto those sheets. It didn't work, and in the next minutes she would learn just how quickly her resolve could crumble.

In quick succession, Maurice sucked her clit, thrust into her opening, then flattened his tongue over her pussy in a way designed to drive anyone on the receiving end of such delightful torment absolutely crazy. Her body buzzed with need, her breaths came in quick pants, and she was certain all the sheets had been ripped from the mattress at this point.

"Say the words," he whispered over her damp skin. "Say it and set us both free, lover. Just say it."

Desta was strung so tight she barely wanted to move for fear she'd spontaneously combust. Dragging her hands away from the comforter, she pushed them through her hair and tried to catch her breath. Tried to think coherently. Then he blew over her clit, a very soft, very warm, extremely erotic breath that sent her teetering over the edge.

"Now, Maurice. Now. Please, now!"

CHAPTER FOUR

MAURICE HAD NEVER stripped out of his clothes faster than he had tonight. His dick was hard, her essence was still warm and spicy on this tongue, and she was lying on that bed totally naked, like a dessert prepared especially for him.

She watched him as he stood at the end of the bed, smoothing the condom down his length. Her eyes were fixed on him, her heated gaze zeroing in on his dick, making it jump in anticipation. When did she start to look better than any pinup photo or adult-movie star he'd ever seen?

He climbed onto the bed, still watching her watch him. Her hair was down around her shoulders, brushing over her lovely golden-brown skin—skin he wanted to run his fingers and his tongue over. First, he was going to kiss that spot at her throat, right where her pulse beat as wildly as his heart was at this very moment. She spread her legs as he continued his trek toward her.

"This isn't going to be slow." The thought just

occurred to him that this was their first time, and women often liked the first time to be slow. So they could commemorate or recall it later. He'd had no idea, but he'd recalled hearing that a time or two from someone he couldn't remember at the moment. "I promise it'll be good, but not slow. Not this time."

When he was close enough, he slid his arms beneath the backs of her knees, lifting her legs to rest on his shoulders.

She reached her hands between them, cupping his dick in her palms once again. "Did I ask for slow?"

That question, coupled with the feel of her hands on him and the look of sheer wantonness on her face, just about drove him over the edge. In the next second he was sliding his dick inside her with one deep thrust that had them both moaning and gasping for their next breath.

As promised, he wasn't slow. He grabbed her ankles, held onto her and pumped fiercely. She was so wet he slid in and out of her with such ease and pure delight. He clenched his teeth to keep from crying out. The rush of pleasure had his eyes closing as he continued to rotate his hips, pull out and then thrust back in. When he cracked his eyes open, it was to see her palming her breasts, squeezing until only the dark brown of her nipples was noticeable between her fingers. They puckered as if they were staring at him, trying to tell him something, to entice him, to drive him insane.

"Yes," she moaned, licking her lips quickly. "Yes. More, more, more."

He gave her exactly what she asked for, holding tight to her ankles as he pushed her legs away from his shoulders, spreading them into a wide V. Her mouth gaped, and her eyes widened as he rotated his hips again, much slower this time. She sucked her bottom lip into her mouth, biting down on it as she stared up at him. The guttural groan that rumbled from her chest was like a reward.

"You want more of this? How much more can you take?" He wanted to pump harder, to go deeper, to release all the desire that had built up in his mind every time he'd read one of her emails. He wanted to feel each one of the words, to make them come to life in every thrust and push of his dick inside her.

"All. I want it all." She'd spoken so clearly and so decisively he'd almost grinned, because for a moment she'd sounded like she was in the boardroom. Except he'd never seen Des naked before. He'd never even imagined her body would look this great without clothes or that she would be so warm and wet. So damn perfect.

Aiming to please, he eased one of her legs down to the bed, still keeping the other one pressed up against his chest, working in and out of her from a new angle. The groan that erupted from his chest with how good that first deeply penetrating stroke felt made his throat feel raw. Her fingers clenched the already-mussed sheets as she mumbled his name.

His name.

Maurice.

Said in the throes of pleasure, in Des's voice.

It was his turn to bite down on his lip as his dick was so deep inside her warm heat he thought he would surely drown. If so, it would be with a smile on his face. But he wasn't finished. Not until she was. To shift positions again, he eased out of her, immediately missing the feel of her tight muscles gripping his dick, milking him. She moved without instruction, as if she knew what she wanted, rolling until she was on her hands and knees.

"Yeah." He grinned and repeated the one word. "Your favorite position."

When he smacked both hands to the plump cheeks of her ass, she sighed and wiggled that ass in invitation for another smack.

She hissed this time as he'd put a little more sting into the second slap. "You know why this is my favorite position?"

He already knew because she'd told him…in a very lengthy email message. "Tell me, lover. Tell me exactly what you want me to do while I'm back here."

"Hard," she whispered. "I want it hard and fast. Make me come, hard and fast."

No sweeter words were ever spoken. Flattening his hands on her butt cheeks again, he speared his dick into her, settling into the space he'd missed in those few moments away. Then pulled back and gave her exactly what she'd asked for.

* * *

She screamed. Grabbed the pillows, buried her face and screamed again, because she'd never come so hard it left her shivering all over. Her legs and arms were shaking as Maurice moved in and out of her slowly, no doubt letting her recover from the intensity of her release.

When had he gotten so thick and long and deeply embedded inside of her? Probably when she asked him for just that. Damn, this was good. Even now as he picked up speed, as the sound of her release mingled with his thrusts echoing throughout the room, all she could think of was how good it felt.

His hands were spreading her cheeks apart, so she was sure he was watching his dick enter and retreat. The thought of what that must look like caused another tendril of pleasure to slip down her spine, until she shivered again and bit down on the pillow.

"So good," he was mumbling from behind her. "You look so good. Feel so good. Des, this is…"

He didn't need to finish; she knew what he was going to say because she was feeling it, too. So. Damn. Good.

When he repeated her name again, his fingers tightening on her butt, she knew he was taking that tumble that had just flattened her. She wasn't a big fan of a guy making loud annoying orgasm sounds, overreacting or in some way trying to prove his own prowess. Maurice grunted and moaned low so that the deep timbre moved over her skin like a warm massage. He gripped, then released her ass, gripped and released it again, until she felt like he was worshipping it. His body had gone rigidly still, except for a couple last, stilted thrusts and the pulsating of his dick still buried inside her.

Moments passed, and she finally turned so that her cheek rested on the pillows and she could thankfully catch her breath. It didn't bother her that she was still on her knees, ass still in the air and in his hands. As far as she was concerned, she could die just like this and it would've been a reasonably good life. But he eventually pulled out and eased her down until she was flat on her stomach.

"Be right back," he said before dropping a quick kiss on her left butt cheek and moving off the bed.

The sound of the bathroom door closing had her thinking she should probably get up, get dressed and head to her room before he returned. But when she flopped onto her back, the itchy feeling easing over her skin signaled a warning.

If she left, would that seem like running?

Admittedly, that had been the ultimate deciding factor in agreeing to this weekend with him. Of course, she hadn't said that to him, nor had she really allowed herself to dwell on it, but now here it was, manifesting itself in physical reactions that her therapist advised was her body's external warning system. Folding her arms over her chest, she ran her hands up and down her biceps, trying desperately to ease the discomfort.

She wasn't running, not again. That wasn't the answer to whatever was making her feel the need to bolt—it wasn't totally clear to her what that was yet. It couldn't be fear of anyone finding out what she and Maurice had done, because he'd been on point when he'd vehemently declared it was none of anybody's business. On the other hand, she wasn't the one in the media spotlight on a daily basis. Still, if he could push that obstacle to the side, she could, too.

Going back to her own room would give her space to reason with all these thoughts, to sort them out and get a grip on what was happening before tomorrow morning. She wasn't going to run out on the weekend: she'd already agreed to stay, and she wanted to stay. But space, yeah, that might be good, and when she saw Maurice again, she'd be in control of her thoughts and her body once more. She was just sitting up, about to throw her legs over the side of the bed and get moving, when the bathroom door opened.

"You need anything? Something to drink, maybe? There's a fully stocked fridge over there." He came out naked, talking and walking around the room until he found the boxer briefs he'd been wearing.

She watched him push each leg through and pull them up over muscled thighs. When they covered his still semi-erect dick, she licked her lips. "Yeah. Um, I'm a little thirsty."

Thankfully, his back was to her by now, and he couldn't see her thirst went well beyond the *I need a drink* stage. Since a stealth getaway was obviously out of the question now, she slid off the bed and tiptoed around until she found her underwear. She pulled on her lace panties and grabbed her bra, hurriedly fixing the clasp. Just as she was about to turn the matching lace material around and slip the straps onto her shoulders, he was there.

"Here, take this and let me help you with that."

The heat circling her body at his proximity was weird. She'd stood next to Maurice a kazillion times at the office, at a runway show, during last night's dinner at the Golds' house. Her body had never reacted to him this way before.

"I got it." She didn't step away from him as she wanted to, but she did continue situating her bra, the way she did every day of her life without his help. Turning to face him then, she accepted the canned soda he offered. "Thanks."

She opened the drink, took a deep gulp and then reminded herself she was cutting down on her soda intake. He had a can, too, but his was beer and he chugged away, just like she'd done. Apparently, he was thirsty, too.

"Normally, I'm a go-all-night kinda guy," he started as soon as he'd finished his beer and tossed the can into the trash. "But I was up late last night and then early this morning to take care of a few things before jumping on the road. So I'm gonna crash. You're welcome to join me."

He'd walked past her while he talked. He seemed

to be moving a lot. She wasn't totally sure what that was about, so she took another drink. "Or I can go back to my room? Is that the option you'd prefer?" Because his offer sounded like it wasn't really an offer, rather like it was something he'd say to one of the women he could take or leave. Why that irritated her she wasn't sure.

In bed already, he pulled the sheets up and folded his arms over his bare chest. "Honestly, it's been a very long time since I've slept with a woman. I mean, actually lay in a bed all night and slept with her."

Well, there was her answer. "I understand."

He didn't want her to sleep in here with him tonight. Turning, she went to grab her dress. She wasn't dealing with the garter and nylons again, so she just pushed them into her purse. She gathered the dress in her hands so she could slip it over her head, but she gasped when he also grabbed hold of it, now standing in front of her.

"This weekend will probably be the first of a lot of things, for both of us," he said, staring at her intently. "We might as well start with sleeping in the same bed."

She could tug on the dress, and he'd let it go. He'd watch her put it on and walk out the door without trying to stop her, because that's the type of guy he was. Maurice didn't push, not even at work. He stated his case, proved his point and moved on. For those smart enough to follow his lead, it paid off. For others who still doubted him, well, it maybe didn't work out so well. Tonight, she was in the position of having to make that decision. Did she follow his lead, or should she walk away?

Walk by her own choice and not from any type of fear or demeaning words, which she'd been so used to in the past. But not run because the pain and disgust had become so unbearable. She wasn't giving in; she was standing for what she wanted. Because deep down she knew she wanted to sleep in that bed with Maurice tonight.

"I'll stay." She let go of the dress. "But I sleep on the left side, closest to the window, and I like more pillows than covers, just in case you like to hog the sheets."

He grinned and tossed her dress onto the chair with her coat and purse. "I'll try my best to accommodate you."

CHAPTER FIVE

IT HAD ONLY been his goal not to take all the sheets last night. Rolling over and staying plastered to the back side of her body wasn't what he'd thought would happen. That's when it occurred to him that maybe he should stop planning and assuming what would happen between them this weekend; so far, he'd been wrong on two accounts.

Maurice wondered what time it was when he opened his eyes and inhaled the sweet scent of whatever type of product she used on her hair. He could've moved a little, lifted his body up to see over her to the alarm clock on the nightstand, but he was really comfortable where he was. His arm draped over her waist, her butt cradled against his morning arousal.

He knew it was morning. They hadn't closed the curtains all the way last night so about six inches of light peeked through. It slashed across her shoulder, giving her skin a shimmering glow. Without thought, he placed a soft kiss on that spot. Then another before telling himself he was being ridiculous.

Tender, romantic, thoughtful—he could be all those things when he wanted to. But he hadn't wanted to in a very long time. He wasn't an ass: he knew how to pour on the charm—it was actually part of his natural personality—and he knew how to say all the right things. The latter was pretty much common sense. Besides, the women he dated didn't require much. They already wanted him. If they hadn't made that perfectly clear right from the start, he probably wouldn't have pursued them. If they weren't looking for flowers, candlelight dinners and gifts on Valentine's Day, then they definitely weren't looking for love—which kinda went hand in hand with all that romance stuff. They could focus on a good time otherwise.

The real point behind his methodology for dealing with women was simple: India Frazier. He'd loved India, as much as an nineteen-year-old could love someone. But his love or infatuation or whatever it could be called had left India paralyzed and him forever scarred. For months after the accident he'd been on the brink of an emotional breakdown, repeatedly going over in his mind the moment he made the decision to pick India up in his new car and ultimately put her in harm's way. Besieged with guilt over the situation he'd so callously put the person he'd loved in, he vowed it would never happen again. He'd never fall in love or put his emotions over common sense again.

Des didn't seem the type to need all those material

proclamations, anyway. And, like him, she wasn't looking for anything permanent. She did, however, demand respect and honesty—which he could definitely do.

"What time is it?" She lurched up in the bed, her shoulder slamming into his mouth, which was still pretty close.

Pride kept him from crying out when he thought he might be tasting a little blood from the collision. Instead he pressed his finger to his lip as he reared back, and a hasty glance at his hand provided relief when there was no blood to be seen. "Not sure. Just woke up." She didn't need to know he'd been enjoying the quiet and the feel of her closeness for a few minutes now.

"Oh no!" She rolled out of his grasp and reached over to the nightstand to grab her phone. "Why didn't my alarm go off?"

He wasn't a morning person at all, so he lay back on the pillows and dropped an arm over his eyes. "What time is it?" He knew she was a morning person because she was in the office by seven every day of the week. Weekends he wasn't sure, but since today was Saturday and she was obviously freaking out, it was a good bet that she woke up at the crack of dawn every damn day.

"Oh no! It's nine forty-five. I should've been up by now." He lifted his arm and peeked out to see her fingers moving busily over her phone. "I can't believe all the messages I've missed. I'm usually up by now checking and…ugh, I just don't know how this happened."

He did, and he tried like hell not to smile. "Well, you know what they say about good sex?"

She glared at him over her shoulder, that slash of sunlight casting her face in an ethereal hue. "No. I don't know what they say." Her lips were tilted upward in the cutest smirk he'd ever seen, and he tried not to grin.

Losing the battle, he replied, "Good sex'll put you to bed right." He laughed so hard at his own joke he didn't see when she reached for the pillow and threw it at his face.

"Nobody says that, you goof." He could hear the smile in her voice, so she wasn't angry. "And I'm serious. I'm usually up by now. Plus, and I'm sure this will interest you, we missed the first activity on the agenda this morning."

He did sober, just a little, at that statement. Enough so that he leaned over to see her phone screen. "What was the first activity? Something about sex, right?"

"Everything this weekend is about sex, Maurice." She didn't bother to grace him with a look this time, just kept scrolling through her emails. "I don't know what it was, I just remember it started at nine."

"You have your inbox open. Just find the welcome email and click on the agenda."

"I'm checking my work emails."

"The office is closed on Saturdays. And this

weekend is a holiday, so you don't need to check any of that stuff."

"Work isn't just relegated to nine to five, Monday through Friday."

"Yeah, it is. That's why it's called the weekend— the week's end, get it? Because it's time for you to rest."

Now she did give him that smirk again. "You're ridiculous, and I know you better than that. Besides, I do sleep in until around six on Saturdays."

"You call getting up at six sleeping in?" That alone should be a criminal act. And her looking as pretty as she did with her hair mussed and her cranky attitude was a little more on the sexy-as-hell side.

"Yep. I'm normally up at four."

The sound he made reflected the pain he felt at simply hearing such an insanely early hour in the morning.

She shook her head. "The early bird gets the worm." Her tone was light, her attention still set on her phone. "That's what my grandmother used to say, and living in a house with five older brothers, it was true. My mom's a nurse, and she worked the night shift for the pay differential. My grandmother was at home with us most of the time, and she got up with the chickens, cooking us a big breakfast every morning. If I wasn't first at the table, my greedy brothers would scarf everything down before I got a plate."

He'd never heard Des talk about her family before. He knew she had one because his mother had mentioned it at some point, but there'd never been a reason for the two of them to have a real conversation about it. "You're from Chicago, right?"

"Mmm-hmm."

"Why don't you go home to be with your family?" Because for the last few years she'd been at his family's house celebrating Thanksgiving with them.

"I'm busy. They're busy." She shrugged.

Her clipped responses told him she didn't want to talk about that subject anymore, and he was happy to oblige. She already knew about his family, and still, if she'd started asking about them while they were lying partially naked in this nice warm bed on a Saturday morning, he wouldn't want to discuss them, either.

Deciding she wasn't going to pause checking work emails to look at the schedule, he rolled over to his side of the bed and grabbed his phone off its charger. Scrolling to the welcome email and agenda only took a few seconds.

"Morning Sex Mania," he announced, unable to hide the rise in excitement from his voice. "That's what we missed. Damn, we could've gotten some tips on great morning sex."

She didn't budge. "I don't need any tips on good morning sex. All you need is the morning and a great partner. Boom. Done."

With that said, he dropped his phone, rolled over again and scooted his very hard dick up against her ass, which was barely covered by those black lace panties.

"Well, we might as well get started."

It had been Desta's idea to forego the morning sex. This time she did need to go to her own room, for a shower, clean clothes and a breather. He'd been right about why she'd overslept, even though she'd never in a billion years admit that to him.

The sex had been great. That orgasm had clearly knocked her ass out for more than ten hours. She rarely ever slept that many hours straight. And then there was waking to the touch of his lips on her shoulder. That had felt too good. And too intimate, which was why she'd bolted up out of bed on her partially exaggerated quest to figure out the time. This weekend wasn't about intimacy, it was about sex. Very good sex, if last night was any indication.

After showering and slipping into fitted gray pants and a matching turtleneck, Desta pulled on black knee-length boots. Working in the fashion industry had obviously worn off on her, because she was at the mirror applying makeup and styling her hair for the next twenty-five minutes. Diamond-stud earrings she'd purchased for herself as a birthday gift last year were quick to affix, as were the three silver charm bracelets she favored with her casual attire. A spritz of perfume and she was walking across the room to grab her phone and Dear Lover ID badge. Her cell buzzed as soon as she picked it up.

Meet me at the elevator in 5 min. We don't want to miss Make-Up and Mimosas!

Initially, she grinned at Maurice's text—he couldn't be that anxious to get free mimosas. But then her body tensed in an all-too-familiar way as she stared at the text and the directive he'd given. Gordon used to give concise directions and expected them to be followed without hesitation. How many times had her snappy comebacks, honed from growing up with bossy brothers, led to heated arguments with her ex and him tossing out her favorite perfume or cutting her nice blouses into shreds? Too many to count. She didn't want to recall any of that right now. With a shake of her head, she decided she was being foolish. She slipped her phone into one back pocket and the ID and room key card into the other, then headed for the door.

"Right on time," Maurice said, tapping his watch when she approached the set of elevators on the far end of the floor.

"We could've taken the stairs." Ignoring another ping of distress, she tried to keep things light. That was the key to this weekend, light and simple. Just the way their email exchanges had gone. If she didn't let all the reasons they shouldn't be doing this together flood her mind, these next couple days would go smoothly. The incessant pricks from her past were another matter, but she'd been able to push them aside for years so far. This weekend wasn't going to test her.

"Let's skip the stairs. I like the R&B station they have playing in the elevators." He winked as the door opened, and waved a hand for her to step inside the car before him.

She did, giving him a playful jab to his gut as she passed by. "You're at the gym every day. Don't slack just because it's the weekend."

"Not all of us are as diligent as you, Des. I go to the gym every morning because there's one in our building. When I travel, I cut back on workouts." He stood right next to her in the elevator, which wasn't necessary since they were in the car alone.

He smelled good. It was the same fragrance with hints of sandalwood she always smelled on him, but today it seemed more prominent, more alluring. His boots today were chocolate brown, pants a shade lighter, and his button-front white shirt showed the RGF emblem on the right-hand side of his chest.

"You're not going for anonymity, huh?"

When he stared at her quizzically, she nodded to his shirt. "Your face is familiar enough, but you could always lie if someone called you out. Wearing an RGF shirt so openly just connects more of the dots."

He glanced down at his shirt and then back up to her when the elevator door opened. Again, he signaled for her to walk ahead of him before stepping out to join her in the bustling lobby.

"The key to not alerting people to who you are is to mingle like you don't care. Besides, as you might recall, every guest attending this weekend was required to sign that nondisclosure agreement." With that he looped his arm in hers and led them through the crowd of people either dressed to hit the slopes or heading to the resort's restaurant for breakfast. A sign next to the front desk showed the Dear Lover logo—a white pen in hand centered inside a gray heart—and the words *Morning Sessions* right next to an arrow.

"We're this way," he told her and led them in that direction.

Five minutes later they were inside another room with wall-to-wall windows and a breathtaking view of the mountains lined with snow. There were crimson-colored beanbag chairs in pairs around the room. On one wall was a long dark wood table filled with mimosas. At the center of the room was a podium and microphone, and behind that was a projector screen.

"Badges?" a petite woman asked before they could fully enter the space.

Maurice pulled his from his pocket and held it up, while Desta was so busy looking around the room, he had to nudge her before she reached into her back pocket to show her own. He'd been right to remind her about the NDA they'd signed. It was part of the registration process, and she'd read it a couple times before affixing her signature. She thought it was a good extra layer of privacy offered by Dear Lover.

Of course, it hadn't occurred to her that someone as notable as Maurice would be a client. Not considering millionaires, celebrities or other well-known people would be searching for companionship may have been naïve on her part. At any rate, this weekend was a private event, so in essence whatever happened in the Finger Lakes stayed in the Finger Lakes. Still, while that form was meant to be reassuring to all Dear Lover's clients, she knew firsthand that rules were often overlooked for the sake of a good story.

They were directed to the side of the room closest to the windows to find a seat. "You okay?" he asked, pointing to an empty set of beanbags.

"Yeah. This is, uh, not what I expected."

"What'd you think it was going to be, desks and chairs? Pencils and paper for us to take notes on the lecture?" He plopped down way too happily onto his bag, then looked up at her with a toothy smile.

She went down a little slower, not because she thought she might fall but because her fitted pants were more fashionable than practical. Bending to sit just about on the floor wasn't what she thought she'd be doing this morning. "Oh come on, you gotta admit this is a different type of setup even for you."

"Yeah," he said, moving around in the chair like he was a kid trying to feel every bean inside the bag. "But it's kinda fun."

With a roll of her eyes, she shook her head and turned her attention to the scenery. The sight of fluffy snow draped over the mountains was like a balm to the turmoil riling in her stomach. Her efforts to combat the memories of Gordon that insisted on flooding her mind were proving unsuccessful. It was strange because this wasn't the first time she'd dated since walking away from him. Of course, she'd never been with a coworker or a man who was the face of an international fashion house, but that was just a small detail. Right?

"You wanna ski after this?"

"Huh?" She returned her attention to Maurice with a start.

He pointed to the window. "You're looking out there like you can't wait to hit the slopes. When this is done, we can change and go out if you want."

"Oh. Sure. I haven't really been anywhere outside the city in a while, so the scenery is pretty nice."

"How haven't you been out of the city? There's a mandatory four-week vacation rule at the company."

"I know. I just prefer to do staycations." Actually, she preferred to save face in front of her family, but Maurice didn't need those details.

"And that means you just sit in your house for four weeks?" Of course, he couldn't believe that she found comfort in solitude and actually enjoyed being in her private space, since he was the party-going, fun-loving Gold sibling.

Thankfully, an athletically built man interrupted them. "Good morning, Lovers." He was standing at the podium with the brunette woman who'd been guarding the door.

"Hush, they're starting." And Desta was glad. The last thing she wanted, after blurting out her family situation to him earlier, was to have him asking more questions about her personal life. It was none of his business for one, and besides that, it had nothing to do with what they were doing here this weekend.

"Okay, we're sure none of you have had a knock-down, drag-out fight yet," the male speaker said. "At least, we hope not." Now that she was staring at him, Mr. Athlete looked more like a hot sports model with his cool blue eyes and blond hair. The crowd of about forty chuckled at his remarks, and he gave a dazzling smile in return.

"But just in case you do this weekend, or some-time later, we want to make sure you're prepared with the best make-up sex tips," said his sidekick, who was almost as attractive as he was. "And oh, we have mimosas!"

Desta leaned over to whisper in Maurice's ear. "Are they really about to give us sex tips?" Of course they were. Wasn't that what this weekend was all about? It was much easier to accept that when she hadn't known who her Dear Lover was.

Maurice's grin was back, beaming at her as he turned so their faces were only inches apart. "We probably don't need 'em, but let's play along, any-way."

The quick kiss to the tip of her nose was a sur-prise, and the uncertainty she'd been feeling mo-mentarily dissipated.

"So, the thing about having a fight is that all the anger you were feeling during the argument makes you really hot." Ms. Congeniality—that's what she was calling the woman—fanned a hand in front of her face. "I mean, physically hot."

"Right, so once you've given in and apologized… guys, this is usually us, especially if we know what's good for us." More laughter. Mr. Athlete obviously had jokes. "It's time to get turned on. The feeling you get when you're angry and when you're turned on is very similar. Body heat rises, and shortness of breath ensues. It's no big deal to just switch that around from anger to what could possibly lead to bliss."

"And it can all start with a touch," Ms. Congeniality said. "So guys, touch your lover. Just something light but arousing at the same time. Assure them that even in the midst of this argument, they're still the one for you."

Maurice was right on task. Desta had leaned back over to the privacy of her own beanbag chair, but now he was invading that privacy. Easing his body over to her, he reached out a hand and cupped her cheek. It was a soft touch, one that didn't necessarily have to be intimate—damn, she really had feelings about that word. Still, she had to resist the urge to jerk back in surprise or pull away after the surprise settled.

"Good. Now, how did that touch make you feel?" Ms. Congeniality continued. "Does it make you want more? Does it make you hotter? Ladies, it's your turn to respond. He's sorry now for whatever he did to piss you off. Don't you want to make him pay by getting him so turned on he can barely see straight?"

No. That was never how she'd felt when she and Gordon argued. Not after the first time when he'd put his foot through their patio door and warned she would be next if she didn't get it together.

But at this moment, at Maurice's touch, a heated flush draped her body. She told herself it was involuntary. While her mind was still trying to keep this class and what was expected of her in perspective, her body was all in and ready to do what she was told. And since she'd agreed to spend this weekend with Maurice, leaning into his touch was simple. His thumb rubbed over her cheek, brushing past the edge of her lips, and a quick spurt of desire took over. She swiped her tongue over his thumb.

His eyes instantly went darker, and before she could speak, he was moving from his bag to hers. Now their bodies were flush against each other, and he was exchanging his thumb for a finger that she promptly sucked between her lips. After all, her payback to him for any argument was supposed to be to drive him wild with desire. The sexual heat that morphed from anger, which Ms. Congeniality was currently describing in detail, was accurate as hell. Wearing a turtleneck today hadn't been the best idea, because Desta was burning up. When Maurice began moving his finger in and out of her mouth, her breasts swelled with the need to be touched, and a tiny moan escaped her throat.

Maurice gasped at the sound, his gaze dropping to her mouth as she continued to suck on his finger with the same fervent hunger she'd had last night when it was his dick in her mouth instead. Why did this feel so good, and how in the hell could she be thinking of stripping out of her clothes so that he could dive deep inside her while they were in this room full of people? None of this was what she'd ever imagined herself doing. But she didn't want to stop.

"That's right, go with it. Let the making up and making out begin," Mr. Athlete said, and she almost expected to hear the crowd cheering him on.

Except the crowd was moaning and groaning instead. She didn't want to glance away to see what anyone else was doing, especially not when Maurice was pulling his finger from her lips, leaning in closer to trade it for his mouth.

His lips were warm against hers, his tongue slipping inside to tangle with hers. She wrapped her arms around his neck, pulling him closer. Obliging, he rolled until he was on top of her and the kiss deepened.

What in the entire hell?

She felt like she was forgiving him for something and repledging herself to him. Giving her all to this kiss, pressing her body against his, while his hands moved up and down her back in a way that conveyed compassion, longing, need.

Before she could figure out what was actually happening, a bell sounded loudly throughout the room. Maurice jerked away from her, and when she looked around many of the other couples looked equally confused.

"I know it's just getting good," Mr. Athlete crooned. "But there's more. Now, there're bound to be instances when the argument you have with your partner is warranted, and a real discussion needs to be had about whatever that issue is. But sometimes, fights can be about something dumb. Maybe someone forgot to clean the shower when they were done *and* didn't empty the dishwasher in the same day, and the other is fed up."

Maurice had settled back, still on her beanbag chair, his arm now wrapped around her shoulders.

"But here's the thing," Ms. Congeniality chimed in. "You love him. You most certainly love the way he goes down on you."

Oh, hell no! She was definitely not spreading her legs in this room with all these people so that Maurice could put his mouth on her already damp pussy the way he had last night.

At the sound of appreciative murmurs from the crowd, Mr. Athlete nodded and grinned. "Yeah, you know he brings it home every time he sets his mouth on you. So when it's a little disagreement, it might be a better use of that energy to let him prop you up on the kitchen counter and have you for dessert."

Desta pressed her thighs tightly together, then

eased them apart when she thought Maurice might've seen her reflexive reaction.

"I'd love having you for dessert." The words sounded so husky and so hot coming from him she almost came right then and there.

Instead, she focused on the steady movement of his hand on her shoulder, so strong and possessive. That last word gave her pause. But then his other hand moved to her thigh, resting there with a punch of searing heat.

"You ever have make-up sex that made you forget what the argument was even about?" he asked. "I mean, sex that just took away every coherent thought from your mind?"

Why was he doing this? Why was he making this so difficult for her?

"No," she said after inhaling a shaky breath. "I haven't had a lot of make-up sex." Gordon's apologetic gestures came in the form of a delivery guy handing her a gift—a diamond necklace, a pair of Louboutin pumps, an Yves Saint Laurent bag. "Sometimes people should have to work harder for forgiveness."

She shouldn't have said that last part. When she looked at him, it was to see him giving a knowing nod. But he didn't know; he couldn't. She'd never told anyone what had truly happened between her and her ex-fiancé, not even her family.

"I don't get a lot of make-up sex, either. Disagreements rarely arise when you make your position clear right off the bat." That's right, he wouldn't have a disagreement about not doing the dishes because he never stayed with anyone long enough to dirty dishes in the first place. "But I'm beginning to think I'd like making up with you."

Okay, this wasn't going well for her. The volleying back and forth between her past and these new and strange feelings his presence was evoking in her were going to drive her nuts.

"Whew! That was something for the first round. Let's take a break before anyone starts to get naked." Ms. Congeniality offered a smile that Desta wanted to smack right off her cute face. "Go grab yourselves a mimosa, and we'll move on to the next round in a few minutes."

"Thank goodness," Desta mumbled, forgetting Maurice was still close enough to hear her.

He chuckled. "You thirsty?"

She shook her head. She was horny and confused. "Not really, but I could use a break. This session is giving a lot of information that I don't think I'll be forgetting anytime soon."

"Really? My kisses are that memorable, huh?" He was smug and arrogant, and too damn sexy when he was being both.

"Hush up and go get us a drink." She really needed some space from him, even if for just a few minutes, to clear her mind.

"Cool. I get it if you need a few minutes to gather yourself after that great kiss."

"Don't kid yourself, it wasn't that great." Of

course, she was lying. "But that line's getting longer for the drinks." His kiss had seared a hole straight through her soul and made the insistent memories of Gordon during this time even more puzzling.

Maurice didn't believe her, anyway. She could see it in the mischievous twinkle in his eyes. But he did get up and walk away, and she watched him go, all the while wondering what she'd gotten herself into and how the hell she was going to train her body not to respond to his touch come Monday morning.

CHAPTER SIX

SOMETIMES PEOPLE SHOULD have to work harder for forgiveness.

Did she know about India and the guilt he carried for months after the accident? She couldn't have. No charges had been filed, and as soon as India was out of the coma, her parents had flown her to some hospital in Switzerland for extensive therapy. As far as Maurice knew, she'd never returned to the States. Which meant he would never have the chance to tell her how sorry he was, again.

No, he was fairly certain Des had no idea of just how reckless he could be. After the accident, he'd spent the remaining years in college—and all of his adult life—trying to forget that night had ever happened. And in doing so, he'd created a totally different persona, the one that was too carefree to look for love…because he didn't deserve to find happiness after what he'd done.

If Des wasn't talking about his past issues, she had to be referring to her own. Had someone done something to her that she couldn't forgive? Or had she, like him, done something unforgivable? It was more than likely the former. Des wasn't reckless, nor was she selfish or inconsiderate. Watching her with staff and his family, whether at his parents' home or when they were out at work functions, she was always the same—calm, cool, compassionate and sometimes funny.

"Okay, I think I've got it this time," she said, and he directed his full attention to her again. He tried to shake off the memories that had crept to the surface. It was a beautiful afternoon on the slopes, and he was helping Des with her skiing.

The white pants, jacket and matching boots she'd changed into after the Make-Up and Mimosas workshop made her look like a sexy ski goddess. Whatever she wore looked great on her, and after years of being surrounded by beautiful women, he knew that meant something.

"You just want to keep your feet firmly planted, bend your knees a little and then…" He paused, watching her blink repeatedly as she tried to take in every word he was saying. Deciding it'd be much better if he showed her, he dragged his feet in his skis until he was standing right beside her. "Like this." He demonstrated the way he wanted her to stand and waited while she mimicked him.

"I've skied before," she said while adjusting the poles in her hands and trying to line her knees up with his. "It's just been a while."

"It's just like sex. Once you've done it, you never forget how to do it." The last words were exaggerated, but he chuckled, as he often did whenever he cracked a joke, because the people around him rarely appreciated his sense of humor. He was caught off guard when she leaned in to nudge him with her elbow and instead turned her leg and subsequently the ski.

He had seconds to reach out and grab her, then try to resituate them both before catastrophe struck. His attempts were a failure, and they tumbled over, falling onto the snow-covered ground with a thump. Both sets of skis clanked together as they rolled a couple times before stopping by a tree.

"Well, I guess my sex comment put some thoughts in your mind, huh? But if you wanted to have sex outside, I'd suggest it not be on the slopes. I don't do too well in arctic temps." She wiggled beneath him, but she wasn't smiling when he stared down at her. In fact, her brow was furrowed, lips pursed in irritation. Sort of how he'd caught her looking a few times during the workshop.

"Hey, it's okay. Everybody falls sometimes. I mean, it could be that I'm not that good of a ski instructor. But you don't have to share that with anyone." Still trying to keep things light, he watched her warily, waiting for the tension to melt away from her features and the stiffness from her movements.

"No. I'll get it." She pushed at him again. "Just let me up. I can do this."

Maurice rolled off her and sat on the ground as he watched her get to her feet. He could've gotten up first and helped her, but instinct told him to let her be. When she was upright and he followed, she adjusted the sticks in her hands once more. He stood close enough to help if she fell, and just far enough away that she didn't have to give him one of her *you're workin' my nerves* looks.

Adjusting her hood, she stared straight ahead. Determination was clear in the serious lines of her face as she bent her knees, planted the poles a short distance in front of her and pushed off. At first all he could do was watch, admiring her tenacity, before finally following her down the rest of the hill. She'd been doing fine until she tried to stop and swerved her body a little more than was required. When she toppled over this time, he wasn't close enough to catch her.

She got up cursing.

Maurice moved in to help her. "Doesn't have to be perfect every time, Des. You did good coming down."

Once she was up on her feet, she pushed his arms away. "Don't talk to me like I'm a child."

There was no mistaking the anger that laced her tone nor the definite scowl she was giving him now. He was used to attitude—Riley gave it to him all the time. He knew independence and confidence were really important to both his sister and Des, especially in the workplace. But this was different. Des was always in control at work, and whenever she was angered, her responses still came calmly, laced with deadly accurate aim. He'd never seen her react to anything or anyone in this way.

"Are you okay?" Because this wasn't just about being rusty at skiing.

She glanced away, then stabbed her poles into the snow and shook her head. "I apologize," she said, returning her gaze to him.

He didn't want her apology; he wanted to know what was going on with her. "Tell me what's wrong. Maybe I can help?"

"You can't."

"You won't know until you trust me enough to tell me."

Shock filled her gaze now, and he realized he'd just said the T word, which could sometimes carry as much weight as the L word.

"It's not a big deal. And you're right, neither is skiing perfectly. It's not like I'm trying out for the Olympics." Her lips curved in a tentative smile that didn't quite reach her eyes. "Let's just head back to the hotel. It's getting cold."

It had been freezing since they'd come out here an hour and a half ago, so he knew that wasn't the only issue here. But he shouldn't push. It was only fair that she have her secrets. After all, he had his.

On Saturday evening, Desta touched a hand to her stomach and closed her eyes as she stood at the door of her room. Just a few minutes more, some quiet time to get her thoughts in order, that was all she needed. Breathe in, breathe out. Slowly. Count down from twenty. Start again, this time from fifty.

She had to get Gordon out of her mind. Truth be told, she wasn't sure why memories of him were popping up left and right during this trip. It had been a long time since she'd thought about him and what had happened between them, and it was irritating as hell to have it coming back now like a tidal wave. But she could do this. She could get over him, just like she'd done before. All she had to do was focus on Maurice and the reason they were here this weekend.

That was so much easier said than done. First because, for whatever reason, so many things Maurice was saying or doing were direct leads to specific memories about Gordon. Like the elevator. For the second time, Maurice had sent her a text telling her to meet him at the elevator. Gordon always gave her instructions: be dressed at seven; have dinner ready at six; call me as soon as you get in the house. So much so that after a while she'd started to feel as if he were a drill sergeant and she was a soldier he had to keep in line at all times. *Demeaning* didn't begin to describe how that made her feel, even now. And while she knew this wasn't Maurice's intent, it still opened the window to those damn memories.

Second, if she just set her mind to having sex with Maurice every second of every day they were at this resort, she'd also go crazy. There was a hunger when she was near him now, a sensation she hadn't felt before, but that was definitely awakened now. A part of her had wanted him to tear her pants off and touch his mouth to her waiting core again, just like they'd mentioned during the Make-Up and Mimosas session this morning. Of course, she hadn't wanted him to do it right there in front of everybody, but the thought of him going down on her again had her pulse increasing and her pussy pulsating. She could have him as much as she wanted this weekend, of that she was certain. It was more how or if they were going to keep this momentum going when their weekend was over.

At any rate, she couldn't think about any of this anymore right now. She needed to get going so they wouldn't be late for the PJs, Dinner and a Movie event. She was starved, and Maurice probably was, too. Finally opening her eyes, she took another steadying breath and left the room.

She stepped out into the hallway wearing a cappuccino silk pajama set. Staring down at the ensemble, she told herself for the hundredth time that choosing to wear the pants instead of the shorty-short-shorts that also came with this set was a smart idea. The top was long sleeved and had a belted waist instead of buttons, and on her feet were her favorite Ugg Cozette leopard-print slippers. She frowned and wiggled her toes because these were the slippers she wore when she was at home. She'd meant to order a pair of more sedate-looking slippers for the pajama party, but she'd had gotten busy at work and forgot. With a shrug, and because the clock was ticking, she continued down the hallway.

Maurice was punctual, and so was she, which was why she told herself that any recollection of Gordon around Maurice was a mistake. This wasn't the same. In fact, it couldn't be more different than what she'd gone through six years ago.

"How is it possible that you make even pajamas look sexy?" The twinkle in Maurice's eyes as she walked toward him was alluring. She'd noted that long ago, which was why she never questioned how so many women were swept away by him, even though they knew he'd never commit to any of them. "I mean, you're not showing a bit of skin. Well, except for your toes, which are mighty cute with that yellow nail polish."

"Sexy Is a Complete Package," she replied, coming to a stop beside him.

"Ahh." He grinned and nodded. "Last year's Women of the World Collection slogan. That was brilliant then, and it's still relevant now."

She couldn't help feeling the flush of pride wash over her as he recalled one of her most recent marketing campaigns. RGF's Women of the World Collection—which featured both upscale business and business-casual wear as well as budget-friendly designs—had given career-minded women more fashion choices than any other line across that season, and she'd been in charge of getting the word out to the world about it. It was one of her favorite projects.

"Skin doesn't always mean sexy. You should know that by now," she told him.

The elevator came, and they stepped inside.

"Why? Because the women I date all show a lot of skin?"

His response seemed defensive and was a little off topic. "I meant because at RGF, we're not all about showing off a woman's body with revealing clothes. We cater to the entire style of a woman."

The look on his face said he was rethinking his words. It should've been the look of someone realizing they'd put their foot in their mouth, but that wasn't Maurice. While he could admit when he was wrong, it was always on his terms. He remained silent for the duration of their ride, and she stepped off the elevator first when the doors opened again.

She already knew which direction to go without the help of the signs and arrows the resort had put up to assist them in getting around. Besides that, she could smell the food coming from the resort restaurant and her stomach churned in response. She was actually following her stomach's lead.

"Hey, there! I sent you a text this morning after the mimosas session, and you didn't respond." Kelli came out of nowhere, stopping Desta in her tracks.

"Oh, hi. Yeah, sorry about that. We went skiing and then I came back and took a nap. Didn't know the slopes could be so exhausting." That was a lie.

After all her tumbles and the emotional upheaval of too many trips down memory lane, she'd gone straight to her room when they were done and taken a hot shower. She'd felt better after that, and she'd checked and answered emails until it was time to get ready for tonight's festivities. She gave Kelli a tentative smile. The woman returned it with a beaming one of her own.

"I'll just bet you were exhausted." With a wink and a chuckle Kelli glanced over Desta's shoulder. "Guess your match is working out?"

"Yes. Yes, we're…working out just fine." *For the weekend*, she wanted to say for clarification. One more day and they'd be back in the city working on something other than turning each other on. "Um, Maurice, this is Kelli. Kelli, this is Maurice."

"Oh, you don't have to tell me who he is." Kelli stared at Maurice, accepting the hand he'd already extended for a shake. "I know exactly who Maurice Gold is. The elusive fashion mogul who loves the ladies but not enough to settle down with one. I recognized him as soon as I saw you in his arms yesterday."

If Maurice felt as uncomfortable with what Kelli just said as Desta did, he didn't show it. In fact, his most dashing smile was in place as he shook and released Kelli's hand. "It's a pleasure to meet you, Kelli. Did you have a chance to link up with your match this weekend, or are you just hanging out solo?"

Desta had wondered that, too, since Kelli had not only sent her a text this morning but had also sent one late last night. Desta had responded to that one after she'd left Maurice's room this morning.

"Oh no, I found my guy. He's right over there getting us a table. Hey, why don't you two join us? We can have a double date." Kelli didn't wait for their response but immediately turned and fast-walked over to the restaurant entrance, where a guy wearing gray sweatpants and a matching T-shirt was speaking to the host.

"We should get out of this," she said to Maurice the moment they were alone.

"Nah, then we look like we've got something to hide. And we don't, so let's just go."

"We don't? Are you sure?" She couldn't help but question him here. "How's it going to look that two RGF employees were caught spending the weekend at a sex retreat?" Because when it came right down to it, regardless of any of the names they slapped on it, that's exactly what this weekend was turning out to be.

Maurice easily took her hand in his and said, "It looks like two consenting adults decided to do some adult things."

Unable to hide her exasperation with his unbothered attitude where the media was concerned, she sighed. "Look, I know you like to believe that you've got everybody eating out of the palm of your hand all the time, especially the media. But this time I'm attached, too. My career's on the line, and unlike you I'm not related to the bosses. I could lose my job."

He stopped, dropped her hand and turned so that they were now face-to-face. "I'm damn good at my job, Desta. No matter what the media prints or says about me, RGF is always at the forefront of my mind. So don't throw my family in my face as if I can afford to be reckless because of them."

She wanted to snap back, but creating a scene wasn't going to help make her point. Besides that, she'd never seen Maurice look as serious as he did right now.

"I'm just saying we should think about this."

"You can think about it. I'm going to have dinner." With that, he left her standing there.

She felt like an idiot as that itchy sensation rippled over her skin again. She closed her eyes, intending to start her breathing exercises to calm herself down, but stopped. She opened her eyes again. Maurice was right: now was not the place to fall apart. If Kelli was going to run to the media with this tidbit of information, Desta's reaction to it would just add fuel to the fire.

Pasting on a smile, she pulled out her phone as she began to walk after Maurice. If it looked like she was reading a message or something, maybe it wouldn't seem like they'd had a disagreement and he'd just walked away from her—something she wasn't going to forget he'd done.

Kelli was waving wildly from a table that was

thankfully toward the back of the restaurant. Maurice hadn't turned back to see if Desta was behind him, but when he arrived at the table, he pulled out the chair closest to the wall and waited until she took a seat. Offering him one of her practiced smiles, she sat across from Kelli and glanced at Kelli's guy as Maurice sat down.

Kelli's match had cocoa-brown hair that was long and curling on top but close-shaved on the sides. Glasses, gray eyes and a full goatee filled out the rest of his face. She'd already noted he was tall and built like a basketball player, and when he smiled as she stared at him, she got the impression he was friendly.

"Hi, I'm Travis." Because she'd been caught staring and she really needed to get herself together if she was going to make it through this meal, she accepted his hand for a quick shake.

"Hi, Travis, I'm Desta. And this is Maurice." She prayed Kelli wouldn't mention his last name.

"Maurice's family founded the largest Black-owned fashion house in the world. I know you've heard of RGFashions," Kelli announced amiably, and Desta's hopes were quickly dashed.

"And Desta's head of our marketing department," Maurice added.

Good thing she'd pulled her hand back from the shake with Travis and let it rest in her lap with the other one. Now she could clasp them together tightly in frustration without anyone else seeing them.

"Really? So are you here this weekend for work

or pleasure?" Travis asked, probably because she wasn't wearing her ID badge.

Glancing over at Maurice in his fitted black T-shirt and black basketball shorts, she noticed he wasn't wearing his badge, either.

Of course Kelli answered the question for them. "No, silly, they're Dear Lovers, too."

"Oh? Wow. How does that work? Were you surprised to find each other here?" Now, all on board with Kelli's excitement, Travis was the inquisitive one.

"No," Desta spoke up. "We knew we'd both be here, and once our matches didn't pan out, we just decided to stay for a relaxing weekend." Where that lie came from she didn't exactly know, but it felt right. The less these two—and possibly, at some point, the world—knew about how she and Maurice actually came to be here together, the better.

"Yeah, but it was quite a coincidence," Maurice added easily. "With the disappointment of not hitting it off with my match, it was an unexpected comfort to see Desta here."

This was the second time he'd used her full name. Since about a month after she'd begun working at RGF, Maurice had called her Des, and because she'd liked him from the start—in a strictly platonic way—she hadn't bothered to correct him. It dawned on her in this instant that he was the only one who called her that, and she liked it.

"That's so cool." Kelli had leaned forward, resting

her elbows on the table. She stared at them as if they were a couple on a reality-television show she was obsessed with. "So, how's it going so far? What'd you think about Make-Up and Mimosas? I only saw you two walking out, but I couldn't catch up with you."

"It was definitely informative." Maurice was sure to answer first this time. "All those tips on how to shift the anger from the argument to sexual desire were quite interesting. Makes you want to pick an argument just for the sake of getting to the make-up sex."

Travis grinned and nodded at Maurice. "I was thinking the same thing, man."

"No," Kelli answered quickly. "No arguments over here, at least not yet." She giggled. "It's too early to say for sure if they'll end with make-up sex or a complete block from my email and my phone."

"That's certainly an option," Desta added. Even though, for her, it really wasn't. If this thing they'd agreed to went south, she had no idea how the work relationship between her and Maurice would turn out.

She couldn't tell if Maurice was thinking along the same lines, and the conversation quickly turned when the server came to take their orders. Cheeseburger sliders, hot wings, fries and beers all around came to the table in the next fifteen minutes. From there, the chatter went to the food, the beer and guesses as to which movie they'd be watching tonight.

Desta managed to relax at some point, and when Maurice put his arm around the back of her chair after they finished eating, she didn't give it a second thought. A stranger walking by might think this was a normal double date, with four friends laughing and talking about things like sports and how many times Desta fell on the slopes in comparison to how many times Kelli had done the same.

Nobody would know that a war was going on inside her—one in which she wished she could actually have this sense of normalcy. Only, the smarter, more experienced side of her knew it was an impossibility. Things could seem good one moment and change completely the next. And because of that, she would never willingly take a chance on a relationship again.

CHAPTER SEVEN

MAURICE HAD GUESSED they'd be watching something like *Iron Man* or some other Marvel movie, because it would've certainly taken the sexual edge off all the other planned events for the weekend. He'd been sorely mistaken.

Twenty minutes after they'd finished eating, he found them a set of beanbag chairs in the far-left corner of a room that had been designated their movie theater for the evening. It had taken a little dodging to unravel them from Kelli and Travis after leaving the restaurant, but he knew dinner had been stressful for Des. When she wasn't eating, she'd been wringing her hands so much he was certain she'd caused bruising.

And he needed to make up for losing his patience with her earlier. He wasn't going to apologize because she'd been out of line throwing his family into the reason why he had job security, especially since she of all people knew that wasn't true. If there was one thing his father, Ron Gold Sr., didn't tolerate it was insubordination on the job, and if his dad for one minute thought something Maurice was doing was jeopardizing the image of the company, he would fire him personally. Admittedly, on the surface, he could see how his philandering ways might be a stain on RGF's otherwise impeccable reputation. But he'd always been the charming Gold brother, a trait which aided in his job as the head of PR. The media reps loved him, which more often than not worked to his advantage. If that meant the media also took a considerable interest in his personal life, he'd been willing to deal with that.

"We're pretty much out of sight back here," he said when Desta only stood next to the pair of beanbags. He had no idea why the organizers of this event thought these were a cute idea. While he got a kick out of them, Des definitely wasn't a fan.

"And we can still see the screen," she added, even though she made no attempt to sit.

"Of course, as soon as they turn the lights down and get started it'll be just like being in a movie theater."

"Without the comfortable reclining seats." Glancing over at her, he saw her tentative smile.

He chuckled. "Yeah, I guess you could say that." He plopped down onto one of the bags. Actually, since they were in the back, their seats had been pushed farther into a corner, putting a little more space between them and the next couple. It was actually a pretty ideal spot for privacy.

When she was still standing, he reached out and pulled the other beanbag closer to his, until the faux leather material touched and they looked like one big blob. "I like it. C'mon, sit down. The movie will be starting soon."

He was certain she wanted to say something else, to make another remark about how she didn't understand why they didn't have real seats, but she declined. Giving up on that argument was a task for her, he knew—Des loved to get her point across. She sat down beside him, moving a little more in the seat than she had this morning. "You okay? Do you need me to find you another seat?"

"No. It's not that." She continued to move until finally settling herself into a groove. "Guess I'll make a note that silk pajamas don't really go with beanbag chairs. I'll probably be slipping and sliding around throughout the entire movie."

Only because the lights went out at that moment, signaling the movie was about to start, did he bite down on the remark about possibly enjoying her slipping and sliding around as long as she ended up beneath him again.

Someone came by with cartons of popcorn and a choice of bottled waters or sodas. Des took a water and popcorn. He only took a water. For the first twenty minutes of the movie they shared the popcorn and sipped on their drinks, both watching the screen with mild interest. It was when the lube, blindfold and whip were revealed that all thoughts of eating or drinking disappeared.

Des's eyes were plastered to the screen, and there was no look of surprise or disgust on her face. For that reason, Maurice turned his attention back to the movie and waited to see how the scene would play out.

The man explained things like safe words and complete submission, pleasure and dominance, all while removing the woman's clothes slowly, one item at a time. Maurice imagined his fingers brushing over Des's smooth skin as he untied that belt at her waist and slid the top from her shoulders. There was a spot right at the hollow of her collar bone that he'd kissed last night and had been thinking of kissing again. His dick jumped, and he thanked the heavens that he'd had the good sense to wear loose-fitting shorts. Even if she looked over right now she probably wouldn't notice his growing erection.

He felt it, though, along with the rush of warmth throughout his body as he continued watching the scene. The actress licked her lips, the same way Des had done last night when she'd been standing in his room staring down at his dick. After Des had done that, she'd been on her knees, taking him into her mouth, and he'd been certain he'd died and gone straight to heaven. When the actor on-screen touched the pad of his finger to her tongue and the woman proceeded to lick around the digit, Maurice sucked in a breath. A glance over at Des and he could see her tongue stroking her bottom lip.

It took a few seconds for him to calm himself enough to not roll on top of her—they were in a room full of people, after all. The Dear Lover staff were crafty and very good at creating a sexually charged atmosphere, he'd give them that. But what was he supposed to do now?

Des had brought up the issue of Kelli telling the media about them being there together. If that were the case, or if anyone decided to phone in an anonymous tip, him reaching over to touch Des would possibly give more ammunition. Then again, it was pretty dark in this room and they were sitting in a semi-secluded spot. Before he could ruminate on it any further, Des's hand moved from where she'd had it resting in her lap up, until it brushed over her breast. The nipple was already hard, and Maurice cursed before extending his hand to touch it.

She jumped when he touched her and then their gazes locked. "Tell me to stop." It was a plea, and he wondered if he should follow that up by giving her a safe word like the guy on-screen had done. "Please, just say the word."

Otherwise he was going to continue to circle his finger around her nipple.

Her lips parted, and she inhaled deeply, releasing the breath slowly before blinking. "It feels good."

That didn't sound like *stop* to him, and in the next instant he palmed her breast, squeezing it in his hand until her head fell back against the beanbag. A tiny gasp escaped through her lips.

His gaze was now focused on her breasts, the one he held in his hand and the other that had a pebbled nipple, as well. She had great-sized breasts, a little more than a handful, high and perfect for suckling. If he closed his eyes right now, he'd see them in his mind—delectable mounds with big dark nipples that beckoned him. Reaching his other hand out, he cupped them both, kneading them until the top of her pajamas began to slide open. He already knew she wasn't wearing a bra, and he wanted to curse his phenomenal luck.

"More?" Asking for permission was a must every step of the way in this precarious situation. There was no plan for what he was doing. He was just following his body's reaction to her, trusting that hers would respond.

"Yes." It was a faint whisper, but he'd heard it and he dipped his head. With his chin he eased the material to the side until he could put his mouth on her bare mound.

Was he really doing this? Right here and right now? The answer was a resounding yes.

And from the sounds of moaning coming from the screen, and some he was certain from right in this room, he wasn't the only one. In all his life he'd never imagined himself doing something like this, never even considered that he might be into an orgy-type scenario, but this was making him hot as hell!

When she slapped a hand to the back of his head, holding his mouth over her breast, he moaned. His dick was so hard, tenting his shorts as it ached to get inside her.

"Can't believe this," she murmured. "Can't stop. Feels so good."

Yeah, he couldn't speak right now because he'd moved to the next breast, but she was absolutely right, it did feel damn good. And he didn't want to stop.

He did, though, at least after a few more moments of sucking on the tautest nipples he'd ever tasted. Lifting his head, Maurice eased over so that his body was just about on top of hers. He cupped her cheek, turning her face into his, and touched his lips to hers. Their tongues instantly dueled as if they'd each been waiting for this exact moment. Again, her hand was on the back of his head, holding him in the position she wanted him.

It was an aggressive move, a dominant act, and lust soared through his bloodstream like a drug. Kissing Des was unlike kissing any other woman he'd ever met. Her lips were so sweet, her tongue so masterful as it stroked his until drops of pre-cum seeped from his dick. He needed to be inside her right now.

"Des," he whispered when he was able to pull back a few inches from her mouth, "we gotta…"

"Yes," she moaned and then pulled him down for another kiss.

This time there was a fevered pitch to the way their tongues moved. She sucked his deep into her mouth, and he moved his hands to bury them in her hair. He was going to climb on top of her and fuck her right here in this room with this damn movie playing and at least twenty other couples watching.

That was an insane idea. No way could he let it go that far. He had to stop. They had to get out of here.

Calling on every ounce of control he possessed, Maurice pulled his mouth away from hers. She didn't try to hold him still; instead she dropped her hands to her side as if touching him had somehow injured them.

"We can't do this here," he said, his whisper husky with desire.

She licked her lips again and nodded. "I know."

"Let's get out of here."

"Yeah," she replied and cleared her throat. "Now."

"I need to feel you."

Desta could hear the urgency in his voice. She felt it in the moment they were in the elevator alone and he pushed her against the wall of the car. His lips were on hers again, and she couldn't think about anything else but falling into the kiss. She'd been trying to reconcile this madness in her mind since last night. How was it that they'd gone from friends and coworkers to insatiable lovers in such a short span of time?

The answer was his hand slipping beneath the

band of her pajama pants, going farther, past her panties, until she could feel his fingers pressing against her mound.

"Just gotta touch you." His words came on pants for air that they were both taking between the heated kisses.

Desire surged through her like a raging storm, making her feel as if her heart might leap right out of her chest it beat so fast. She was limp against the wall, held up by the arm he'd wrapped securely around her waist. When his fingers inched lower, parting her, sliding easily inside her, she gasped. Her head fell against the wall, back arched, eyes closed.

"Maurice." His name was a whisper. A breath she had to breathe in the midst of this tumultuous wanting.

Two fingers—she was almost positive that's how many he used—pressed inside her, and she clenched her teeth so hard flashes of light sparked behind her still-closed eyes. He didn't give her a second to acclimate herself to the feel of him stretching her but instead began pumping his fingers quickly in and out, while his lips fastened over her neck.

Desta held him tightly, her low-cut nails digging into his back through the T-shirt he wore. She lifted one leg and wrapped it around him.

"Hell yeah. Thank you. Thank you. Thank you." His words tumbled over her as he thrust faster and deeper now that she'd given him even more access.

Her hips moved now, meeting his thrusts and silently begging him for more. How could this feel so good? It wasn't his dick penetrating her and yet the feeling was almost as intense as if it were. Her body was taut with anticipation, her nipples so hard she wanted to reach up and rub them herself.

"Need you to come for me. Right now, just please come."

She'd never been begged to come before. On a few occasions she'd pleaded with her body to simply cooperate so that things would go smoother, but she knew that didn't count.

Her eyes fluttered open as she panted. "Please don't stop. Please. Just. Wait." Pleasure ripped through her so fast and so intensely that it rendered her speechless.

Maurice moaned, holding her even tighter, his fingers slowing inside of her but not stopping.

The elevator, however, did stop on their floor at that moment. A light dinging sound told them the doors were about to open, and Maurice hurriedly pulled his hands from her. She let her leg slide down and was ready to walk out of the car as soon as the doors slid apart. He followed her off, grabbing her by the hand.

"Hurry" was all he said as he continued in the direction of his room.

She stopped, shaking her head when he turned to look at her quizzically.

"My room tonight." She didn't say anything else but turned to walk in the opposite direction. He would follow her; she knew without having to turn around and check.

Her fingers shook a little as she found her key card in the side pocket of her pajama pants and walked into the suite. The door had barely closed before Maurice was grabbing her and pushing her back up against it. He blinked quickly, a look of shock or maybe apology on his face.

"It's okay, I can take a little roughness." In fact, she liked it. Even though she hadn't before and had sworn she'd never allow it from another man again. But this was different. There was no anger, no need to scare or intimidate. No, this, with Maurice, was pure desire. It was mutual, and rising so fast and potent between the two of them she reveled in the rush of anticipation.

A hungry groan was how she'd best describe the sound coming from him just before he ordered, "Off!" Meaning her pajamas, she surmised by the way he pushed the top of the pajama set off her shoulders. She remembered the belt and tore at that until it was loose. That piece of silk hit the floor in seconds, leaving her breasts bare to him.

He palmed one in each hand before bending down to take a nipple into his mouth. Then, moving quickly, he switched sides. All the while, she squirmed with the desire building inside her once again. This time she made the next move, reaching for his shirt and forcing him to stand up and release his hold on her breasts so she could remove it. His top fell to the floor, as well. He pushed her pajama bottoms and panties down past her hips, and she stepped out of her slippers, then eased each leg out.

Mimicking his motions, she pushed his shorts and boxer briefs down while he hastily stepped out of the leather slipper moccasins he wore. Now they were both naked, her body quaking beneath his in-depth perusal.

"I never imagined you naked," he said while shaking his head. "I don't know why. I should've known." His hands were moving up and down her torso now. "I just should've known."

Then he was pushing her against the door again, hiking up one of her legs to latch around the back of his waist. She pulled him to her, running her nails along his back as she waited with anticipation for him to sink deep. "Wait. Condom."

The litany of curses that tumbled from his mouth at that moment would've seared any other person's eardrums. If that other person hadn't grown up in a house of crude brothers who thought swearing was a measure of their manhood.

Maurice backed away as if he'd been scorched, and she frowned when he dragged his hands down his face.

"Condoms are in my wallet." If this were a cartoon, now would be the moment when question marks popped into the air. "My wallet is in my room." That statement settled around them like a lead weight.

"Oh." That didn't seem like much of a response, but then— "Oh! Wait! I have some!" She shot across the room, not giving a damn what body parts jiggled as a result, and went straight to the duffel bag she'd brought with her in addition to her suitcase. Digging inside she found the box and stood holding it in the air like it was the prize of the decade. "I have some!"

He did a fist pump in the air and then paused. "You always carry a whole box of condoms when you travel?"

"No." She frowned and tossed the box at him. "Only when I'm coming to meet the guy who talked about making me come numerous times a day."

Maurice didn't respond. He was too busy ripping the box open, dropping the torn pieces of cardboard onto the floor. When he plucked one packet out of the box, the box met the floor as well. A moment later so did the condom wrapper as he hurriedly sheathed himself.

He reached for her and lifted her off her feet. With a gasp she wrapped her arms around his neck and her legs around his waist.

"This is gonna be fast again," he growled and then walked them to the nearest wall—which was actually the bathroom door—and pushed inside her.

"Yes!" The one word was loud and echoed throughout the room. "That's what I want, hard and fast and so good. So damn good."

Mutual gasps echoed through the air at their joining as she took him in deep. There were no more words, no more quips from either of them as only the sound of their bodies pounding into each other resonated throughout the room. He was driving into her so hard and so fast that her back slammed into the door, her mind whirling around the delicious thrill of this heated taking.

"Sorry," he groaned and thrust inside her once more before his body stilled. "So. Sorry." Two more of those stiff thrust-and-stop movements and she was shattering around him again.

Her eyes closed and her head tilted back, her fingers still digging into his skin as her muscles contracted around his pulsating dick.

"Dammit." Moaning, he dropped his forehead to rest at her neck. His body jerked with his release moments after hers, as she continued to tremble.

"Tomorrow," he whispered after a few minutes of them both trying to catch their breath.

"Tomorrow?" That was a weird word to use after sex.

He nodded. "Yeah. We're gonna take it slow, tomorrow."

CHAPTER EIGHT

MAURICE GRABBED TWO towels from the closet by the bathroom door and dropped them on the end of the soaker tub.

She was still standing in the doorway, a sheet from the bed wrapped around her body, and her arms folded over her chest to hold it in place. When he'd suggested they take a bath, the languid after-sex sensations that had been filtering through her body switched places with a clammy feeling that now pricked her skin. This was different and yet it was the same, even her body could get that message right.

Maurice was not Gordon, and this wasn't a real relationship—that much was clear in her mind. But taking a bath was intimate, and intimacy blurred the lines. She needed those lines, the barriers she'd carefully built around her in the years since the worst breakup she'd ever experienced.

Unfortunately, she didn't see a way of wriggling out of this that didn't make it seem as if she were overreacting or, worse, weak.

"I'm not gonna bite. It's just a bath. After all the falling we did on the slopes this afternoon and the other, um, very vigorous activity we just enjoyed, I figure a nice soak will do us both good."

"You sound like an old man," she quipped and then figured, the hell with it, and stepped completely into the bathroom.

"Nah, not old, baby." He stepped into the tub and lowered his body into the water. "Just a ski coach whose student couldn't grasp the idea that the skis remain on the ground, not her pretty little ass."

Rolling her eyes at his smug smirk and keeping a lid on how irritated she'd been earlier today on the slopes, she dropped the sheet and walked over to the tub. Definitely large enough for the two of them. It was positioned close to a window that, when open, boasted another glorious view of the mountain scenery. She'd closed the electronic blinds when she'd been in here getting dressed earlier. Going to the opposite side of the tub, she hurriedly stepped in and sat down. Not because she was modest about him seeing her body—they'd obviously been there and done that. She just didn't want to chicken out at the last minute.

"You aren't the best at everything," she said once she was settled in the pleasingly hot water. Maurice was a tall guy, six feet two and a half inches, to be exact. She knew how tall each of the Gold siblings were because she'd seen their measurements on a spreadsheet during a show where the family were all wearing specially designed outfits. He sat with his legs spread open and pressed against the edge of the tub. She sat with her legs between his, her cheery yellow painted toenails almost hiding his crotch area. A bubble bath might have been a better idea.

"Never said I was. But the things I am good at I like to boast about. Just in case there's someone who needs to know." His juvenile grin relaxed her. It also made her look around for something to throw at him. "Besides, I can't help it that you're a perfectionist and it annoys the hell out of you when you can't get something right on the first try."

Only because in the past whenever she messed up, she paid for it dearly. "I'm not arguing with you about this." She leaned back, letting her neck rest on the lip of the tub. If she closed her eyes and focused solely on the water, she wouldn't have to stare at him and his naked body, a stark reminder that they'd totally changed the dynamic of their friendship.

A few moments passed in silence. Moments when she knew he was watching her, and she told herself not to feel uncomfortable about that.

"Why'd you sign up for Dear Lover?"

Hadn't they already talked about this? No, not really. She sighed and lifted her head so she could look at him. "It was something to do. I saw the ad one night when I was doing online research. It was just there on the side of some website I was on, and the name caught my eye, so I clicked on it."

"You weren't looking for an online hookup?" He

was staring at her skeptically, his eyes narrowing. Damn, when did he start looking so sexy?

From his tawny skin tone to the thick dark eyebrows that were so naturally neat that she couldn't help but envy them to the low-cut goatee and his perfectly tapered fade haircut, he was quite possibly the handsomest man she'd ever seen. And that was just from the neck up.

"Were you?" She shot the question back at him because her mouth was going dry.

"No." He rubbed a finger over his chin and then shrugged. "Like I told you before, I wanted to try something different."

"But how did you know about the site?"

Again, his eyes narrowed, but this time it was as if he were contemplating what he should say.

"I searched dating sites online. And before you ask again, no, I wasn't looking for a date. I just wanted someone to talk to."

"Wait," she said sitting up so that water sloshed with her movement. "Were you lonely? *The* Maurice Gold was lonely."

Now he shook his head. "Don't do that."

"Don't do what?"

"Don't act like the rest of the world. You know me. You knew me before this." Moving a hand back and forth between them signaled what *this* was. "You know I'm not the way they paint me out to be."

He was right; she did know. Which was why she sat back again and decided to give him a better answer. "It can be hard to figure out who you can trust enough to just be yourself with. I think that happens to everyone who reaches a certain level of success, because with it comes notoriety and expectations. You don't always know where you fit into the mix."

"That's exactly it." He nodded. "Major's married, and Riley's in a committed relationship. And here I am, still dating the flavor of the month, according to *FYI Update*."

The tabloid he spoke of was one of the worst, and their reporters had a fixation with the Gold family. A few months ago they'd run a malicious piece claiming Major's wife, Nina, had left her father to die in a nursing home so she could come to New York and marry into money. In truth, Nina's father lived in a facility Major had found nearby and would be spending Christmas with the Golds in a few weeks.

"If it's any consolation, RJ's still happily single." Bringing up the oldest Gold sibling was sure to invoke a bit of levity into a conversation that had taken a weirdly serious tone.

Maurice's soft smile only made him sexier. "RJ's going to die single. Do you know, one day he said he'd rather lie naked over hot coals than even consider getting seriously involved with another woman again."

She chuckled. "Yeah, I think I was there when he said it."

"Right." He was nodding and grinning now, too. "Come to think of it, you've been around a lot."

"I work for your family's company." As if that needed to be said.

"No. I mean, you've been around in my personal life a lot. Linking up with you on that app has to be some kind of strange coincidence."

"Fate. That's what my grandmother would call it. She doesn't believe in coincidences." And Desta no longer believed in things happening for a reason. If that were the case, what the hell was the point in all she'd gone through with Gordon?

"You miss her. I can hear it in your voice. I heard it this morning when you mentioned her, too. But you don't want to go back to Chicago and visit her. That's odd."

Not liking where this conversation was going, Desta reached over and snagged one of the loofah sponges from a gold-wire basket on the back edge of the tub. "Not as odd as the two of us sitting in this tub."

He shrugged again. "I don't know, I'm kinda liking the two of us sitting here together."

"You would," she said with a roll of her eyes. The water was growing warm, so she grabbed the bottle of liquid soap and was about to pour it on the sponge, when he moved.

"Let me do that for you." He didn't wait for a response but took the bottle and loofah from her hands.

Scooting closer and causing water to slosh over the rim of the tub, he chuckled. When the sponge was lathered up, he reached for her.

"This is crazy. You know that, don't you?" It was crazy good, she could admit that to herself the moment he touched the sponge to her chest.

"Yeah, I know. And no, I don't know how it's going to turn out, but right now I'm gonna wash you up and put you to bed. Is that okay with you?" Asking a question while he dragged a soapy loofah ever so seductively over her nipples was a trap if ever she'd heard of one.

Still, all Desta could do was smile. "Yeah, that's okay with me."

"This is gonna feel so good." There wasn't much that didn't feel good where Des was concerned.

"I take it you're used to getting massages." She was sitting on the bench beside him, her body covered by the plush white robe they'd each been handed five minutes after walking into the spa area. It was midafternoon on Sunday, and they'd signed up for the Relax and Relate session.

There were two other couples sitting in chairs across the room. The guy carrying a clipboard who seemed to be in charge of the schedule had just left the waiting area with another couple.

"I used to have a monthly in-home appointment." Maurice paused a moment recalling Hannah, the masseuse who'd turned into a date that went disastrously wrong. The memory made him frown. "But it's been a while."

"Did she quit or did you fire her for the new flavor of the month?" Normally, coming from Des, that question would've been presented as a joking jab or just a flippant remark, but the way her face paled before she glanced away implied she was feeling something different today.

Which made sense, because he wasn't feeling his normal nonchalance, either. Instead, he was sure his cheeks had heated at her words in what he could only describe as embarrassment. Did Des really see him as a callous philanderer? It appeared that way, considering her question. The thought made him feel like crap. That wasn't the impression he wanted her to have, and he wasn't ready to explore why the hell it mattered at all.

"Oh hey, y'all!" Looking toward the door he saw Kelli walk in, Travis right behind her. "You guys sure do sneak out of a room fast. We couldn't find you at all last night after the movie. We wanted to have nightcaps and discuss the show. But I guess you two had better things to do." She giggled.

Yes, giggled like a teenager before looking over her shoulder at Travis, who did not giggle. Thankfully. The guy did, however, look at Maurice with a nod and partial smile for a greeting.

"So you decided to do the Relax and Relate, too." Des's voice was less than enthusiastic, and he knew why.

After sleeping in this morning—his idea, not hers—they'd decided to once again go off script of the retreat's agenda. They'd opted for breakfast in her room and had then headed out to visit some of the souvenir shops in the quaint little ski town. Considering all the other Dear Lover workshops and exercises, they'd assumed the couples' massage session might be the least attended one. In any case, it didn't seem like something the gregarious Kelli and Travis would consider doing.

"Of course," Kelli said, happily taking a seat on Des's other side. That made Des move over, closer to him.

He didn't mind, but since Travis was also going to try and squeeze onto the bench with them, Maurice scooted down until one side of him was at the edge and the other was pressed against Des. Her hair smelled like vanilla ice cream. It was the oil he'd watched her squeeze out of a small bottle and rub into the center of her palms before smoothing over her thick bouncy curls this morning.

"We're trying to take advantage of everything we can this weekend and figured we'd squeeze in the massage, too. This morning's sessions were a little physical." Kelli nudged Travis.

He looked slightly uncomfortable at the implied meaning behind her words, but he smiled and nodded again.

"What did you two do this morning? I didn't see you in any of the sessions. What are you doing after this one? We're going to the Sweet Talk Tasting because I hear they're having a dessert bar, in addition to the open bar." This time Des was the one Kelli nudged. "Nothing like free drinks, right?"

"You plan on drinking at three in the afternoon?" Des asked her.

Kelli waved a hand, shaking her head so the ponytail she wore bopped back and forth. "Girl, please. It's five o'clock somewhere, and I did say free."

Clipboard Guy came from the back and called the next names on his list. Maurice hoped they were next because Des wasn't going to last very long sitting with Kelli. He'd had a hard time trying to figure out why Des had given the woman her number in the first place. Kelli was the exact opposite of the type of person Des would normally tolerate.

"We're probably not going to attend that session," Des told Kelli. "We were thinking about maybe doing a little more sightseeing and then going out to dinner."

That was partially their plan. What they'd actually talked about was dinner in the room and renting some movies to watch if there was nothing on TV.

"Oh wow, you two are just like a real couple already. Aren't they, Travis? Don't they look like they've been in love for years and years?" Kelli was looking from Des to him and back again.

"Years and years," Travis echoed, now with a big grin on his face.

"Dear Lovers 1687 and 1288." Clipboard Guy was back.

Maurice jumped up, and Des followed right behind him. "That's us!"

"Follow me." They did as the organizer said without looking back at Kelli and Travis and chuckled when they finally walked into the private room.

"That's your friend," he said to Des when she stood next to one of the massage tables shaking her head.

"Oh no, as soon as I leave here tomorrow, I'm blocking her number. We're definitely not going to be friends. Nessa is the most cheerful person I know, and she's not even as bad as Kelli. That's probably why I can deal with her, at least during work hours."

He nodded at the mention of her assistant and wondered if that was the only friend Desta had. While it had never occurred to him before, he realized now that he'd never seen Des with anyone outside the office.

"You can both climb up onto the table," Clipboard Guy said. "The object of this exercise is to encourage open communication between couples. You'll be receiving a Swedish massage and can talk freely about anything you wish, just so long as you're sharing, becoming closer."

Maurice climbed onto the table after making sure Des got up all right on her own. Not that she wasn't capable, but after yesterday on the slopes he had a new protective instinct where she was concerned.

"You're encouraged to let the relaxing of your muscles coax you into opening up with your fellow

Lover. Releasing all anxieties or inhibitions to freely be together. You may remove your robes." Clipboard Guy finished softly and moved closer to the table where Des was, immediately pulling a sheet up over her body so that she could remove the robe and still retain privacy.

Maurice was already lying facedown with his robe off, and he'd pulled his own sheet up to his waist by the time the man turned to him.

"Well, all right, then. The masseuses will be in momentarily. And don't fret, they've also signed NDAs with Dear Lover. Nothing you say in here during the session will ever be repeated."

"Does this feel like forced communication to you?" she asked as soon as they were alone in the room.

He turned his head so they were staring at each other. "Definitely."

They both laughed. The beds were about three feet apart, and the only light in the room came from two lanterns on a table in the corner. The golden haze was weirdly comforting, and the faint sound of a waterfall added to the ambience.

She reached back and grabbed her hair, pulling it away from her face. "What do you want to talk about? Because we might get in trouble if we don't cooperate."

He knew exactly what he wanted to talk about; it had come to him the second she asked the question. His response had to wait because their masseuses entered. It always took him a few minutes to become totally relaxed in a massage, so he didn't speak until the woman's oiled hands were moving expertly over his shoulders and toward the center of his back where most of his tension seemed to rest.

"Why don't you go home for vacations?" he asked when he thought she'd had enough time to relax as well.

There was no immediate response. In fact, she took so long he wasn't sure she was going to answer him at all.

"I don't want my family to see me." Her voice was quiet, and he slowly opened his eyes to glance over at her.

She had her eyes closed while the second woman worked her shoulders.

"You don't want them to see how successful you've become?" He was almost positive that wasn't what she meant, primarily because it didn't make any sense, and Des was one of the most sensible women he knew.

"No. I don't want them to see how badly I messed up." She opened her eyes then. "I didn't listen to my mom's and my grandma's advice."

"They told you not to come to New York because you might get lost in the big city," he joked.

"Chicago's a big city, too," she replied with a half smile. "They told me not to move to Denver with Gordon, my boyfriend from college."

Those last three words had his gut clenching,

more from his own personal memories than any sort of unwanted jealousy. Then there was the guarded look on her face, as if she were wondering if she could continue while knowing it was too late to stop.

"Tell me about it," he said in as even a tone as he could manage. Never, ever had he had a conversation with one of his dates about their former lovers or boyfriends.

"His name was, or is, Gordon Thomas." She closed her eyes again, but this time he suspected it was because her masseuse was applying kneading strokes up and down her back, a move he knew could be particularly relaxing. "He was the star of the basketball team in college, leading our school to the NCAA Championship two years in a row. I tutored him during our sophomore year."

That last sentence explained a lot because he definitely hadn't pictured Des as the star athlete's girl. He knew from reviewing her CV when she'd been hired at the company that she'd graduated summa cum laude in undergrad and went on to be in the top five percent of the class to achieve her master's degree. She was a brilliant marketing strategist.

"To make a long story very short, we fell in love and when he was drafted to the NBA, I went with him to Denver. My mother and my grandmother weren't thrilled with the idea of me packing up to go follow some man's dream, but in the end, they respected my decision. He played professionally for one season before sustaining a foot fracture that benched him." She'd had her arms down by her sides, but now she moved them to fold under her head before resting her cheek on them. During the movement, he'd seen that her hands were shaking.

His arms were by his sides, and his hands fisted. If she was getting ready to say what he was thinking she was going to say…he wanted to find Gordon Thomas and punch the bastard in his face.

"I gave him six years, four of which were hell on earth. Exactly when he'd gone from the attentive, loving guy with the great smile to the controlling maniac who'd taken his injury and subsequent fall from the NBA out on me in all the worst ways possible, I have no idea." She took a deep inhale and released it so slowly he could see her entire body vibrating with the action.

It took every ounce of control he possessed to keep still on that table. Des wouldn't want pity, and that's exactly how she'd take it if he went to her now and tried to console her in any way.

"Anyway, when I finally decided to leave him, I didn't go home to Chicago, and when my mother asked what happened between him and me…" She paused.

"You didn't tell her because you didn't want her to know you'd been in an abusive relationship." Finishing the sentence for her was one of the hardest things he'd ever had to do. Saying those words in relation to Des had a ball of hot fury resting in the pit of his stomach.

"I didn't want my family to know that I'd been weak and foolish. I especially didn't want either or all of my brothers hopping on the first plane to Denver and catching a murder charge for putting Gordon out of his misery."

Which was exactly what Maurice was contemplating at this moment.

He'd almost forgotten they were getting massages when the woman lifted his left leg, bending it at the knee slowly and pulling it back. Clearly there'd be no jumping off the table now, so he extended his arm between the tables to her. Waiting a beat for her to release her arm and accept his hand was like holding his breath just over the two and a half minutes Major had clocked him doing when they were kids.

"You're not weak or foolish." He hoped those words were enough. There was more he could say but not while he was feeling such insurmountable rage.

"I know I'm not. At least, now I do. But my mother was a very no-nonsense woman, which is why she remained a single mom. My father was an alcoholic, and she took no pity on him or the disease he suffered when she still had six kids to take care of. My grandmother had been a single parent as well, passing on that same strong Black-woman pride and resilience to my mother and supposedly to me. There's no way I could tell them all that Gordon had done to me."

He understood. No, dammit, he didn't. He'd been furious when he'd read the vicious lies Riley's ex had given the media when they broke up years ago, and now that rage seemed to triple as he thought of Gordon physically harming Des.

"You're a brilliant woman, Des. That's indisputable. And he was trash."

She smiled. It was quick and put the light back into her eyes, so he smiled, too.

"You're right, he is trash." Then she moaned. "And this feels sooo good."

He agreed. As if both masseuses knew from the heavy topic of conversation they'd been having that it was time to step up the massage, it soon became too much for either of them to speak. But he didn't release her hand, and she didn't do anything to change that.

CHAPTER NINE

HAVING DINNER IN her room wasn't running. It didn't mean that she was in the midst of a situation she couldn't control. But Kelli's recognition of Maurice and them being seen together so much this weekend had her feeling cautious. When she'd suggested a quiet dinner tonight after last night's interlude, Maurice hadn't pushed the point.

"You're really not afraid of anything the media says, are you?"

Maurice sat across from her at the small table by the window. He'd changed out of the gray polo shirt he'd been wearing earlier and now wore a black T-shirt that fit tightly against his muscled chest. She hadn't expected him to go to his room before dinner and show up at her door with his duffel bag in one hand. His only comment before walking around her and into the room had been that it was pointless to keep going back and forth. He was right.

After taking another swig from the bottled beer

he'd ordered, he lowered it to the table and sat back in the chair. "I can't control the media."

"But you can control what you feed them." Why this was bothering her this weekend, when it hadn't in the years that she'd known him, Desta had no clue. Maybe because now she was attached to him in more than a work capacity. Just like she'd been attached to Gordon. Once the media had learned of his injury they'd dogged him unmercifully and when his anger about being cut from the team began to spill over into brawls at the club and rumored affairs, she'd been looped right into the headlines.

Maurice shrugged, lifted his hands up in exasperation and then let them fall to his lap. "What am I feeding them? Do I call or email them every day with a story?"

His mood had been on the edge of agitation since the massage that had been meant to relax them. Part of that was probably her fault since she'd dropped the details of her messy past on him, but she hadn't felt like dodging his questions about her family again. That was the first time she'd told anyone the truth about what had happened in Denver.

"No. But every time you step out of your house, you know they're watching you. Every date you pick up and take to a restaurant, a Broadway show, a Knicks game and then to a hotel, you know they're right there taking notes. So basically, you're giving them all this ammunition to write stories about you."

"And what would you suggest I do? Not go on

dates? Stay locked up in my house?" He sucked in a breath, holding his lips together tightly before letting it out on a whoosh. "I learned a long time ago that I can't control everything, that sometimes things just happen—and I adjusted my life accordingly. That's the extent of any changing I plan to do for the sake of anyone else." Dragging a hand down his face, he pushed back from the table and stood.

This wasn't how she'd meant for their dinner to go. It was the end of their fun, sex-filled weekend, after all. But something had changed, and if she wasn't oblivious to that fact, she knew Maurice wasn't, either.

"You're not the only one with painful stuff in your past."

His comment shocked her because she'd thought by walking away he was finished with the conversation. Desta turned in her seat and looked at him.

"I guess college must have been the time to mess up, because that's when I invited my girlfriend, India, out for a ride in my new car. She'd just graduated from high school, and I was home for the weekend. I figured it was a great time for us to celebrate." He stood near the window with his back to her.

"What happened when you went for a ride?" A sense of dread had already begun to lodge itself in the center of her chest, but she waited.

"Long story very short," he repeated her earlier words with a smirk, "I was speeding, and so was the eighteen-wheeler that came around that bend and smacked into us. I got twenty stitches for a gash in my leg, had a mild concussion and some bruised ribs. India was paralyzed from the waist down."

She gasped. "I didn't know." Sorrow for what he and India had gone through slammed into her.

He turned slowly, slipping his hands into the front pockets of his jeans. "How could you? It was before the press took an interest in me." The partial smile and choked chuckle couldn't hide how shaken he now appeared. "The bottom line is I could've not been speeding. I could've taken India to dinner and brought her right back home. The accident didn't have to happen, and I own my part in it. It took me a long time to shake the guilt, but I own it now. And I swore I'd never put anyone else I cared about in danger that way again. So I don't get involved past a few dates. I keep it casual, no emotions, no recriminations. If the media wants to continually use my choice as their headline, then that's their business. I only deal with the things I can control."

Hadn't she decided to do the same after walking away from Gordon? Only have dealings with other men on terms she could control, only focusing on doing her job well because she could order those steps as well.

"We make a perfect couple." The words were out before she considered them, which was unlike her. "I just mean that we both carry these loads from our pasts like backpacks."

"Not tonight…" he said softly. "Can we just drop

those backpacks and leave them by the door for to-night?" As if in answer to his question, his cell phone buzzed. He pulled it out of his pocket, glanced down at the screen before turning it off and tossing it onto the chair by the window. "Just for tonight, can we leave everything else behind?"

Desta stood and crossed the room, closing the space between them. Reaching up, she touched her palm to his cheek and warmed all over when he turned slightly to press his lips against her skin. "We can have tonight," she whispered because that's what they both needed.

Just one more night to be in each other's arms in the way they wanted to, on the terms they'd created. It was what they both deserved.

Stepping closer, she tilted her head until her lips touched his. Nothing else, just the touch of her lips to his as she stared at him and he stared at her for what felt like endless moments. When he touched her hair, pushed his fingers through the curls until he was clutching the back of her head and holding her to him, she whimpered. Not a favored sound coming from her, but a moment of relief, of letting go and giving in to this moment and all that she was feeling in it.

"We were just coworkers," she whispered as his other arm slipped around her waist. "Just friends."

"Not anymore," he answered before thrusting his tongue into her mouth and dragging her into the swirl of emotions that had started to churn in the pit of her stomach.

This kiss felt different from the others. His voice was different, the feel of his hands on her was…different. She laced her arms around his neck, tilting her head to deepen the kiss. He was holding her so tightly, and she was leaning into every part of his embrace. Her legs would most assuredly give out if she didn't lean on him, but she'd never leaned on anyone before. She'd decided not to give that part of herself again.

Before that thought could take hold, he was easing his mouth away from hers, moving until he had her scooped up in his arms. She almost protested, almost told him he was being unnecessarily silly. But she remained silent, and he calmly walked her over to the couch and gently put her down like she was the most precious thing in the world. She knew they were entering new territory.

"I'm gonna take your clothes off, slowly," he said staring down at her.

She didn't know how to respond to that, and as it turned out, no response was necessary. He sat on the edge of the couch beside her, his fingers going to the buttons of the pale pink blouse she wore. Easing up from the couch so he could completely remove it seemed more sensual than anything she'd ever experienced before. It was the touch of his fingers on her skin—light, there and then gone, purposeful, not intentionally sexy but still erotic as hell. The rest of her clothes went in the same fashion as he moved methodically but not rushed, until she was lying naked on the couch, every part of her body—and she feared a part of her soul—open for his perusal.

She watched him undress in the same way, with gradual and deliberate movements he had to know were torturing her at this very moment. "What are you doing?" He was naked now and had taken a condom from his wallet and set it on the back of the couch.

"Adoring you." She wasn't expecting that reply nor the punch of something much more powerful than lust.

The kisses came next and not just the fevered and sensual ones to her lips that she'd come to enjoy. No, his mouth was apparently on the same mission that he was, moving with unimaginable tenderness over every part of her body. Down the line of her neck to her shoulders, over her breasts where his breath whispered above each puckered nipple. Down, down, until she was breathless with arousal as his tongue moved masterfully over her tender flesh, dipping inside her just as her release exploded from her.

Then he was over her, no words, no preamble, just the motion of his very toned body, his actions paused for the seconds it took him to tear into that condom package and smooth that latex over his thick length.

"In me. Now." Her lips trembled as she spoke. "Now. Please."

He obliged, lifting her legs and propping them onto his shoulders before angling his dick and driving into her with one smooth stroke.

She took his breath away.

Everything about her, from the way she looked chewing her food at dinner tonight to the pensive gaze she'd had when she questioned him about his intentions toward the media and finally to that look of pure delight that washed over her face, flooding her cheeks with color the second he pushed into her.

Now her eyes fluttered, naturally long lashes fanning out with each blink. The amber color of her eyes went darker with every stroke in and out of her. She was so responsive, her muscles tightening around his dick, pulling him in deeper and holding him there. Tongue snaking out the swipe over her lips before that sexy little whimper escaped from her throat.

He'd been right about what he'd said a little while ago. There weren't just friends or coworkers anymore. That ship had sailed, leaving behind this delicious connection that was draining him of every ounce of his resolve.

"I won't stop wanting you tomorrow." The words tumbled free even as he turned his face to kiss her ankle, circled his hips and pumped deep into her again. "Or the next day or, dammit, even the next." It was the simple truth.

Coming here to this resort in search of the woman who'd intrigued him from the first moment she'd responded to his email had been the beginning of the end.

"I know." Her hands were moving over her breasts, gripping them, squeezing until her taut nipples poked between her fingers. "I won't stop, either."

He didn't want any of this to stop and so he kept moving, continued with the circular movement of his hips and buried himself and his emotions even further into her. His hands tightened on her ankles as he spread her legs apart. In and out of her, that's all he could think about. The warmth, the wetness, the weightless feeling of falling. He accepted it all, holding onto it for dear life because for the first time in a really long time, that's exactly what it felt like. After all this time, he was living when he was with her, alive, breathing, feeling, and only with her.

She came again with a gasp before arching up off the couch, arms falling to her sides. It was a surreal sight to see pleasure take over her body so completely and to know that pleasure was wrapped up in him in what they'd shared not only this weekend but over the last three months of emails, and even before that in the years they'd been just friends and coworkers. That thought, coupled with the clench of her walls around his dick, pulled his release from him in a powerful surge that had him cursing and yelling her name.

It was a long time before either of them returned to normal breathing. "This couch is terribly uncomfortable."

He agreed and eased out of her. "Sorry." Standing now, he grabbed his underwear and was going to head to the bathroom when her words stopped him.

"Don't be." She sat up and let her legs fall to the floor before standing. "There's no need for either of us to be sorry about anything that's happened. In our past or right now."

He really needed to get to the bathroom before he made a mess on this terribly uncomfortable couch, but he moved to her once more, leaning in to kiss her. "You're absolutely right."

On his way to the bathroom, he glanced at the chair where he'd tossed his phone and cursed. He'd turned it off when he didn't want to be bothered while they were together, but he never kept it off for long. For family and business purposes, he knew the value of being reachable. Grabbing it, he turned it on while he was walking but stopped upon seeing the multiple text messages and email notifications on the screen. He swiped the first one titled *Urgent*.

"Is something wrong?" He looked up from the phone to see she'd already collected her clothes from around the couch and was holding them in a bunch in front of her. Probably waiting to get into the bathroom as well.

"Uh, no, not wrong. Just surprising." When he noticed the guarded look on her face, he added, "Riley's getting married."

CHAPTER TEN

One Week Later
Gold Mansion

"DON'T BE NERVOUS."

"Are you saying that for my benefit or yours?" Desta asked when they stood on the top brick step a few feet away from the double white doors of the Gold Mansion.

Maurice smirked. "Don't be funny."

Lifting a hand, she gave him a salute. "Yes, sir." She hadn't given the words or the action any thought, but the moment she saw concern flicker in his gaze, she chuckled. Nervously. Damn him. "I've been to Sunday dinner at your parents' house before, Maurice. It's silly to feel any type of way about being here now."

She'd been to lots of functions at this house. In the beginning, turning down invitations had seemed rude and quite possibly career suicide, so she'd attended one Sunday dinner and then a cocktail party, a cookout, Ron Gold's sixtieth birthday party and eventually more Sunday dinners and poker nights. Before long, she'd begun to feel as comfortable around the Golds as if she were an adopted part of their family. So much so she'd recently chanced turning down some invites, claiming she had other plans. Unfortunately, that wasn't going to work tonight.

"We hadn't slept together all the times you'd been here before." He was right about that.

And they had been sleeping together—a lot—in the last week since returning to Manhattan. In fact, Maurice had stayed at her place three out of the past five nights. Her queen-size bed was no match for the king-size they'd slept in at the resort, but she'd kind of liked the feeling of him that close through-out the night. Exactly when they'd decided to continue whatever it was they were doing, she wasn't sure. Neither of them had said anything definitive, nor had they stopped.

"Well, there's no sticker on my forehead saying we slept together, so if nobody asks that particular question, they'll never know." He arched a brow, and she sighed. "You're not helping."

"It's going to be fine. We're not hiding anything." When she shivered from the cold, he rubbed his gloved hands up and down her arms.

He wore a black leather bomber jacket over a navy-blue sweater and turtleneck combo. His pants were dark gray, cuffed at the ankle, black leather loafers on his feet.

What he'd just said made perfect sense; they hadn't been trying to hide anything. The nervousness she'd had about them being seen together at the Finger Lakes hadn't surfaced here because being together here could easily be connected to their jobs. From the time they'd returned after driving back from the Finger Lakes late Monday afternoon, until early Friday evening, they'd walked in and out of the office together more than they ever had before. They hadn't offered any explanation, nor had anybody asked. But they'd never arrived at his parents' house together. This affair they were having could backfire, and losing her job would be the consequence of acting on emotion and not common sense.

"You're worried about what they'll say, too, aren't you?" she asked.

He frowned and, as if to quiet her discomfort, leaned forward to drop a light kiss on her lips. "It's freezing out here. We're going in."

But before he could turn his attention to the door, it opened. "I thought I saw your car." Major stood just inside the foyer, a wide grin on his face. "Hey, Desta."

Her heart was beating frantically, but she managed to move like she was as unbothered as Maurice was, stepping toward his twin brother and walking inside. "Hey, Major. Nice jacket."

He wore a deep burgundy velvet sports coat over a black shirt and pants. Commenting on his outfit was what Desta would've done on any other occasion. Of all the Gold brothers, Major was the least interested in switching up his black, blue, gray and brown color palette, so whenever she saw him in other colors—which had come more and more after he'd met Nina—she was sure to notice.

"Thanks. Nina picked it out. She said it's festive."

Desta had walked past him and was removing her coat. When she turned back to face Major, he was brushing a hand down the front of the jacket.

"It's not Christmas yet," Maurice added when he came into the house.

Major closed the door and laughed. "You two teaming up on me? Wow, that's cute."

Was it? Were they? Had Maurice told Major about them? In addition to being twins by birth, these two were thick as thieves in life. Maurice was insistent about not keeping their affair a secret, and she was on board with that decision, but had he hurried home to tell his twin about their weekend rendezvous?

Kemp, the Golds' long-time butler, came into the foyer at that moment. "I'll take your coats." The very slim, older gentleman with smooth almond-toned skin appeared as fit as any of them, even though she knew from Maurice he was in his late seventies. He'd been with the Golds for decades.

"Hi, Kemp." She gave him her coat, but her attention was still attuned to Major, who was staring at her with an odd look on his very handsome face. Even though they were fraternal twins, there was a close resemblance between him and Maurice.

Since Major no longer worked at RGF full-time—he and Nina ran their own company, the Gold Service, on the outskirts of the city—she hadn't seen him this week.

Yet, the grin he was giving Desta right now was definitely a knowing one.

After Kemp took Maurice's jacket, she leaned over and whispered in Maurice's ear. "Does Major know about us?"

Maurice's response was a glare in Major's direction and dismissive shake of his head. "No. But come on inside, we might as well get this over with."

Yes, they might as well—as in this was going to be a very long evening.

"Oh, this is gonna be good." She heard Major's comment from behind them and refused to look back.

The Gold twins could be quite an annoying pair when they were together. Normally, she wasn't bothered by their inside jokes or suspicious looks during their monthly poker games, but tonight she wasn't in the mood for the tag-team effect. It was going to take all her practiced calm to get through the always-scrutinizing gaze of Marva Gold.

"There you are, Desta. I was wondering when you were going to get here. I told Riley you're never late." Speaking of the matriarch of the Gold family, Marva came toward her the moment Desta stepped into the family room.

Wearing winter-white trousers, a shimmering

rose-colored blouse and nude pumps, the woman was the fashion industry's Black royalty. Impeccably dressed, pleasantly composed and timelessly beautiful. She had the same tawny complexion as Maurice, and her thick silver-streaked hair hung in big neat curls to her shoulders while diamond earrings glittered at her ears.

"No, ma'am, I would never be late for your Sunday dinner. I had a few reports to finish up before I left, and there was some traffic." Her words died as Marva embraced her.

The woman always smelled fantastic, no matter the fragrance she chose. Marva was such a contrast from Desta's mother, who usually smelled like the hospital where she still worked twelve- to fourteen-hour shifts four days a week.

"I want you to stop working so hard. You're too young and too pretty to have your face buried in papers and that computer all the time."

Not used to extra attention from Marva, Desta quickly glanced around the room. She could see RJ—or Ronald Jr.—standing near the classic grand piano, a drink already in hand. Ron Gold Sr., RJ's older and wiser look-alike, sat astutely on one of the two ivory-colored couches in the room, while Nina and Riley were already parked in the taupe side chairs. Riley's fiancé, Chaz, stood near her, holding a drink that looked to be the same as RJ's. So, the gang was definitely all here.

"Are you all right, Desta?" Marva asked, the hint

of concern in her tone so noticeable, just about everyone in the room paused their conversation to look in her direction.

Major came around at that moment, talking as he made his way across the room. "She's fine, Mom. Stop hovering. After driving all the way out here with Maurice, she's probably just a little windblown. You know how he likes to speed through traffic."

If she were closer she would've punched him in the arm. Not only was she certain Major knew something about her and Maurice—even if Maurice hadn't confirmed it—but his remark about Maurice speeding immediately touched a nerve with her now that she knew about the car accident with India. She pasted on a smile. "I'm good, Mrs. Gold, really. Just trying to get back in the swing of things after being away last weekend."

"Oh," Riley said, her tone a bit too perky, "you were out of town last weekend, too? When I finally heard from Maurice last Sunday night, he said he was away on a ski trip. Where'd you go?"

Wishing for a hole to open up in the floor right now and swallow her was probably too much to ask for, but Desta wasn't looking to Maurice for help. Brushing the strands of hair she'd flat-ironed a couple hours earlier behind her ears, she squared her shoulders and looked Riley directly in the eye. "You know, it was the strangest thing. I had this brochure for a luxury ski resort in the Finger Lakes and realized it was getting closer to the end of the year and

I hadn't gone anywhere yet. With our busiest season coming up, I figured a long weekend was my best bet."

"So, you went skiing, too?" Riley asked.

Maurice moved from where he'd been standing right behind her, leaning in to kiss his mother on the cheek. "We ran into each other at the ski resort. Seems the place is extremely popular this time of year." He spoke as casually as if he'd just said, "Hey, Ma, what's for dinner?" She clearly wasn't as aloof as Maurice about all this.

"Dinner is served," Kemp announced before anyone else could speak.

The questioning gazes coming from everyone in the room spoke volumes, but Desta followed Maurice's lead and walked toward the dining room.

Tonight's catered meal was an array of fresh salads, lemon pepper chicken, curry rice, sautéed string beans and buttered rolls that smelled heavenly. Hungry and determined to get through this evening, Desta took her seat between the twins where—coincidentally—she always sat. Ron said the grace and bowls began passing between everyone. Same as usual. Inwardly, she was relieved.

Five minutes after they began eating, RJ dropped his fork to his plate with a clatter. "When I called and texted you repeatedly on Sunday to tell you about Riley's engagement, you were at a ski resort…with Desta?"

Maurice and Desta both looked at RJ, but neither had a chance to answer before Riley asked her, "Wait, you knew before I called you on Monday?" The accusatory tone in Riley's voice made Desta feel like crap.

It had been almost six Monday evening when Riley had called, brimming with excitement about her engagement. Desta had thought it best to act surprised, especially when Riley quickly continued to discuss business and announcing the engagement.

"I didn't want to take any of the joy that was so apparent in your voice away." Desta's throat was suddenly dry, so she lifted her glass of wine and took a gulp. "By the way, my team and I have already laid out all the preliminary steps to marketing the engagement in the same way we did Nina and Major's."

"Yeah, Desta filled me in on the details of that new strategy," Maurice said. "You sure you want to invite the media into your personal life in that way? I mean, inviting them to the engagement party and into the wedding planning?" Maurice was so calm, and Desta gritted her teeth in frustration. Another gulp from her glass should help her feel more in control.

Riley blinked, probably confused by the shift in conversation. Or possibly annoyed. But she continued with a nod. "Chaz and I discussed it, and it makes the most sense. The media was going to be poking around trying to find out all that they could, anyway. So, why not give them a certain amount of access during the planning? The wedding itself will be private."

Chaz added, "We don't even want the location known. They can have all the pictures of dress fittings, cake tastings and parties that they want, but it stops there."

"Have you decided on the venue yet?" Nina asked.

"No, actually we're considering a destination wedding," Riley said cheerfully.

For the next twenty minutes the conversation was all about the wedding. Who would and shouldn't be invited, who Marva wanted to cater it, what Ron and the other guys didn't want to wear. It all seemed so normal and at the same time so foreign. Desta hadn't thought about getting married in a very long time, even though her grandmother mentioned it almost every time they spoke. Why, Desta still couldn't figure out. It wasn't as if Edna Bell's marriage had been successful. To the contrary, she'd caught her husband and their neighbor in the backseat of his truck at a drive-in movie.

Her mother hadn't fared much better, but Sheryl Henner had appeared genuinely happy on that long-ago spring weekend when Desta and Gordon had gone to Chicago to announce their engagement. As the conversation around her continued, Desta's skin began to tingle at the memories it evoked. She'd started to plan her own wedding. A venue, brides-maids, groomsmen and a date had been selected. Her dress search had been taking longer than expected, and she'd been online searching designers the night she got the call that Gordon had been hurt.

"You okay?" She startled at Maurice's voice. He'd leaned over to whisper in her ear, and when she turned to him, he grasped her hands.

She hadn't even realized she'd dropped her hands to her lap, linking her fingers together and holding tight. His hand covered hers now, warm and familiar.

"Yeah," she sighed. "I'm good. Just taking in all the details." He didn't believe her. She could tell by the set of his jaw, the gentle squeeze of his hand and the way his eyes had grown dark with concern. "I'm good." If she said it more than once, maybe he'd believe her. Maybe she'd believe it herself.

"You know what might be a cool idea?" Major's voice seemed a bit louder than it had been, and Desta forced a smile as she turned in his direction. "What if Riley and Chaz get married at the same ski resort Desta and Maurice stayed at?"

Desta held her breath because in that moment she was totally sure Major knew, and he was having a good time teasing.

"That's probably not a good idea," Nina immediately replied.

"It was a really nice resort," Maurice said. He still had a hand over hers beneath the table, and when she pulled one away to reach for her glass again, he laced his fingers with hers. "With a terrific view. Once Des and I realized we were both staying there, we spent the weekend together exploring the little ski town and enjoying the slopes. There's a wonderful restaurant at the resort, but the place within walking distance has more of a selection. Des and I thought their food was great."

It was the way he'd said *Des and I* followed by the curious stares that had her picking up the glass and emptying it of every drop of wine. She was tempted to reach for the bottle but stopped when Maurice lifted their entwined hands from beneath the table, resting them atop the white linen tablecloth for all to see.

"Well," Marva said after a brief silence, "it seems things just keep changing around here." She used a napkin to dab at the corners of her mouth before sending Desta a luminous smile.

"I knew it! You owe me ten dollars," Major said to Nina, who smiled at Desta before shaking her head at her husband.

Ron had been holding a butter knife in one hand, a roll in the other. Now he pointed the knife from Maurice to Desta. "You two? Spent the weekend together, as in *to-gether*?"

Desta sat motionless, waiting for him to say she was fired. She kept her shoulders squared and her eyes on Ron because if that was how this was going to play out, so be it. What was done was done, and she wouldn't undo it now if she could. The wine was definitely beginning to kick in.

"Yes, we're together." She was glad Maurice didn't mimic the way his father had said the word.

"It just happened last weekend," she added. It shouldn't matter, but she knew for certain there wasn't enough wine in this house that would make her comfortable explaining this had really started via an online-dating site.

"I think it's wonderful," Nina added. "You two make a great-looking couple."

"Well, at least now the sexual tension that was always brewing between you two can finally be resolved." RJ looked bored and immediately changed the subject to who would be traveling to each of next year's Fashion Weeks.

"Sexual tension brewing between us? Where'd that come from?" Maurice had been holding that question in, waiting for the moment he could get his brother alone to ask him about it.

They weren't technically alone now, but since the women had all gathered in the living room to discuss wedding plans, the men had retreated to his father's study where there was a full-scale bar on one side of the room and a large-screen TV on the other. There was a massive cherrywood desk in the center of the room, and across the space were more leather chairs, high-backed and deep-cushioned. They circled a glass table loaded with classic magazines that noted high points in RGF's history as leaders in the industry.

RJ shook his head and propped his ankle up on his knee. "It came from all those meetings I had to sit through with you two barely being able to stop snipping at each other."

"We did not snip at each other during work meetings," Maurice insisted.

"Yeah, you did. And during poker games," Major added. "I just thought you'd have the good sense to get over whatever thing you had for her, considering how close she is to the family. But when I saw the two of you leaving her office the other day, I knew something was going on."

"Wait, what exactly did you see?" He'd been to Des's office so many times throughout the past week. Not all the visits were work-related, but he'd been pretty sure they kept it G-rated, at least when the door was open. No matter how hard he'd tried to stay away from her, the effort had proven futile, especially since being with her helped to take his mind off the non-work-related stress he'd been experiencing this week.

"Yeah, but you don't usually leave with your arm around that person's waist, so low it could've been considered on her butt." Major grinned with that announcement as RJ rolled his eyes.

"See, that's the part I'm stuck on," Ron said to his son. "Not your hand inappropriately on her in the office. But the fact that she's been around us for all these years like she was a blood relative. And you, in your position at RGF, work particularly close to her. I'd have thought you would steer clear, as well."

"Love chooses," Chaz interjected. "Not business

dealings, family relations or any of the other social trappings we tend to get into."

"Whoa. Wait a minute. Hold up." Maurice was shaking his head vehemently. "Nobody said anything about love." He certainly hadn't. And he wasn't thinking it, either.

"You've never brought a woman home to meet the family before." The corners of Major's mouth wavered as he fought off another grin.

"I said we spent the weekend together. And okay, we were together a lot this week. But that's it, we're just having fun." He shook his head because he didn't like the sound of that, like what they were doing was trite and inconsequential. It wasn't. "I mean, we're just dating. Casually." As opposed to seriously— something he'd sworn never to do again.

"Well, I'm not saying you can fall in love in that span of time. You know I don't give a damn about love, anyway. All I'm saying is it's about time. Now we can move on to more pressing matters." The director of sales at RGF, RJ was always about business. As driven as every member of the Gold family was, the company was all RJ had, especially after the infamous proposal so long ago.

Chaz got up and went to the bar to refresh his drink. Riley had been bringing him to as many family dinners as he would attend over the past year since they'd been together, so he was already used to moving around the house. "A relationship can easily jump from sexual desire to love in the blink of an eye. Especially if that connection was already there in the form of a friendship. Or even an opposing relationship."

He was referring to the feud that had since been squashed between the Golds and Tobias King, the owner of King Designs and Chaz's uncle. Despite the companies being in direct competition—and Ron's and Tobias's refusal to speak to each other for more than thirty years—Riley and Chaz had started a secret affair that hand grown into a relationship and now an engagement.

"No!" Major said and pointed a finger toward Chaz. "We are not going to mention you and my sister in the same conversation as sexual desire."

RJ closed his eyes and shook his head. "Yeah, I agree with that one."

"I definitely agree with that one," Ron said. "We've accepted you into our men's club, Chaz, but there's a line that can't be crossed, and it starts with my baby girl."

Chaz chuckled. "All right, I get that. But for real, I'm speaking from experience here. It's not about time or duration, it's always about the depth of the feelings."

RJ made a gagging sound. "Spoken like a guy newly strung out by a woman. That's why you bought that ring and are about to have a billion-dollar wedding on your tab."

"It's cool," Chaz said coming back to sit down with drink in hand. "I can afford it." In addition to working with his uncle at King Designs, Chaz was also owned a multi-billion-dollar company.

"No, young man, paying for my daughter's wedding is my job. Always has been and always will be." Ron was a proud man. He could be hard at times, was tough as nails when it came to his company but was all about love and his family underneath.

Maurice was uncomfortable with this entire conversation. In fact, this was turning out to be one of the weirdest family dinners he'd ever attended. As much as he'd tried to assure Des that everything was going to be fine, he hadn't been totally sure of that himself. He'd been the one to make the obvious clear to his family, but that was because they were asking so many questions. He should've anticipated that, but he honestly hadn't thought he and Des had been giving off any signs. It'd only been a week since they'd started a physical relationship—how could so many people notice that so soon? And why did any of this even matter? His temples throbbed.

"All right," Maurice began, "I don't know what we're doing. There, I said it." Admitting the problem was the first step to recovery, or so people said. But what was he trying to recover from? He liked being with Des. He liked it a lot. There shouldn't be any problems with that, nor should there be any other questions or concerns. And yet, he was full of questions and concerns right now.

"That's usually how it starts," Ron said with a nod before sticking his cigar between his teeth.

"He's right," Major added. "I started out thinking Nina and I were just working for the company, and the next thing I knew I was buying her a ring."

"Your mother had me going to concerts where men sang nothing but love songs. She smelled like fresh-picked flowers and, man, I couldn't get that scent out of my mind to save my life." Hearing his father talk about falling in love with his mother made Maurice respect his parents and their marriage even more. Once upon a time, when he was very young and mostly stupid, he'd thought that was what his adult life would look like.

It was a good thing he'd grown up.

Almost getting India killed in that accident had been a sobering and maturing experience. While hooking up with Des online was something akin to fate, if he were prone to believe in that type of thing. All he knew for certain was that this thing with Des was unexpected and tempting as hell. What if it continued? What if they ended up in love or engaged, or...could he even allow himself to think like that?

No, he couldn't.

No matter how good it felt to be with Des, he knew he couldn't risk it. After all he'd been through, he couldn't get entangled like that again.

His phone vibrated in his pocket. Standing, he pulled it out and read the message. He felt a boiling rage at seeing the message for the tenth time this week. It must've showed on his face, because Major noticed.

"What is it? One of your exes trying to come back for seconds?" his twin asked.

"Now, that's gonna be his biggest issue. Turning down all those women he still had waiting in line for their chance with him." At that, RJ laughed.

"Maurice, man, you all right?" Chaz asked.

"Is there a problem at the office, son?" Ron chimed in when it seemed like something serious was going on.

Maurice heard all their questions, but it sounded like they were traveling through a tunnel. His ears had begun to ring, and he clenched his teeth as he read each word again. Now was not the time for this. His sister was getting married, his brother had just celebrated his first holiday with his new wife, and his mother was elated about him and Des.

Des.

How would she react if she found out about this?

When his father called his name again, Maurice looked around the room, noting all the people he was closest to in life. If there was nobody else in the world he could trust with this, he could trust these men, and he knew that unequivocally.

"I'm being blackmailed," he said solemnly. "Twenty million dollars or they go to the press with a paternity scandal that could derail the entire plan we're putting in place for Riley's wedding."

CHAPTER ELEVEN

On Tuesday, Desta sat at her desk looking at the digital ads her team had composed using pictures of Riley and Chaz. She had until four this afternoon to decide on one to send to *Infinity* magazine in time for their special holiday edition. She'd reviewed all five designs at least twenty times in the last hour.

"Knock, knock." Not moving her hands from the keyboard, she glanced up at the open door to her office to see Nina walking in. "Hey. You ready?"

Dressed in black jeans, knee-high boots and a leather jacket, Nina looked more like a classy biker than the co-owner of a multi-million-dollar tech company.

"Hi. Ready for what?"

With a sigh and half smile, Nina came to the edge of Desta's desk. "Lunch. We scheduled a lunch date Sunday before you left the house. Today's the day, and I'm just about on time." Nina checked her watch. "With five minutes to spare."

"Oh crap!" She'd totally forgotten about that, even

though she'd seen it on her calendar this morning. The slipup was slightly embarrassing, and she shook her head. "I'll be ready in five minutes. Just let me shut this down and grab my purse."

Nina laughed. "Girl, no rush. I'm free for the rest of the afternoon so I can get some of my Christmas shopping done."

Groaning, Desta shook her head and minimized the open tabs on her screen before locking her computer. "Don't even talk about it. I haven't done any shopping yet. Well, that's not totally true. I got a few seasons of *Murder, She Wrote* for my grandmother. She loves that show."

When Desta stood, Nina was shaking her head. "I was going to ask what that was."

"Oh yeah, a television show from the eighties and nineties. I grew up watching it with her." Desta grabbed her coat from the chair she'd tossed it on this morning, and they headed to the elevator.

Twenty minutes later they were seated in a Manhattan restaurant with two mountain-size steak salads in front of them.

"So, we've talked about work, Christmas shopping or lack thereof and the wedding." Nina used a napkin to wipe her hands before taking a drink from the glass of soda she'd ordered. "Now, let's talk about you and Maurice."

Desta knew she couldn't have been lucky enough to get through this entire outing without Nina broaching that subject. There'd been a few questions while she, Nina, Marva and Riley had sat in the living room after Sunday dinner, but mostly that conversation had revolved around Riley and the details of her destination wedding. Now, she figured Nina thought it was time for her and Maurice to be in the spotlight.

Throughout her life, Desta had never had a lot of girlfriends, so this should've seemed odd. She and Riley were coworkers and friendly, but like Desta—at least before earlier this year—Riley hadn't been the girlfriend type, either. Nina, on the other hand, had sisters and so was more inclined to close female friendships. Besides that, Nina wasn't a blood member of the Gold family, so Desta felt a certain kinship to her. And to be honest, she needed to talk. So much had been going through her mind in the days since that dinner, having a sounding board would be a blessing.

"We're seeing each other," she said as if that had to be announced.

Nina laughed. "I think I got that much. How long have you been seeing each other? Major really did guess that you two were involved, but I swear I never saw it coming. Was it really just the run-in at the ski resort?"

"No." It was the truth, and she needed to say it out loud. "I'm starting to think it's been brewing for a long time. As I look back over my time here at the company, I've been around Maurice the most, and whenever I was at the Gold mansion we were always together. I guess I never paid much attention to that at first." She hadn't been able to get it out of her mind in the past few days. "The ski resort was a shock to both of us, but then things just sort of clicked." With the help of three months' worth of very graphic emails, but still, Desta knew there was much more to it than that. There was no way she would've done the things she did with Maurice in the Finger Lakes with a guy she'd just met face-to-face for the first time. Sex, sure, but being so open in those sessions, sharing those private parts of herself and then giving herself the way she had each night… No, that was all because she'd known Maurice for so long.

"Like a real-life friends-to-lovers story. Oh, this is so sweet. You know, you usually only see this stuff in movies." Nina had started poking her fork into her salad again.

"I guess." Desta wasn't hungry now. She was conflicted or confused, not sure which.

Nina paused before taking another bite. "You don't sound so sure. Are you in love with him?"

That word rendered her still. Her mind was freezing as it wrapped around the sound of those four letters together. She couldn't be in love with Maurice. It was too soon, and Desta had never been a believer in insta-love. But hadn't she just recalled how close they'd been for the last five years? What if her true feelings for him were just manifesting? "I wasn't looking to fall in love." Then, what had she been looking for? To reclaim control of her life? Well, she'd done that by being successful in her job. What else was there to claim? Her heart, she thought with a gasp. All this time, harboring the anger and resentment toward Gordon was like letting him keep her heart.

"Well, for what it's worth, I don't think Maurice was, either." Nina chewed the forkful of salad she'd put into her mouth and then shrugged. "Neither were Major and I. And from the stories she's told me, I'm positive love was the last thing on Riley's mind when she and Chaz hooked up."

"What are you saying?" Desta played with her food while Nina took another drink from her glass.

"I'm saying that nobody ever plans love. That's not how it works."

No plan meant no control. Desta had experience with love, and she hadn't liked it. How was this situation any different?

An hour later she was back in her office, trying her best to stop thinking about the conversation with Nina and all its implications. The new Mrs. Gold was quite smug in her assessment of Desta and Maurice's relationship, and if she weren't so close to the truth—at least where Desta was concerned—Desta might've had the nerve to be pissed off at Nina's presumptiveness.

It was close to four, and she still hadn't made a decision on the mock-ups, so Desta was extra irritated when her cell phone rang.

Taking a deep breath before answering, she pushed the button and said, "Hey, Ma."

"Hey, Dessie." Once upon a time this had been the only nickname Desta answered to. Now, her heart warmed each time Maurice called her Des. "Didn't get a chance to talk to you over the Thanksgiving weekend so I thought I'd call now. Mama said she talked to you and that you'd had dinner with your boss's family."

"Yeah. I worked right up until it was time for their annual dinner, so I just joined them, and then I went away for a weekend." She knew that was a mistake as soon as she'd said it.

"You went away, but you didn't come home?"

She didn't know how to answer that.

Sheryl moved on just fine without a response. "I want you to come home for Christmas. No excuses, Dessie. It's been too long."

What was it, Slap Desta in the Face with All Her Truths Day? It *was* time for her to go home. Truthfully, she'd been foolish to stay away for so long. Her family loved her; they wouldn't have judged her. But she'd judged and blamed herself for something she knew hadn't been her fault.

"Yeah, Ma. I'll come home for Christmas." Saying the words lifted a weight from her she hadn't known she'd been carrying. Desta wondered about those other words she and Nina had discussed. She considered the possibility that she might be falling in love with a guy who'd been her friend for the last five years. More importantly, she wondered how that guy was feeling about her.

"Thought you'd still be here." She hadn't heard his voice all day. Not since they'd stepped off the elevators this morning and walked in different directions to their offices.

Glancing down at her watch, she sighed. Once she'd finally decided on the picture and sent it off, she'd jumped right into the next project to be completed. She sat back in her chair and looked at him. "Lost track of time."

"I see, back to your usual pace." Pushing away from the doorframe where he'd been leaning, Maurice closed the door behind him and made his way into her office.

She recalled watching him dress in the heather-gray suit, light blue shirt and tie this morning. When he'd gone to his place and grabbed a change of clothes yesterday, she'd had no idea. But after last night's dinner meeting with Parker Donovan to discuss the exclusive articles on Riley and Chaz to be printed in *Infinity* over the next six months, they'd gone directly to her apartment. And straight to bed like an old married couple, because they'd both been working nonstop since seven that morning. Now he walked his sexy self across the floor of her office as if he totally belonged here.

"You've got nerve. You're still here at seven thirty at night, too," she pointed out.

Normally, when he came to her office, he'd sit in one of the guest chairs positioned across from her desk. Tonight, he came around the side and perched a hip on the corner by the sleek speakers she'd purchased last year during a Black Friday sale. "We're both workaholics. There's a remedy for that, though."

She rested her hands on the arms of the chair, settling into the comfortable ease they'd had around each other for years. "Yeah? What's the remedy?"

"I'd say another one of those massages we had at the resort. But for tonight, a hot bath. Order-in dinner. Football game on TV, or in your case one of those sappy holiday movies you bribed me into watching the other night." Even taking a deliberate jab at her, he was charming. From the even tone of his voice to the sexy grin that punctuated his words and the casual way he lounged his toned body on her desk as if that were the only place in her office for him to sit, his allure was incomparable.

"I've got a better suggestion," she said, and he raised a brow in question. "I'll pick the takeout, and you pick what we watch on TV."

His nod of agreement came quickly. "Your place or mine?"

Maurice had a very nice and spacious apartment in the NoHo neighborhood of Manhattan. She'd been there twice—once to drop off files from work and another time to pick up a painting she'd won from him in one of their monthly poker games. He hadn't invited her there since they'd returned from the Finger Lakes, and she hadn't minded. Her place was her comfort zone. It offered her complete control over when the date would end. Or at least, that was how it'd worked on the past few dates she'd had.

"Don't overthink this. It's not that big a deal," he said, tapping the lines she knew appeared on her forehead when she was deep in thought. "We'll go to your place. Did you drive today?"

"No." She rarely ever drove her car to work. The subway was easier than fighting traffic.

"Then, gather your things, and we'll get ready to leave." While the Golds all used the company car service for transportation to and from work, Maurice always drove his car. He called it an extension of his daily routine and noted he'd be lost without Sweet Sally—the name he'd given his black Porsche 718 Boxster.

She didn't move when he eased off the edge of her desk and started walking toward the door. She couldn't—the sense that something was crawling just beneath her skin had started again, and she clenched her teeth in an effort to ease the discomfort.

"You okay?" She heard him ask through the haze of emotion swirling around her.

"No." A lie would've been easier, and then she could've pushed past the occurrence and told herself she was making progress. She had been, at least during the past week. Between work and spending her evenings with Maurice, she hadn't thought about her past, until today during her conversation with Nina about falling in love.

"Hey." He was back, circling around her desk this time, grabbing the back of her chair and turning it so she faced him when he knelt in front of her. "What's going on? You were drifting away like this on and off at the resort. Is it about your ex?" A muscle twitched in his jaw.

There was concern in his tone and sincerity in his eyes. She knew those eyes, had known them for a long time. They'd never made her feel the way she was feeling right now, though. The change was a bit discomforting.

"It's this. Us. What we've been doing since the trip." There, she'd said it. The thing that was stopping her from fully grasping all that Nina had talked about earlier. He was right: it had been right there between them from the moment she'd spotted him at the resort.

"I don't understand."

He wouldn't, and not because he didn't have the capacity to. That would be leaning on that reputation he'd carefully constructed. She knew him better than that, especially now after he'd told her about the accident with his first girlfriend.

She flattened her palms on her thighs, rubbing them back and forth. He gently placed his hands on top of hers, ceasing their movement and turning them over so that he could lace his fingers through hers. "This is me, Des. Not Dear Lover, not the guy in the tabloids, it's just me. Tell me what's on your mind. Please."

"I'm not comfortable taking commands from men. Being controlled to suit their needs, directed to do only the things that please them. It just doesn't work for me." A flush went through her body, and she shivered against it. "It probably sounds silly to you, but it's a very real thing for me."

"What do you need me to do, or stop doing?" That was it? All it took was for her to tell him what not to do. Why hadn't that worked before?

"It's so natural for you to lead and control. It's the way you were brought up, and you don't use it in an aggressive way. I've always known that about you." So why couldn't she stop this foolishness? "You think I'm controlling, bossy, and that might be true on some level, but it's because I've had to be. Like Riley, I have very domineering brothers, so I always had to stand my ground." She'd also had Gordon, but she didn't want to bring that up again. Telling him about that very dark time in her life had been a huge step for her, but what she'd told him hadn't been everything.

It didn't matter whether she said it or not, the sorrowful look in his eyes said he was thinking it, anyway.

"I won't ever try to make you do anything you don't want to do. You know that. If you don't want to have dinner tonight, that's fine. Just tell me what you want."

She shook her head and cleared her throat. "You're right. I know that." Giving his hands a light squeeze, she took a deep breath and then stood.

He stood with her, still holding tight to her hands. "I'm always here to listen whenever you need to talk. That doesn't change when or if we decide it's time for this new aspect of our relationship to end."

He didn't wait for her to respond, just released her

hands and headed for the door again. She thought he might walk through it and not look back, but he simply waited for her to decide what would happen next.

She wasn't running. Never again—that's what she'd told herself when she'd finally come through the darkness after the breakup. But Maurice wasn't Gordon, not in looks, demeanor or any other aspect that mattered. It took her a few minutes to save and close her documents, shut down her computer and grab her briefcase and purse.

"I'm starving. There's a great restaurant near my house. They have the best spicy seafood pasta. It's like a British-Jamaican cuisine, but I know you like spicy food." She talked while she walked to the door to meet him. "I have the menu saved on my phone."

He waited until she passed him before replying, "You know me too well. I'll even trust you to pick something off the menu for me."

They chatted amiably about the menu and the Netflix movie his assistant suggested he watch called *The Holiday Calendar*. By the time she was seat-belted in the passenger seat of his sporty little convertible, her skin irritation had subsided, and that comfort that she normally had with Maurice had returned. They debated whether radio stations should play Christmas music all day so early in the season, and for the first time today, she relaxed and let her mind clear of all worries and doubts. She let herself just be with the man who was steadily becoming an even bigger part of her life.

CHAPTER TWELVE

DESTA MOANED LONG and deep. Her head fell back against the pillows on her couch, where she'd stretched out, her feet in Maurice's lap. He repeated the motion that elicited such a pleasing sound from her, pressing his thumb into the ball of her foot.

The movie had gone off about twenty minutes ago, and they were still stuffed from the delicious dinner. The jerk chicken wings with a side of sweet plantains she'd ordered for him was fantastic, and he'd had her text him the name and number of the restaurant for future use. The local news was on now, and Maurice wasn't ready to leave.

"You like that?"

"Oh. My. Goodness." She enunciated every word, her eyes still closed as he continued to massage her foot. "Don't ask silly questions."

He grinned, satisfied with the relaxed and appreciative tone of her voice. She'd rebounded from the episode in her office, talking through dinner and watching the movie as if nothing had transpired between them. As if she hadn't compared him in some way to her ex. Giving himself accolades for taking it so well, he'd continued throughout the evening as if the struggle he'd seen so clearly etched over her face earlier didn't still bother him. That situation managed to override the blackmail issue he was still dealing with, so maybe he should take it as a partial win.

"Next," he said as he moved from one foot to the other.

"Do you charge for this service? 'Cause, damn, I'm sure you'd make a killin'." She lifted her head and stared at him from beneath hooded eyes. *Lovely.* That's the word he'd use to describe how she looked at this moment.

When they'd walked into her apartment, the first thing she'd done was take off the heels she'd worn to work. They'd both removed their coats and walked farther into her home. It wasn't a big place, but the building had been expertly renovated. And she'd made it a comfortable space, filled with things that represented who she was.

Paintings on the wall, including the one of the jazz musicians she'd won from him last year, statues of angels and a multitude of peach- and cream-colored pillows on her couch. *Cultured, feminine, complex*— all words he'd use to describe Des.

"Seriously, though, if you're doing this to all the women you sleep with, I'm confused as to why they take your end dates so easily." Running her hands through her hair, he couldn't help but continue to stare at her. Even when he wanted to ease her feet from his lap, get his coat and go home.

The problem was, he couldn't blame her for that comment or others like it that she'd made. A few months ago if she'd said something like that to him, he'd have given some blithe response and gone on his merry way. But something had begun to change in him in these past weeks, even before he'd gone to the ski resort and found out he'd been sending erotic emails to his coworker.

Looking away from her to stare at the TV screen, he continued rubbing her feet. "Never gave any of them a massage like this." He'd never even thought about doing it.

"Oh." Did she have to sound so shocked?

"Ask your next question."

"How do you know I have another question?" she asked.

"Because I know you, Des. I think we keep going round and round with that fact. Let's face it right here and now. I knew you pretty well before I ever sent a Dear Lover email."

"I don't argue that fact. I know you as well as I know my brothers—probably better since I haven't seen them in a while." Clearing her throat, she continued. "Okay, I was going to ask why you never did this with them. Actually, no. I *want* to ask you why you were with so many of them. Did you really think it was necessary to keep your guilt at bay, or was part of it ego?" She was more interested in this part of his life than he would've preferred.

He shook his head. "None of those women meant enough to me to stroke my ego. And for the record, I didn't sleep with every one of them." He held up a hand because he knew he hadn't fully answered her question. "Every woman I've ever gone out with intrigued me on some level. Some more than others, and those were the ones I slept with. Dating, socializing, *partying* as some would say, it was a good distraction. If I was out with them, I wasn't sitting in my apartment thinking about what happened to India."

"Do you still love her?"

He hadn't expected that question, but after a few moments, he could understand why it seemed that way. "On the contrary—it's because I've been so afraid of ever feeling that emotion again that I've used all those women. I know they like to judge me in the tabloids, and that's fine. Why shouldn't they? Even though I'm not doing anything wrong now, I did before."

"So destroying your personal reputation, or rather building a false one, is your penance for an accident that you didn't cause." She sighed. "That's just as ridiculous as me blaming myself for what Gordon did to me."

He clenched his jaw upon hearing the man's name, and because her words were partially correct. He didn't mind the press bashing him, mainly because if his name was in circulation, so was the name of the company. And since the worst they could do was call him a playboy, it didn't negatively affect RGF. But he didn't see the life he'd chosen to live as doing penance. He saw it as taking responsibility in a way he'd failed to do so long ago. "I think we've already discussed how well-matched that makes us." Were they really well-matched? If he were on the outside looking in, he wouldn't have thought so. And now he wondered how that thought made him feel.

"Well, we're certainly two of a kind."

He looked away when seconds ticked by with neither of them speaking.

"Maurice?"

He looked over at her again. "Yeah?"

"What comes after the foot rub?"

Maurice carried her into the bedroom. Another first for him. He'd responded to her question by turning off the TV and lifting her into his arms. When she looped her arms around his neck and stared at him with a look hot enough to sear his eyeballs, he'd tried like hell not to run in.

Tonight, unlike too many of their nights together, he wanted to do things differently. Probably because things between them had begun to feel different, even more than their last night at the ski resort. As if this thing between them was taking steps, moving from one level of involvement to another. If so, what step were they on now?

It was dark in the room when they entered so

when he set her down, she went to the nightstand beside her bed and switched on the lamp. Now that the space was cast in a golden glow, he walked to her, cupping her face in his hands before leaning in to kiss her.

His lips touched her tonight as if for the first time. The warm connection came as an easy prelude, and he dropped another lingering kiss on her closed mouth. Her hands came up to clasp his biceps, and he took the kiss a step further. This time he swiped his tongue over her lips. She sucked in a breath, the action parting her mouth so he could slip his tongue inside. They played a game with their tongues, delving deep, pulling back, needing the connection again, so going in once more.

Eventually his hands moved, fingers slipping through the silken strands of her hair. She slid her hands down from his biceps to his waist, gripping his shirt between her fingers as she tilted her head and opened her mouth wider. His body had grown warm all over. Not an instant flash of heat but a slow fever of satisfaction that began at his feet and rose slowly with a tender sweetness.

When they both needed to take a breath, he pulled back, still gradually, letting his hands fall from her hair and down to the buttons on the pale gray blouse she wore. Undoing one button at a time, he watched the inhale and exhale of her breathing, the rise and fall of her chest. When he was done, he pulled the blouse from where it was tucked into her skirt and pushed it off her shoulders, his gaze rested on the blushing mounds of her cleavage.

Wait.

The word was a gentle whisper in his mind. An instruction he was determined to follow. Letting the blouse fall to the floor, he reached around her, pulling her body flush to his. She gasped and wrapped her arms around his waist while he worked the zipper on the back of her skirt down. When he stepped away from her to push it over her hips, she pulled the tail of his shirt up and undid the button and zipper on his pants. The feel of her fingers lightly grazing over his already-stiff erection was pure bliss, and he momentarily closed his eyes to enjoy it.

She left his pants undone and went to his shirt, unbuttoning it before pushing it down off his shoulders. The undershirt he wore went next, and her hands immediately went to his pectoral muscles to squeeze.

With her hands on his chest, she pushed him down to the bed where he removed his shoes and socks. As he angled up toward her, she nudged his shoulders again until he was lying back on the bed. She removed his pants and boxer briefs, rubbing her hands along his legs and brushing a kiss over his hard dick. She eased away from him then, going to find his wallet where she retrieved two condom packets that she tossed onto the bed before straddling him.

"Okay, you can have a bit of control, Ms. Des."

She smiled, a slow lifting of lips, a glimpse at

straight white teeth and that light he loved to see rising in her eyes. "I like the sound of that."

Yeah, he was sure she did. Des was definitely a woman who liked control—he'd known that from the first day he'd met her. Tonight he'd learned that she needed the control to keep from believing she'd lose herself if she didn't have it.

Coming partially off the bed, he reached around her back and undid the black bra she wore. All that was left was a slip of lace that was supposed to be her panties—but was more like the bane of his existence at the moment. She reached for a condom packet then and eased off him while tearing it open.

He knew what was coming next, and still his mind exploded with pleasure as soon as she wrapped a hand around his dick. Expecting her to glide the latex down over his length, he almost passed out when she moved quickly, covering his tip with her mouth instead.

"Shit!" She had a perfect mouth. There was nothing else he could say about it, and no other words were coming out, anyway. Only the moans and groans that coincided with just how good it felt when her tongue swiped over his slit, then slid down his length like she was enjoying a favorite lollipop.

"You gotta stop that," he murmured when it felt like his eyes were going to get stuck as they rolled to the top of his head. "Please, Des. You gotta stop."

She pulled her mouth from him with a plopping sound that had him groaning one more time. "Payback's gonna be a bi—" The word was cut off as she came forward and kissed his mouth.

This may have been the hottest kiss he'd ever experienced, with full open mouths, twisting tongues, and her hand still wrapped around his dick.

Wait.

There was that damn word again. He was getting pretty tired of it right about now. Flipping her over easily, he ran his hands down her torso when she was on her back. Climbing between her legs, which she eagerly spread wide for him, he dipped his head and took each puckered nipple into his mouth for a quick suck. He freed them with a sound reminiscent of the one she just made when she'd released his dick.

"This is killin' me," he grumbled and lifted her legs until her ankles were on his shoulders.

She didn't have a chance to respond because in the next second he was burying his dick inside her.

What the hell was she doing?

Was she falling for him? For Maurice?

The way he eased in and out of her so excruciatingly slow, his dick hitting every spot deep inside that made her shiver in delight. The way his hands held her legs tightly against him while staring down at her as if he could see straight through to her soul. The way he whispered her name as he circled his hips and continued to dive in, pull out and then dive in again.

What would happen if he wasn't falling for her? How would she survive that?

But then he was spreading her legs wide, easing out of her, and then moving ever so slightly so that when he sank in deep again, it was from a different angle, pressing against a different spot that had her biting her bottom lip with the same urgency. Why was he doing this? Why was he stroking her, spending time with her, understanding her, acting like this was more than just sex?

And why did him doing all those things feel so good? He was filling a space in her she'd purposely left empty, making her feel alive again in a way she'd sworn she'd never do.

The urge to give him something he'd never had before filled her with desire. She wanted him to feel what she was feeling. "I want to ride you," she said. The unexpected push and tug of an unnamed emotion bubbled in her chest. The eerie sense that this was where they both belonged. It was foolish, it had to be. This was exactly what she'd tried not to do again.

"I want you to ride me." The raspy growl came just as he began moving their bodies once more.

When he was on his back and she over him, she went still and just stared down. His muscled body made her bed seem smaller. The splatter of dark hair over his much lighter skin was sexy as hell, especially as it narrowed into a line that disappeared just before his navel. Her mouth watered again as her gaze rested on his dick, thick and long and waiting for her. With a light touch she ran her fingers over the line of hair at his groin, then moved up his abs until she was circling his nipples. He grabbed her wrist then, bringing her fingers to his mouth where he sucked each one. Her legs trembled, her nipples hardened to painful peaks, and she sighed.

As she angled her hips, positioning herself over his length before he pistoned into her, all she could think of was that this was perfect. This night. This man. This moment. It was absolutely perfect.

Circling her hips, she began moving over him, lifting her hands to cup her heavy breasts.

"Lovely." He was staring up at her. "That's what you are, Ms. Des. You're absolutely lovely."

That wasn't a word she heard every day. It wasn't even a word she thought men used, yet the sound of it coming from him had a light flutter rising and settling in the pit of her stomach.

Leaning forward she flattened her palms on his chest and began to work herself over him, bouncing her ass up and down, until he couldn't speak any other words except *damn*, *so good* and some other indecipherable things.

Rising, she leveraged herself on her knees this time. Desta continued to stroke him, feeling the fever pitch toward climax mounting with each move. He reached up then and grasped her breasts, kneading them. On a ragged moan he let his hands move down her torso until he was holding her hips, guiding her motions to meet his thrusts.

"Come for me," he said, his throat hoarse with desire. "Come for me, Des."

She couldn't speak. She wanted to, but her head had rolled back, her eyes half-closed, and her body was in that place drifting steadily toward release. That was all she could focus on, all she could think of. And when he eased a hand down between her legs, pressing the pad of his finger to her clit and circling it, she screamed. As if all the life drained from her with the blast of pleasure shooting through her body, she screamed his name more times than she could count.

"That's my baby. Come all over this dick. Yes." He made another sound of satisfaction, but all she knew was that she felt as if she were falling apart. Had exploded into a billion pieces and was just fracturing from delight.

"C'mon, baby, let me get back there."

He was moving them again. Her body was so pliant she hardly had to expel any effort to ease off him and remain on her knees. But Maurice was behind her now, grabbing her hips before sinking deep into her once more.

Now his grunts were loud, with each thrust of his hips his dick pressed harder into her, the sound of their bodies meeting a clapping sound that reverberated throughout the room. Then he stopped moving, holding himself planted fully inside of her, his fingers dug into her hips, and he came.

Desta had no idea how much time had passed since Maurice eased out of her and lowered both their bodies to the bed. She barely recalled what day of the week it was.

"Bathroom," he groaned the one word but only fell to his stomach on the bed beside her.

She rolled over onto her back, her legs still partially spread, every part of her body on display and not a pinch of modesty. A sound buzzed through the room. It took her a second to realize it was a phone—Maurice's. He got off the bed where he'd presumably been gathering his strength to get up and go to the bathroom. Grabbing his boxer briefs and jeans in one hand, he used the other to dig his phone out of his pocket.

Her eyes drifted closed after that, her mind still floating in the aftermath of what was arguably the best sex she'd had in her entire life. The sound of Maurice cursing ripped her from that pleasurable thought. With his phone and clothes in hand, he disappeared into the bathroom. For endless moments she simply lay there staring at the door, convincing herself that there was no reason for her to think anything other than he'd gotten a message he didn't like.

That didn't mean the message was from a woman. But he'd never rushed out of a room with his phone before. Not like Gordon had.

She sat up on the bed. Maurice wasn't Gordon. Desta knew that without a doubt, and she refused to let any more thoughts of her past invade the happiness she'd finally found.

CHAPTER THIRTEEN

DESTA'S HEART DID a quick flutter and start the moment Maurice walked into her office on Wednesday morning. Today's suit was a rich cranberry hue, paired with a caramel turtleneck. The smile he gave her after stepping inside and closing the door made her want to leap out of the chair and wrap her arms around him.

The fact that she was at work, wearing another long pencil skirt—this one a yellow and gray African print—with four-inch heel boots, held her still. "Good morning," she said as he passed behind her desk to where she sat.

He turned her chair, dropped a hand on her desk, and threaded the other through her hair, pulling her closer to him. "Mornin'," he whispered just before his lips touched hers.

It never failed, that twist that happened in the pit of her stomach the exact moment his tongue tangled with hers. She reached a hand up to slip behind his neck, holding him to her in the same urgent way that he was holding her. Could this be sustained? This feeling, his scent, his touch, this moment? Could it stay like this forever?

She didn't know, and the not knowing was driving her crazy.

"Missed you last night," she whispered the moment he eased his mouth away from hers. It was what she'd been thinking all last night after he'd left and she was alone in her bed.

For six years, since the day she'd walked out of that house she'd shared with Gordon, she'd lived alone and slept alone. Dates that turned into sex never turned into overnights at her house or theirs. Until Maurice, who'd slept beside her for the majority of the nights since the ski trip.

"Missed you this morning." His smile was intoxicating.

With a grin of her own, she tapped a finger to his chin. "Why, because I've become you're personal alarm clock?"

"Hey, you can't blame a guy for enjoying when a woman like you straddles him at four o'clock in the morning."

She had been doing that, after vowing she could make up for the workshop on morning sex they'd missed during the Dear Lover weekend. And she'd been enjoying it just as much as he had. So why had he left after getting that message last night?

"Obviously you didn't enjoy it too much. You opted not to stay last night." Did that sound too controlling? Clingy? Needy?

Maurice backed away from her then, moving around her desk and taking a seat in one of the guest chairs. She tried not to take that as a bad sign. "Had some things to take care of at home last night, that's all. No big deal. But I want to cook for you tonight. Are you available?"

"You? Cook?" She laughed. "This I've gotta see. Sure, I'm available."

"Oh, don't act like you don't know I've got skills in the kitchen. You remember those pizza bagels I brought in for that birthday luncheon for Betty down the hall."

"I remember they were overcooked and actually tasted a little store-bought."

He clapped a hand over his heart. "You wound my tender pride. I definitely pulled those out of the box and added extra cheese and oregano for a home-cooked touch."

"You're definitely a goofball." And she was unequivocally falling for him. "Your mother was amazed that I'd ever see past your silliness to be attracted to you."

His face contorted. "What? You talked to my mother about me?"

"No." She shook her head. "Briefly on Sunday when you and the guys were closed up in Ron's study, the women talked to me about you." That had been the first family girl talk she'd had in a long time. Since she was a teenager to be exact—that was the last time she, her mother and her grandmother had spent an evening talking, drinking lemonade and eating popcorn.

Maurice waved a hand distractedly. "I don't want to know what else was said during that little discussion."

He wasn't looking at her. He was much more consumed with whatever he was reading on his phone. Just like last night.

"Listen, I gotta run. Just wanted to stop in and see you before I got started with my day."

Shaking herself free of the questions looming in her mind, she smiled when he stood. "Well, thank you very much for the visit."

He leaned over the desk now, and she came up out of her chair to meet him halfway. "No thanks necessary," he whispered before one quick kiss. "I'll talk to you later."

She nodded and went in for another kiss, this time tracing her tongue over his lips. "Yeah, I'll talk to you later."

With a grin he backed away and headed for the door. Desta watched him leave, resisting the urge to follow him. With an irritated shake of her head, she wondered when she'd decided reclaiming her life meant falling right back into her worst nightmare?

She didn't like feeling this way. Wanting to be with Maurice all the time, needing to hear his voice, to feel his touch. It was insane. And it was the beginning of a very slippery slope. Like the one she'd slid down when she'd thrown all of herself into her relationship with Gordon, only to be shocked later when he'd wanted to keep her in a cage, doing his bidding and punishing her whenever she rebelled. Just when she'd convinced herself this was different, that Maurice was different, doubt eased back into her mind. But she didn't have time for this. Whatever was going to happen with Maurice would happen whether she spent the next few minutes worrying over it or not. There were better things she could do with her time. Work, for instance.

It was after four when Desta was able to tear herself away from her desk long enough to grab herself a bottled water and a bag of trail mix from the lunchroom. An impromptu call with the Donovan brothers had morphed into talks with their sister, who was a TV producer and had expressed interest in a reality show featuring Chaz and Riley. Normally, Desta's job didn't take her into the world of TV, but she was in it now. Back upstairs, she chewed a handful of trail mix and finished her email to RGF's legal department with all the questions she needed answered before going further with the discussions.

Nessa, her assistant, came through on the line. "Yes, ma'am?"

"I know it's late and you don't have anything on your schedule for the rest of the afternoon," Nessa began. Desta was less concerned with the woman's cryptic words and more concerned with why she was whispering through the phone. "But there's a woman here. She says her name is Kelli Boston and that she needs to see you about a personal matter."

Kelli Boston? Did she know someone by that name? Oh wait, yes, she did. "Yes, send her in."

Grabbing a tissue from the box on the other side of her desk, Desta wiped her hands of the trail mix and closed the bag just in time to watch Kelli walk into her office with the same cheerful smile she'd given her when they'd met.

"Hi!" Kelli said, waving as she came closer.

"Hi," Desta responded with less enthusiasm as questions pressed in. "How'd you know where I worked?"

"Oh, well, once Maurice said the two of you were coworkers, it was a no-brainer."

She was right about that, so Desta relaxed a bit. "Well, are you from New York? We didn't really get a chance to get to know each other during that weekend." The times they had been together, Kelli had done most of the talking, and truth be told Desta hadn't gone to the Finger Lakes to make another female friend.

"Oh no. I'm originally from Louisiana, but my parents moved to Miami when I was sixteen. Then I went to college in Delaware and ended up in Virginia."

None of which explained why she was sitting across from Desta right now. She didn't know how to say that without being rude.

"But the ski resort was so nice, I decided to stay on another week after the event ended. And then when I saw this while I was on the road, I knew I just had to make a detour and come make sure you were all right." Kelli had been pulling her phone out of her purse while she talked. Now, she was leaning over to hand the phone to Desta.

For endless moments Desta just stared at the woman wondering what in the world was going on. She didn't know Kelli well enough for her to be sitting in her office, hadn't even known her last name until Nessa said it a few minutes ago.

"I find it hard to believe you'd see something on your phone that warranted a detour from Virginia to come here and show me." Yet, Desta reached for the phone and pressed the Play button at the center of the screen.

It started with music, some slow, dramatic orchestra piece, and then the words *Breaking News* scrolled across the screen in bright red letters. She was about to ask what type of foolishness this was when the first picture of Maurice appeared on-screen. He was helping a woman get out of a car, taking her by the hand, then bringing that hand up to his lips to kiss. The music faded, and a woman's voice she didn't recognize began talking about the night she'd met Maurice Gold. For the next two minutes and twenty-seven seconds, Desta's heart slowed to an almost nonexistent beat.

Throughout the video there'd been many pictures of Maurice with other women, but the clincher was the pictures of *her* with Maurice, which had been taken during the ski trip. Her chest constricted, and she struggled to remain calm as the woman speaking on the video continued to narrate. "I'm taking this time to share with the world the type of man Maurice

Gold really is. He's the father of my child, yet he refuses to acknowledge it. That's the man these women are dating. That's the man selling clothes to you and smiling at you, mesmerizing you through a camera."

Desta dropped the phone, and it clamored across her desk. "What the hell is this? And why would you come all the way here to show it to me?"

"I thought you should see it before the rest of the world does." Kelli picked up the phone and looked down at the screen. "Well, I guess that might be a little late because it's had half a million views already. Traffic was really tight on the highway today."

In the next seconds Desta recalled how Kelli always seemed to pop up where she was during the Dear Lover retreat. When Kelli had admitted she knew who Maurice was, Desta had been alarmed. But when she'd tried to tell Maurice they should be careful about being seen together, he'd dismissed her concern. Now she wondered if that'd been a mistake. "Who are you?" she asked before standing.

Kelli smiled sweetly. "I'm your friend, Desta. Looking out for your best interests. You wouldn't want to get tangled up in another very public love triangle, would you?"

Desta's heart pounded, her hands fisting at her sides. "I don't know what you're talking about," she said through gritted teeth. But she knew exactly what Kelli was referring to. The question was, how did Kelli know about the press conference in Denver when Gordon was officially cut from the team after his affair with the coach's wife?

"Come on, now. I know you're too smart to play dumb with me. I really am just here as your friend. But I see you're not really welcome to that idea." Kelli reached for her phone and shrugged. "That's a pity. Anyway, all you need to know now is that this could've been avoided. Maurice could've saved you, his family and this company the embarrassment, but he chose not to." She was walking to the door now, still smiling brightly. "Oh, and when you see him, because I know you're gonna run right to his office and tell him about this, tell him I said hello!" With a wave of her hand Kelli walked out of the office, and Desta struggled to breathe.

After a few moments of thinking she might actually hyperventilate, she picked up the phone and dialed Maurice's extension.

"Yeah, I can't talk right now. I'll get back to you."

"What? No. I need to talk to you. It's serious."

"Okay. Okay. We're meeting at my place at six. We can talk then."

"Maurice, I mean it. We need to talk now."

"I can't right now. I'll see you at my place."

The sound of him hanging up on her sent Desta into a tailspin. Her hands shook as she tried to put the phone back into its cradle. She swayed as the room seemed to tilt around her, and she finally dropped down into her chair to keep from collapsing. So many thoughts were going through her mind right now, so many questions. All she could do was drop her head in her hands and close her eyes.

What was she doing? Was she really reliving everything that had happened when she was back in Denver?

She wasn't naïve—she'd known what she was getting into by continuing to date Maurice. His entire job was based on being the public face for this company. He knew reporters and photographers by name. There were always pictures of Maurice with women in the tabloids, so seeing some of them in that video wasn't what had shocked her. It was the pictures of her and Maurice taken while they were at the ski resort that caused alarm. Despite not trying to keep their relationship a secret, having it revealed that they'd been on a dating app meet 'n' greet wasn't something she wanted the public to know.

What had made her entire body tremble was hearing that unknown woman talk about Maurice fathering a child. She'd never imagined him as a father, and the thought of him being a father to someone else's child sent a quick jab of annoyance and pain through her chest.

Sitting back in her chair now, she let loose a nervous chuckle. She couldn't make this stuff up: her life might read like a movie script, but it was real. And now she needed to get home and change for this dinner with Maurice, where she'd have to tell him that their secret was not only out, it was exploding for the entire world to see on social media.

CHAPTER FOURTEEN

"You missed the deadline? I thought you said your guy was going to have the IP address of the blackmailer this morning and you'd have this wrapped up by the end of the day." RJ slammed the door to Maurice's office a few minutes after five that afternoon.

Major was already there standing across from Maurice's desk, and Chaz was in the far corner talking on his cell phone. RJ was technically late to the party.

"He had some kind of tech failure this morning, so I called Major and Chaz. They've been working all day to track the IP address and get us the name of the owner." He was trying to keep the cool he was known for, trying to let this play out the way it needed to so he could get to the desired result. It was hard. He wanted to punch somebody, but he didn't know who, and then he wanted to scold himself for making the same mistake over and over again and not listening to anyone who'd tried to warn him about the way he dealt with the press. His jaw hurt from clenching it so tight each time he thought about how insane this situation was. The woman mentioned in the blackmailing emails and who he suspected was narrating that video—which he now knew had been viewed over a million times—was a liar. He'd definitely dated her. There were pictures of them in the video that could prove it, but he'd never slept with her—a fact she wasn't thrilled about in the end. He wasn't the father of her child.

"We found the IP address, and Chaz has his people working on getting us the name and location now," Major said.

"So all we can do is wait? This thing is spreading like a virus. You're gonna have to make a statement. Tell them about the blackmail attempt and that the paternity thing is all a lie. Dad's already called the lawyers, so they're standing by ready to go after whoever's behind this." When it came to family scandals, RJ was just like their father. He went into action immediately, doing any and everything he could to protect his family first, the company second.

"I can't believe this is happening," Maurice said, dragging his hands down his face. And of all times for it to happen, why now? Why when he'd finally realized the player lifestyle he'd adopted because he didn't think he deserved real love and happiness was a total mistake? When he'd just found Des.

Leaning back in his chair, he closed his eyes and tried to ignore the pressure in his chest at the thought of how she'd react when she got wind of this. How long before she saw the video and came storming down to his office to curse him out?

"Okay, let's just all calm down. We're actively working on the situation. As soon as we get a name and an address, we'll be able to get the ball rolling toward prosecution. And this will all blow over just like the other failed attacks against us," Major interjected.

Opening his eyes and sitting up straighter in his chair, Maurice nodded. He believed every word Major had said, but those weren't his only worries. "I gotta tell Des."

"You mean you haven't told her about this yet?" The stunned tone in RJ's voice caught his attention, and he looked over to where his older brother stood. "I thought that was some kind of code for you people in love, that you had to tell each other everything."

"I never said anything about being in love," Maurice countered, but his temples throbbed as if to reject the words. He stood from his chair and started to pace, something he never did.

Major shook his head. "Did you think you had to? You haven't been like this with a woman since India."

RJ slipped both hands into the front pockets of his pants, his brows lifting. Chaz was still in the corner of the office with his back turned to them while he talked on the phone.

"If you're not in love with her, why risk sleeping with someone so close to all of us with the intent of walking away from her like you do every other woman? What's going to happen when this is over? How are the two of you going to continue to work here?" RJ asked way too many questions.

"Des isn't every other woman, and how we deal with our relationship is our business." After this, he prayed they'd still have a relationship. Hadn't he been trying his best to show her he wasn't like her ex? He'd told himself a million times that he'd never hurt her, not the way he knew that guy Gordon had. Now, because of him and his reputation, she was part of a paternity-suit scandal gone viral.

"It is your business, but you're our brother," Major told him. "What happens to you happens to us. That's why we're all sitting here now."

"Got it!" Chaz yelled, clapping his phone in the palm of his hand. "IP address is out of Virginia and belongs to a Travis Milhouse. I called the detective who helped us out with that ex-employee who helped steal designs, and he's doing a search on the name right now."

"See, we're going to get to the bottom of this," Major said.

Maurice walked back behind his desk. He didn't sit in the chair but placed his hands on the back of it, squeezing as he continued trying to hold in his rage.

RJ moved from where he was standing close to the door and stopped beside the chair Major sat in. "Good. Now, it's time for damage control."

"I'll make a statement." Maurice nodded. "A written one for now, and we'll get it out to all outlets. A presser can come later."

"I think we should probably do the presser sooner, Maurice," RJ said. "We have to get ahead of this. Think about our stocks. The customers. The overseas buyers. Riley's wedding."

Maurice pushed his chair back and stood, rubbing his hands down the back of his head as impatience rushed through his body.

"I've already got my team working on getting the video taken down from all social-media venues. It might take a few hours, but they're good, and they can get onto the Dark Web, too, if need be. It'll be gone by tomorrow," Chaz said. "And as far as a press conference, what if you make the written statement now, and tomorrow morning we do one without you." When nobody spoke immediately, Chaz looked around the room. "A united front, remember. What better look of unity is there than the brothers standing in for him, even the brother that's coming from the outside."

Maurice was liking Chaz more and more every day. "It's a good angle."

"Yeah, it is," RJ said.

"Then, we'll make it happen. Your assistant knows how to get the press conference rolling. I'll go out and talk to her."

When Chaz was gone, Major clapped a hand on Maurice's shoulder. "It's going to work out, man. Just go home, talk to Desta, and chill for tonight. We'll handle this."

Hearing Major say her name again had him glancing at his watch. Cursing because it was almost six, he pulled his chair back and sat down. "I gotta type this statement up."

"Good. We'll get out of here so you can take care of that," his twin said. Maurice was already pulling up a blank document on his computer, preparing to compose a statement to the world about how he'd been a reckless playboy who'd set himself up for this type of false paternity claim and how he'd regret his decisions forever because of the pain and embarrassment he was sure this video had caused his family.

Desta.

Had she seen it?

He cursed again, slamming his hands down on his desk. It was RJ who came to stand beside him this time. "Look at me," he said. When Maurice didn't, his brother clasped his shoulder and gripped it until he did.

"You're better than this. I know it, and you do, too. Don't you ever think I was saying you weren't. You're my brother, and I've got your back no matter what. You understand?"

Staring into RJ's intent dark brown eyes was something Maurice had been doing all his life. He'd looked up to both his brothers and his father, and he'd never wanted to disappoint any of them. Tonight, he was afraid he had, again.

"Now, handle your business here, and then go home like Major said. We'll do the rest."

"I'd never walk away from my child, RJ. No matter what other mistakes I've made in my life, I'd never do something like that."

"I know, man. You didn't have to tell me that."

Maurice shook his head. "I had to say it."

And he needed to say it to Desta, too. So the moment RJ left his office, Maurice typed his statement. He read it over three times before emailing it to his assistant, who Chaz was discussing next steps with. From there he went straight to the elevator and down to his car. He was running really late now, and he needed to get home to see Desta.

Forty minutes later Maurice was still sitting in his car, stuck in traffic. He'd started calling Desta immediately after leaving the office, but she hadn't answered. It was ten minutes to seven now, and he'd sent her four text messages as well, but still no response. Slamming his hands on the steering wheel he cursed. To say he was having a bad day was an understatement.

Finally he was a block away from his house. He was just about to turn the corner when he saw flashing lights from police cars and fire trucks.

"What the hell?" His speed had slowed because traffic was backed up here due to the accident up ahead.

While he waited, he tried calling Desta again. Still no answer. His phone was loaded with text messages and missed calls, but none of them were from her. Another ten minutes passed before he was able to edge his car closer to the street he needed to turn down, but before he could do so he glanced over at the three cars involved in the accident. His breath caught at the sight of the gray Volvo. Desta drove a gray Volvo, and she was supposed to meet him at his house at six.

The next few minutes passed by in a blur as he jumped out of his car toward the crash. He pushed past bystanders and was finally stopped by an officer when he tried to get close enough to the car to see if it was hers.

"My… She's my—" He tried to speak but his chest was full of white-hot pain. "I think this is my—" His head throbbed, their conversation this morning replaying over and over again in his mind.

I want to cook for you tonight… Just wanted to stop in and see you before I got started with my day.

That's what he'd said to her this morning. She'd looked so beautiful sitting behind her desk. He'd told her to come to his house and she'd agreed, just like India had agreed to go for a ride with him that night.

"Sir, we need you to get back in your car and move along," the officer yelled.

Now it hurt to breathe. The sound of the police sirens echoed so loud his ears began to clog. "No, you don't understand," he said, each word laced with the sting of guilt circling back to him once again. "I think this is…my…my girlfriend. This is her car." It *was* Desta's car. He knew it without having to get closer, and he sank to the ground with the weight of guilt and grief.

CHAPTER FIFTEEN

"Hey, man! Where've you been?" Maurice turned at the sound of Major's voice as he was walking toward the elevators on the first floor of the hospital.

"I had a few things to take care of." He didn't want to talk to Major right now. He only wanted to see Desta.

"It's been three hours since you called to tell me about the accident. I expected to find you here pacing or yelling at the staff when I got here." By the sound of his voice, Major was irritated about that.

Maurice was doing a good job of pissing people off today. He took a deep breath and released it. "I came here straight from the scene, but they wouldn't let me see her." He'd been tempted to run through the doors separating him from where she was, damn the consequences. But at the last minute he'd thought better of that idea. "She was being evaluated, so I knew that would take a while. I figured if you and Nina came, at least she'd have a friendly face if I wasn't here." Because he might also be the last person she wanted to see right now.

"A friendly face? Not the face of the man she's in love with?" His twin sounded agitated, but before Maurice could reply, Major continued. "Mom, Dad and Riley are up there in the waiting room now. They've called her mother and grandmother, and Dad sent the jet to pick them up. So, you're welcome for having us take care of your girlfriend."

Desta *was* his girlfriend. He'd told the police that at the scene of the accident.

A muscle twitched in Major's jaw, and Maurice knew he was angry. He had that same telltale sign when he was upset. His twin was probably thinking Maurice had screwed up again today. Not long after they'd found the idiots trying to blackmail him, he'd caused Desta to be in an accident and then left her at the hospital alone. He could definitely see how that would piss off Major and probably the rest of his family. Being the Gold family screwup wasn't fun.

"I called every thirty minutes for a report," he told Major. "I knew she wasn't awake yet. Or is she? What happened?" Fresh fear coursed through him.

"Why the hell wouldn't you just stay here with her, Moe? Is this about India? Are you still guilt-tripping over that at a time like this?" Major shook his head with exasperation. "You're acting like such a jerk about everything lately. I don't even know what's going on with you."

His brother's nickname for him, coupled with those harsh but true words almost sent him reeling. But he knew now was not the time to fall apart.

Major was right: he'd been messing things up lately, and he didn't fully understand why. All he knew now was that making sure Des was all right was his first priority.

"I know what you're thinking and where you probably thought I was." He locked gazes with his brother. "I did go back to the house, to my room." Where he'd locked himself for days after India's accident. "But I know what happened to India wasn't my fault. I know, Major. So, I left there and went straight to Desta's place. I had to show the landlord a billion forms of ID, then prove that she worked at our company, convince him that she was in an accident, and then, finally, I thought to call Nessa who had a key to her place so I didn't need to deal with the landlord anymore. I wanted to make sure she had things she was familiar with when she woke up."

Major looked down at the duffel bag and the pillow he had stuffed under his arm as if just seeing those things for the first time. "You went to her house to get her things?"

"Yeah. Because India and the guilt from my past aside, I still hate that Desta was in an accident on her way to see me." She was hurt and while there was nothing he could do about that physically, he would do whatever possible to make sure she had everything she needed and was comfortable. "So I'm gonna go up and see her now. Is that all right with you?"

Major gave him a half smile before shaking his head.

"What's so funny?"

"You, man. You're funny." Major continued to stare at him.

"That's a wonderful thing to say to your brother after the day I've had."

Major put his arm around Maurice's shoulder and walked him onto the elevator when it opened. "If you think this was a day, wait until you let yourself realize you're in love."

He was in love. As he'd sat in his childhood room thinking back to that night he'd come home from the hospital—while India had been going in for her first surgery—he knew what he felt for Des was totally different. He'd been so young when he was with India, and the trauma from that night had blemished his soul from that point on. But the moment he'd begun that anonymous email exchange with Des, everything changed. The way he thought about his life, all the women he was dating, how his behavior affected his family, the more he'd realized he had to change. Des had been that change, the second he saw her at the ski resort.

"And to top that wonderful news off, we found out that guy, Travis Milhouse, is a freelance reporter looking for his big break. He tried to sell the paternity story to the *New York Post*, but his girlfriend was the one who came up with the blackmail idea."

Maurice didn't know who Travis Milhouse was, and right now he didn't care. He just wanted to see

Des. He needed to see the woman he loved and to tell her how sorry he was, for everything.

Desta had a terrible headache. That was her first thought when she opened her eyes. Her second thought was to quickly close her eyes again because opening them hurt far too much.

"Just take it slow, sweetheart." A woman's voice and a hand over hers soothed some of the edges around the blinding pain, but not all. "Did they give her something for the pain? It seems like she should have some type of medication?"

"Relax, Mom. They will. They wanted to wait for her to wake up first so they can check all her vital signs again."

She knew that voice and took a chance on cracking her eyes open slowly once more.

"Hey, there," Riley said, waving a hand.

The action made Desta moan as memories floated back into her mind, and she saw Kelli with her goofy grin.

"Maurice." It hadn't hurt to say his name, but damn, the light in the room was causing all kinds of tingles to shoot from her temples down to the rest of her body. "Turn out the light. Where's Maurice?"

Riley looked to someone, but Desta wasn't going to risk turning her head because she had a sinking suspicion that would only cause more pain.

"He's on his way, dear. Do you need something to drink? Do you want to sit up?" She knew now the voice belonged to Marva, and Desta sighed slowly, accepting her motherly presence.

"No," she finally managed. "Where am I?"

"In the hospital. There was a three-car pileup about a block away from Maurice's house. You were car number one so you got the least amount of the damage." Riley shrugged. "Even though that still landed you here with a concussion."

"A concussion." She moaned because saying the word triggered more spikes of pain.

"Yes, dear. The doctor said you'll need to stay here at least for tonight. So Ron and I thought it was best that your mother and your grandmother be here with you. They should be arriving soon."

Oh joy, Edna and Sheryl were on their way to New York to see her lying in a hospital bed. That was going to be a treat.

"My car?"

"The good news is you're awake and talking and your prognosis is good," Riley said and waited a beat. "The bad news is your car's totaled."

She groaned, fully expecting the pain that followed. The doctor and a nurse came in soon after that, poking and probing, and asking her all sorts of questions. They said she was going to be fine, before finally giving her something for the ferocious headache and leaving the room.

There were a few minutes of silence, when nobody was in that room with her, that Desta simply lay there thinking about all that had happened. The accident had occurred so fast. She'd been waiting for Maurice to arrive one moment and then the next she'd been thinking that maybe he'd stood her up.

Recalling those moments made her irritated, and she frowned when she looked up to see him walking through the door.

"You hung up on me." That's the first thing she thought to say, even though the warmth rolling over her skin indicated she should probably say something else.

He came closer. "I'm sorry."

"I had to tell you something really important."

Dropping the bag he was holding on the floor, he came closer to the bed. "I'm sorry."

How was it possible that he looked worse than she felt? His eyes seemed a little puffy, like maybe he'd been crying, and his shoulders were slumped, like he was carrying a heavy weight. "I waited for you, and you didn't come."

He shook his head. "I was late, and I'm so, so sorry." Leaning over her when she thought he would've kissed her, he eased the pillow he'd been carrying beneath her head instead.

Then he went to the duffel bag and took out her phone charger and the unicorn figurine that sat on her nightstand. "You went to my house?"

"Nessa let me in." When he set her favorite tumbler with the bright blue straw on the table beside the unicorn, she wanted to cry.

"I have to apologize now."

"No, baby. There's nothing you need to apologize for. I was late. If I'd been there when I said I would, you wouldn't have been in the accident. And Des, I need you to know I'd never do anything to hurt you. I'd never be careless with you in any way. I didn't father a child and walk away, and I'm not interested in dating multiple women anymore." He'd taken her hand and was holding it tightly. She could feel his fingers trembling in hers.

"I thought I had to be that way after the accident with India so many years ago. I felt so bad about what happened to her that I didn't believe I deserved to be happy or in love again. I messed up back then, and I messed up again today. But I want to do better, I want to be better." He kissed her fingers before looking up to her again. "I'm better when I'm with you."

How could he be breaking her heart and filling it at the same time? She ached for the pain he'd carried all these years. It was foolish of him to think he had to be punished for an accident that wasn't his fault. Just as it was foolish of her to hold what had happened with her and Gordon so close that it spilled over into everything she did. Once again, the fact that they seemed to be a perfect match was not lost on her.

She tried to lift her free hand up to his face, but the effort was painful, and she winced. He immediately leaned over so he was closer, and her palm finally met his cheek for a slow stroke. "We're quite a pair, you and I. Walking around here acting like martyrs, holding our feelings back because of some nonsense in our past." She shook her head. "Last night, when you left, I thought back to when I found out Gordon was cheating on me. And then after I saw that video I remembered when the owner of the team Gordon had played on held a press conference to announce that Gordon was being released from the team after sleeping with the coach's wife." She took in a shaky breath, forcing herself not to cry over events that didn't deserve any more of her tears. "I felt like it was happening all over again, but this time the pain was surreal."

"Des—" She shook her head to stop him from speaking.

"No. I know that this is different. You're not Gordon, and I'm sorry for comparing what we have to what I had with him."

"I would never intentionally hurt you. Not ever," he insisted.

"I know."

Revisiting her life with Gordon was tough, but it was also cathartic, because in that moment she looked into Maurice's eyes, she knew deep down in her soul that he'd stand by his word.

"I would never treat you badly. Next to Major, you've been my best friend these past five years." He was shaking his head now. "I didn't realize that until now."

"Well, you may rethink that when you find out

I was responsible for that video going viral." She figured he had to know about it by now. He was in charge of PR at the company, so someone would've reached out to him once they saw it.

"What are you talking about? When did you see the video?" He looked as perplexed as she'd felt when Kelli had walked into her office. But after telling him about that entire exchange, his look of confusion shifted to pure rage.

"Dammit!" He released her hand and stepped away from the bed, turned his back on her and then ran his hands over his face. "That's where I knew that guy's name from. When Chaz first said it, I didn't make the connection."

"The connection to what?" Despite the pain meds her head was still pounding as she tried to process everything.

He turned back to face her and shrugged. "It seems that Dear Lover was responsible for bringing us together and was almost responsible for tearing us apart. Travis Milhouse was the one who sent me the blackmail messages I started getting that Sunday while we were still at the resort. He and Kelli must've concocted the plan once they figured out who we were. And if I wasn't the consummate playboy, they wouldn't have had the opening."

"Oh no, you're not about to accept the blame for that, too. I knew Kelli was a little off when I met her."

"Nah, I'm not taking the blame for anybody but myself at this point. I just can't believe we had to go through all of this…just to realize our friendship was meant to be more."

"Is it more for you, Maurice?" It was a brave question, one she'd been struggling with asking him all day long.

When he walked over to the bed again, this time brushing his knuckles over her cheek and bending down to drop the softest kiss on her forehead, her skin rippled once again with warmth. It traveled throughout her body now, comforting and calming.

"Yeah, it's definitely more now."

EPILOGUE

Three Months Later

MAURICE HELD HIS cards tight, watching as Major decided what he was going to do. Chaz and RJ had already folded, leaving their money to add to the hefty pot up for grabs. Desta was sitting prettily with her cards facedown on the table. She'd already added her bet to the pot.

He watched her while he waited, recalling all they'd been through in the past several months. After she'd left the hospital, they'd both given statements to the police about meeting Kelli and Travis at the ski resort. With their lawyer beside them, they hadn't needed to go into too much detail about why they'd been there in the first place. Arrests had occurred about a week later, and Maurice had done a press conference explaining the falsehood to the media.

Desta, along with the legal department and a talent agent they'd hired, had negotiated a lucrative reality-television special deal for Riley and Chaz.

The new development kept her busy for the bulk of her days, but the nights were reserved for him. Just after they returned from spending Christmas with her family in Chicago, they'd decided that her place was just too small for both of them. He'd wanted her to move into his place, but she'd insisted on them searching for a place where both their names could be on the lease. He respected her need to maintain her independence while being part of a relationship.

Maurice had been in a relationship for three months now. Not three dates, but three months. Who would've ever thought he'd change his ways so drastically and so quickly? Who would've ever thought his best friend would turn out to be the woman of his dreams?

"Damn, Major, quit studying the cards. Make a bet or bow out," RJ complained, and he wasn't even in the game anymore. He was getting grouchier, and the family hoped traveling to the private island they'd booked for Riley and Chaz's wedding in June would relax him a little.

"All right! I'm out." Major had been taking a long time deciding, but Maurice was patient. At least, he'd been telling himself that for the last hour and a half.

"So it's just you and me," Des said from across the table. "Or are you about to concede to my superior poker skills like the rest of them?"

He loved her smile. He loved the way she didn't take any mess from him whether at work or at home.

And he especially loved the way she loved him completely as he was.

"Oh, I'm in," he said and then set his cards down on the table to reach into his pocket. When he knew everyone in the room was expecting him to pull out more cash to toss into the already large pot to bet, Maurice instead removed a little black box.

He opened the box under the table and stared down at the three-karat pear-shaped diamond ring sitting against the cushioned interior. Taking a slow breath and releasing it, he extended his arm across the table, sat the box on top of the cash pile and waited.

Desta looked down at the black box and the brilliantly shining ring inside. She struggled for a moment to catch her breath, yanking her hands from the table for fear she might touch it and it wasn't meant for her.

"What's going on?" That may have been a silly question, but it was the first thing that popped into her mind.

"I love you, Des." Maurice stood up and walked around to the side of the table where she was sitting. "I think I've loved you since I've known you. It just took me a while to figure that out and act on that love."

"A long while," Major joked from the sidelines, and Chaz chuckled.

She couldn't believe this was happening, and on poker night of all nights!

Maurice knelt down on one knee, taking her hands in his. "I love everything about you, even the fact that I know in my heart you're a cheater when it comes to playing poker."

Now everyone chuckled, even her while her eyes filled with tears. Her heart was beating so fast, and her hands were shaking. Until he lifted them up to his lips and kissed each finger.

"But what I love most about you is the way you love me. Everything you've given me has taught me how to love you in return. You're my world, and I don't want to continue on without you. So will you please marry me?"

The tears fell—there was no use trying to hold them back. "I love you. I love you so much for showing me it was okay to love again. You're my best friend."

There was a pause and then, "So is that a yes or a no?" RJ asked.

Everyone looked at him in surprise.

"I mean, if all of you want to be married, that's fine by me," RJ continued with a shrug.

"Yes!" Desta answered without waiting for anyone to say anything else. "Yes, Maurice Gold, I'll marry you."

"Well, all right, then!" Major yelled and began to clap along with the others.

Maurice stood, pulling her up with him and wrapping his arms around her for a tender kiss. When the kiss broke, she laughed nervously. "Oh, I forgot about the ring and the rest of my winnings."

Releasing her, Maurice took the box off the table and removed the ring. He lifted her left hand in his and slid the ring onto her third finger. "I'm the biggest winner in this room tonight because I've won you."

Staring through tear-blurred eyes at the man she was going to marry, Desta wrapped her arms around him for another hug. "And I've won you."

* * * * *

THE LOVE CURE

CARA LOCKWOOD

MILLS & BOON

This book, my last Dare,
is dedicated to all the Dare fans.

Thank you so much!

CHAPTER ONE

LIAM LANGE JUST wanted this damn day to be over already and it was barely five. He rolled up the sleeves of his canvas work shirt as he slid onto the peeling leather barstool in the dark dive bar in Hoboken. The blinds were down so he didn't have to stare at the silver cityscape of Manhattan, his least favorite place on earth.

He ordered a cold Pabst Blue Ribbon to try to cool his temper, still simmering from the run-in he'd had with the foreman on the condo build he'd worked on down the street. The foreman—all mouth and no brains in Liam's opinion—micromanaged his work on the roof all day—from the ground. As if he could tell anything from down there. It had taken all of Liam's patience to finish the job, which thank God was now done.

Liam's lower back ached, since he'd been working double time to get out of there, and he could feel the singe of a sunburn on his neck. The mid-May sun had been unforgiving all day, but it was nothing that a cold beer or two wouldn't fix. The bartender opened a longneck and slid it to him, and he took it with a small nod of his head and drank deep.

No. His real problem had nothing to do with the sun or that moronic foreman. Or his aching muscles. It had everything to do with that damn message on his phone.

Hey, brother. Happy Birthday. WL.

WL for Wilder Lange. As if he wouldn't know that this unlisted, blocked number would be his asshole half brother's. It doubly irked because his full brothers, Seth and Stuart, hadn't yet acknowledged his birthday. They were still pissed off about him taking Mom's side against them in the last run-in with Wilder, clearly. Well, they could be pissed all they wanted. They were the ones who'd picked the wrong side.

He took one more look at the text, his finger hovering over the reply button. What could he even say?

How's the money grab going? Stolen all of our father's money yet? Want to bleed me dry, too? Ha, sucker. There's nothing you can take from me.

That's where Liam had already won. He'd walked away from the Lange Communications fortune long ago. Nothing but vipers and vampires hanging around hoping to get a drop of their dead father's power and money. All Liam had to his name was a few thousand dollars, and whatever this last job would pay—if the foreman didn't dock him like he'd threatened. What he needed to do was save all his money and head south. Florida, maybe? Somewhere away from Manhattan and New Jersey, which on days like today just seemed populated with the world's worst assholes.

Liam was halfway through his PBR when the door to the dive bar slid open, letting too much of the late afternoon sunlight in. He squinted, annoyed at the flash of light in the otherwise shuttered and darkened bar, light that seemed not to be waning. Some idiot was holding the door open. He could feel the blast of hot air from outside on his back. Liam turned, half expecting to see that asshole foreman, as he'd be the kind of guy who'd swing open a door wide to a darkened bar.

Instead, he saw the most beautiful woman he'd ever seen in his whole life, ringed in a halo of light. She was delicate and blonde, her hair gleaming like spun gold. She wore an airy white sundress, which, backlit with the sun, showed her amazing thighs in nearly perfect detail. She kept her elegant hand, nails painted a shell pink that matched her soft bow lips, on the door as if wondering whether or not to come in. This kind of bar was not the place for a woman as gorgeous as that. Her white linen dress wouldn't stay white long against these faded and peeling barstools. Her delicate strappy-heeled sandals would no doubt find it hard going on the pitied concrete floor.

It's no wonder she looked so uncertain, so confused, as she let in the summer heat.

"Hey, in or out! You're gonna melt us over here," one of the less than savory characters on the other side of the bar yelled, his Jersey accent as thick as his belly. He was almost entirely bald except for a wisp of dark hair he'd tried unsuccessfully to sweep over the center of his head. Liam scowled at the man. He wasn't wrong, but still, that was no way to talk to a woman. Liam glanced over at her, sure she'd exit the place, realizing her mistake, but instead, she stepped inside, letting the door swing shut behind her.

Interesting. So she was going to double down on her mistake. She either had guts or lacked the sense to turn around and leave.

"Hey, sweetheart. Come sit by me!" the man called out, clearly turning in time to realize he was yelling at a gorgeous model. Liam scowled again. Okay, so he was going to be a problem. And the bartender wasn't doing anything about it. He had his head buried in the ice at the end of the bar, ignoring the ruckus. Liam stretched his neck, its joints popping. He wouldn't mind getting into it with some jerk. Might help him work out the day's stress.

"Leave her alone. She can sit where she wants," Liam said, voice low but steady. "Let her decide." The man saw Liam for the first time and seemed prepared to pop off. But then Liam stood, to his full height of six-three. He was also a wall of muscle, a benefit of working with his hands all day. The man suddenly found something interesting to look at on his phone.

Uh-huh. Thought so.

The woman's gaze darted from Liam to the man and back again. Maybe this was the time she'd choose to bolt. Instead, she moved closer to Liam, and laid her hand hesitantly on the ripped stool next to his.

"Mind if I...?" she asked, her voice sweet like honey. Her clear blue eyes held his a minute. Damn, they were pretty. Fringed with thick dark lashes. Liam wasn't exactly in the mood for company, but there was no way he could say no to that voice, to those small, pink, rosebud lips. Whatever the lady wanted, she'd get.

He nodded at the seat, and she perched on it, the hem of her sundress inching above her knee. He tried not to stare at her legs, which she crossed at the knee. The hem rode up a little farther, giving him just a glimpse of pale thigh. She set her small straw clutch purse on the bar.

"I'm Cecily," she said, holding out a dainty hand with those perfectly pink nails. He dragged his focus away from her legs with difficulty.

"Liam," he replied, taking her hand, which seemed childlike in his. He worried she'd shrink from his calloused paw, but she shook it gamely.

"Nice to meet you." She flashed him a dazzling white smile that nearly blinded him. God, the woman was even prettier close-up. Barely wore a stitch of makeup, and had a few freckles across her nose, but otherwise, her skin was flawless. Her clear blue eyes, like a gorgeous calm day on the Atlantic, stared at him, and seemed…friendly. It had been a while since a woman this pretty had been this interested in him. Not that it didn't happen, but normally, he attracted the punk chicks with the smoky eye shadow and heavy liner, with extra piercings and tattoos, the ones who didn't mind his calloused hands. Beautiful blondes who looked like they ought to be shopping on Fifth Avenue with limitless platinum cards typically didn't go for him.

"Can I buy you a drink?" she asked, nodding to his now, near-empty longneck. He almost choked on the last sip.

"*You* want to buy *me* a drink?" He had to laugh. Who was this woman? First, she strides into a dive bar where she clearly doesn't belong, and then she offers *him* a drink? Every man in here would buy her two or three or ten.

"Is there something wrong with that?" A playful—even flirty?—smile crossed her lips.

Clearly, Cecily was a woman who flaunted convention. Well, that worked just fine by him. He didn't care much for convention, anyway.

"Nothing at all wrong with that," he said.

"Good," she added, and signaled the bartender, ordering him another PBR, and her one, too. When the bartender put the bottles before them, she clinked her neck against his. "Hell with this day. Here's hoping it turns around." She took a big swig from the bottle and he wondered what could ever go wrong for a beautiful woman like this. He always imagined gorgeous women got pretty much whatever they wanted.

"You had a bad day, too?" he asked her, a bit of amusement in his voice.

"Sure did. I mean, did anyone *in here* have a *good* day?" She indicated the few grumpy patrons around the bar. Liam had to laugh at that.

"I bet not," he agreed. People didn't come to this dive to celebrate.

"So, how about you? Your day…was it bad…or the worst?" She seemed actually interested.

"The worst," he admitted.

"Well, then, we'd better add Jameson shots to these, or we're never going to get anywhere." She signaled the bartender as Liam laughed then, despite himself. He liked this woman. She leaned over the bar to talk to the bartender and Liam noticed a flash of smooth skin at her neckline, the hint of cleavage visible. One of the straps of the dress fell down her left shoulder and she absently tugged it up again. He studied her shoulder, wondering if her skin was as soft as it looked. He felt want in him stir. *Down, boy*, he told himself. *Not the right time.*

The bartender set the Jameson shots in front of them, and the woman handed over her credit card for an open tab. Liam shook his head. He'd have to argue with the bartender later about who was paying for these drinks. He couldn't very well let this beautiful woman carry him tonight.

"What should we drink to?" she asked him, blinking fast.

"Well, it is my birthday."

Her pink lips parted. "Your birthday? Seriously?" She looked joyful, as if he'd just given her the best news. It had been a long time since anybody had cared about the day he was born, and probably longer since they'd been happy about it. He had a flash of his older brother Wilder scowling at him, the day the two nearly tore each other's heads off, the last day he'd ever stepped foot in the Lange family mansion. "Well, then, to you, Liam. On your birthday. Sorry it's been the worst."

She gently clinked her shot glass against his, and their fingers touched as she did so. Was it just his imagination or did a current run straight up his arm and right to his groin? She put the shot glass to her delicate lips and drained it, then thumped it on the bar with a clunk. Damn, the woman was sexy. Liam followed suit, the Jameson sliding down his throat with only the slightest twinge of a burn. His eyes never left her. Part of him thought she was just a mirage and she'd disappear if he didn't keep an eye on her. He still couldn't believe she was sitting next to him, her exposed knee inches from his own. He probably should try to talk to the woman, but he kept thinking if he opened his mouth, she'd fly away, like a beautiful songbird.

"So, tell me, Liam," she said, leaning forward. "Why's your day been so bad?"

Terrible boss. Worse brother. A family feud that he'd long since grown tired of managing. And the fact that this day marked two occasions: his birth and his father's untimely death. Where to start? "Birthdays aren't really great for me," he admitted.

"Why not?" Her blue eyes studied him with real concern. She seemed to actually care.

"My dad died. On this day, years ago." Liam glanced down at the bar. "So, every day, I'm reminded that I was born, but he's not here."

Cecily's face crumpled a bit. "Oh." She bit her lip. "I'm so very sorry."

Liam had been barely a teenager when his father passed, when he'd gone from being incredibly wealthy to having next to nothing nearly overnight. His oldest brother, Wilder, took over the company, mostly cut out his mother and his brothers. He'd listened to his mother complain bitterly about this for years, and he knew it wasn't fair.

"I'm not talking to most of my family." Liam shrugged. "After my dad died, well, my half brother kind of became a prick. And…" Liam couldn't believe he was even getting into this. And with a perfect stranger. He never talked about Wilder. Never talked about the Lange dynasty. The millions, no billions, stolen from its rightful heirs. "Well, we disagreed on what should happen with Dad's…uh…belongings. Wilder thought he should get most of it. I thought Dad would want it split between all four of his sons and his wife."

Liam remembered trying to argue with his grown brother. He'd been just a kid, really. He never would get any traction. Then, his older full brother, Seth, and Liam's twin brother, Stuart, they'd all just bought into Wilder's lies. Took his side. Against him. Just because they were happy to take Wilder's meager payouts. Liam felt the rest of the family deserved more. Much more. There wasn't much point in staying in the family after that. As soon as Liam hit eighteen, he was gone. All he'd taken with him was a voting seat on the board of Lange Communications. Wilder had offered him millions for it. Liam had taken great joy in telling him to go to hell.

"Your brother took it all?" Cecily looked aghast.

"He took all that mattered." Liam stared at the label of his beer bottle. "He took the valuable stuff." As in, taking over Lange Communications, the cash cow and divvying up the tiniest of cash and stock payouts for the rest of them, which wasn't nearly enough for his mother to live on or to pay for Liam's private school tuition. His father never would've let that happen. But Wilder was a different story.

Wilder said Dad wanted him to take over the business, but Dad never mentioned that to Liam. Or anybody else. So, as far as Liam was concerned, Wilder could've simply made it all up. Liam was the one who'd convinced the board he was the natural choice to lead the company. And knowing his eldest brother, the control freak, the bossiest brother of all time, it was simply a straight-up power grab.

Cecily put her hand on Liam's. The soft touch startled him.

"I'm sorry," she said, eyes full of empathy. "That had to be terrible, fighting with your brother, especially after you just lost your dad."

"Half brother," he corrected. But Liam couldn't stop staring at the woman's delicate hand on his. There seemed to be more than comfort there. Something more like…an invitation. But was he imagining it?

"But grief does terrible things to people. Maybe he didn't mean to do the things he did."

Liam studied Cecily. She was a woman, he decided, who just tried to see the best in people. And maybe that was because people always put their best faces on around her.

"You're being kind to him, but he doesn't deserve it." Liam waved a dismissive hand. Some people were just rotten. There was no helping them.

"Well, we can all use a little kindness, right?" She beamed at him, undeterred. "So, what can we do to cheer you up today? Nobody should be sad on their birthday." She flashed another brilliant smile at him. Suddenly, all he wanted to do was have her naked in his bed. That would set things right. Maybe for all time.

He took a swig of beer to distract himself from those thoughts. She was too good for him. Too pretty. Too sweet. He hadn't even showered from his day of sweaty outdoor work, and he was thinking of taking

this lovely princess to his bed? His cramped Hoboken apartment with a stunning view of the brick
building next door would *not* impress.

"It's okay. Besides. I'm not the only person who's
had a bad day. Didn't you say you were having a
rough one? How come?"

Unease flickered across her face. "Yeah. I had a
pretty rough day." She bit her pink lip, as if trying to
decide how much to share. He almost worried she'd
blurt out something about a powerful rich husband.
But, glancing at her left hand, he saw no ring. Nor,
even, a white imprint of one she used to wear. "I got
some bad news."

"What kind?"

She studied him for a second, her resolve waver-
ing. "I…uh. Lost my job. And my health insurance."

"Seriously?" What crazy person would fire this
gorgeous, sweet woman? A fool. That's who. "Who
would fire you? You're…you're…so…" Perfect.
"Nice."

"Aw, thanks, Liam." An appreciative smile tugged
at her mouth. "It was just layoffs. Nothing personal.
It's just about the corporation's bottom line. I worked
in HR for Yancy's. The big department store chain?"
Liam nodded. He knew it. Everybody knew it. They
had a store at every mall, and in every downtown in
America. But retail had taken a hit lately, especially
with the economic downturn.

"Or, I guess I should say, *worked*." She stared at
her own beer bottle then, as if it were a crystal ball.

"I can find another job—probably. It's losing the health insurance…" She trailed off, as if the words had become lodged in her throat.

"Oh, you'll be fine," he told her. "Bet you get a new job and new insurance in just a month or two."

She sent him a brave smile. "Yeah. Probably."

Liam didn't know what he'd said, but now she seemed sad. Despondent, even. *Great job, man. You've brought her down somehow.* But didn't he always bring the mood down? Wasn't that his specialty?

Why do you always have to be such a problem? Why do you always have to push everyone who cares about you away? Wasn't that what Wilder had told him, the last fight they'd had face-to-face?

"I'm headed to the bathroom," Liam said, standing. He glanced at Cecily's pensive face. He figured he'd just give her time to slip out of the bar, and out of his life. She already had one mental foot out the door anyway, he could tell. Besides, she was out of his league. Way, way out of his league. The longer he sat next to her, the more likely he'd be to start getting his hopes up. And the way this day was going that was just a recipe for disaster.

"Oh? Okay." She watched him as he headed back into the even darker parts of the bar and walked to the small, narrow hallway with the old bathroom sign on the wall and an arrow pointing to the basement downstairs. He barely made it to the basement, his work boot hitting the ground floor when he felt a soft touch on his elbow.

He turned then to see Cecily there, big blue eyes wide, pink lips parted. His brain didn't understand what she was doing there, didn't understand why she hadn't taken the opportunity to sneak out the dive bar and be on her merry way. His brain didn't get it, but his body seemed to instinctively understand exactly why she was standing on the steps above him, the extra height still not quite making her taller. She studied his eyes, then his lips. No explanation came. No reason why she'd followed him down this dark staircase.

But he knew then, suddenly, exactly why she'd come. The realization dawned just as she closed the distance between them and pressed her soft lips against his.

CHAPTER TWO

WHAT THE HELL are you doing, Cecily Morgan? It was the only clear thought banging around in her head the second she kissed this big mountain of a man, this straight-from-a-construction-worker-calendar man whose tanned, taut muscles were evident even through his canvas shirt rolled up to the elbows. He was gorgeous, and beyond sexy, and so very, very far out of her league. Yet, she was kissing him brazenly right here in the basement of this bar, near the restrooms, as if coming on to strange men was something she did all the time. It was something she never did. Never in all her life.

He was frozen, probably in shock, and who could blame him? She was kissing him, and he was standing there like a statue, and…oh, God. This was going to be bad. Would he push her away? Declare her a brazen hussy who needed to go get a life? She didn't know what happened in these kinds of situations, because she'd never kissed a stranger before. Never done anything like this.

But her clock was ticking. And she had a bucket list. And this was number five. *Kiss a handsome stranger, a guy you'd never in a million years think you have a chance with, and just...see what happens.* And what she needed to happen was to turn this horrible day around. Kissing a handsome stranger was one way she hoped to do it.

Of course, what was happening was she'd scared this chivalrous man to death and now he was patiently standing here waiting for her to *get off him*. But just when she thought he would push her away, tell her that her pass was decidedly unwanted, he began to kiss her back. He moved slowly at first, cautiously, but his lips parted, matching hers. He tasted like Jameson, but also, something else, something sweet and savory. Something she wanted more of. She opened her mouth, so her tongue could meet his, and the second they began that old ancient dance, every single coherent thought in her brain evaporated.

His big hand slid behind her lower back, and suddenly she was instantly lifted off the last step, and her body pressed tightly against his. He pulled her to him, and she went, eagerly, tasted the salty residue of sweat near his upper lip. A man who worked with his hands, who smelled like the outdoors, and so gorgeous he might as well be a walking sexual fantasy, muscle-bound edition. She put her hands in his thick, dirty blond hair, and he released her mouth, his lips finding the delicate skin of her neck. Oh, God, that felt good. His tongue caressed her, tasted her, and she wondered what else his tongue might be good at doing. Her entire abdomen felt on fire, her thighs had melted into one another. He nuzzled her neck, and she almost cried out right there. In seconds, this had gone from a single kiss to a white-hot make-out session. His hand was working its way up her skirt, and she wanted it there, wanted his calloused hands on her skin. He cupped her hip beneath her dress and she sucked in another hard breath. He covered her mouth with his again, his tongue lashing hers, promising much more to come. One hand was up the back of her neck and in her hair. He grabbed a bit, loosely, but protectively, as if to better maneuver her head. He was taking control and she liked it. Liked it too much.

God, why did he taste so good? Why did he taste like everything she'd ever needed her whole life? Now her own back was against the brick wall, and she felt it, hard and unforgiving. He was pressed against her, and she raised her right leg, he pulled it upward, ever upward, and pressed into her. She could feel him through his jeans, feel his need growing there, hard and determined. Feel him pressing against the thin fabric of her delicate underwear.

Were they going to do this right here? All he had to do was unzip and… She couldn't believe she was even thinking about it. A hot quickie with a perfect stranger outside the bathroom of a dive bar? She didn't even know his *last name.* They'd met mere *minutes ago.* And she was contemplating letting him take her, right here, right now. This was not the Cecily, she nor anyone else knew. This was not the prim human resources executive, who'd just been laid off. The one who never did anything risky. Never did anything spontaneous. That was, until life threw her the curve ball of all curve balls.

The doctor's visit today had been the worst.

I'm sorry, Miss Morgan. There's nothing more we can do.

And then she'd gone back to her office, only to be told that second quarter growth had stalled, that layoffs would take place immediately, and she was out. Along with her health insurance. But, she guessed, if there wasn't any treatment for her, then why even worry about health care?

Why was she thinking about that now? She had a gorgeous man running his hands up her skirt. She should be thinking about that. She should think of nothing but the feel of his mouth on her skin, nothing but the sure way his hands roved her body. She'd lose herself in him, just for a few moments, and she wouldn't have to think about the horrible reality of her future. Or lack of one. This was about her damn bucket list. She needed to do this.

"Excuse me?" The strange voice came from somewhere behind her. She broke away from Liam then, in time to see a busboy carrying a big plastic bin full of dirty cocktail glasses. She realized with a start that they were blocking the swinging door to the kitchen.

"Oh, uh. Sorry." Cecily moved to one side, Liam's hand still protectively on her waist. Liam studied the busboy, who worked hard not to make eye contact as he walked quickly by. Cecily's face grew hot, as she glanced back up at Liam. No doubt her lipstick was all over her face now, and her hair felt untamed, and she could still feel the rivets his fingers had made. She probably looked like the world's biggest slut, but she didn't care. She had a bucket list.

She glanced at Liam, who seemed also to be catching his breath. Was he as surprised as she was by the electric current between them? Like a pulse of energy that couldn't be diverted, nor contained. The old Cecily, the conservative, shy Cecily, would have probably run off at this point. Ducked into the bathroom before things could get weird. But this wasn't the old Cecily. It was Bucket List Cecily.

"I want to do something special for your birthday," she said, trailing her hand up the buttons of his shirtfront.

"You do?" Liam's voice came, but breathless. His brown eyes looked darker, the need in them sharp. "And what's that?"

"Do you live around here?"

Liam didn't answer at first. Then, he nodded.

"Good. Take me there, and I'll show you."

Cecily still couldn't believe she was doing this, even as Liam led her into the small three-story brick building where he lived, around the corner from the dive bar, the setting sun only just penetrating the narrow staircase that led up to his apartment on the raised first floor. She followed him, wondering whether or not she'd be able to go through with this. It wasn't in her careful planner DNA. After all, going to the home of a perfect stranger was pretty much risking being killed or worse. They were a stone's throw from Manhattan, and hadn't she been schooled on stranger danger since she was a kid? Not to mention all those stories about those poor women. The ones that told her not to jog alone, not to walk alone at night, not to go to a stranger's house…at six in the evening.

But this was her bucket list.

And, according to the doctors, she had less than a year to live anyway. So, why not take the risk? Still, her heart hammered in her chest. Was she really going to do this? She didn't even have any condoms. Did he? And how was she supposed to ask? Then again, what did she care about STDs? She almost laughed out loud. She was *dying*, and she was worried about catching something? That had to be a first. Cecily needed to shut off her damn brain. She needed to just let this amazing hunk of man explore her body all night, and forget about all the things she used to overthink. The time for overthinking was done. The time for living was right now.

Liam swung open his apartment door, and she stepped into the small, but very neat apartment. She was impressed. It was well kept for a guy's place, she thought. The sink clear of dishes, the couch free of even a discarded jacket. It was a single room, but felt larger than your average efficiency, and based on what she could see, he had no roommates. His place was simple, but she could tell he was a man who took care of what he had. That meant something. Her attention then went to his bed, a queen, neatly made, sitting on a slightly raised platform in the corner of the room, head against big, loftlike windows. The light he flicked on was attached to one above the steel gray comforter, and it almost felt like the bed was a stage. She felt a bolt of nerves as she thought about performing there. A calico cat mewed then, distracting her, and Liam ducked down and gave the feline a quick pat on the head.

"This is Molly," he said.

"Nice to meet you, Molly," Cecily said, feeling suddenly as if she knew Liam better. He was a tough, muscle-bound guy who owned a cat? It made her feel safer, somehow. She didn't know why. In her gut, she'd always known Liam was a good guy. From the second he'd sounded off against that heckler at the bar, she'd known it in her bones. That's why she was here. But now, standing in his apartment, she suddenly felt uncertain.

"I've got a cat, too," she said, as she dipped down to pet his. Molly laced her body through Cecily's legs, rubbing her face against her shins. "A Russian blue named Tripp. Or at least part Russian. The shelter wasn't a hundred percent sure. He always tries to get out of the apartment whenever he can. He's determined to get lost. I guess you probably know about that, too?" Cecily was babbling now, showing her nerves. Her mouth was on autopilot, and why was she talking so much about her cat?

"Yeah," Liam said, noncommittal.

"I mean, Tripp once got out and was roaming my building, until I found him in the boiler room. He was probably looking for rats!" She swiped Molly's head, but the cat got tired of her attention and wandered off. God, she was blowing it. Babbling. *Shut up, Cecily*. She took a deep breath and willed herself to silence. She straightened, and glanced at Liam. What happened now? She had no idea. Did she jump on him? Take off her clothes?

God, this was suddenly awkward.

"Do you…uh, mind if I take a shower?" Liam asked. "It's been a long day at work, and I want you to… I mean…" Liam almost looked sheepish.

"No, of course." He was showering *for her*, she thought. It was a sweet gesture. That's what kept surprising her about this seemingly tough guy. She'd half expected him just to rip her clothes off, cave-man-style, but he was acting more like a gentleman. Wanting to get clean for her? He was sweet. And naughty, like the way he'd run his hands up her skirt. She liked it. The dichotomy.

"I'll be quick," he promised. "There's beer in the fridge."

He stepped into the small bathroom, and Cecily was free to snoop. The shower came on, and she heard the metal rings of the curtain being pulled back. She headed to the fridge and opened it, finding a six-pack of beer and not much else. Bachelor fridge, she thought. She took one of the twist-offs and opened it, hoping to gain a little more courage. Her heart was still hammering in her chest. She'd never done this before. Never been with a stranger. Never had sex with anyone she hadn't known for at least a few weeks, if not a few months. She overplanned everything and that included her sex life.

She wandered to the shelves hanging near his couch, and saw only one photo: him and his dad, she presumed. He was young, just a kid, and his dad was holding a swordfish, an enormous game fish. They were standing on the back of what looked like a yacht. Maybe not his dad? But there was a definite family resemblance. His brown hair was longer, curlier, but his eyes, his nose, were exactly the same. She glanced around the humble apartment. She squinted at the photo again. No, the older man definitely had Liam's eyes. They were related. Why was she so hung up on the photo? Probably just a rented boat, anyway. None of her business.

She glanced about but found that was the only photo in the place. She took another sip of the beer, and moved to the next shelf, where she found a row of books, including Dostoyevsky and Nietzsche. Not exactly the kind of reading she'd expect from a construction worker. Interesting. So he didn't just have a body. He had a brain.

Huh.

Before she had time to really process that, the bathroom door opened, steam flowing out. She turned in time to see Liam there, wearing only a towel around his waist, his dirty blond hair wet and slicked back. Her jaw went slack. All she could do was gawk at the man. His chest, still wet from the shower, glistened in the light. His full pecs and clearly defined abs made her mouth go dry. Her focus rested on the impressive V, the muscles that pointed down beneath the knotted white towel. Her breath caught in her throat. She didn't know the last time she'd seen a man this…gorgeous. Had she ever? Cecily wanted this. She needed this. She wanted that man in a way she hadn't wanted anyone in a long, long time.

Liam ran a hand through his wet hair, his dark eyes finding hers. A whole lifetime of conversation passed between them then. If Cecily had any doubt that she'd go through with this little adventure, those doubts fled right in that moment. She took a step toward him, like a magnet drawn to metal. He was a force she couldn't resist. And she didn't want to even try. He stood stock-still, eyes locked with hers as she strode to him, putting her hand on his massive chest. She traced the edge of his muscles, her eyes following her own fingers and then lifting up to meet his gaze. She saw want there, and something deeper, something even more primal. All awkwardness evaporated right in that moment.

"Are you sure you want to?" he asked, as if still not quite sure how she'd come to be standing here in his apartment. And she didn't know, either. All she knew was that this was exactly the medicine she needed right at this moment.

"I'm absolutely sure," she said, and it was the truth. She craved this distraction. A way to finally, at long last, turn her brain off, forget about her worries. For just a night. Or hell, just a few minutes. With her hands on this man's skin, she wasn't thinking about the cancer diagnosis. The grim prognosis. She was just thinking about what she'd be doing in the next few moments. And that was a delicious gift.

She stepped back from him then, realizing that she was still fully clothed, and he was…nearly naked. She unzipped the side of her white linen sundress, and then she gently pulled one strap down, followed by the other. The dress's built-in bra meant that as the dress pooled at her feet, she stood before him wearing nothing more than her lacy boy shorts. His dark eyes drank her in, slowly, appreciatively, as if he was attempting to memorize every curve. He took a step to her now, his eyes intent on her body. She almost felt worshipped with his gaze, but instantly dismissed the thought. She was sure he had gorgeous women throwing themselves at him all the time. But then, he put his hand on her face, delicately, gingerly, and pulled her in for a kiss.

His mouth touched hers and set off an electrical charge through her whole body. Every nerve ending came alive with his touch, as she pressed herself against his muscled chest, as she felt her soft body mold to his hard one. His tongue explored her mouth and she opened for him, wanting more of his lips, more of his tongue, more of his hands. She'd never felt so free before in her life, and she wondered if that's because she only had a little time left. Cecily brushed the thought away as she wrapped her arms around his neck, thick with muscle. His calloused hands ran down her bare back and she shivered, loving the rough touch. She could feel the knot of his towel against her stomach, as he walked her backward, toward his bed. She went, willingly, her bare feet tracking on his clean, maple floor. She hit the bed with the backs of her knees and then sat down on it. She leaned forward and kissed a ridge of his abdomen, gently, provocatively, as he watched her trail more kisses downward, to the edge of his towel. His strong fingers undid the knot and the fuzzy terry cloth dropped away.

She saw him, full and at attention, bigger than she'd guessed. Cecily's hands found him, wrapping around his amazing shaft. Normally, she'd never be so bold, never be so brazen, but if this was the last sex she might ever have in her life, then she damn well better make it count. She dipped down and flicked her tongue along his thick head. She never did this, but now, here, wanted to do it. For this beautiful man. Also, because, what were the chances she'd ever see him again? She could be as dirty, as naughty, as over-the-top as she liked. Liam groaned, and his head fell back, his brown hair still wet. A droplet of water rolled down his chest. Cecily could barely fit even the tip of him in her mouth, but did so, gladly. She loved hearing his moans of pleasure, loved hearing how she could make him groan. She worshipped him this way for a few more moments, relishing it, trying not to tell herself this could be the last time she ever had a man this way.

Then, Liam grasped her shoulders and pushed her backward, ever so slowly. She fell against his soft gray bedcovers, her back against his firm mattress. His eyes bore into hers, as he reached down and tugged at the waist of her pink lacy boy shorts. His big fingers pulled them downward, past her knees and ankles, then he tossed them on the floor.

"Your turn," he told her, a command that reverberated in her chest. He knelt in front of the bed, pushing her knees open, and then he buried his head between them, his tongue finding her white-hot liquid center. Now it was her turn to gasp, a million different pleasure centers in her brain lighting up at once. He found the perfect rhythm: soft, amazing. She could no longer think about anything else but his tongue on her, nothing at all but his perfectly soft and wet tongue. She'd never had a man so skilled, never had a man like this, who seemed to know exactly what she needed, exactly how to touch her. She almost laughed out loud thinking about how she'd deliberately avoided casual sex her whole life, how she'd always been a "good" girl, never going home with a stranger. Why had she been avoiding *this* all her life?

She wrapped her hands in Liam's thick, damp hair and held on for dear life. His gentle touch lured her body ever closer to the edge. She felt like she was on a roller coaster now, strapped in, ticking ever closer to the peak. With each swipe of his hungry tongue, she found herself closer to the top, and then the ground fell out from below her, gravity disappeared and she was soaring, her body awash in wave after wave of pleasure. Pleasure lit her up from the inside, seized every nerve ending in her body, as she rode the wave. She heard a loud cry, and realized, with a start, it was coming from *her*, ripped from her throat. Her body lay exhausted, as she panted, sucking in air, her heart thumping against her rib cage. Liam lifted his head, a cocky smile on his face.

"That good, huh?" he quipped. And that's when she realized that scream probably alerted the entire building to just how good it was.

"I didn't mean to be so loud," Cecily said, embarrassment warming her face.

"Be as loud as you want," he murmured, kissing her inner thigh. "I like it. Tells me I'm on the right track."

"Oh, you definitely are." She'd never come so fast in all her life. Never been so swept up in the moment.

He reached over to the small drawer of his side table and pulled out a condom. "Good. Because now I'm headed to the finish line."

He rolled the length of latex along his thick self, and then he positioned himself between her legs. She couldn't believe it, barely could wrap her head around the fact that she'd just met this man, and now here she was, ready to accept him, ready to take him in. She knew most adults did this—casual sex—but she'd always been one to overthink everything. To worry about the *what-ifs*, to talk herself out of anything that carried even a little bit of risk. But not anymore. Not now, not when she might have such little time left. Right now, she couldn't think about it. Her whole body felt so electrically alive, pulsing with pure energy. She didn't feel sick. She didn't feel like she was dying.

She felt, a little, like she was only starting to live.

Liam entered her then, and she gasped, rising to meet him as she clutched at his shoulders, holding on for dear life. This, she realized, as her body opened for him, as they became one, was exactly what she needed. This might not be her cure, but it damn sure would be her painkiller.

CHAPTER THREE

LIAM STILL COULDN'T believe this was really happening. Sure, he'd had many willing women in his bed, but Cecily…she was different. She was gorgeous, she was perfect and she held absolutely nothing back. She was free in a way he'd never expected, giving of herself in a way that took him completely by surprise. She didn't try to hide her want, either, as she arched her back, pressing her pelvis against his. Women who wore expensive shoes, like she did, typically didn't care for his calloused hands. She couldn't seem to get enough of them. And in this moment, their bodies pressed together, merging into one, he couldn't imagine a more perfect fit for him. He'd never been with a woman so open, so uninhibited, so alive in the moment. He felt drawn to that take-no-prisoners spirit. He wanted to sit in her light for as long as she'd let him.

Her tongue lashed his, her mouth hungry, and she clung to him as if he were the only man in the world, the only person she'd ever want. Her grip drove him wild, her body melding to his. She trailed her nails down his back, sending shivers down his legs. His whole body felt alive, felt like one vibrating nerve ending, awash in sensation. She was soft, she was wet and she wrapped her legs around his waist, pulling him ever deeper into her warm center. He'd be a fool not to go. The dam holding back his want for her, his need, cracked. He wouldn't be able to hold himself back anymore. He came in a hot, wet, molten explosion, every ounce of him pouring into her, every last bit of himself drained.

He collapsed on top of her bare chest, her soft, amazing breasts pressed into his chest, and tried to regain control of his own heart thudding like mad in his chest. His whole body pulsed, twitched, with the aftereffects of his earth-moving climax. He never, in his life, had come like that. Never felt as if he'd pumped every ounce of himself, every bit of his essence into a woman. He felt now like an empty shell. He held his weight on his elbows, as he buried his face in her neck, in her delicious smell, the air thick with the scent of her perfume and their bodies, with sweat and want and a need satiated.

"God," she murmured into his ear.

"I don't know if God had anything to do with this," he quipped, and she laughed, deeply and vibrantly, her whole body shaking. He pulled back and looked into her eyes, shocked again by how blue they were, how clear. He caressed her perfect heart-shaped face, sweeping golden hair from her forehead.

Her eyes, full of light, searched his own. For a second, he thought she might be about to deliver bad news, that she might roll out of his bed and out of his life right then—spoiling all hope that she might spend the night here with him. He'd never wanted anyone's company more than he wanted hers right this moment. He still couldn't believe this amazingly beautiful and delicate woman was in his bed. Still couldn't believe his luck.

"Thank you," she told him then, as they were nose to nose. Again, she surprised him. She was thanking him? He was the one who should be on his knees, thanking her.

"You shouldn't be thanking me." Liam rolled off her. After all, Liam was a whole lot of complicated. He'd walked away from his brothers—the good ones and the bad. He'd left them all. That wasn't a selfless act, either.

"I should be." She perched herself up on one elbow, miles of her flawless skin on display. She touched his face gently. "Thank you. That was amazing."

He glanced at her, guard up. That's what women usually said when they were about to leave. His stomach tightened and he realized he didn't want her to go. Not now. She rolled over to him, trailing a delicate nail down the middle of his chest, she curled into him, and he opened up his arm, pulling her to him, their bare bodies lying together.

"Can I stay awhile?" she asked, her voice almost so low he didn't hear her.

"Of course," he murmured into her hair, pulling her close. He wanted her here, wanted her in his arms. Because the second she left, he knew he'd not believe it had happened at all. Lying here, he suddenly wanted to know everything about her: where she was born, where she'd grown up, did she have brothers? Sisters? And more importantly: Why? Why had she picked him? Of all the guys in that dive bar, hell, in all of New Jersey, or Manhattan, why him?

And…what was it she was trying to get away from?

He knew it had to be something. He wasn't sure he wanted to know. A bad boyfriend? Or worse… A bad husband? This was a woman trying to drown her sorrows in his body, distract herself from real life, because a woman like this didn't hop into bed with a man like him without a reason. A woman like this didn't cling to him like he was a damn life raft, unless she felt like something—or someone—in her life was drowning her. And she definitely didn't cuddle up in his arms, tucking herself into his side as if hoping he'd take the shrapnel, just for a little while.

She was hiding something. But what?

The question bubbled up in his mind, but he shushed it. Talk, he feared, might send her to the door. If he prodded to find out her secrets, she'd most definitely flee. Instead, he tucked his other arm protectively around her. She would talk when she was ready, he figured. And he'd be there to listen.

"You sure it's okay that I stay?" she asked him.

"Yes," he replied, without hesitation.

"You're not just saying that?"

Liam pulled away a little so he could meet her gaze. "I don't lie. It's too much hard work. The truth is easier."

She laughed a little. "So you won't lie to me?"

"Nope," he said, pulling her close. "I'll always tell the truth. You can count on that."

Cecily awoke the next day to dim early sunlight filtering in through the blinds. She blinked, staring at the window, her mind feeling muddled. She didn't have blinds in her condo. She had curtains. And… there was a big warm arm tucked across her waist. The entire night flooded back to her then: the dive bar, Liam, her amazing night of…could that even be called sex? More like *naked fireworks that blew her mind.* She'd never in her whole life realized sex could be so…amazingly hot, so mind-numbingly showstopping. She'd never in her life been able to shut off her brain during sex, always worried about whether the light shone on that one patch of cellulite on the back of her thighs, or whether her partner would *ever find* the right spot, or what weird sounds either of them might be making. Sure, she'd had decent sex before, but there was always a part of her logical, detached mind in play. Last night, Liam had shut off every single logical circuit, and all that had been left was pure instinct, pure desire, pure white-hot pleasure.

And that had everything to do with Liam.

She barely knew him. Hell, didn't even know his last name. And yet, after last night, part of her wondered if he now knew her better than most of her ex-boyfriends combined. He knew her body, that's for damn sure. Knew it better than she even seemed to know it himself. His tongue. His hands. Lord. But now, in the gray light of morning, that other reality she'd tried so hard to keep at bay came trickling in.

She was dying.

Liam might have made her feel alive again, for a single night, but now, she had to face the reality of it: She wasn't young and full of life. She was young and dying. And now she had no job, either. No health insurance to even try to get a second opinion, see if there were other treatments out there. And, hell, no insurance or money to pay for them even if there were. The reality hit her like a cement block, and tears suddenly stung the backs of her eyes. What would she do? Tell Liam about the cancer prognosis? Tell him, hey, if he played his cards right, he might have eight or ten months? Maybe even a year? Even the best of men might not be able to handle that. She could lie, of course, or just not mention it, but then what? If they really continued on, after a few weeks or a few months, she'd have to tell him.

All of it was terrible.

Liam's deep breathing next to her told her he was still asleep. The steady rise and fall of his chest meant maybe she could sneak away. Maybe she could leave without him knowing, and maybe she could

get herself home without any awkward goodbyes.
Or lies. He'd promised to be honest with her, so she
would try to do the same.

Even if it meant sneaking out and not saying
goodbye. Technically, that wasn't a lie.

If she waited until he woke up, she'd have to lie
and tell him she'd call him, when she knew this could
only be one night. She couldn't string him along
for more. That was, even if he wanted that. Who
knew if he even wanted that? A man as gorgeous
as him probably wouldn't even miss her, probably
had a dozen women right now waiting in his phone
contacts or DMs, who wouldn't mind keeping him
company tonight.

The very thought of that sent an ache pulsing
through her chest. But it was just one more disappointment she'd have to learn to deal with. Cecily
told herself to focus on the fact she'd had one amazing night with him. One she'd think about often
through the dark days ahead.

Take joy where you can. Isn't that what her grandmother always told her when she was little? Now she
knew the importance of those words.

She eased slowly out away from his embrace.
Liam's breathing continued, soft and steady as she
gently shifted his arm. She inched her way to the
edge, careful not to move too quickly, as she put her
bare feet on the floor. When her butt left the mattress, it creaked a bit, and the sound woke Liam. He
groaned and reached out.

"No, shh. Go back to sleep," she whispered. He wasn't awake enough to really hear her, she decided. He rolled over to his side, tucking his face into his pillow. *Yes, that's it, don't mind me. Go back to sleep,* she willed him, and once more his breathing grew steady. She stood there, at the side of the bed, admiring the strong muscles of his back as it rose and fell with every deep breath. She didn't know how long she stood there: A few seconds? A few minutes? She was trying to fuse the memory of his perfect body into her brain. Then, she grabbed her discarded clothes from the floor and quietly, ever so quietly, pulled on her underwear and her dress. Her sandals lay near his door, with her small purse. She crept over to them, careful, picked them up, and gently slid the bolt open on his door. She turned the knob, freezing at the sound of the creaking of the door—unnaturally loud in her ears. Cecily glanced once more at the bed in the corner. She watched Liam moan a little and shift. She froze, her heart racing, but then he went still again, his breathing steady. She tiptoed out the door and shut it slowly behind her, the click of the latch making her cringe. She stood on his doorstep a second, but heard no creaking bed telling her he'd sat up. No determined footsteps marching to the door. Cecily darted away, moving quickly down the steps, barefoot, shoes still in hand, lest the clack of her heels on the wooden steps give her away.

She went past the glass door, pushing through it and letting it swing shut behind her. Then, she knelt and slipped on her wedge sandals. She dug into her small white bag, looking for her phone, so that she might be able to call a rideshare. That's when she realized her phone wasn't there.

What the…? And then she remembered: last night. After many rounds of amazing, world-changing sex, she'd checked her phone and saw the battery nearly dead. Liam gallantly offered her his charger. Her phone was likely still sitting there.

"Dammit," she cursed to herself. She turned, grabbed hold of the front door of the building, but found it predictably locked. Of course it was. And what would she do anyway? Sneak back up the stairs to get it? Buzz the buzzer of his apartment? She glanced at the names on the silver buzzer box. They were handwritten last names on small white tags.

In that second, she realized she didn't even know Liam's last name. Hadn't even asked. She didn't know which name was his on the directory. Petrie? Jules? Laures? Lange? She had no idea. Would she just buzz them all? And then what would she even tell him if she did find him? *Not trying to sneak out or anything, but could you get me my phone?* She shook her head. She had special insurance for her phone. Maybe she'd just say she lost it, and get a new one. She liked that idea a whole helluva lot better than seeing Liam's face when he realized she'd snuck out.

Just then, a yellow cab turned the corner. It let someone out down the street. She had her wallet, and she had cash. She could just get in that cab and in minutes be home. It felt like fate was pushing her in that direction. She trotted down the stairs and hailed the cab. As it pulled up, she opened the back door and slid in, glancing once more at Liam's second floor window. She kept staring at the window as the cab pulled away, her heart heavy as she wondered if she did the right thing.

CHAPTER FOUR

LIAM WOKE AN hour later, wondering if the night before had been a dream. Cecily—gorgeous, passionate, amazing Cecily—in his bed all night. He'd explored every inch of her body and yet his fingers itched to do it again. He stretched out his arm and grasped only cool, abandoned sheets. He sat up then, blinking. Where was she? He swung his feet off the side of the bed. He wore only boxers as he padded over to the bathroom. He found it predictably empty. Her shoes, which she'd kicked off near his door, were also gone as were her clothes. A pit formed then at the center of his stomach.

She'd snuck out.

Why was he surprised? She was just trying to save him the awkward breakfast-or-no-breakfast conversation, the lie about how, of course, they'd get together again. Because she had no intention of getting together with him again. Of course she hadn't. What would a woman like that want with a man like him? But he also sort of admired her determination not to lie to him. Not to tell him, of course, she'd see him around. When she already knew she wouldn't. He knew he should feel lucky to have gotten one night. She was a million miles out of his league. He sat back down on his bed and fell backward, her scent still on his sheets, filling his nose, reminding him that, no, it hadn't been a dream. She'd been here. And he'd had the most amazing sex of his life. At least he'd taken advantage of it. They'd been up nearly all night, falling asleep sometime just before dawn. How she'd managed to even wake up was beyond him. He'd been dead to the world. It had been a long day of work yesterday on the roof and then a long night in bed with the most amazing woman he'd ever met. He'd been bone-tired. No wonder she'd been able to sneak out.

And now she was gone.

Just one more woman he'd scared away. Good things didn't stay in his life for long. He should know that by now. He pulled himself up on his elbow and surveyed his simple and stark apartment. Nothing in it was there purely for decoration, except for the one photograph of him and his dad. Everything had a use. He glanced at the breakfast bar of his kitchen, which served as a breakfast, lunch and dinner bar since he had no dining room table in his small efficiency apartment. Waste not, want not. Something he hadn't learned growing up in one of the country's wealthiest media families. He glanced at the phone lying on the countertop and froze. That wasn't his. It must be Cecily's.

He laughed out loud. Her sneaking-out skills clearly needed work. He pulled himself from bed and grabbed the phone. He swiped at the screen, expecting to find it password protected, but instead, found the entire thing unlocked. How trusting was this woman? Everyone knew you needed a password to protect your phone. Otherwise, you drop it on the street and people could access your email, or worse, bank account. She hadn't even bothered to activate fingerprint or facial recognition protection. He shook his head. He shouldn't snoop through her phone, but also, how else was he supposed to figure out how to return it?

He dug into her text messages first, figuring that maybe she'd have a friend or relative he might be able to text. He saw a message from her mom, first. Hi, honey.

So, he had her mom's number. What could he say? *Hi, there. Your daughter left her phone at my house after a one-night stand of hot and dirty sex?* Probably wouldn't leave the best impression. He scrolled deeper into the conversation, though, not even meaning to do so.

How did it go today? Any good news?

Hmm. Wonder what her mom meant? He hoped it wasn't about her job. Because he remembered she'd mentioned she'd gotten laid off. He dipped out of that conversation and back to the message list. He scrolled through a few marketing messages, and then stopped when he saw Anderson Oncology Center. He opened the text. It was a bot confirming her appointment. And it looked like that appointment— was for yesterday. And this was one of several in the last month.

Liam felt his throat go dry. She'd told him at the dive bar yesterday that she'd been having a bad day. He thought it was because she'd lost her job, but now he was beginning to realize she was hiding worse news. Only people who were sick went to the oncology center, only people who had hard cancer cases. He knew that because one of the guys on his last roofing job had mentioned it, that his dad went there for advanced prostate cancer. Liam felt a little nauseous. And a little betrayed. Why hadn't she said something?

But what would she say? It's not like *Hey, I've got cancer* is what anybody means when they ask about talking dirty.

Of course, now he knew why she'd come so eagerly into his bed. Why worry about consequences of having sex with someone clearly below her when she had other, bigger things on her mind. His own head filled with a dozen questions at once: How serious was the cancer? What kind was it? What was the prognosis? And was there anything he could do?

He almost laughed to himself. He was a roofer, not a doctor. What could he do?

First, he needed to get her phone back to her. Because she didn't need to have to worry about buying a new phone on top of everything else. It hit him then that the loss of her insurance probably felt like another kick to her gut. He shook his head. Damn, heartless corporations. Always about their bottom line, never caring about the human carnage they left behind.

He opened up her email on her phone, trying to figure out where she lived. Right at the top he found a confirmation of an online order, and her delivery address was right there. Turns out, she lived pretty close. And Liam had nothing to do today. He had some time off before his next job started. No better time than today to return her phone—and get some answers.

Cecily sat on her modern gray couch in her own small condo a few blocks away, and reached down to pet her Russian blue, Tripp. He mewed softly, and rubbed against her ankle. Normally, his attention meant that he wanted a kitty treat, or that it was mealtime, but lately—since her cancer diagnosis, or if she were honest with herself, even a little before—he'd been hovering around her, his concern evident. Maybe it was true what they said about animals being able to detect sickness in people. Tripp certainly seemed unnaturally attuned to her. He followed her everywhere now, keeping his gray eyes fixed on her, as if afraid that if he didn't, she'd fade away and disappear.

Thinking about what would happen to him when she was gone made tears spring to her eyes. Where would he go? Her sister's? Mother's? Would they know what kind of treats he liked? Which ones he didn't? And he was super picky about his cat litter. They'd need to know that. Tripp leaped up on the couch, burrowing his head into her lap as if to tell her not to worry, it would all be okay. He then curled up on her legs for a quick nap. His rumbling purring comforted her.

She needed to talk to her mother and her sister. Neither one knew how bad things were. They knew about the cancer, but both had assumed there'd be treatments. Chemo. Surgery. Something. Just like she had. She needed to call them both. She promised herself she would. But not yet. She planned to avoid telling them about the bad news. What was she going to say? Better come visit me while you can, even though you live hundreds of miles away near Cleveland?

It seemed an impossible blow, especially since her father had died of a heart attack a few years before. Now her mother and sister would lose her, too. The thought made tears sting her eyes. She sniffed them back. She wasn't going to cry today. She'd promised herself no moping today. No pity parties. There'd be plenty of time for those when her health really started to fail. Right now, she had to not waste the time she had left. She needed to do more things like she did last night: get out of her comfort zone. Be daring.

She thought about Liam's strong hands exploring her body and missed them suddenly. She still couldn't believe she'd been so bold as to fall into his bed minutes after meeting him, but then again, she hadn't met a man that sexy, that strong, in who knows when. The old Cecily would've been too scared even to sit next to him, even after he'd been kind in the bar by shushing her heckler. Hell, the old Cecily would've been too scared even to *go* into that dive bar, much less buy Liam a drink.

She kind of liked the new, Bucket List Cecily. Reminded her more of the woman she used to be, the college undergrad who'd packed up her beat-up hatchback and driven all the way to NYU, the first in her family to move out of state in at least three generations. She glanced at her watch, realizing she'd just missed her usual train, a twenty-minute ride to the corporate HR headquarters of Yancy's, where she used to work. She'd given them seven hardworking years, and they'd repaid her by letting her go when she'd needed health insurance the most.

She glanced around her small, modern condo, kept mostly neat, except for her dirty gym clothes peeking out of her gym bag, and her discarded shoes near the couch. Her place was about half or a third the size of what she'd be able to afford if she'd stayed in Cleveland. She might even have a house by now and a husband, like most of her high school class-mates did. They all had yards and endless baby show-ers, reminding her that taking the leap and moving to a bigger city meant putting some of those dreams on hold.

Of course, now she might never have a family, or a yard of her own. No, not *might* not, she reminded herself. *Would* not. Sadness filled her heart as she cuddled Tripp in her lap. He seemed to sense she needed a little more comfort as he stood, stretched and nuzzled her neck.

"Thanks, buddy." Tripp mewed, staring into her eyes with concern. She stroked his back. "It'll be all right," she told him, not at all sure it would be.

The buzzer sounded at her front door then, star-tling them both.

"Who's that?" she asked Tripp, even as he leaped off her lap and flicked his tail, his ears flattening just a little at having his petting session interrupted. Ce-cily stood and padded over to her intercom, pressing the button. "Hello?"

"Hi, Cecily." The man's low voice hit her straight in the solar plexus.

"Liam," she said, startled and a bit panicky. Her hand flew to her hair. Had she even combed it since she'd been home? She glanced down at her outfit: gray sweatpants and an old NYU shirt, grub clothes that she'd hastily changed into the second she'd got-ten home that morning. She'd scrubbed her face of the residue of makeup from the night before. In short, she was a shiny-faced mess. "Uh, what are you doing here?"

"Just wanted to return your phone."

Dammit. Her phone. She ought to be happy, but facing Liam, in the early afternoon light of her condo after she'd snuck out, was the very last thing she wanted to do right now. Yet, part of her was flattered he'd made the trip to her place the same day. Or that he'd made the trip at all. If he were a worse guy, he could've sold her phone. Pocketed the cash. But she already knew Liam wasn't that kind of guy. She remembered him taking a shower the night before, considerate of her, a surprising gentleman.

"Uh, can I come up…or…?" Liam hesitated.

Cecily paused, too. Should she let him in? What should she do? She glanced down at Tripp who busied himself by leaning against her right leg, still purring.

"If you want me to just leave the phone here, I can do that, too." Liam sounded resigned. Sad even.

"No!" Cecily shouted, a bit too forcefully into her intercom, so that she got a buzz of feedback. "I mean, here. I'll buzz you up. I'm on the third floor. First door on the left." She hit the buzzer as her heart thumped in her chest. What was she doing? She ought to have just let Liam walk away, but the thought made her heart freeze. She didn't want him to leave. But she didn't exactly want him to stay, either. Cecily quickly checked her reflection in her foyer mirror, patting down an errant bit of blond hair, and frowning at her shiny forehead. Oh, well. Too late to do anything about that now. She heard heavy steps outside. She swung open the door and Liam was standing on her landing, looking even more gorgeous than he had last night.

He wore jeans and a plain black T-shirt that clung to his defined chest, his muscled shoulders stretching the fabric to its limits. He held her phone in his big hand, and she remembered exactly what those hands had felt like on her body the night before. Gentle, yet strong. He studied her with his serious brown eyes, his dirty blond hair looking perfectly combed, which made her want to put her hands in it.

"Hey," she said, voice lower than she intended. She kept the door mostly closed, feeling Tripp still near her legs. Sometimes he'd bolt if she let the door open too wide, and then she'd have to lure him back with the offer of treats. He had an adventurous spirit, that cat. Hard to keep inside.

"Hey. So, I found your phone on my counter." He handed it to her, and she took it, the phone feeling heavy and cold in her hands. He stared at her a beat and she wondered what else she'd seen there. She glanced downward.

"Thanks. I, uh…" *I'm sorry for sneaking out? I should've at least said goodbye?* She didn't know what to say.

He stared at her, waiting. He made no move to leave, nor did she want him to.

"Want to come in?"

"Do *you* want me to?" he asked. Touché.

She nodded, as she gently moved her cat backward with the heel of her foot. She left the door open a bit, and he slid through. He spied the cat on the floor and raised his eyebrows.

"Hi, Tripp," he said.

"You remembered my cat's name?" she asked, surprised. She'd only mentioned it once, she thought, during her nervous babbling the night before.

"I remember everything you said. I pay attention." He flashed her a smile, and suddenly Cecily felt warm. She wondered if that meant he remembered everything she'd shouted in his bed the night before, too.

Tripp seemed to take an unusual interest in Liam. "He must smell Molly on you," she said.

"Maybe our two cats would fall in love," he joked, and she laughed a little.

"Wouldn't that be something?" she said, and then immediately regretted it. She didn't think they had a future. Had no intention for their cats ever to meet. "Uh, have you always liked cats?" she asked, desperate to change the subject.

"My mom loved them," he said. "She had three Persians."

"Really?" she asked, surprised. "Those are usually expensive cats."

"Yeah." The tone of his voice suggested that he wasn't interested in answering more questions about his mother and her cats. Maybe she bred them, Cecily thought. Or maybe she'd picked them up at a shelter. They might not have been purebred Persians. And Cecily wasn't one to pry. She moved to the kitchen. "Want something to drink? Tea? Wine?" And then, after a beat, added, "Whiskey?" It was a joke, and she expected Liam to laugh, but he didn't.

Liam shook his head as he followed her to her gray, granite-topped eat-in kitchen. "You drink whiskey?" His tone was serious. He stood near her glass-front white-framed cabinets in her modern condo, leaning his big body against her fridge.

"My father loved the stuff. I guess I inherited his tastes. He passed away a couple of years ago from a heart attack."

"I'm sorry."

"It's okay," she said. "I guess we're both father-less."

"I guess we are." Liam crossed his arms across his chest. "And no whiskey for me. Not yet. It's too early."

"Yeah, I know. It was a joke," she said, but felt that awkwardness wanting to creep in again, that reminder that they were still two strangers, that despite having spent the night together, they were still learning things about one another—like how humor worked between them.

"Oh." He looked a little sheepish. "Right."

"Water, then?"

"Sure." She poured him a glass and then they stood awkwardly for a second in her kitchen. She wondered if she should offer him a seat on her couch, but then it just suddenly seemed too odd. Mere hours ago, they'd been naked, entwined in his bed, and now, in the bright light of day, that memory faded. She didn't like the feeling. "Want to sit?" she asked him, moving into her small living room.

Tripp, she saw, had already taken up roost on her chair, wrapping himself into a tidy little circle, watching them both with amusement. That left only the small love seat. It would be a tight squeeze with the both of them. Cecily couldn't help but think Tripp had done it on purpose. After all, he usually picked the love seat corner for his day naps. The cat, how-ever, simply cocked his head to one side and yawned, feigning innocence. She took a seat first, and he fol-lowed. They sat together on the love seat, facing the switched-off flat-screen TV against the wall, their featureless reflections in it. Cecily was more than aware of how close together they were on the couch, how his big knees were so close to her own. If she shifted just a little bit, their legs would touch. She almost felt as if she were holding her breath for what might come next.

"Thank you for bringing my phone back," she said, trying to get some control over the moment.

"You're welcome. I hope you don't mind I looked through it. To get your address."

She shrugged. "What's done is done."

He put down his water on her glass-topped coffee table. "There is one thing I wanted to ask you." He shifted toward her, and his knee bumped hers. The contact sent a jolt all the way up her spine.

"Yes?" She glanced at his stark, honest brown eyes. His dirty blond hair threatening to fall across his forehead. She studied his full lips and his rugged jaw.

"How bad is the cancer?"

CHAPTER FIVE

LIAM ALMOST REGRETTED asking the question. All the color drained from Cecily's face and he felt like he'd blindsided her. Which he had. After all, he'd come here with an agenda beyond just returning her phone. He wanted to know. Needed to know. How bad was it? He wanted the truth. Unvarnished.

"I'm sorry. I saw the oncologist's appointment on your phone. People don't usually go see one of those unless they're sick. So, how bad is it?" Liam was the kind of man who wanted to get all the bad news up front. He didn't see a need to sugarcoat anything. But as he watched her gnaw at her lip, eyes refusing to meet his, he realized she was trying to figure out a way to lie. Or, at least, try to figure out a way to round out the edges of the truth.

"Why do you want to know?" She was hedging. It was obvious.

"Because…" She was the first woman in a long time he truly cared about. . "Because I want to know."

"We're practically strangers, though."

He tried not to think about how little of her body was strange to him. He'd explored every inch of her bare skin. How he'd made her moan. How, right at this moment, he wanted to hear her moan again. But he needed to know the truth.

"Because we haven't known each other for very long, you don't have to spare my feelings, okay? Just be honest with me."

"But…"

"Look, I'll be honest with you, if you are honest with me. Let's make that promise, okay? We can't get anywhere if we're not honest with each other."

"Okay." Cecily sucked in a deep breath and sighed. "I've got a rare form of liver cancer. The problem is that they can't operate. The tumor is too entrenched, and taking it out would pretty much destroy my liver."

"Why not get a liver transplant, then?" Liam asked.

Cecily shook her head. "The cancer spread to a blood vessel. That means even if I did get a transplant, there'd be cancer cells left in my body. Doctors fear it would be a waste of a transplant organ that could save someone else's life."

"What about chemo? Radiation?" Liam couldn't believe this. There wasn't a treatment option for someone as young and vibrant as Cecily? He couldn't wrap his mind around it.

"It would just shrink the tumor. Not get rid of it." Cecily shrugged. "And the way it's growing, doctors say that there's not enough chemo or radiation to give me a fighting chance. Those things would just make me sick, and probably make the time I have left miserable."

"Time you have left?" Liam's stomach twisted into knots. He didn't like where this was going. Not at all.

"Doctors gave me eight to ten months."

"To live?" Liam blinked fast, stunned. Cecily appeared healthy, despite her diagnosis. She looked nothing like the cancer patients he always saw on hospital fundraisers. She had luscious, thick blond hair, and clear blue eyes, and nothing about her seemed weak or frail.

Cecily nodded, glancing at the hands folded neatly in her lap. How was she so calm about this?

"You're dying." He didn't believe the words even after they were out of his mouth.

Cecily glanced up at him, eyes luminous, a sheen of tears on them. She nodded.

Liam reached out then, and pulled her into his arms, as if by holding her, he could keep her safe. But the danger was invisible, was inside her, was something he couldn't fight. She sagged against him, her resolve fading as the tears came, silent sobs that shook her small body. He hugged her tighter, still not believing this beautiful woman—this perfect woman—could be so sick.

Cecily clung to him, wrapping her thin arms tightly around him. She needed him, needed a safety that he wanted to give, but knew he couldn't ultimately deliver. He'd never felt so helpless in all his life.

"Did you get a second opinion?" he asked her, quietly, trying not to find hope where there wasn't any.

"No," she sniffed, and pulled away from him a little. He reached out and grabbed a tissue from the box on the end table nearby and handed it to her. She took it gratefully. "I've seen the specialist in my network, and there aren't a whole lot of other doctors on my plan." She shrugged. "Or what *used to be* my plan. COBRA is too expensive for me. No way can I afford it. It costs more than half my rent." She sniffed. "Everything from here on out is out of pocket."

"That's not right. They laid you off and you have cancer?"

"Technically, they didn't officially know yet, so it's not discrimination," she said. "I'd kept the diagnosis to myself for a couple of weeks while I tried to figure out what kind of treatment—" She stopped abruptly and swallowed. "How much sick leave I'd need. But then the layoffs happened. I was among three hundred people laid off nationwide, so I can't claim it's because of the cancer."

"Still. Maybe they'd hire you back?"

A bitter laugh escaped Cecily's throat. "Hire me back so I could take indefinite sick leave and drain the health benefits? No. That would hurt profits. No way would they do that."

Liam shook his head. He understood the bottom line, but that still didn't prevent him from wanting to call up her HR department. Give them a piece of his mind. "It's not right. It's not fair."

"Yeah. There's a lot in life that's not fair." Cecily seemed remarkably calm about all of this. Liam wanted to punch something, but she sat with her fingers on her lap. Her cat jumped up next to her then, purring, and she stroked his dark gray fur.

"Yeah, but cancer is expensive and…"

"And there's no treatment for me, so it won't, actually, be as expensive. I'll have end of life care, of course, but—"

"But do you really know that? If you've only seen one doctor?"

"Would a second opinion really be so different?" Cecily asked, studying her cat.

"It might be," Liam said, careful not to let hope into his voice. "You never know." He knew about how his mother complained about doctors. Also knew that her stints in and out of rehab and with one counselor after another meant that he knew for a fact that some treatment centers were far superior to others, and not all facilities were equal. His mother, Lucinda, had battled alcoholism for most of his life, though now she'd been sober going on at least three years. The alcoholism, too, he thought could be traced back to his father's death. At least, he thought her drinking got worse then, anyway. Who wouldn't want to drown their sorrows after Wilder had cut them out?

"Are you going to try?" he asked.

"I can't afford it." Her mouth tensed a little.

Liam knew all about difficult times. He'd been there. Lost jobs, too. He didn't have a safety net to fall back on, either. He thought about his rich half brother. Asking him for help had always been out of the question. Plus, he'd likely not give it anyway.

"I could help you." He didn't have much, but what he did have, he'd be happy to share. Cecily shouldn't be alone. Not now.

She shifted uncomfortably on the couch. "I don't want you to feel you have to get involved." She picked at a piece of lint on her gray sweatpants. "This is my burden, and we're strangers. I don't even know your last name. Technically." A small blush crept up her cheeks at this admission.

Liam sighed. He hated to bring up his name, since so many people knew Lange Communications. Most asked about the connection right away. "It's Lange. Liam Lange."

"Lange?" she echoed. He hoped she didn't ask about Lange Communications or Wilder Lange. Everyone knew his half brother. He was one of the most famous billionaires in the world.

"Yes, and you are Cecily Morgan. I saw it in your email." He held out his hand for a shake. She took it, confusion and amusement warring on her face.

"So, nice to meet you. Now we're not strangers."

She laughed a little at that.

"But still, we only just met."

Intellectually, he knew why she kept reminding

him of that, and yet, part of him worried she was just trying to shuffle him out of her life. He didn't want to go. She needed him.

"But you need someone on your side here. You need someone to talk to about this. What does your family say about your prognosis?"

"It's just me, my mom and my sister. And…" Cecily sucked in a breath. "I haven't told them yet."

Liam remembered the upbeat text messages from her mom, as she asked about her daughter's doctor appointment.

"Why not?"

"They live in Cleveland and… I don't want to crush their hope." She glanced up at him, her blue eyes full of pain.

"Then don't." Liam reached out and grabbed her hands. They were soft and delicate, dainty in his big palms. "Get a second opinion, and maybe you won't have to."

Cecily stood, and walked across her small living room to her window, glancing at the street below. She hugged herself, as if chilled. Liam left the love seat, too, following her.

"I need to think about it," she told him.

For Liam, there wasn't anything to think about. A second opinion meant the possibility of a second chance, and he couldn't see how anyone would ignore that. But it wasn't his place to push her. He understood that. What he did know was that he couldn't just leave her to fend for herself. He knew exactly what it felt like to be a lone fighter with no one on his side.

"I want to help, if you'll let me."

She rubbed her arms as she turned to look at him, her blue eyes luminous. The sunlight hit her golden hair just right, making it seem to shimmer. For a second, he felt rooted to the spot.

"I don't want you to feel obligated," she said.

"Look, I don't do anything I don't want to do. You should know that about me right now." Liam moved closer to her. He brushed a wave of hair from her forehead. In that moment, he'd never seen a woman as beautiful as Cecily. He'd do whatever he could to help. "But know that I'm here for you as long as you need me. You shouldn't have to face this alone."

"Thank you," she said, and then he pulled her close to his chest, inhaling the sweet smell of lilacs in her hair. "But, right now…the best thing you can do for me is to distract me. I need…something else." She pulled away from him. He knew that look on her face right then and felt blood rush to his groin. She kissed him, slowly at first. Gently. Almost a nibble.

Part of him wondered if she simply planned to distract him with sex, if this was all little more than her way of changing the subject. If so, he wasn't going to object. She crawled into his lap then, straddling him, and he could feel her warmth through her sweatpants. He grew painfully against the zipper of his jeans, as she flicked her tongue against his. Blood pounded in his temples, as he could think of nothing more than her on top of him. He wrapped his hands in her hair, as she deepened the kiss. Damn, the woman could kiss. Even after the entire night, he still needed her. Still wanted her. She wasn't like any other woman he'd ever met.

And she was dying.

He wanted it not to be true. Even as he pushed the thought away, he found himself leaning her back on the love seat and tugging at her sweatpants. They came off and he saw she was completely bare beneath, her knees slightly open, her eyes gazing at his, filled with want. She needed this, needed the distraction he could give her. He licked his finger and gently touched her, a gasp escaping her lips as he rubbed her swollen clit. He felt it swell, felt her desire rise. He slipped his finger inside her, finding her gloriously, deliciously wet. So very wet.

His own desire grew. He wanted her, badly, despite the fact he'd just had her last night. Or, maybe, it was because he'd just had her. He knew exactly how delicious her tight little body was.

"I want you inside me," she groaned. She reached up and unzipped him, freeing his thick cock.

He grabbed his wallet from his back pocket. He had a condom in there, albeit an old one. Who knew when he'd last put it in there? He kicked off his pants and underwear, and then unwrapped the latex and slid it on.

"Hurry," she told him, and he did. The next second, he was deep inside her, and they both felt the urgency, the need. In this moment, nothing else mattered but their bodies, moving together, perfectly in sync. Who needed to talk about the future, when everything that mattered was right here in this moment, her desire and his, a white-hot sensation, and nothing mattered except releasing the pent-up energy. He wanted to save her, wanted to erase all her problems. The sex felt frantic, desperate, somehow, as she clawed his shoulders, nails digging into his flesh. She wrapped her legs around his waist and pulled him in ever deeper. He wanted to hold off, wanted to wait, but he didn't know how long he could last. She clutched him harder, and somehow, they rolled straight off the love seat, him hitting the floor first and then her on top. He didn't even care about the glancing blow to his elbow, the shock of the rugged carpet against his back.

Now she was on top of him, her eyes wild, her face flushed. She whipped off her T-shirt, revealing she'd been braless. Her rose-petal-pink nipples stood at attention in the cool air of the room. She leaned forward, as if offering them, and he took one in his mouth. He licked her salty skin gently, reverently. She moaned, as she dipped down to kiss his neck, sucking there. Cecily rose up then, and rode him, gently at first, but then her blue eyes grew dark, her pupils widening in pleasure, as she picked up the pace. Her hips rocked with a determination he'd rarely met, and certainly never expected from a woman as delicate as this. But she wanted him, and she drew him in, ever deeper, always deeper.

The stiff rug pressed into his shoulder blades, but he didn't care. He was glad the floor lay beneath him, or otherwise, he felt he might get lost in her body. He reached up, caressing the soft roundness of her breasts. She closed her eyes and lifted her face to the ceiling, as his eyes roved her perfect body.

Her trim waist, the flare of her soft hips, the small indent of her belly button. He tried to memorize every detail of her body, here in the sunlight, just in case this was the last time he was allowed to see it. Women like Cecily didn't fall for guys like him. Even if they had cancer. Or especially if they had cancer. He needed to treat this as the miracle it was, and know that like all miracles, this, too, would disappear.

He grasped her hips then, moving her with his hands, meeting her thrust for thrust. She was so beautiful, a delicate pink flush ran down the front of her chest. She lifted her golden hair, and tendrils of it fell downward, her breasts defied gravity as she rocked back and forth. He could die here beneath her and be happy. Cecily let her blond hair fall to her shoulders and pressed her palms against his chest. Her breathing grew more rapid, as her eyes met his.

"Come for me," he challenged her.

Her full pink lips parted, as the flush on her cheeks grew deeper. She sucked in a breath and cried out, her body urgent against his. He could feel the climax building in her, feel her tighten around him.

"Yes, that's it. You need this," he told her, voice low.

"Yes, yes, I do," she replied, and ground against him even harder. He'd never had a woman who wanted this so badly, a woman who needed what he could give.

He might not be able to cure her, but by God, he could make her feel like her diagnosis was a million miles away. He met her, each thrust, syncing to her rhythm, and watched as the climax overtook her. Her eyes flicked open, her gaze meeting his, and he saw the raw, honest pleasure there as she cried out. In that moment, in that perfect moment, she wasn't sick. She seemed as if she could live forever. And then, he came, too, unable to hold back any longer. He wanted to make her his, and he wanted her for as long as he could have her. Then, she collapsed against him, breathing heavy. He wrapped his arms around her, his own heartbeat loud in his ears. He wouldn't think about tomorrow right now.

"Who cares about cancer? You're going to kill me with orgasms," Cecily murmured into his chest.

He laughed then, hugging her tightly. "It would be a better way to go," he told her hair.

"No doubt," she said, and then Cecily rolled off him, snatching her shirt from the ground and tugging it on. He took the opportunity to grab a tissue from the dispenser on the coffee table and wrap up the used condom in it. He padded over to the bathroom trash and dumped it. Cecily watched him, blue eyes wary. Liam tugged on his underwear, and then picked up his jeans.

"You know, you can still go. Not bother to call me again. I would understand."

Liam froze, one leg stuck in his jeans, one out. "Why would I do that?"

"Because…because of…" She spread her arms wide. "Everything."

He finished pulling up his jeans and zipped them. She seemed so fragile then, so delicate. "I'm not leaving unless you want me to," Liam said. And he meant it. She needed him. Needed protecting, if he could do it, needed distraction if he could give it. "Do you want me to leave?"

Cecily bit her lower lip. "No," she admitted. "But I… I just…" She sighed. "But I don't want special treatment, okay? Just treat me normally, okay? Like any other one-night stand."

"Who said this was a one-night stand?" Liam sure as hell didn't want it to be.

"I mean, I'm sure you pick up girls in bars all the time, and I mean, just do what you normally do."

"For the record, *you* picked *me* up." Liam's lip curled into a slow grin. "You were the one buying *me* drinks, trying to get me wasted so you could take advantage of me."

Cecily barked an indignant laugh. "I was not!"

"And then you lure me back to my apartment, take advantage of me and leave without a word."

"You know why I left." Hurt flashed across Cecily's face. He knew why. She'd been trying to spare him her drama. But he didn't want to be spared. "And, anyway, I'm sure you've snuck out on your share of women. I'm sure you have one-night stands all the time."

"I don't. For the record." Sure, Liam got his fair share of female attention, but Liam hated casual. Hated everything about casual—usually. He didn't work like that. It was why he couldn't casually accept that his brother had taken over the family empire. He didn't do things by halves. He was all in, or all out. "I don't do casual."

"You...don't?" Cecily's eyebrows raised in surprise. "Why not?"

"I don't see the point," he said. "Either you're into someone, or you're not. Why have sex with someone you don't think you can love? I never understood that." It was why, if he were honest, he'd scared away women in his past, women who had no intention of settling down, of having a real relationship. They'd wanted something casual. He couldn't deliver.

Cecily blinked fast. "But we just met."

"Right." Liam went to her on the couch, sitting next to her. "That's why I want to get to know you better. So this isn't casual."

"But..." He could see all the excuses well up in

her eyes, all the ways she wanted to tell him that wasn't possible. He put a finger on her lips.

"You wanted me to treat you normally," he said. "So this is my normal. Let me at least do that."

"What *is* your normal?" she asked him, tentative.

"How about we start with a date?"

Her eyes brightened, but then she hesitated. What was holding her back? "I don't know. I promised myself…"

"Promised yourself what?"

"Well, I have a bucket list. Of sorts. I'm trying to get through it all, before…" She trailed off. "That's why I kissed you. At the bar."

"It was?" Liam almost laughed. He wondered what item that might be. Kiss a jerk at a bar? Throw herself on the first schmuck she saw? "What was the item you were trying to scratch off?"

"Kiss a handsome stranger that's out of your league at a bar and see what happens."

"You think I'm out of your league?" Liam couldn't believe that. If anything, the opposite was true.

"Yes," Cecily admitted, but wouldn't look him in the eye. He felt amusement well up in him. He didn't know what planet she lived on to think *he* was out of *her* league. Clearly, it was the other way around.

"What else is on your bucket list?"

"Tons of things. Seeing the Eiffel Tower in Paris. Buckingham Palace in London. Skydiving. Horseback riding. Ice-skating at Rockefeller Center." She ticked off a few items on her fingers. "Oh, and at some point a super fancy, super expensive dinner at one of those places that only foodies go where nobody knows what they're eating?"

"Okay. How about this? We work on your bucket list together," he said. Hope flared in her eyes for just a moment.

"Seriously?" she asked him, and the hope in it nearly split his heart in two. He felt right then determined to tick off every last item on her bucket list, so help him.

"Absolutely," he said. "Let's start with that fancy dinner."

CHAPTER SIX

CECILY CHECKED HER reflection in the full-length mirror of her bedroom one last time later that evening. She wore an eye-popping poppy-red strapless sundress that clung to her curves, the A-line skirt flaring just above the knee. She'd wondered for the briefest of seconds if it was too daring, too Marilyn Monroe, but that was exactly what she was going for: daring and bold. Bright red lipstick marked her lips, and a cat-eye liner completed the look. Liam had told her the dinner was formal, so she wore black patent-leather peep-toe heels that in her mind screamed sex. As much as she was looking forward to a nice dinner, what she really wanted was to get Liam back into her bed, melt into his arms and let her problems burn away.

She leaned in closer to the mirror, carefully fluffing her hair, trying to infuse body into her delicate gold waves. She tried not to think about what would've happened if the doctors had told her the chemo or radiation would work. She hadn't wanted to imagine her hair coming out by the handful. *It'll only make you sick, but we don't think it will help. You might get six more months, maybe ten. But those won't be good months.*

She ought to be worried about how she'd pay for her half of dinner tonight, but she'd decided just to put away her worries for a while. If she didn't live while she still had good days left, then what was the point? She had a small bit of retirement savings, and since she wasn't going to be old enough to enjoy retirement, she might as well use it now.

She took a deep breath, willing herself not to think about it. Tonight, she would be normal. She would forget her troubles because she was going out. Like normal people did. Except, she reminded herself, she'd be with one of the most gorgeous, amazing men she'd ever met. Nothing about Liam Lange was normal—not his intense brown-eyed stare, or the fact he was a walking bundle of contradictions. Gruff on the outside, a soft heart, she was beginning to suspect, on the inside. Most men would've gone running for the door at the very hint of a complication as serious as cancer. Not Liam. Instead of running, he'd asked her on a date. There was something grounding about Liam, something solid that she desperately needed right now.

Her apartment buzzer rang then, and she skipped to it, eagerly hitting the button that would let Liam in. She grabbed her small black leather cross-body bag and slipped it over her head, noticing that Tripp sat at the door. He sat licking his paw. He glanced up long enough to give her a quick once-over. He yawned, uninterested, but she took it to mean he approved.

Cecily heard heavy feet on the stairs and swung open the door in time to see a freshly showered and shaved Liam stride up to her door. He wore a pristinely tailored suit, complete with tie, and for a full second, she forgot to breathe. He didn't look like the rough-around-the-edges roofer he claimed to be. His eyes widened as he saw her, and his pace slowed.

"You look…beautiful." The way he said it, awed, almost with a reverential tone, made her heart tick up a notch.

"You don't look so bad yourself." He'd made it to the landing and now she glanced upward, more than aware of how tall he was, how broad. Could he feel the current between them? Built-up electricity, like a living thing, a live wire, unpredictable and dangerous. Who needed a date? What she wanted was to rip his clothes off and take him to her bed.

"I clean up okay," he admitted, as a sly smile crept across his face.

"More than okay."

"You're…gorgeous, Cecily." She knew he meant it, as his eyes drank her in. She could see the thirst in them, the want. It made the backs of her knees tingle.

She moved closer, and he took her into his arms, unable to resist the pull any longer. She tilted her head up for a hello kiss and he pressed his lips to hers. Soft, insistent and so very, very welcoming.

The contact sent a bolt of electricity down her back, landing at her knees that felt a little like jelly. God, the man could kiss. She entwined her hands behind his neck, pressing tighter against him.

He broke free, breathing hard. "If you keep that up, we'll never leave," he said.

"Maybe we should stay in."

He looked tempted, more than tempted, but he shook his head. "No. You wanted normal, and you're going to get normal." He took her by the hand and tugged her out of her apartment. She laughed as she went. "Besides, we can't let you sit at home looking that stunning. It just wouldn't be right. I want everyone to see you on my arm. Every straight man out there will die of jealousy."

She laughed. "Where are we headed?"

"I told you. It's a surprise." They trotted down the stairs, to the waiting rideshare below. "I thought we'd have wine at dinner," he added, nodding at the car.

"Sounds wonderful to me." She slid into the back of the car, stomach buzzing with excitement, as Liam took a seat next to her. The driver gave her a swift nod, and then they were off. Liam squeezed her hand.

After a short drive, they pulled up to GNT. Cecily's eyes grew wide as she stepped out of the car. "We're going here?" she asked, still not quite believing it. GNT was a five-star, uber-expensive, gastropub restaurant that had a two-month waiting list to get in. It was the kind of place that had no prices on the menu because everything was expensive. The kind of place she wouldn't dream of going herself. "How did you get a table?"

"I have friends," he said mysteriously, and then held the ornately carved wooden door open for her. Inside the darkened, small and intimate space, a maître d' in an expensive, tailored suit met them, ushering them to a small corner table, where the candlelight flickered. She took the seat the maître d' held out to her and then he slid her in, as Liam sat down. A small, paper-thin menu was presented to them then, a list of a prix fixe menu, and the only prices on the list were an added wine pairing. Her throat went dry when she saw that the wine alone with dinner would add $150 to the bill. She wondered what the actual food would cost. Several patrons of the restaurant glanced over as they sat down.

"Any allergies, mademoiselle? Monsieur?" A waiter appeared, wearing a black shirt and tie.

"No, not for me," Cecily said, as Liam, too, shook his head.

"Sparkling or still water?" he asked.

"Still, please," Cecily managed. If wine cost $150, she didn't want to know what soda water might be. She pressed her red skirt down, as the waiter reached over and draped a white napkin across her lap.

"Wine pairing tonight?" He glanced at Liam.

"Yes, please," he said before Cecily could argue. The waiter nodded and left.

"But it's so expensive," she said. "How can you…"

"I just got paid, and you deserve a nice meal."

Cecily blinked fast. "Yes, but…" She turned the menu over, as if hoping the prices would magically appear. "But this seems…extravagant. This isn't… normal."

"Sure it is. It's the normal you deserve." Liam flashed a smile and Cecily's stomach warmed.

"Are you trying to butter me up? Flattering me like this?"

Liam shrugged. "I just tell the truth." He leaned forward, and beneath the table their knees touched. Cecily felt a bolt of electricity run up her spine. "Did you see how everyone looked at you when you came in? And some, even now, can't take their eyes off you." Liam subtly nodded to a table of two couples. The men were staring at her, but the women, she noticed, seemed intent on Liam. As did the waitress of the table next to theirs.

"You're getting just as much attention," she pointed out, as she reached across the table and took his hand.

"They're all looking at you," Liam insisted. She wondered how a man so gorgeous also seemed so humble. The waiter brought the first course, a delicate small white ball with a sprig of green, and rattled off quite a lot of words, many French, and none that Cecily understood.

"He said it's crab with butter and herbs," Liam said.

"You speak French?"

"I learned it in grade school." Cecily stared at

Liam, surprised. She never took a foreign language in grade school. A little bit of Spanish in high school, but that was about it for Cecily.

"Where did you grow up again?" she asked, curiosity piqued.

"New York," he said, vaguely. Too vaguely. The waiter came then, pouring a white wine in their empty wineglasses.

"What part?" Cecily glanced down at the many forks and knives by her plate, including two small forks at the top of her place setting. She bit her lip. Which one should she use? She rarely ate at fancy restaurants, and when she did, normally they simply changed out utensils with each course. Cecily reached for the inner fork, but hesitated. It looked too big for an appetizer.

"Start on the outside, and move your way in," Liam suggested, picking up the small fork on the outside.

"Oh, thanks." She took the fork, wondering how he knew that. Then she felt a tad guilty. Why wouldn't he? Because he was a roofer with calloused hands? So what. Since when had she gotten elitist? "Where in New York did you grow up?" she pressed, even as she gently spooned some of the small appetizer into her mouth and nearly forgot she had asked the question. It was like perfection on her tongue: beautiful buttery goodness. She'd never tasted anything so wonderful. She snatched up the other bite, and then realized with acute disappointment her plate was empty.

"Upper East Side," he said, so softly that she almost didn't hear him.

"Upper East Side?" Cecily echoed. "But that's…" She stopped herself. That was where rich people lived. Cecily had never lived in Manhattan, had not even been able to afford a decent apartment there, which is why she'd landed in New Jersey. But she knew enough about New York to know where the expensive neighborhoods lay.

"Yeah. It's…that." Liam finished his appetizer, and then dabbed his mouth with a napkin. He looked as if he wanted to change the subject, but Cecily wasn't sure she could let it go.

"I thought only the super wealthy live there."

"They mostly do," Liam said, noncommittal.

She then remembered him talking about the fight over his father's estate. Okay, so there was probably more to that story. She'd made assumptions about him, about his background, that weren't true. When he said his brothers fought over the will, she thought it was maybe a few thousand dollars. Or the family's modest home. "But now you prefer dive bars in New Jersey." Cecily couldn't help but tease him. She was still trying to process the fact that he knew French and which fork to use in a fancy restaurant.

"Definitely." Liam grinned.

"So, tell me. What was that like on the Upper East Side? I grew up near Cleveland in a blue-collar neighborhood. Everyone in my family thinks I'm a little crazy for moving out here."

Liam sighed. "I'd rather not talk about my family." A wall came up then, a big no-trespassing sign right there on the freshly laid brick. She'd hit a sore spot, and she knew it. Still. This was supposed to be a get-to-know-you dinner, wasn't it? Wasn't Liam the one who claimed not to do casual?

"I'm sorry. I didn't mean to pry." But at the same time, who got so defensive about one's family? It made Cecily want to know more. But the determined set of Liam's jaw told her she wasn't going to get more. At least, not now.

The waiter came then, whisking their empty plates away.

"Let's talk about you," Liam said, raising his wineglass. She'd forgotten about the white wine. She took the thin glass stem between her fingers and raised her glass and clinked it against his. "Cheers," she said, as the awkwardness floated away.

She stared into Liam's brown eyes and felt at home there. She wondered how she already felt like she'd known him a long time. Cecily didn't believe in reincarnation, not really, but part of her couldn't shake the feeling they'd met before. Or they were meant to meet. One way or another, she felt fate was involved. She'd never felt as connected to a person in so short a time before. Even a person who seemed determined to keep some secrets, determined to keep the spotlight on her instead of him.

Liam's eyes brightened again as he took a sip of wine. "Tell me about your childhood."

"I had one older sister, and we both shared a bedroom in our small house," she said, hoping that if she divulged more of her own background, he'd do the same. "Mom worked in a hair salon, my sister as a cashier at the local grocery. Neither went to college. Dad, before he passed on, was a plumber. I was the first one to go on to college, and the first one in a couple of generations to move out of Ohio."

"Felt like you didn't fit in there?" Liam studied her as if he understood. He'd referenced his own family troubles, and the fights that had left him on the outside looking in.

"Right," she said. "I didn't have a big blowup or anything, I just… I just wanted more from life, I guess. I love my family dearly, but they're all so focused on exactly what's all around them. I wanted to live in a big city, you know? In the town where I grew up, it was all hamburgers and chicken fingers. Nothing like this." She glanced around the fancy French restaurant, knowing exactly how her sister would see it. Too upscale, too fancy for her tastes. But Cecily, even when she was a kid, yearned for adventure. Yearned for something different, something exciting. That's what drew her to New York. "There's nothing wrong with where I came from, it's just not the life for me."

"You're kind."

"I love my family. And I'm glad they're happy

where they are. And they're happy I'm happy where I am." *At least, until they hear the cancer isn't treatable.*

"How much do they know? About the cancer?" Liam's dark eyes grew soft as he leaned closer, his knee against hers offering a reassuring pressure.

"They know I have cancer. Neither one knows there are no good treatments."

"That you know of," Liam corrected, sipping his wine.

"Right." She laughed, rueful. "Do you know of some kind of expert or something? You're a roofer *and* a medical expert?"

"I have friends," he said, vaguely. "I also know not all doctors are equal."

"Right." She nodded. She reached for her wineglass but found it nearly empty. She swallowed the last sip and sighed. The last thing Cecily wanted to do was spend time talking about her cancer over this amazing dinner. Thankfully, the waiter brought the next course: once more, something unidentifiable, but that looked delicate and delicious.

"It's the salad course," Liam offered, even as Cecily stared at the small round yellow circle on top of the white circle.

"I don't see any greens," she exclaimed. "What kind of salad is this?"

"A root vegetable salad," he said, as the waiter filled up their glasses with a new wine, this one a rosé.

"Oh." Cecily wasn't even sure what that meant.

She took a crunchy bite, though, and instantly her mouth fell in love with the citrus vinaigrette. "Mmm," she moaned, as she finished the last bite. She glanced up to see Liam studying her intently. The focus of his stare made her feel suddenly warm. She laughed a little uneasily. "Sorry. I just never have tasted a salad that good."

"You shouldn't apologize," Liam said. "You're beautiful. That's why I'm staring."

Cecily shifted, a little uncomfortable, in her seat. "I bet you say that to all the women you date."

"Only if it's the truth. And, besides, I don't date that many." Liam shrugged.

"You don't take them all to fancy restaurants like this?"

Liam laughed. "No. I'd be broke."

Cecily laughed, too.

"But, seriously, I don't date around."

"Right. You told me you don't do casual." Cecily still couldn't quite believe it. Who was this perfect man who'd fallen into her lap? Saved her from a heckler at a bar, and now when he ought to be running for the door, was stubbornly staying put. She would've thought he loved to play the field, make women fall in love with him.

"No, I don't." He reached across the table and took her hand again. It felt warm, strong and steady. "I'm just not wired that way. Life is too short to play around when you're not serious. I don't have time for people I don't want in my life, and I go after the ones I do."

Cecily felt her throat go dry. The way he was looking at her right at that moment was like a collector of expensive art, and she was the masterpiece he'd been looking for. She felt rooted to the spot, but also, strangely flattered. He could have any woman he wanted, most likely, and he seemed to want her.

"How do you know you want a person in your life?"

"I just know," he said, with a confidence Cecily wished she felt. "I want you in my life, Cecily."

Cecily suddenly felt overcome with emotion, surprising her. "You do?"

"Yes, for as long or as little as that may be."

Why was this man, this beautiful man, so determined to be with her? She had no time. She had no future. Yet, she could see the promise in his eyes, and that made her heart both swell and feel heavy all at once. Could she, at long last, have met the man meant for her? Just at the very point in her life when she found out she had little time left. It seemed cruel. Beyond cruel.

"Excuse me, I…uh. Just need to go to the bathroom," Cecily said. She pushed back her chair and headed to the ladies' room, tears pricking her eyes. How had she gotten so involved with a man she'd only just met, when she knew, without a doubt, she had nothing to offer him?

CHAPTER SEVEN

LIAM WATCHED CECILY sprint away from the table and inwardly kicked himself. What the hell was he doing? He was supposed to be taking her mind off her illness, not reminding her at every turn that the clock was ticking. He was trying to be supportive, telling her he didn't care what time they had left, as long as they had some time together, but that only brought up the specter in the room, the thing she was trying so hard to ignore. If only she'd consider a second opinion. Surely, there were other doctors, other treatments. Why listen to the first one who told you it was hopeless?

While Cecily was so strong, so courageous, she was also fragile. Dealing with the emotional trauma of having to face the possibility of her life being cut short wasn't easy for anyone. Liam couldn't begin to understand how that felt. He should stop bringing it up. He should just let her deal with it on her own terms.

That, or she'd be just another woman he'd scared

off with his intensity. Hadn't the last woman he'd dated told him to loosen up? Stop being so serious? He couldn't help who he was, though. He'd been born this way.

The waiter came by and replaced their small salad plates with the third course. Another artistic, gastronomic phenomenon, no doubt, but Liam was losing his appetite. He'd grown up with food like this, food that was hard to pronounce, and looked nothing like it ought to: salads that weren't green, meat covered in delicate sauces and bookended with tiny baby vegetables. Plates that looked more like art than food.

He was surprised how easily he fell back into old habits, how fine dining felt like coming home. He'd spent most of his life running from the money he'd grown up with, and yet, here, in these places, he was reminded that money did, indeed, have benefits.

He took a sip of the wine and as the rosé met his lips, he remembered his mother. His mother loved her rosé, and the smell of expensive wine always clung to her, especially in the days when she drank too much. He tried to bury that memory. She'd been a good mother, or at least, tried to be a good mother to him. It wasn't her fault she buckled under the pressure of being a single mom to them. Besides, alcoholism was a disease. She'd needed help, and he was often the only one there to help her.

A few moments later, Cecily returned from the bathroom and Liam felt a sense of relief. Part of him had been worried she'd just sneak out the back and never return. As she crossed the restaurant in her fire-engine red strapless sundress, the breath caught in his throat. She was the most gorgeous woman he'd ever seen. As in, beauty queen, head-turning stunning. He observed how the patrons and staff in the restaurant turn to watch her as she walked through: diners, waiters, busboys, she claimed all of their attention.

Liam leaped to his feet when she approached the table, a habit gleaned from years at boarding school. Rise for elders and women, help them with their chairs. He hurried over to pull out her chair, and she seemed a little taken aback. She sat and he got a whiff of her perfume. Roses, maybe? Lilacs? Something delicate and beautiful, just like her. He took his seat across the small table. He studied her face, but saw her eyes were dry, though her nose seemed pink. He damn well hoped he hadn't made her cry.

"I'm sorry about that," she said. "I'm just an emotional wreck these days."

"Please don't apologize. It's my fault. I'm supposed to take your mind off things. Not remind you of what you're trying to forget."

She reached forward and grabbed his hand, hers feeling cool and soft. "You do take my mind off things. Believe me, you do." She sent him a brave smile that squeezed his heart a little bit. He was still not sure how a woman this perfect, this glowing, could be sick. She didn't look sick. Didn't act sick.

Maybe, he thought, the doctors were wrong. God, he hoped they were wrong.

The waiter returned, this time bringing a small melon sorbet, a simple bite. Cecily blinked hard, staring at it, then she leaned over. "Is this dessert? Already?" She was no doubt worried that dinner consisted of only several bites of delicious, but not-so-filling food.

"It's a sorbet," Liam explained. "To cleanse your palate. So you can better taste and enjoy the next course."

"Oh." Cecily took the small spoon on the plate and dipped into the single green ball. "Mmm. Honeydew," she announced. Then, she watched him do the same. She studied him, as if trying to figure out a puzzle. "How did you know it was sorbet? The waiter didn't tell us."

Liam shrugged. "Lucky guess."

"About sorbet and cleansing palates? You are a mystery. Is this what people on the Upper East Side eat all the time?" she teased, but he didn't go for the bait.

She dabbed her mouth. He shifted, suddenly uncomfortable in his seat. Why had he decided to tackle "fancy dinner" on her bucket list? There were a ton of other things he could've done. But he knew why. He'd wanted to impress her, wanted to spoil her with a magical meal. That's why he didn't mind blowing cash on an expensive dinner. But now, with all the questions popping up in her mind about him, he was beginning to regret the decision. He might as well have just worn a sign that said, "I come from money. Why not ask me about it?"

Thankfully, the waiter came with the next course. Their beef course—the "main" course, though the delicate food on the small plate was hardly bigger than four bites—was the largest portion yet. Cecily was so busy staring at the beautifully plated meal that she was temporarily distracted from asking him about sorbet. Thank God.

"So," he said, as the waiter filled a new glass with red wine. "I want to know everything. Favorite movie. Favorite band. You go."

"You first," she challenged him.

"All right," he said, glad to be in safer territory. "Favorite movie? *The Godfather*. Favorite band? Tough one. I like all kinds of music. But a killer guitarist is my thing. Stevie Ray Vaughan, Gary Clark, Jr. Guys who can rip on the guitar."

"I saw Gary Clark, Jr., in concert. He was amazing."

"You like Gary Clark, Jr.?"

"'Bright Lights, Big City' is my favorite song." Not only was the woman gorgeous, but she also had amazing taste in music? She might just be the perfect woman.

"Mine, too." The two of them stared at each other for a long beat. He couldn't believe he'd found a woman who loved a wailing guitar as much as he did. "And, personally, *The Godfather* is great, but if you're talking amazing mob movies, you've got to give it to *Goodfellas*. Scorsese runs circles around Coppola."

"You like mob movies, too?" Liam couldn't keep the skepticism out of his voice. Now, she was too good to be true.

"What? Do I amuse you?" she said, quoting from the movie. "Am I a clown? Am I funny to you?"

"What's your second favorite mob movie?"

"No question, it's *The Departed.*"

"I might love you," Liam blurted.

"Might?" She batted her eyelashes at him, and he laughed. A big belly laugh that took him by surprise. Cecily was full of surprises, wonderful delightful, surprises.

"I can't believe you love mob movies."

Cecily laughed. "Is that so weird?"

"But you're…" Sexy. Hot. Delicate. Feminine. Not the kind of person he'd expect to want to curl up on a couch on a Friday night with a bowl of popcorn watching gruesome mob hits by tough guys spouting pithy one-liners.

"I'm…?" She let it lie there between them as a teasing smile played at the corners of her lips. God, had a woman ever been this sexy?

"Maybe the most amazing woman I've ever met." She laughed then, flashing her even white teeth, her beautiful smile. All he wanted to do was make her laugh again and again, see that smile on her face every day for as long as they had together.

"You're easily impressed," she managed, catching her breath.

"Not that easy." It had been a long time since a woman had piqued his interest quite so much. Maybe never, if he were honest with himself.

The rest of the dinner flew by in a blur, and Liam barely acknowledged the meal of amazing food. He was too busy focused on the amazing woman in front of him. Her quick wit, her daring nature, the way she seemed to tackle every challenge in her life with a kind of rare and quiet fortitude.

Most people who'd gotten a diagnosis like hers would be bemoaning their circumstances, and crying, *Why me?* Cecily didn't seem to have a self-pitying bone in her body. She was smart, full of light and laughter, her eyes bright with excitement about every little dish put in front of them. Her curiosity about the world, about him, about everything, spilled out into everything she did and said.

Liam wasn't used to this kind of sparkling company. They talked about everything from movies to politics, the conversation never lagging, the connection between them growing deeper the longer they talked. It felt like they shared a brain, they had so much in common.

Outside the restaurant, they held hands beneath the silvery moonlight. "Want to go for a walk? The waterfront is just over there." Cecily nodded in the direction of the Hudson River, not far from their restaurant.

"Is that where you take all of *your* dates? All the men who fill up your dating inbox with messages about how they can't wait to sweep you off your feet?"

Now it was Cecily's turn to laugh. "I don't date around, either," she told him as they walked, hand in hand. Her delicate hand was so soft, so small in his. "I did have a boyfriend."

"Knew it."

"But things didn't work out. He was in the finance industry, and, well, let's just say he didn't believe in monogamy."

Liam felt a rush of anger toward a man he'd never met.

"He was an idiot."

Cecily shrugged. "Yeah, that's what my sister said." They turned the corner and before them was the dark water of the Hudson, and in the distance, the glittering gold lights of Manhattan, the skyline lit up in the night sky. Liam tried not to frown when he saw the big buildings, a reminder where his brother and family still lived.

"You don't like the skyline?" Cecily asked, glancing up at him with concern. He must have had his distaste written all over his face. They began walking along the path, which was mostly empty. A few stragglers still walked or jogged by, though the sun had long set.

"Not really a New York guy," he said.

"But you live in New Jersey, a stone's throw away."

"Yeah. I know." He glanced away from the water. He had his reasons. One of them was a promise he'd made to his mother not to go too far. She'd always need him: in case she relapsed. Someone would need to take her to rehab, and his brothers had long since washed their hands of her care. "My mom lives in Manhattan, and she's a recovering alcoholic. I promised I'd stay nearby. In case she needs me."

Cecily raised an eyebrow. "That's being a dutiful son."

"I guess." Liam shrugged.

"Are you two close?"

"Kind of." Their relationship was complicated, like most son-and-mother relationships, made all the more so by her chemical dependency. There were times in his life she hadn't been there for him, times when he was much younger that he had to fend for himself when he shouldn't have. She often missed meals, missed teacher conferences and missed his baseball games. But he knew that wasn't her fault. That was the addiction. It was a semi-manageable problem until his father died, and she spun out of control. "She always struggled a little with drinking, but things got worse when my father died."

"I'm sorry to hear that," she said, squeezing his hand. Something about the tone of her voice, or the way she was holding his hand, made him want to share. He never wanted to share details about his life or his family with anyone, but he wanted her to know.

"Yeah, she's sober now, but for a while, I didn't think she'd be able to get clean," he managed. "After my father died, the drinking was by far the worst. It got bad."

"How bad?"

"She was so hungover, I missed my first day of middle school," he admitted. "She was supposed to drive me. I tried to get her out of bed, but she wouldn't budge. So I missed the first day. My twin brother, too. But he didn't care as much as I did."

"That's terrible," Cecily exclaimed.

"Yeah. Alcoholism is a bitch of a disease," Liam said. "And my half brother didn't make it any easier for her. I think he thought it was just a personal failing, a weakness of character. But it is a disease."

"I'm so sorry." Cecily moved closer to him, and he was acutely aware of her slim body next to his, the warmth of her arm now entwining in his.

"She got sober eventually, and has been sober for a couple of years, but I don't know how long that will last. When things get to be hard in her life, sometimes she falls off the wagon." Liam shook his head, trying to press down all the many terrible memories from his childhood: her showing up late and drunk to his graduation. Her being so hungover that she missed saying goodbye that morning he left the family estate and never looked back. "And my half brother, he took advantage of her. Of her being out of it. That's how he took over my dad's business."

"Doesn't sound like a very nice thing to do."

"He's not a nice guy." Liam ground his back teeth together as he thought about Wilder. "He never really liked that Dad remarried, never liked my mom."

"How do your brothers get along with him?"

"Fine, I guess. They don't see him as I see him." As the money-grubbing, backstabbing traitor he was. "They think he's doing what's best. But Wilder is persuasive. He's brainwashed them."

"Or maybe he's not all bad," Cecily offered. "If he's taking care of your brothers…"

"No." Wilder shook his head. "He's only taking care of them so he has their votes on the board. It all comes back to what he can get. What's in it for him. He stole my dad's business."

"And what's that?"

Liam balked. He didn't know why. Why not just tell her it was Lange Communications? One of the largest media companies in the world? The conglomerate that owned one in three newspapers, and three out of five television networks? Yet he hesitated.

"It's an old family business," he said, not wanting to get into the fact that it started out with his grandfather launching a few magazines in the 1950s, but sixty years later, the company had gobbled up airwaves and some broadband, too. "Boring stuff, really. Networking and stuff." Not a lie, but not the truth, either.

"Oh, okay," she said, but her eyes told him that she knew he was holding out on her. And why was he holding out? Why didn't he want to tell her? But

then, he knew why. He was enjoying her not knowing. Once women found out he was one of the possible heirs to Lange Communications, something
always changed in the relationship. Something
shifted. Even women who claimed not to care about
money in the least, still somehow did. In theory they
agreed, until they realized he'd left millions, or even
billions, on the table. Many questioned his sanity;
others tried to convince him maybe it wasn't too
late to make amends. But he knew it was beyond
too late for that.

He didn't want to ruin whatever time he had
with Cecily arguing about the foolishness of walking away from such a substantial fortune. Or have
the disappointment in knowing that she would think
it was foolish.

"Look at that moon," he said, drawing her attention to the crescent in the sky, hanging above the city
skyline like a ready-made postcard.

"It's pretty," she agreed.

"Not as pretty as you."

She turned to face him then in the moonlight, her
delicate features illuminated by the moon and the
streetlights. In that moment, she was the most beautiful woman he'd ever seen. She seemed transfixed
by him, too. Their gazes locked, as her mouth parted
just slightly. He dipped down and kissed her gently at
first, reverently. She was the one who quickly deepened the kiss, lacing her delicate hands behind his
neck, pressing her soft body against his. Instantly, he

felt his whole body react to her, his primal self come alive. She was no delicate flower, as she kissed him, her tongue lashing his, awakening a need in him he didn't even know he had. Instinctual, essential. His hands roamed down her back, finding her hips. He just wanted more of her. More of her mouth. More of her tongue. More of her frantic hands in his hair. Just…more.

He almost forgot they were making out in public, on the waterfront, until a passerby whistled. A jogger sped by.

"Get a room," he yelled as he ran.

Cecily pulled away from him, her eyes bright and full of mischief. "Well, shall we?"

He could feel his want pressing uncomfortably against the zipper of his pants. "Yes. Let's."

Cecily couldn't believe she was having Liam over at her apartment. Couldn't believe her luck that a one-night stand had turned into…what was this, anyway? No, she told herself. Don't think about it. Don't label it. Just be in the moment. All she wanted was to be naked in his arms, forgetting all about what might lie ahead. There was no better way to put off thinking about the future than Liam's amazing body, his talented mouth and his expert hands.

She'd always thought that stories about sex addiction sounded so crazy. Who could possibly be addicted to sex? But then she met Liam and her mind was completely changed about the subject. Though she'd known him so little, she felt herself needing him more and more. Could feel the hunger for him, and only him, rising in her. Could it become an addiction? Yes, she was sure it could.

They were barely inside her apartment before Liam had his own shirt off and was working on hers. Clothes became obstacles to get off as soon as possible, barriers that must go immediately. They didn't even make it to her bedroom before he took her against the wall of her entryway. Neither one of them could wait. He was holding her easily against the wall as she spread herself, wrapping her legs around his waist.

Waiting through dinner and then the walk had been torture. All she wanted was his body, his mouth, because with him inside her, she could think of nothing else but the desire growing in her, the white-hot want, building, ever building, inside of her, reminding her that she was the furthest thing from dead. She was alive. Her whole body was alive. She was almost there, but then he came, too quickly, in a groan of defeat.

"God, Cecily," he cried, slumping against her. "I am so sorry. I didn't mean to—"

But she silenced him with a kiss. Something about him not being able to hold off seemed incredibly hot, as well. That she'd made him lose a little bit of control, a man she could tell prided himself on that very control. On not letting his feelings run away with him. But her body had done this. Made all discipline fall away. She loved it, the control, the power. He gently set her on her feet, and before she could move, he was kneeling in front of her, his mouth on her juicy mound.

"No, wait…" she cried, but he was there, his mouth eager to please, his tongue warm, slow and deliberate. She was pressed against the wall, and her knees felt weak, even as he lifted one of her legs in the air and placed it over his shoulder, the back of one knee now near his ear. She pressed both arms against the wall for support, and because the whole world felt like it was spinning out of control. He slipped two fingers inside her, and together with the amazingly light strokes of his tongue, she could feel the pleasure building, pent-up beneath some invisible gate. She forgot about everything but his mouth and his fingers that hit nerve endings she didn't think she had. Pinned against the wall, his head between her legs, she reached the tipping point. There was no turning back as the climax came. A cry tore through her throat, as a tidal wave of pure pleasure washed over her, again and again.

Liam kissed her inner thigh gently before he rose and found her mouth, covering it with his. Her knees felt shaky and weak, her bones disintegrated into jelly. He picked her up then and carried her to her bedroom. She barely noticed that her blinds had been halfway open. They'd been so focused on one another, on the pleasure they'd get, that neither had bothered to shut the blinds. Cecily didn't care. Liam carried her to the bedroom, laying her down on her bed and running feather kisses down her body. Worshipping her, drinking her in. She'd never felt as if a man took such care with her body before.

"That was amazing," she croaked, still not able to believe the chemistry, the electric pleasure that had pulsed through her. She'd never felt something that powerful, that real, before. "I thought you promised me 'normal.' But there wasn't anything normal about that."

"True," Liam said, and chucked low, as he lay down next to her. "Should we try again and see if we can be 'normal'?"

"No way," Cecily cried, curling up around his body, Liam's arms closing around her. "I never want normal ever again."

"Good, because you're not going to get it," Liam said as she laid her head on his chest. She could hear his heartbeat, steady, a calming rhythm. She felt safe there, as if he offered her a perfectly protected bubble. Here, in his arms, she didn't have to think about the future, about her failing body, about the cancer eating her from the inside. Here, everything was perfect. She had no worries.

"Thank you," she muttered, suddenly feeling completely overcome with gratitude. What had she done to deserve this comfort? This amazing peace?

"For what?" Liam asked her hair, as he stroked her back with his free hand.

"For this." She curled against him. He hugged her tighter, wrapping his hands around her.

"I'm the one who should be thanking you," he said, and sounded as if he meant it. "I didn't think I could find anything like this." He stroked her hair.

"Me, neither."

Gratitude for Liam, and sadness, too, bubbled up in her. She squeezed back tears. She wouldn't think about what would happen in the future. She would just live in the now. Wasn't that on her bucket list, too? Live in the now. Don't worry about the future.

"You don't have to stay the night, if you don't want to," Cecily said. She didn't want him to feel hemmed in. Trapped.

"Why wouldn't I want to stay the night?"

"I mean…" There were a million reasons, but the biggest was that this relationship really couldn't go anywhere.

"Why would I leave, when we're just getting started?" Liam promised, and she knew he wasn't lying. They wouldn't be getting much sleep tonight and that was just fine by her.

CHAPTER EIGHT

Two weeks later, Cecily zipped up her skydiving suit, her stomach squadron of butterflies flying a zigzag pattern. Was she really going to do this? She adjusted her helmet and wondered if she was actually losing her mind. Skydiving *was* on her bucket list. She glanced over at Liam, handsome as ever, as he gave her a casual thumbs-up. The roar of wind snapped in her ears, as the operator of the indoor sky-diving facility hit the go button. Soon, she and Liam were propelled upward in the clear plastic wind tunnel, made weightless by a huge fan. The wind buoyed them up, and she spread out her hands and legs, feeling as if she were flying. Because she *was* flying.

"This is insane!" she shouted to Liam, who just grinned and reached out for her hand. They linked fingers and for a second, floated at least two stories above the ground, flying in perfect circles in the wind tunnel. "I'm flying!" she cried, feeling pure, absolute joy rush through every vein in her body. Liam squeezed her hand and as she met his dark gaze, she wondered if it was the fan lifting her up, or Liam's solid presence, the way he made her feel like anything was possible. She glanced at him, and saw the surprise in his eyes, which were protected beneath his blue plastic goggles. She wore pink goggles, and tried not to giggle as she thought that everything she saw now was rose-tinted.

Cecily felt overwhelmed with joy and gratitude, as they both floated together, defying gravity. He laughed and so did she, but the sounds were drowned out by the whirring tornado of air, the thunder in their ears of wind pushing them ever upward. She didn't want this moment to end. She wanted to pause right here in her life, holding Liam's hand, twirling high in the air, weightless. If only they could live in this moment forever.

After the whirlwind—literally—ride, the fan gently slowed, and they were once more lowered to the ground, her feet feeling the solid ground beneath her as they hit the latticed floor. The operator opened the airtight hatch, and the two climbed out, Cecily feeling breathless and…completely and utterly alive.

"I want to do that again!" she cried.

"And we can, anytime you want." Liam pulled Cecily into his arms and kissed her. What breath she had left he took away. No man she'd ever met could kiss like Liam. No man made her feel pure electricity in her toes. She only thought she'd been flying inside that vacuum tube. Now, right here, she felt like she was soaring.

He broke free and she grinned up at him, unable to contain her excitement as she ripped off her rose-colored goggles. "Could you believe we were flying? We were *flying*!"

He lifted his own goggles, resting them in his mussed dark-blond hair. He gingerly caressed her cheek, looking at her with a kind of reverence.

"And one of these days, we'll do the *real* thing," Liam promised, and in that moment, Cecily knew he meant that promise. Since meeting him, he'd been attacking her bucket list like a man on a mission: they'd hit the roller coasters on Coney Island and taken pictures on top of the Empire State Building. Every day with Liam had been a new adventure, every day bursting with *life*. Liam had been deadly serious when he said he didn't do things by halves. The man was all-in.

"You're amazing," she told Liam, and meant it. Who else would take her bucket list so seriously? Who else would help her plan all these adventures? "One of these days, you'll have to get back to work!"

"I've got a little time before my next roofing project," Liam said. "And we're going to make the most of it."

There it was. That reminder of the ticking clock, the hourglass with a finite amount of sand. She tried not to let it deflate her excitement, but it was impossible not to feel the shadow looming over everything they did. Liam was looking on the bright side, and she appreciated that. She blinked away the sadness that threatened to overtake the moment.

"That's right," she said. "We're going to make the most of it." They walked toward the locker rooms then, where they could change back into their street shoes and return their jumpsuits. "In fact, why don't we do that right now?" He moved them both into a single-stall changing room. Liam closed the door and flicked the flimsy handle lock.

"What on earth are you going to do?" she whispered, but felt giggly, felt decidedly like breaking the rules was exactly what they ought to do.

"Kiss the life out of the most beautiful woman I've ever seen," he said, voice low. He moved closer, and then his mouth was on hers. She wrapped her hands around the back of his neck, pressing her body against his, her lips parting for him. His tongue flicked over hers, and her whole body came alive. With the adrenaline already buzzing through her brain, this just added fuel to that fire. She managed to remember they were in a public place, though the locked door told her they were safe. For now.

"What if someone catches us?" she murmured, as he trailed kisses down her neck.

"We'll just tell them we're ticking off items on your bucket list," he whispered into her ear.

"Oh…right." She'd forgotten number twenty-five: adventurous sex, maybe even in public. "I forgot how seriously you take my list."

"Damn straight, I do," he said, sliding the zipper of her jumpsuit down. She wore just a one-piece jumper underneath and he quickly freed her of that, as well. Her hands were on his clothes, too, tugging them off. He spun her around, so her palms were against the cool tile wall. He kissed the back of her neck, and she felt as if her whole body were on fire. This was wrong, but so very, very right. Her heart hammered in her chest, and her breath came in short, shallow gasps.

He gently spread her legs, and she stood, splayed, breath coming fast. He teased her first, the head of his hard cock against the back of her thighs. Just when she was going to tell him to do it, he took her from behind then, hard, fast, possessive, filling her up. She groaned, unable to help herself. This was what she needed. She needed him, inside her, along with the promise of everything yet to come. He pressed his hand against her mouth, and then she remembered they were in public, in a changing room, and people were walking back and forth in the small hallway outside.

She'd need to be quiet, but how could she? Especially now that Liam's hands were cupping her aching breasts, squeezing her nipples, which came to life with the pressure. She wanted to cry out but bit her lip instead. Liam's hand traveled lower, pressing against her belly, gliding downward. The tip of his finger found her clit, swollen and needy. She nearly gasped again. She sucked in a breath and held it, trying to be quiet, fighting the urge to scream. The pleasure built in her, and she wondered how she'd ever be able to keep silent, as her want, as her need, grew. He had her now and he knew it, as he began his gentle caress. The combination of him filling her, rubbing her, driving her wild, she couldn't concentrate on anything but his amazing cock, his hands, the way he was pushing her, no—carrying her—to an inevitable climax.

"Come for me," he urged her in a low whisper. It was a command and a promise, as he worked harder, faster, and the urgent need in her built. She could feel it, the slow climb, the steady build, as the pressure grew. It had to be released. She felt the cool, hard tile against her palms, braced herself against every one of Liam's thrusts, each new one deeper than the last. She loved it, this feeling of being taken by him, being pinned. His mouth was on her neck, driving her wild. His hands on her body, teasing, commanding.

Had she ever been with a man like Liam? A man who set her very soul on fire? She'd never wanted a man like this. Never needed a man like this. He would make her come, just as he had before. There could be no resisting him. Her body tensed as the climax ripped through her, his hand was on her mouth, muffling her cry of pleasure. And then, he came, too, one last deep thrust inside her, running over the last vibrations of her own come, as the two of them collapsed, gasping against the wall.

A hard knock came on the door then. The two,

half-naked, froze. Cecily stared at the doorknob and watched someone try to turn it.

"Hello?" a strange voice asked outside.

"This one is occupied," Liam managed, voice loud.

"Everything okay in there?" Whoever was knocking seemed like an employee of the place. That couldn't be good.

"Yeah. Just one minute."

Cecily bit her lip to try to suppress a laugh. "We'd better get out of here before they call the cops," she whispered, as she hurried to put on her street clothes. Liam jammed his feet into the legs of his jeans.

Another knock came at the door. "One second!" Liam cried again as he scrambled for his shirt on the ground.

He gave her a lopsided smile. "I think you're right," he said, tugging the T over his head.

They giggled all the way into the parking lot. Cecily felt carefree and amazing as she held Liam's hand, walking toward Liam's steel gray pickup truck.

"We almost got arrested," she breathed.

"I doubt he would've arrested us," Liam added. But Cecily wasn't so sure. The burly manager at the Fly High Studio didn't look pleased when the two of them hurriedly exited the dressing room, shirts untucked and bags in tow. "Probably does happen all the time. Adrenaline rush and all that. Still, he's not likely to complain too much. I gave them all a good tip."

"Good," Cecily said, as Liam pulled his remote key fob from his pocket and unlocked his truck. The lights flashed and the telltale beep told them the doors were open. Liam went around to open her door and Cecily only just put her toe on the running board, when she suddenly felt light-headed. A sharp pain struck her temple, and she pressed her palm against her forehead as she leaned against the truck's door.

"Are you okay?" Liam asked, strong hand on her elbow. She was grateful for the contact, and glad for the literal support. Her legs suddenly felt like spaghetti.

"I just…" Her eyes clouded with stars as she tried to shake her vision clear. Her doctor had told her that fainting spells, light-headedness, might come with the territory.

"Here, let's sit." Liam lifted her up into the truck bed, sitting her on the plush seat.

She nearly collapsed.

"I'm sorry. I just…" She felt like she couldn't breathe in that moment.

"Here. Maybe this will help." Liam helped her lie down, so that her head was on the driver's side and her knees were propped upward, the loose fabric of her jumper accommodating the position easily. "Maybe you need more blood to the brain."

He moved then, jogging around the front of the

car so he could be near her head. She glanced up at him, frowning. Stars still bounced around her vision. But they slowly cleared. "How did you know this?"

"My little brother always got light-headed when we played sports. Doctors said it was because his brain was starved for oxygen. Happens if you get your heart rate up too fast."

Or if you're dying of cancer. The thought popped into her brain and she immediately squashed it. She could be light-headed from anything, right? From the sex. From the adrenaline of flying. This didn't necessarily have to do with cancer.

"Oh." Cecily covered her eyes with one arm and breathed deeply. She remembered, though, the conversation with the doctor who told her this could be a symptom. That as her liver failed, her blood wouldn't be cleaned as well. Fainting spells could occur. Or worse. Was her body already failing her? What if she *couldn't* complete her bucket list? What if she got too sick too fast?

"Hey." Liam brushed a bit of her hair out of her face. "You okay?"

"Yeah. The light-headedness is going away." She inhaled slowly. "I can't believe I can skydive and…" She felt a hot blush creep up her neck when she thought of the delicious quickie they'd just shared in the changing room. "But a short walk in the parking lot did me in."

"We did a lot today. Maybe we pushed you too hard."

"No." Cecily reached up and grabbed his wrist.

She met his dark, worried gaze. "We didn't do too much." She refused to believe she was already getting weak, already losing her battle. She had a lot of living to do yet, and she planned to do it.

"Are you sure you're okay?" Liam repeated. "And I don't just mean physically."

Cecily peeked out from under her elbow, meeting his concerned brown eyes. Why couldn't she hide anything from this man? He seemed to know her every thought. Every mood. Every feeling. It was as if they shared the same brain.

"I just… I guess I'm not fine."

"That's what I thought." He stepped into the cab of the truck, sitting next to her head. He stroked her face. "I know we haven't mentioned this much, but have you given any more thought to a second opinion?"

Cecily sat up, wanting to flee this conversation. The stars came back and she felt woozy.

"Whoa," Liam said, pulling her against him. "Easy now."

She cuddled into him, glad for his strength, his warmth. "I don't know—about another doctor. It's expensive."

"I'll pay."

"I don't want you to have to."

"Besides cost, what's the reason?"

Cecily paused, thinking. She wasn't sure how to explain it, but she was just starting to process the idea that she only had a limited time left. She had her bucket list. She had Liam—in this moment. Thinking about a second opinion, or more treatments, scared her. She knew that sounded crazy. Who wouldn't want hope? But sometimes if she felt like she let hope in, and then was disappointed again, she might not survive it.

"Let's just try?" Liam's voice was soft. Honest. "Let's just *see* if there's a different treatment. If there's not, there's not. But at least we tried."

"What if it's all just false hope? The idea of seeing a new doctor. I don't know. I'll get my hopes up and then what…just to be told the first one had it right all along?"

"Doctors rarely agree on anything," Liam said. "My mother saw tons of them. For all kinds of ailments, including her addiction. Believe me, there's not always a consensus."

"But what if…they do have a treatment, but it doesn't work anyway? And it's painful and it makes me…sicker?" Cecily felt fear choke her. The idea of losing what little time she had left in bed, unable to move… It just made her feel hopeless. So helpless. She'd never seen herself as either. She was a planner, and she liked having a plan. Liked making the most of the time she had left. The idea of anything shortening that time terrified her.

"But what if there is a treatment and you can beat this thing?" he asked. She gently pulled away from him, meeting his gaze. In it, she saw all the hope he had, all the desire to prolong her life.

"But what if going to the doctor means that it

shortens what time I have left? Or at least, shortens the quality of the time I've got left? I don't want to lose *any* time."

"And you won't." Liam sounded so certain, but Cecily knew in life certainty didn't exist.

"Besides," she said, grasping for straws. "I don't even know any specialists."

Liam squirmed then, looking a little uncomfortable as he glanced out the windshield to the half-full parking lot. "I might know one. Dr. Kelly is an oncologist with a pretty impressive résumé. Groundbreaking studies, cutting-edge stuff."

"Really?" Cecily felt unease at the pit of her stomach.

"Yeah, and I *might* have made a call for you."

"You did? When?"

Liam wouldn't meet her gaze. "I know you've been hesitant to talk about second opinions, but I've been thinking. What if a second opinion meant that we had *more* time for the bucket list? If we had more time together?"

"Yeah, but what if it meant we had less?" She didn't want to risk what time she had left on unproven treatments that could make her worse. "If it's experimental, then it's not proven. It might make me worse, or...even kill me faster." She hated to admit that, but it was a real fear.

"Look, Dr. Kelly is the best of the best."

"You just happen to *know* the world's leading oncologist?"

"I have friends in high places." Liam shrugged.

"If you don't want to do this, I get it. But the office had a cancellation this week, and can get you in. Dr. Kelly is normally completely booked."

Cecily told herself *not* to be angry that Liam had been making calls to a doctor's office. He was only trying to help. Looking at his face, she knew this. Cecily let out a breath. Maybe Liam was right. Maybe she should get a second opinion. What could it hurt, really? Yes, she was scared that the doctor would tell her exactly what the last one did: that there was no hope. But wasn't she already trying to come to terms with that?

"And, look, if the doctor tells you there's no treatment, then I won't push you to find another doctor, okay?"

Cecily knew Liam wouldn't let this go. He never let anything go. It was one of his most infuriating and admirable traits.

"Okay," Cecily said. "I'll go to see your doctor friend. But on one condition?"

"Name it." He grinned.

"You're staying at my place tonight."

He leaned in. "I was already planning on it," he said, and kissed her so deeply that she nearly forgot why she'd been so stubbornly against a second opinion in the first place.

CHAPTER NINE

LATER THAT WEEK, Cecily sat in the waiting room of the expensive specialist's office in the Upper East Side, holding Liam's hand. She still couldn't believe she was here, about to see Dr. Kelly, the so-called legendary oncologist who had a typical waiting list of at least six months to get in, or so Liam had told her. The office almost had the feel of a spa, rather than a medical suite: a small bubbling fountain lined with smooth black rocks sat in the lobby, and the soothing sounds of instrumental music percolated from some hidden speakers. The expensive, modern white couches and armchairs in the waiting room looked better suited for a high-end hotel than a doctor's office.

"How do you know Dr. Kelly again?" Cecily asked, as she glanced at original modern artwork on the walls. She wondered how much the oversize paintings had cost.

"We went to grade school together and a bit of high school." Liam shrugged, noncommittal. "Lost touch a few years ago. You know how these things go."

Cecily quirked an eyebrow but said nothing. Grade school was supposedly where he'd learned French. She remembered that from him ordering in French at the fancy restaurant where they'd dined.

"Public or private grade school?"

"Actually, it was a private school," he said, sounding evasive. "Not far from here." The well-kept sidewalks outside, where they'd walked, had been lined with very expensive residences and high-end boutiques. "And we both spent freshman year together at Jordan Prep."

"Jordan Prep?" Cecily knew of that school. One of the most exclusive—and expensive—prep schools in New York.

"Yeah." Liam didn't meet her gaze, and Cecily got the impression he didn't want to talk about it. Just like he never wanted to talk about his past. An invisible wall would always come up, muting any hope at conversation. But the more Cecily learned about Liam, the more she suspected that he was a man full of secrets. She actually didn't know much about Liam, or his family, at all.

Just then, the door adjoining the front office staff opened, and a beautiful woman with sleek dark hair walked out, her skin like perfect porcelain, marred only by a few well-placed freckles on her nose. She looked like she ran marathons—as she swung open her slim, fit arms.

"Liam!" she cried. "Haven't seen or heard from you in years!"

"Hey, Rebecca." He stood and hugged the gorgeous doctor. "You look great."

The way Rebecca pressed herself against Liam's chest made it seem like she wanted to stay in that position permanently. Who the hell was this? Cecily wondered, temporarily confused. Rebecca wore a white doctor's coat, and that's when Cecily glanced down at the stitching on the left side. *Dr. Rebecca Kelly.* Wait a damn minute. *This* was Dr. Kelly? This amazing, gorgeous bombshell was *the world-famous oncologist*? Why hadn't Liam mentioned she was model-beautiful?

The good doctor then put both her hands in Liam's hair and mussed it.

"What happened to the buzz cut?" she cried, combing her fingers possessively through his dirty blond hair. That was when she noticed the signature sterling silver Tiffany bracelet and matching ring on her right hand. On her left, she wore a diamond-encrusted Rolex. Okay, so Dr. Kelly was doing well.

"Got tired of it. And I stopped playing football." He shrugged.

She laughed, deliberately giving him a flirty shove. "Figures. Whatever happened to you? You, like, disappeared after freshman year! Did you all move somewhere? There were all kinds of rumors—"

"They were just rumors," Liam said curtly. Rebecca backed off immediately, and the two old friends stared at each other a minute, and Cecily felt the need to clear her throat to remind them both she was still in the room. Liam's gaze darted to her face, and he quickly pivoted to include her in their little circle. "Rebecca, meet Cecily. She's why we're here."

Rebecca offered her hand for a shake, and Cecily almost flinched at her surprisingly cold palm against hers. Rebecca smiled, but Cecily didn't miss the quick sweep the woman did of Cecily's simple flowered sundress, the assessing look the doctor gave her. Did Rebecca see her as competition? Cecily wondered. Then, she almost laughed out loud. Why was she worried about whether or not Liam and Rebecca were involved? She was dying. It wasn't like she could expect Liam to be exclusive, not when she couldn't offer him more than a few months at best, before she got too sick to do much of anything.

"Glad to meet you, Cecily. Shall the two of us head to the exam room?"

"Liam can come with us. It's okay." She suddenly didn't want to be alone with Rebecca. The idea made her uneasy.

"You might have to undress," Rebecca pointed out, as she sent a not-so-subtle glance in Cecily's direction. Cecily wanted to tell the doctor that Liam had already seen her naked and up close, but she refrained. She didn't know the history of these two.

"It's okay," she reiterated.

"Fine, then," Rebecca said, brightly—almost too brightly.

Liam reached over and clasped Cecily's hand. The feel of his strong, warm fingers wrapped around her own soothed her. Who cared what Rebecca might or might not feel for Liam? This was a new hope at a treatment. And, probably, there wouldn't even *be* a treatment for her. Hadn't the doctors told her the cancer had spread too far, too fast? That there was little that chemotherapy would likely do, except make her sicker, weaker and die faster? This visit, Cecily reminded herself, was really just to help Liam feel better. To make him feel like he'd done all he could to save her. Because deep in her gut, she already knew, she couldn't be saved.

Yet, still, a nagging little hope festered in the core of her heart. No matter how much she told herself she was dying, that this was it, still that tiny flame remained. Maybe the doctors were wrong. Maybe things weren't that bad. With Liam by her side, she felt for the first time that maybe she *could* beat this thing.

Cecily sucked in a deep breath, telling herself she ought not to get her hopes up, that it was just as likely that this doctor would tell her the same as the last. Hope just made the disappointment later that much harder to bear. Hope was the worst kind of torture.

Liam squeezed her fingers and she glanced over at him as they walked down the narrow corridor of patient exam rooms. He smiled, and she felt the warmth of it in her toes. God, she was glad he was here. She couldn't imagine herself in this upscale office alone.

"Here we are," Rebecca chimed in, showing them

into an unmarked exam room with a dark, sleek door. She wondered how anyone told the difference between one door and another, and wondered if marking doors with numbers was just too tacky? Cecily walked into the relatively small exam room with the paper-covered recliner, and the elegant black leather chair nearby. The room had a single window that faced the trees lining Central Park. She glanced at the brochure sitting on the small countertop near the exam table. It read "Concierge Service," and Cecily wondered what that meant. She guessed concierge service was something only the very wealthy got from doctors.

"Please, have a seat." Rebecca nodded to the exam table. Cecily hopped up on it, and smoothed down her skirt. She felt strangely on display, her sandal-clad feet swinging. Liam took a seat nearby. Rebecca took the file from the small sleeve on the door and began thumbing through it. Then, she turned to the computer nearby and logged in.

Cecily glanced around the small room, looking for the hospital gown she usually needed to change into, but found none. "Should I change for an exam?" she asked, hand hovering near the strap of her sundress.

"You know what? I don't think that will be necessary after all for this visit," Rebecca said, shrugging. Cecily wondered about the change of heart. But decided not to press. Rebecca turned back to her computer. "I did look at the images you emailed me.

But, honestly, I'd like to take new scans. If you're up for doing these again, I can set up the appointment at my hospital and…"

"I'd rather not," Cecily said. All she could think about was the fact that she'd been laid off from her job and had no insurance. She couldn't afford another CT scan. It would come entirely out of her pocket, and right now, she needed every penny to keep her apartment. And what would a new scan really tell her? That the cancer had grown?

Rebecca glanced at Liam. "New scans would be better," she said.

"They're too expensive," Cecily said.

"Can we work with the old ones?" Liam asked, playing peacemaker.

"They'll have to do, I guess," Rebecca said, backing off. "Well, I did look at these scans, and while they're not the best quality, I can tell a few things. I take it that doctors have told you there's not a treatment they'd recommend."

"That's right. They said the cancer is too far gone, and that surgery can't get it all. Chemo and radiation might give me a little more time, but I'd feel sicker. And the chemo and radiation wouldn't save me in the end."

"Right." Rebecca nodded and studied the screen in front of her. Then, she looked up, taking a deep breath. "The bad news is that he's largely right. The medical protocols as they are now mean that there aren't many viable treatment options for you."

"Is there anything you can do?" Liam asked.

Rebecca focused her attention on him. "Well, the *good* news is, a colleague of mine in Japan is doing cutting-edge fluorescence imaging surgery. It's not approved in the US, but the technique basically lights cancer cells up, so surgeons can remove the tumor more efficiently, without ruining the liver. The preliminary results are promising. But…"

"But what's the bad news?" Liam asked.

"Well, no US health insurance is going to cover an experimental surgery in Tokyo. There's also the cost of getting there, and then recovering there, of course." Rebecca clicked her mouse on her computer screen and a website, all in Japanese, came up. Dr. Nimura, it seemed, was the lead surgeon on the procedure. "But Dr. Nimura is the very best. And she's probably your best shot."

"How much are we talking here?" Liam asked. Cecily almost didn't want to know. She only had about twenty-five thousand in her 401(k), and she'd been planning on using that to live out what time she had left.

"Easily two hundred thousand." Rebecca glanced down at the folder on her lap. "Maybe more."

"More?" Cecily squeaked. That was much more than she had.

"You're saying maybe a quarter of a million dollars?"

"Easily." Rebecca shrugged, as if money didn't matter. But then again, she was an oncologist in a very wealthy neighborhood. Cecily was sure that maybe to her, it wasn't that large an amount.

"And there's no way insurance could cover it?" Liam asked.

Cecily already knew the answer to that. She'd already spent hours on the phone arguing about co-pays with her insurance company and that was after seeing doctors in her own network, in New Jersey, not halfway around the world. And that was *before* she'd been dropped.

"I don't have insurance, anyway," she pointed out.

"We could get you on mine," Liam suggested. And then she wondered what that meant. How would she become his dependent? Rebecca frowned, shaking her head.

"Wouldn't matter," she said. "No. Insurance companies aren't going to cover surgery in Japan. It's an unproven treatment in the United States."

"How successful is it in Japan?"

"Very promising so far." She stood, opened a cabinet above her head and pulled out a medical journal. Cecily glanced at the cover and saw the promise of the surgery plastered across its front page. She felt a little bit of hope rise in her chest. Could this be it? Could this surgery actually work when her other doctor said surgery was impossible? She wasn't sure what to think.

"What happens if it doesn't work?" Liam asked. She glanced at him, surprised he'd ask such a pointed question.

"There are risks. Like progressive liver failure," Rebecca said.

Cecily knew what that meant. It meant death. Maybe in days. Maybe in weeks. But death, all the same. Was she willing to trade in the months she had left on the hope the treatment might work? She wasn't sure. That was the honest truth.

"But this is your only shot, in my opinion," Rebecca said.

"Her only choices are a risky surgery or nothing?" Liam asked.

"A risky—and expensive surgery," Cecily pointed out.

"All surgeries are expensive," Rebecca said sharply, glancing at Cecily as if she were slow. Cecily didn't appreciate the sidelong glance, or her tone, for that matter. "There is no guarantee it works, but it might. And *maybe* is a better answer right now than *definitely* not. With Cecily's condition, there's very little to be done. It might not work, but what do you have to lose?"

"That's all well and good, but I don't have that kind of money." Even if Cecily cashed in her 401(k), she'd still be short.

"Liam might be able to help you with that, I imagine," Rebecca offered.

Liam frowned at her. What the hell did she mean? That Liam just had a few hundred thousand dollars lying around?

"Let's not talk about that," Liam said, voice low

and gruff. Rebecca raised a slender eyebrow in surprise but fell silent.

"Well, I can give you Dr. Nimura's contact information. You can follow up with her and she can tell you if you're a good candidate for the surgery or not. How about that? You can argue about how you're going to take care of that bill later."

Liam left the doctor's office feeling as if he was carrying a four-ton elephant on his back. Of course, it would all come down to money. Hadn't he learned growing up in one of the wealthiest families in Manhattan that money both caused—and solved—almost all problems? He felt anger bristle the back of his neck. He vowed never to ask his family for a dime. Not after he'd seen them try to tear each other apart over it. He knew the evils of greed, knew how it could destroy families, and he'd walked away from it because he believed, in his heart of hearts, that money corrupted people. Money made people forget their humanity. Turned them into greedy monsters.

And now here was Cecily next to him, pensively biting her lower lip, the most perfect, most beautiful woman he'd ever met, and a quarter million dollars might just save her life. How could he or anyone else put a price on a human life? He wished there was another way. Something else. Why did it have to come down to money?

"Are you okay?" Cecily asked, blue eyes bright as they left the doctor's office and made their way to the elevator. The hem of her flowered sundress fluttered as she walked, distracting him with flashes of her leg above the knee.

"Just have a lot on my mind," Liam said, noncommittal. That was the understatement of the year. How could he tell her that with a mere phone call to his half brother, he might get the funds to save her life? Except, he knew there'd be strings attached, there always were. And that was if for the first time in his life Wilder did the right thing. Then what? He hated that he even struggled with this decision. It should be a no-brainer. He ought to just call Wilder and ask to borrow the money.

But after calling him a son of a bitch and telling him he hoped he rotted in hell, the chances were probably slim he'd agree to it anyway.

And Wilder would be the only one, he knew in his gut, who'd likely be able to come up with that kind of cash on short notice. His mother probably didn't have the cash. She was perpetually broke. Liam's twin brother, Stuart, and older brother, Seth, were hardly better. Seth was on his yacht halfway around the world spending everything he got from the trust on fuel, and then there was Stuart, and who knew what he was up to lately. Spending money as fast as he got it. Plus, neither brother was happy with him for always siding against Wilder.

There was one sure way to get cash, but Liam didn't want to think about it, didn't even want to consider it. He wasn't going to ask Wilder for a thing.

Not now. Not ever. And he shouldn't have to. If his father's will hadn't been amended right before his death, then Liam would have had the funds to help Cecily. He wouldn't need to beg and borrow to do it. Old resentments flared in his chest.

The elevator dinged, announcing its arrival at the lobby.

"Are you going to say anything?" Cecily asked him.

Say what? That if his backstabbing half brother hadn't stolen his father's money, then he could simply write her a check and send her to Japan and save her life?

"I'm sorry. I'm distracted. That's not fair to you." Cecily didn't deserve his pity party. She deserved his attention. He reached out and grabbed her hand. She took it.

"What's wrong?" she asked.

"Nothing." He didn't want to talk about it. "How are you? What did you think of the experimental surgery?"

"It's too expensive."

"If we could get the money?"

"You planning on robbing a bank?" She laughed at her own joke, and slowly shook her head. "Even if we did win the lottery somehow, I just… I don't know if the surgery is the right thing to do." She bit her lip, glancing up at him with her clear, cornflower blue eyes. They reached the bottom floor and the elevator doors slid open. The two walked out to the lobby, lingering near the door. "That's my honest answer."

"But it might help you," he said, and reached out and touched her shoulder. "This might save your life."

"I can't afford it, Liam." She shook her head. "Where am I going to get that kind of money? Even if I cash in my retirement savings, it won't be enough." She swallowed, hard. "And I need that money. If—when—I need to go to hospice."

That was the very last thing Liam even wanted to think about. Hospice? That was a place where they made the dying as comfortable as they could. No way.

"You have hope now. You might not need hospice."

"It's a Hail Mary pass and you know it."

"It's something. We have to try," Liam offered.

"So you're saying you have the money? You just have a couple of hundred grand just lying around?"

He paused, his chest feeling tight. "No. But…"

"But what?"

He could tell her about his family right now. But the words lodged in his throat. Cecily clutched her bag and hurried out, her body tense as she headed for the lobby door. Liam found himself chasing her out to Sixty-Fifth Street.

"Cecily, wait." He reached out to grab her arm as she sped ahead of him on the sidewalk. She whirled.

"I don't get you."

"What do you mean?"

"I mean, you promised to be honest with me, but you're not. You think we can somehow magically get a couple of hundred thousand dollars. You went to a fancy private school on the Upper East Side? And you hang out in dive bars in New Jersey? What's the deal?"

"There's no deal."

Hurt flickered across Cecily's eyes. "So much for being honest."

Dammit. "Look. It's a long story."

"That you don't want to tell me."

"It's not that I don't want to tell you…" He stopped. That was another lie. He didn't want Cecily to know the truth because he didn't want her to look at him any differently. He didn't want to see the expression on her face when she realized he walked away from millions. Everyone was sympathetic until they realized just how many zeroes were involved. Women, men, everyone judged him and usually found him wanting. Or crazy. Few people thought he'd made the right decision. He didn't want to see Cecily's disappointment.

The hurt in her eyes blazed at him. He didn't want to hurt her anymore, either. She hurried away from him now, toward Central Park.

"Cecily, wait…"

"It's fine if you don't want to tell me. You don't owe me anything."

He caught up to her, jumping in front of her. She

had no choice but to stop. She let out a frustrated breath. "Stop saying that. I'm trying to help."

"And…and I appreciate it. But…this surgery. It sounds great. But there's no way I can afford it. I don't live in *this* neighborhood." She spread her arms wide to encompass the Upper East Side.

"I don't, either."

"But you used to."

Liam let out a frustrated sigh. "Yeah. I used to."

"Are you going to tell me who you are? Because you're not just some roofer from New Jersey. I'm not dumb. Tell me the truth."

He realized then that he did owe her the truth, no matter how painful that truth might be. He'd promised to be honest. He needed to honor that promise. He owed her that much.

"I'm Liam Lange, as in Lange Communications."

"Wait." She tried to process the new information, as both hands flew to her temples. "Lange Communications, as in, They Own Everything Communications?"

As if to drive home the point, a big white cable utility truck with Lange Communications blazed across the side lumbered down Sixty-Fifth Street. One of this half brother's new expansions of his ever-growing empire. That didn't even cover the fact that the company also owned at least half the magazines at the newsstand across the street. He frowned.

"Yeah." He felt a deep heat at the back of his neck, as he always did when he talked about the family business. The business Wilder stole. "Remember when I told you that there was a fight in my family over money?"

Cecily nodded, still looking a little dumbstruck.

"Well, the fight was over a lot of money. And Wilder won. He's my half brother."

"The playboy? The guy always dating new pop stars?" Cecily began walking again, and Liam followed. He shoved his hands in his pockets.

"Yeah, the same. Although, I heard he settled down with someone. I don't know much about what he does now. I don't talk to Wilder anymore. And my mother is only interested because it could be someone else to dilute whatever money is left in the company. That's why I walked away. I was offered a job, but I didn't want it. All I kept was a seat on the board. I wanted a vote, at least."

"I see." Cecily had grown quiet. It was just what Liam had been afraid of. That she'd judge him poorly. "I just… I didn't put two and two together. I knew the name Lange, but I just never thought…"

"My half brother was a billionaire."

Cecily glanced up at him. "Never occurred to me."

"He offered me millions, to pay me off, for that seat. But I didn't take it. I wanted him to have to look me in the face."

"I see." She seemed to be mulling over all the new information. It was a lot to process, no doubt. But he worried that she'd be like most of the other women who'd walked in and out of his life. They never understood why he didn't just take the money.

"Do you see me differently now?" he asked her.

"No," she said. "But it explains a lot." She reached out and took his hand as they walked down the sidewalk.

"Like what?"

"Like how your mom could afford Persian cats. And how you knew which fork to use at that fancy restaurant. And how you learned French in elementary school. That especially has been bugging me." She glanced up at him, a teasing smile tugging at the corners of her pink lips, her blue eyes bright with mirth.

"Really? *That's* what you think about when I tell you I walked away from a fortune?"

"Yeah." She giggled, looking up at him through her thick lashes.

"You're not going to tell me that I'm crazy?" he asked. "You don't think that I should've worked it out? It's a lot of money I walked away from."

Cecily shrugged. "Look, my whole family thought I was crazy for leaving Ohio and heading to Manhattan. They thought I'd get murdered. Or would go broke. Or both. Sometimes, if you don't fit somewhere, you leave. Even if that means leaving a family. Even if that means turning down a fortune."

As she stared at him, the sunlight hitting her golden hair and making it shine, he knew he'd never seen a woman more beautiful than her. She always tried to see the best in everyone, including him. To hear her talk, she was a hero. Not the villain. It was a welcome relief. As the wind ruffled her golden waves, a bolt of desire rushed right through him. He had the urge to take her straight home to his bed.

"That's not how most people think."

Cecily tightened her grip on his hand. "I'm not most people."

"Ain't that the truth."

Liam glanced up and saw a sign pointing the way to a path that would take them to the Central Park Zoo. "If you want to hear more about my family, maybe we should head to the zoo. They're more dangerous than any grizzly bear or snow leopard."

"Are they really that bad?"

He chuckled a little. "You have no idea. It's amazing they didn't eat me when I was young."

Cecily wrinkled her nose. "Ew."

"You're the one who wanted to hear about my family."

"Maybe I'm regretting that decision," Cecily teased as she laced her delicate fingers in his.

"Oh, you definitely will regret hearing about the dysfunctional Langes. Come on, you." He led her down the path. He tried to figure out just *what* to tell her about his backward childhood, about how everyone loved money, but few people loved each other. But the worst of it all, if he were honest with himself, was that the worst regret he had right at this moment, was not having a Lange bank account that could cover Cecily's surgery. He'd never missed money before now.

He entwined his fingers with her, as they headed into Central Park and wondered what he was going to do about making sure he got that money. He'd have to figure out a way.

CHAPTER TEN

CECILY HELD LIAM'S hand as they walked through the Central Park Zoo, meandering their way through the small crowd of tourists that bunched together around the sea lion exhibit, watching the animals lounge on rocks and dive into their glassed-in pool. Above them, the late afternoon sun sank closer to the horizon, and the sky was perfectly blue, with barely a cloud in it. It was an abnormally cool June day, a breeze making the afternoon feel particularly welcoming.

But all Cecily could think about was Liam's bombshell news. She'd no idea he was related to *those* Langes. Lange Communications touched nearly every household in America.

"So why didn't you tell me about your family before?" she asked him, as they both watched a sea lion swim past, seeming to grin at them both as he glided along the glass. She pressed her hand against the glass, awed by the quick, graceful animal.

"It's the kind of news that usually doesn't go over

very well." The loud bark of a sea lion claiming one of the high rocks above them caught their attention. Liam frowned at the big guy making a show of owning the rock. "Besides, my half brother, Wilder, is a lot like that guy." He nodded in the direction of the fat sea lion, who nudged another lion trying to claim the top rock out of the way. The animal bellowed again, mouth open wide in a defensive stance.

"He wanted to be king of the hill?" Cecily asked.

"Yeah. King of everything." Liam sighed. "When my father died, I was still a kid, barely a teenager. Wilder was much older. He took over the family business, cut most everyone else out."

"How could he do that?" Cecily looked appalled.

"My father wasn't there to stop him. And my mother tried to fight him. But she had a drinking problem that just got worse when my father died. And Wilder said there was a new will. The court found it valid, but then, Wilder could afford better attorneys."

"That's awful."

"Yeah, but the worst part is, my mother didn't want to let it go. She's still fighting him. My brothers are trying to stay neutral. Wilder bribes them with gifts and money—it's less than they deserve, but they don't care. They're fine with that."

"But not you."

"I had to withdraw from high school. There was no more money to pay my tuition. No college fund, either. There would have been *if* I'd kissed Wilder's ass harder. *If* I'd signed away my seat on the board. Everything came with strings. I didn't feel like being tied up by them."

"That's terrible." Cecily remembered Rebecca's line of questioning. How she'd asked him what happened to him after ninth grade. "What was it like? Leaving high school?"

"Embarrassing. I still remember the looks of pity and derision. Some people knew why I left. Others didn't."

"Like Rebecca," Cecily said.

"Exactly. It was just too embarrassing. I told everyone we were moving. It seemed easier. And it wasn't exactly a lie. Mom couldn't afford her penthouse anymore. She'd sold the furniture out of it, but eventually there was nothing else to sell. Wilder took it all over then, bought it out from under her. We did have to move to a cramped apartment in Brooklyn."

Cecily could see the pain in Liam's face, and could only imagine what it must have been like to grow up wealthy, with every advantage, only to have all of them stripped away without warning.

"Why didn't Wilder help?" Cecily asked. She didn't want to believe the worst in people. She always wanted to think there was more to the story.

"I don't know. He hated me? Hated my mom?"

"What did you do after Wilder turned his back on you?"

"I graduated from a local public school. Took a

few college classes, but, honestly, the tuition was too much. I'd been working summers helping a local roofer named David Garcia. He took me under his wing, made sure I got the training I needed. He was more a parent to me than my parents were. And now I work honestly, for everything I get."

Cecily was suddenly grateful for the man.

"And the more I worked with my hands, the more I understood the value of money. And I knew that too much of it, well, it just corrupts people. Makes them crazy."

They walked away from the sea lions then, and toward the grizzly bear exhibit.

"So you didn't want to challenge Wilder? If he was wrong, then…"

"You'd need an army of lawyers to do it," Liam said. "And my mother…well, she decided it was best not to fight him directly, and to try to outmaneuver him. Keep her seat on the board. Play her games."

"And you?"

"I kept my seat on the board out of principle. I felt like Wilder was trying to bribe me to give it up, but I wasn't going to."

"I get it. I think there's something noble in that." She paused, considering.

"Is there? I mean, I'm broke." Liam laughed then. Cecily tucked her arm in his.

"Everything you earn is yours. And you don't owe anything to anyone. That's something to be proud of."

"Well, I know Wilder and my other brothers think I've…fallen. That I'm lower than my potential."

"Why? Because they had everything handed to them? You've made your own way. There's no shame in that."

He flashed a grateful smile that made her belly warm. If possible, she was falling deeper in—like? love?—with Liam right at that moment. Could she be falling for this man she'd just met? Yet, she couldn't help but admire that he had principles. That he stood by them, even at great personal cost. That he wanted to live his life a particular way, and had done it, even if that path was scary and uncertain. She thought about all the many kinds of people she'd met in her life and she knew they wouldn't have had the courage to do what Liam had. To walk away from a fortune because he thought it was the right thing to do.

"You know," Cecily said, as they walked along the winding concrete path, the sun moving closer to the horizon and their shadows growing longer. "You might be one of the bravest people I've met."

Liam just laughed. "Brave? How so?"

"Because you didn't just talk about the right thing. You did it. Even if it was scary and new and terrifying. You did it."

Liam shook his head. "I'm just a stubborn SOB. That's all."

"You're more than that."

Cecily turned to face Liam, his strong jaw, his determined brown eyes. He wasn't just stubborn. He was something special. And Cecily knew it right in that moment. The words *I love you* bubbled up in her throat, wanting to leap out into the air, but she caught them just in time. She couldn't get attached. It would be crazy. She couldn't offer him what he deserved: a future.

She didn't want to think of any of that right now, so she pushed that awful thought away. She just wanted to live in the moment. That was all. She didn't want to think about tomorrow. Didn't want to think about experimental treatments for cancer or any of it. All she wanted to do was think about his hand covering hers, and the whole evening ahead of them. How she couldn't wait to get into his bed once more, because that was the only way she knew of to truly turn her brain off, to lose her worries beneath the careful attention of his expert hands and mouth.

She saw a stand selling ice cream and tugged him over to it, eager for a distraction. "Ice cream?"

"You read my mind."

"Chocolate?" she asked.

"Is there anything else as good?" Liam teased, brown eyes looking almost amber in the late afternoon sunlight. He ordered two chocolate soft serves and handed her a cone and then took his. The two lapped at their cones as they headed on to the bear exhibit. The bear was lounging on one of his rocks, napping in the sun.

"He looks comfy," Cecily noted, licking the sweet

chocolate and trying to savor the moment. In the sun with Liam, she felt like any other girl on a fantastic date. Just a normal girl, having a normal date, in a completely normal life. With the most extraordinary man she'd ever met, she reminded herself. Gorgeous, brave and serious, a man who didn't take things lightly. And she appreciated that. Admired it.

"Easy to rest when you're at the top of the food chain," Liam noted. He tackled his ice cream with gusto, and Cecily remembered the night before. How ravenous he'd been for her body—all her body. The thought made her belly grow warm as they walked. A small toddler wandered over to the bear exhibit in front of them, pressing his face against the glass. The parents, busy with trying to strap in his younger infant sister into a baby carrier, had their backs turned. The toddler, wearing a check white-and-blue shirt, ambled over to them, stopping in front of Cecily.

"Ice cream?" he asked, hopeful, raising two pudgy hands toward her cone.

"Oh, I'm sorry, this is mine," she said, just as the dad realized his son had wandered away.

"So sorry," he said, whisking his toddler son into his arms.

"It's no trouble," Cecily said, shrugging. "It's hard to resist ice cream."

The dad gave her a grateful smile. Liam tightened his grip on Cecily's hand as she watched the family move away. She might never have a family of her own. It hit her, suddenly, as these thoughts do. She was still dealing with her own grief about her diagnosis, and these terribly dark thoughts popped up without warning. Suddenly, she felt bone-tired and a little bit dizzy.

"I think I need to sit down," she told Liam, whose brow instantly furrowed with worry.

"You okay?"

"Yeah," she managed as Liam steered her to an empty bench nearby. "Just tired." Suddenly, she didn't have much of an appetite to finish her cone. She tossed what was left of the bottom of the cone into a nearby trash.

"Dizzy like last time?" he asked.

"Just a little. But…" She glanced about, getting her bearings. No stars clouded her vision. She wouldn't faint. Not this time. "Maybe I just need to rest a second."

Was her strength already starting to falter? Was the cancer already catching up to her, choking her body? She didn't want it to be this soon. She didn't want to face the reality. Not yet.

"Let's sit, then." He took a seat next to her and held her hand. He ate the last bit of his cone, and sat next to her, his attention focused like a laser on her. "You're sure you're okay?"

"I just always wanted kids," she said, nodding at the retreating family, the toddler pointing at a nearby balloon vendor.

"Maybe you can still have them."

"Come on." A rueful laugh escaped her lips. "Be serious."

"I am. Maybe, with this experimental surgery… Maybe you will."

"I can't afford it. And neither can you." Hurt clouded Liam's eyes for a moment. Instantly, Cecily felt like she'd said exactly the wrong thing. "I'm sorry. I didn't mean it like that. *No* one has that kind of money."

"I know someone who does." A muscle twitched in the side of Liam's jaw.

"You can't be serious. You can't seriously be thinking of asking your brother."

"Half brother," Liam corrected.

"You don't have to ask him. You promised yourself you wouldn't, right? That you wouldn't go back to the family? You stood by your principles."

"Right," Liam said, squeezing her hand. "But suddenly principles seem pretty cold and lonely."

"You don't have to for me," she said. "We don't even know if the experimental surgery would actually work. It's experimental."

Liam glanced at her, brown eyes serious. "I could ask him. See if—"

"No." Cecily squeezed Liam's hand. "No. Absolutely not. I won't let you do this." She didn't want to see Liam betray his own principles, or to see him beg for something from someone who'd hurt him and his family so much. "We can find another way."

She wasn't at all sure they could, but she couldn't ask Liam to make this kind of sacrifice for her.

"Maybe," Liam said, not quite convinced. "Maybe."

"You know, this doesn't have to be your fight."

Liam glanced sharply at her. "What are you talking about?"

"You don't owe me anything."

"I know I don't. I just want you to *live*, okay? Is that so wrong?" The way he said it, exaggerated, made her almost want to laugh. Except nothing about this was funny.

"Do you have a thing for lost causes or something?" she asked him, trying for a joke, but even to her ears, it came out sounding a bit lame.

"No," he said, dark eyes serious. "I've got a thing for *you*."

She glanced up then, sharply, and saw no guile in his expression. He was serious. She felt rooted to the spot then, struck speechless. Things felt so serious suddenly. And could she even do serious now?

"You just met me."

"I know you better than you think," he said. "And I think you're incredibly brave."

"How do you know? Maybe lying in the fetal position is what I do in my free time?"

Liam chuckled, flashing his even white teeth. "No, it's not. You're fierce. Why else would you burst into that dive bar?"

"Because I was moody and desperate, and because maybe *that* was my version of a pity party."

"Well, I'm glad you decided to come inside." He met her gaze and pulled her close for a kiss. Their lips met, and in that moment Cecily forgot all her worries. Forgot about pity parties and the lack of children in her future, and the experimental surgery, and everything else. When Liam kissed her, she felt like maybe, just maybe, everything would somehow work out.

CHAPTER ELEVEN

TWO DAYS LATER, Liam stood in the glassy penthouse office of the Lange family's attorney, Maria Moreno, of Leisten and Moreno and Associates, glancing at the gorgeous view of the Brooklyn Bridge out her window. Maria, who'd turned fifty that year, had finally started to gray, with a silver streak through her otherwise jet-black hair. She wore little makeup except for a slash of red lipstick. Her appearance was, as usual, impeccable. She wore her tailored black suit and matching sensible pumps and a string of white pearls.

As always, she looked ready for a courtroom or a funeral. Liam couldn't even imagine the woman in jeans. He'd never seen her in anything other than Brooks Brothers. It's no wonder Wilder liked her so much, Liam thought. This woman was a bulldog about details, and sharp as a tack.

Her light brown eyes studied him now, and he could almost see the calculations happening behind them, even as she kept her face stoic and unreadable.

She cleared her throat as she steepled her fingers on her glass desk that sported only a closed laptop.

"I'm surprised to see you," she told Liam.

"Not as surprised as me."

An amused smile tugged at the corners of Maria's mouth. She barely broke character even to acknowledge the joke.

Liam felt jittery as he sat in the black leather chair in front of her desk. His right knee bobbed with a life of its own, fueled by nerves.

"How long has it been?"

"A long time." Liam couldn't remember the last time he'd seen Maria. Probably at Wilder's flat, probably when he'd drawn up those papers asking Liam to sign away any future stake in Lange Communications along with his board seat. That had been a dark day. Liam had told Wilder to go to hell. Then he'd stormed out. He'd never asked for a dime, but then again, he'd never promised not to sue for his share, either.

"I hope you don't mind, but I invited Seth to this meeting." Maria looked to the door. "Seth? You can come in now."

At that cue, a door nearby swung open, and Liam's older brother, Seth, strode out, looking tanned and healthy. Happy, even. Liam supposed living on a yacht and sailing around the world probably did go a long way to improving one's mood.

"Seth." He grinned, happy to see his older brother, though feeling a little guarded. "Forgiven me yet?"

"Never was mad at you, brother," Seth said.

"Is that why you've been giving me the silent treatment?" Liam said. It had been about a year since they'd last talked on the phone.

Seth just shrugged. "I was giving you your space. *You* were the one who was pissed at *us* if I recall. And phones work both ways, brother."

Liam guessed he was right. He'd been ticked off after Seth and Stuart voted against him and Mom in their last-ditch effort to muster enough support for a board vote of no confidence in Wilder as CEO, and get him out of Lange Communications for good. He hadn't expected them to take his request seriously. He'd assumed they were pissed.

"So what are you doing here?" Liam asked.

"Trying to look after my little brother." Seth grinned, and the two embraced in a tight, quick hug. "I'm not in town long. Maria reached out, and I was around, so I came."

Liam frowned. "Are you sure it was Maria who called you?" Liam suspected it was actually Wilder. Seth took Wilder's side early in the inheritance battle. They'd always been close, especially since Wilder had helped him come out of the closet. Liam got it. He'd realized that was a tough time for his brother, but Liam had always thought Seth had it covered. Seth didn't need his help. Plus, he'd been twelve at the time. Not much a twelve-year-old could do, one way or another.

"Wilder might have mentioned it." Seth shrugged.

"But I'm here because you want to talk, and Wilder wants to listen."

The way Seth said it rubbed Liam the wrong way, as if Liam ought to be grateful that he'd get an audience from his half brother, the dictator, the one who demanded everyone lick his boots. "Am I supposed to be grateful?"

"Yeah. You did tell him to go to hell, and not in a nice way."

"I know." Liam knew the shouting match hadn't been his finest moment. But he'd been young then, hot-tempered, and still nursing grudges. Come to think of it, little had changed since then, if he were honest. "Look, I just want to sell him my damn seat and be done with it."

Seth and Maria exchanged glances. It seemed the two spoke volumes in a single look.

"You're serious about this? You really are here to reconsider your brother's proposal?" Maria looked amused. No doubt, she thought he'd finally seen the error of his ways. Finally gotten tired of earning an honest dollar.

"Half brother. And…yes. I am." God, it sounded like he was waving the white flag of surrender. Seth studied him, growing quiet. Maria cocked her head to one side. He hated this. Hated even being here. It went against every single thing he stood for. But, he reminded himself, being in Maria's office was better than seeing his half brother again. He never wanted to see Wilder. Not ever. That was why Liam chose to talk to Maria. He hoped he might simply be able to send a message to Wilder through her. Neat and clean, and without having to worry about trying to keep his temper in check.

"Why now?" Seth asked.

"None of anybody's business," Liam said, biting off the last word.

"Friendly as ever, I see," Maria murmured, so softly Liam almost didn't hear. He didn't care if she or anyone else thought he was rough around the edges. He wasn't here to make anybody feel good. He was here to get money for Cecily's surgery.

Maria and Seth again looked at one another. God, maybe this was a mistake. Then he thought about Cecily's beautiful face.

"Is he still interested in my seat on the board or not?" Liam asked.

"I do not know, to be honest." Maria gave a little shrug. "So much has changed at the company since he offered to buy your seat."

"I know." His own mother had called him out of the blue a year or so ago, saying that it was vital he vote to oust Wilder. Liam hadn't even thought twice about it. He'd cast his vote without a second thought. It was one of the reasons he'd refused to sell his seat on the board. He could've used the money. Oh, could he have used it. But he hadn't wanted the many millions Wilder had offered him back then. He hadn't wanted a dime. All he wanted was the tiny little bit of power that his father had given him and Wilder hadn't managed to wrest away from him. The seat was the only part of his inheritance that was left. But now, with Cecily's life potentially on the line, he didn't care about keeping Wilder in check. Besides, his one measly vote hadn't mattered in the end, anyway. Wilder got what he wanted.

"Maybe he's not interested anymore," Maria suggested. "Or maybe he'll offer less."

"Oh, he's interested," Seth said. Liam was suddenly grateful for the honesty. At least Seth didn't a hundred percent take Wilder's side on everything. It was good to know. "If Liam signs, that means he also gives up the right to sue for future earnings. I assume that would be in the fine print of the deal."

Maria frowned at Seth. Liam guessed he wasn't supposed to mention that, even though Liam hadn't forgotten. The fear of Liam bringing a costly lawsuit was something Wilder would definitely want to avoid.

"So Wilder hasn't changed, then. It's always about money for him." Liam wasn't sure why he was surprised. Money always did all the talking with Wilder Lange.

"You've always been too hard on him," Seth chided. "He saved the company."

"From what? From being run by *all* of us?"

Seth shook his head. "He's done the best he can by the family. He tried to do the best by you."

Liam thought about him getting kicked out of private school. Of the humiliation of leaving midyear his freshman year, holed up in the penthouse, where little by little, his mother sold things like furniture and jewelry to pay for food and booze.

"Where was his care when I had to withdraw from Jordan Prep?"

"He tried to help you with that."

Liam let out a sour laugh. "You mean he tried to corner a fourteen-year-old boy and get him to sign away what inheritance he did have in order to go to school."

Seth sighed. "You know he was afraid Mom would use you against him. He had to make sure that didn't happen. He wanted to care for you. Wanted you to graduate school."

"Only if I agreed to do whatever he wanted." Liam shook his head, bitterly remembering feeling taken advantage of. "I was *fourteen*. Mom at least saved me from making that mistake. If she hadn't come home, hadn't broke up that meeting, I would've signed everything away."

"Look, if you just would talk to Wilder. He can explain. Really. He's not a bad guy. He's done the best he can."

Right. Sure. Liam couldn't believe how brainwashed Seth had become. "Listen, I know you and he are close, but we're not ever going to be close," Liam said. "Either he wants this seat or he doesn't."

"He has control of the board already," Maria said, almost trying to sound bored. "He's made alliances.

You know that, just from you and your mother's stunt last year."

Maria took a seat behind her large desk, arms resting softly on the armrests. She glanced at Seth, who frowned, ever so slightly.

"You have to admit it's tough to ask Wilder a favor when you tried to steal the company away from him last year," Seth said.

"I wasn't stealing anything. Mom needed my vote, so I gave it to her, end of story."

"What if she needs your vote again?" Seth asked, as he perched on the edge of Maria's desk and crossed his thick arms.

Liam stared out the window to the Brooklyn Bridge beyond and for the briefest of moments, wondered if was doing the right thing or making a huge mistake.

"Clearly, my vote didn't really help her last time. Probably won't the next time, either."

"Then, why did you cast it?" Seth asked.

"To get under Wilder's skin." There was some satisfaction in that, at least.

"Maybe you succeeded a little bit too much at that," Maria said, rearranging a stack of papers on her desk. "Maybe he'll remember the insurrection and hold you accountable for it."

"Insurrection? What is he? A monarch? Of course, I'm sure he thinks he is." Still, Liam felt a little bit of panic rise in his throat. He hadn't thought that Wilder would be petty enough to turn down Liam's offer out of spite. He just assumed his half brother was the same power-crazed narcissist he always had been. If he wasn't interested in the seat, then Liam had no bargaining power. No way to get the money he needed for Cecily's surgery. Unless he begged.

Maria just smiled, but the expression didn't reach her eyes. "Why are you looking to sell now?" Maria asked, light brown eyes sharp.

"That's none of your business. Or his." He wasn't going to bring Cecily into the backstabbing world of the Lange family.

"He'll want to know," Maria prodded.

"Debts? Spend too much?" Seth studied Liam. Liam glared back.

"No. Nothing like that. What kind of loser do you think I am?"

"It's not what I think that matters," Seth said. "It's what Wilder is going to think. You know these are questions he'll ask."

Maria quirked one dark eyebrow, intrigued. "He'll want to know," she repeated.

"He doesn't get to know. Either he's interested or he's not. I just need to know if he'll honor the old deal." Liam suddenly wanted to leave. He needed to get out of there. His knee bobbed again. He wished he wasn't so nervous. Wished he never had to do this. But it was for Cecily. All for Cecily.

"I'll call him," Maria said. "And then we'll let you know."

"Tell him he has to decide by Friday," Liam said,

standing. Forty-eight hours should be plenty of time. He headed for the door, not waiting for Maria or Seth to respond. He couldn't wait to get out of her sterile office, couldn't wait to get to the fresh air outside. His heart was thumping as he headed straight for the stairwell, not caring about walking the twenty flights down. He just needed to get out of there. He wasn't sure if he hoped Wilder offered him the money, or told him to go to hell. Then he remembered perfect Cecily. She needed that money. Period. And he'd do whatever he had to in order to get it.

He glanced at his phone and realized that he should get a move on if he was going to get to Cecily's apartment on time. He promised her one more item off her bucket list this afternoon, and he couldn't wait to see her face when she saw the surprise.

"Horses?" Cecily managed, her jaw dropping, as Liam steered his pickup to the stable in Woodland Hills, New Jersey. "Are you kidding me?" Cecily felt her face glow as she saw the big barn in the distance. "How did you manage to find this place?"

"I've got my sources," Liam said, an amused grin on his face. "Actually, I did roof work a few years back. The barn and the house."

"You did?" She glanced up at the huge barn and the big white two-story farmhouse next to it. "That's a lot of roof."

"I know." Liam parked the truck and then hopped out, walking around to open her door, but she was already out of it before he could get there. She felt like she was ten again, a girl buzzing with excitement and her whole life ahead of her. Liam brought that feeling to her, and she was suddenly so grateful for him. She reached out and grabbed his hand, tugging him to the front door of the barn and office, an old wooden structure, complete with extra wide porch and rocking chairs out front. She felt like she'd stepped into the Old West.

She couldn't believe how excited she was about the prospect of riding a horse. She'd never done that before, and it had been a dream of hers since she was a little girl and used to sleep beneath pink horse sheets, back when she liked to draw unicorns on her school folders, and now here she was in an actual barn.

They were barely inside the door when a tanned, dark-haired middle-aged man came out to great them.

"Liam! Good to see you, man," he said, shaking Liam's hand.

"And you, Carlos," he said, smiling. "We still good for that trail ride today?"

Carlos laughed a little, showing even white teeth. "Sure thing. It's been a few years for you. You sure you remember how?"

"Ha. Funny." Liam rolled his eyes.

Cecily quirked an eyebrow as she studied Liam. "You know how to ride?"

"A little."

Carlos gave him a playful punch in the arm. "He's being modest for no reason," Carlos said. "He grew up with horses. His father owned many."

"You owned horses?" Cecily couldn't believe it. She knew Liam came from a wealthy family—whose father built a company everyone knew—but the idea of owning *multiple* horses just took that wealth to a whole new level. She wondered if she would ever really get used to hearing about the wealth he was born into.

"My father did. My half brother sold them all when he took over." The sadness in Liam's eyes struck Cecily hard. "He always hated horses. Thought they were a waste of money."

"Probably because he couldn't ride to save himself. Didn't you tell me he always fell off?"

Liam laughed. "Yeah. He did. It's lucky he wore a helmet."

Carlos nodded toward the stable. "You ready to meet your horse?"

"Am I!" Cecily could barely contain her excitement as Carlos led them to the stables. Once inside, she found herself in front of the stable of a brown mare.

"This is Cupcake," he said. "Speak softly to her and offer up your knuckle."

"Like this?" Cecily mimicked Carlos, who offered one knuckle, and then two, to the horse's nose. Cupcake nuzzled her hand in greeting. "Hi, there, Cupcake."

"She likes you," Carlos noted as the horse nuzzled her hand.

"You're beautiful, Cupcake," Cecily said, reaching out to touch the mare's head. The hair was so soft. She wasn't expecting that.

"Want to give Cupcake a treat?" he asked, offering her a carrot.

"Sure do." She fed the horse and watched it gulp down the carrot in just a couple of bites.

Carlos's pocket rang then. He picked a phone out of it. "I'm sorry. I've got to take this. I'll be back in just a few minutes to saddle her up for you." Carlos turned away. "Hello?" he answered, as he walked back to the main office. Cecily stroked Cupcake's muzzle again, in awe of the big animal and her big doe-brown eyes.

"She's so pretty," Cecily breathed.

"Not nearly as pretty as you," Liam said. She glanced up at him, met his gaze. She felt a shiver all the way down her spine.

"You're too good to me," she said. "How much did this cost?"

"Don't worry about it. Carlos and I go way back."

"Do you know *everyone* in the tristate area?" Cecily laughed. "Oncologists and horse breeders?"

Liam laughed a little, too. "You know, just the important people."

"I guess so." Cecily grinned at him. Liam seemed to grow thoughtful then. He glanced up at Cupcake and gave her snout a stroke. "By the way, Dr. Kelly called me."

She saw Liam stiffen. "And?"

"And she said she made some calls to her colleagues in Japan, and that I'm approved. As a candidate for the experimental surgery. They have an opening in a month." Cecily didn't want to think about it, actually. Didn't even want to consider that she might really have a chance. If she could only come up with a quarter of a million dollars.

"You have to do it," Liam said.

"I can't afford it." Cecily shrugged. She'd been planning this speech for Liam since she got the call. She was just going to gently, but firmly, help him see that she was, truly, a lost cause. She didn't want him asking his family for money, and she wasn't going to ask her family for it, either. They'd have to mortgage their Cleveland homes. Cecily was just going to enjoy what time she had left. She was slowly starting to resign herself to the fact that her life would be cut short.

"We can work on it. *I* can work on it."

"Liam. No. That's too much to ask of you." She shook her head. Liam frowned.

"No, it's not." Liam studied her face. She could see how determined he was, how stubborn. It would be hard to convince him this wasn't his fight. But she'd have to find a way. "Besides, I already reached out to my half brother."

"You called Wilder?" Cecily felt bombarded with a range of emotions: shock, dismay, anxiety. "You can't ask him for this money."

"He has it," Liam said simply.

"No. That's too much money."

"It's nothing for him." Liam shrugged.

"But you walked away from him. From his money." Cecily didn't want Liam to sacrifice his pride for her.

"I don't need it, but you do."

Cecily shook her head. "No. I can't ask you to do this."

"You're not asking me. I'm doing it. He owes me at least this much," Liam said. "Besides, I might have something he wants."

"The board seat?" Cecily shook her head. "No. Liam. You can't." Panic welled in her. "You wanted to make him look you in the eye. You wanted to make him feel badly for what he's done. That's what you said. You didn't want to give up that seat."

"I know. I *used* to want that. But now I want something more."

Cecily bit her lip. Giddy excitement and weighty guilt battling it out in her chest. "What's that?"

"I want you, Cecily. I want *you*." Liam took her hands in his. "Cecily, I love you."

CHAPTER TWELVE

CECILY'S FIRST INSTINCT was to flee. He couldn't love her. She was dying. This wasn't supposed to be forever. She couldn't offer him a life, and now he *loved* her? Yet, part of her knew she loved him, too. Had loved him that night he'd brought her back to his place, that night he'd taken her to a different world, one far away from here. He'd given her a most dangerous gift: hope.

Cupcake the horse whinnied behind her, bringing her back to reality. They were standing in a barn about to ride horses because this was on her bucket list, a list she was trying to speed through before her cancer caught up to her.

"Liam—" She needed to tell him that he couldn't love her. Not now. That he needed to go find himself a healthy woman, one who could give him years, not months, in his life. Even if by some miracle they scrounged up the money for the experimental surgery, that was still no guarantee.

"You don't have to say it back," Liam said quickly. "I know this is happening fast."

"Light speed, you mean," she said, suddenly feeling dizzy, feeling off-balance. The smell of the horses in the barn overwhelmed her. As did everything Liam was saying. "Liam, you barely know me. You can't just...throw everything away for me."

"I'm not throwing anything away. I'm selling my board seat so you have a chance. It's a trade I'm willing to make."

"Liam, I—" How could she make him see that she couldn't take that gift? She could not allow him to beg for money from the family who stole from him, the one he'd worked so hard to get away from his whole life. She couldn't ask him to betray his principles. Not for her.

Just then his phone rang. Liam glanced at the face of it and scowled. "It's Wilder," he said.

"Don't answer it," Cecily implored, tugging at his arm. But he hit the answer button.

"This is Liam," he said, pressing the phone to his ear, even as his jaw muscles twitched. He listened for a beat, and turned, walking away from Cupcake, just as Carlos appeared again in the barn, carrying two saddles, ready to saddle their horses for their ride. Cecily followed Liam out of the barn. "I'll be there," she heard. "Yeah. Okay." He hung up without so much as a goodbye.

"What did he say?" Cecily asked, her boots crunching on the gravel driveway.

"He wants to meet. Tomorrow. His place." Liam

looked as if he'd eaten something bitter. His mouth puckered in distaste.

"I'm coming with you," Cecily said.

His eyes flashed fire. "No, you're not. You don't want to meet them. They aren't nice people."

"That's why I want to meet them. You shouldn't go back there alone."

"I'm not going to let you go," Liam said, crossing his arms.

"Then I'm not going to get that surgery." Cecily turned back to the barn. Two could play this game of chicken.

Liam followed. "I really don't want you to do this," he said, as seemingly one last attempt to convince her this was a bad idea.

"I know," she said. "But I won't let you go back alone. This is about me, so I should be there. I should have a say."

The next day, Cecily stood in the high-speed private elevator that was taking them up to his half brother's Manhattan penthouse high above Fifth Avenue. She'd never been inside the mammoth glass-and-chrome building that towered over the street, far above the noise of traffic below, and wondered if this was how the other half lived. Or she noted the fact that the private elevator went straight to the top of the building with no stops in between and corrected herself: this must be where the other half of the *one percent* lived.

Liam grasped her hand and squeezed it gently.

"Are you sure you're ready for this?" he asked her. "There's still time for you to go."

"I'm not going anywhere." She held his hand tightly in hers. She glanced down at her striped shorts jumper and her gladiator sandals, wondering if she'd gone too casual. Outside, the hot and muggy June air demanded something summery and light, but in the cool confines of the chrome elevator, she wondered if her bare, tan legs might be too much. "Are you sure I'm dressed okay?"

"We're not here to impress them," Liam said, voice curt. He wore a simple blue polo and cargo shorts. His whole body was tense, though, as if he were gearing up for a fight. She pressed her face against his shoulder.

"It's going to be okay," she said, even though she really had no idea whether it would be or not. She wasn't sure at all what to expect, but what she did know was she wasn't going to let Liam give away his board seat for her. She wasn't going to let him betray his principles.

The elevator arrived at the penthouse, and opened up directly into a beautiful foyer, with sleek gray walls and marbled floors. A butler—she assumed— was waiting for them, because he wore a gray suit, *gloved* hands clasped in front of him.

"Jacob," Liam said, recognizing the mostly gray-headed man. "How are you?" Liam extended his hand but the older gentleman crushed him in a big hug. She was surprised at the show of affection. This was not the standoffish reception that Cecily was expecting.

He beamed as he stepped back, his gaze sweeping Liam from head to toe. "Good to see you. You look well."

"Jacob, this is my *girlfriend*, Cecily." The word took her by surprise. *Girlfriend.* It felt so permanent somehow, so decided. She liked it, though. Liked the way he put a little emphasis on the word.

"Hello, Jacob." She extended her hand for a shake and Jacob took it gently.

"So very lovely to meet you," he said, flashing her a warm smile and dipping his head a bit. "I haven't seen Liam since he was…what?"

"Eighteen," Liam said.

"I used to watch over him when he was a boy," Jacob offered, eyes bright with the memory. "I had to keep my eye on him because he was always sneaking cookies from the pantry."

"Who? Me?" Liam grinned. Cecily glanced between the two men, and then around them in the huge foyer with high ceilings and original modern artwork on the walls. She wondered how much that cost. Beyond one of the open doors in the hall, she caught a glimpse of the magnificent view out the floor-to-ceiling windows: smaller skyscrapers, and beyond, a small thatch of green. Central Park.

"Wilder is excited to see you," Jacob told Liam, who frowned ever so slightly, his enthusiasm clearly dampened.

"Is he?" Liam sounded suspicious.

"He's missed you these many years." Jacob lowered his voice. "He hopes that you and he…might reconcile."

Cecily felt hope flicker in her chest. She knew there were two sides to every feud. Liam had been hurt and felt betrayed, but maybe a small part of her hoped it had all been some terrible misunderstanding. Sure, she would always take Liam's side, but she wanted for the two brothers to get along.

"Wilder wants to reconcile," Liam repeated, but his tone suggested he didn't believe Jacob. Not one bit.

"You know he's changed so much since he got married last year. Love has changed him. Warmed his heart."

Liam snorted, unimpressed. "Sure, it has."

"Please. Come see for yourself." Jacob pivoted, and led them down the long hallway to what appeared to be a study. Jacob walked through the doorway and they followed into a library of chrome shelves, all boasting vintage books. The walls and furniture were a combination of everything modern: white, chrome and gray, except for the traditional paintings hung in various places and the antique pieces of furniture that complemented the room. The place felt like a bundle of contradictions that somehow worked. The room was old and new, antique and modern, Cecily thought.

But soon enough her attention was drawn to the

far corner of the room, near the massive windows showcasing the blue sky beyond, where two figures stood: a man and a woman. Wilder, she recognized instantly, because he looked so very much like Liam. The two had the same athletic build, and the same dark brown eyes, but their hair was slightly different: Wilder's was darker and slicked back. Liam's was lighter and highlighted by all the time he spent in the sun. Wilder looked like he lived indoors in sleek boardrooms, and he wore an expensive suit and tie. Not like Liam, whose tanned face and calloused hands told a different story. Liam tightened his grip on her hand.

"Liam. Good to see you," Wilder said, walking forward as if to offer his hand. Liam tensed, so Wilder stepped back, dropping his hand. "I'd like you to meet my wife, Harley." Cecily glanced at the gorgeous brunette, her light brown eyes smart and assessing, her face tinged with just the hint of nerves. Cecily knew how she felt. They were both women in a room with two men who may hug or fight. The outcome was far, far from certain.

"So nice to meet you. I'm Cecily." Cecily released Liam's hand. She wasn't going to let Wilder's wife get the cold shoulder. She hadn't done anything. Relief flooded Harley's face.

"So nice to meet you, too, Cecily." Rather than offering a hand for a shake, Harley pulled her into a warm hug. Her silk printed dress felt soft and she smelled like the barest hint of a flowery perfume.

Cecily liked her right away. They pulled apart, and Wilder was there.

"Nice to meet you, too," Cecily said, offering her hand. He took it, and she noticed his palm was smooth and his nails neatly manicured. Not a man who likely ever worked with his hands.

Liam, for his part, stayed rooted to the spot, eyeing both Wilder and Harley as if they might be rival predators, looking for the right angle to attack.

"How about we just get down to business, and then we'll be on our way?" Liam asked, his voice gruff, his manner all defensive.

Wilder's dark gaze, a little dangerous now, met his brother's. "Harley? Would you like to show Cecily the rooftop garden? I think Liam and I have a few things to discuss."

Cecily clutched Liam's hand, not wanting to let go. She glanced at him, but his profile was stoic, unreadable. He looked down at her.

"It's okay. You can go."

"But—" She didn't want negotiations of any kind to go on without her. She was here to make sure Liam didn't do anything foolish in her name.

Liam bent down and kissed her forehead. "It's okay," he repeated. "Go look at the garden."

"Cecily?" Harley asked, unsure. Cecily glanced at the woman, who'd clearly been given instructions by her husband to distract her while the brothers talked. She supposed she wouldn't really be able to fight it.

Maybe talking to Harley would help her get a better lay of the land, anyway.

"I'd love to see the garden," Cecily said, smiling at Harley, even as she sent an uneasy glance backward at Liam as she moved to the door. She just hoped the two didn't brawl the second she was out of the room. Liam looked like he'd wanted nothing more than to land a right hook to his brother's jaw. She sent up a silent prayer that nothing crazy happened in her absence and followed Harley into the hallway.

Liam felt the adrenaline already rushing through his veins, the fight-or-flight instincts warring with each other as he stood in his brother's study. He hadn't been in this room since he was barely a man, but mostly still a boy, back when this massive two-story penthouse served as the family home when they weren't staying at the massive mansion upstate, or at one of a half dozen or so properties around the world. Liam had renovated it, of course, the modern chrome bookshelves nothing like the big oak ones their father preferred. The only thing that remained the same, he noted, was the marble floor and the big oak door. Everything else was Wilder's. Somehow, the transformation of the room and the penthouse made Liam bristle. What Dad made, what he'd created, was never good enough for his oldest son.

"Want a drink?" Wilder asked, walking over to the rolling glass bar cart near the corner. He picked up a decanter of amber liquid. "Bourbon? Scotch?"

"No. Thanks." Liam ground out the words. He told himself he needed to be nice. After all, he was here to ask a favor. But niceties dried up in his throat when he thought of all the ways Wilder had wronged him. The last year of private school, unpaid. The humiliating move. The way he'd tried to trick him when he was just fourteen.

"Suit yourself." Wilder poured himself a generous serving of bourbon and moved to the overstuffed chair near his desk. "Please. Sit." He indicated the sofa. Liam chose the hard-back chair instead. A small act of defiance, but he wasn't going to be told where to sit.

"So, I heard from Maria that you're interested in selling your board seat."

"That's right." He crossed his legs, trying to remain calm, even though his heart had ticked up a notch.

"Why?" Wilder stared at him, his sharp eyes focused, his facial expression revealing nothing. Liam suddenly remembered that hard look from when he was a boy, back when Wilder was twice his size, and able to wrest away sweets from his little boy hands, lecturing him on ruining his appetite for dinner. But, Liam reminded himself, he was that little boy no longer. If push came to shove, he could take Wilder. He had more muscle, and he was used to working with his hands. Wilder was athletic, yes, but so was Liam. Wilder was no longer the oversized, intimidating big brother of his old memories. Not anymore.

Except he did have the advantage. He was the one who could write the check that could save Cecily's life. *Be nice. Get this done and get out*, he told himself. *For Cecily.*

"The reason doesn't concern you."

"Are you in trouble?" Wilder said it as if he expected Liam would be.

"No." Liam realized his hands were shaking a bit. Nerves? Anger? He wasn't sure. He clasped them tightly in his lap.

"Drugs? Gambling?" Wilder raised a slim, dark eyebrow.

Liam frowned. "Hell, no. Why would you say that?"

"Your mother—"

"Leave her out of this." Liam uncrossed his legs and grabbed the arms of his chair, all the while trying to rein in his rage. Just because his mother was an alcoholic didn't mean he was an addict. And he resented the implication. Besides, she was sober now. Had been for years. Not that Wilder cared to ever check in on her.

Wilder held up one hand as if surrendering the line of questioning, the amber liquid in the glass held in his other hand sloshing a bit. "Okay, okay," he said. "I just have to ask. I was surprised to hear from you. You didn't come to the wedding."

"I didn't think it was a genuine invite." Also, he wasn't much in the mood to celebrate how Wilder planned to start his own family, direct even more of the Lange wealth to a new branch.

Wilder frowned and took another drink. "Look, Liam, I know you don't think highly of me. I know we haven't always gotten along."

Liam had to hold in a snort as he remembered how they'd never clicked, how nothing Liam ever did was right, how Wilder always picked his brothers' company over his. That had been Wilder's doing. From the start.

"But I am trying to do what's best for this family. I'm trying to build on the company Dad built. I'm trying to make sure we're all safe. That we all do well." Wilder set down the half-empty glass on a nearby side table.

Liam studied his older brother, amazed at how well he could lie. He wondered how often Wilder had practiced that speech in the mirror. Probably so often he'd started to believe it.

"Do you really believe that?"

Wilder blinked. "Yes. Because it's true."

"You are talking to the wrong person if you want me to believe you're a hero. I think we both know that's not true." Liam stared at his older brother. "You can act like the patriarch of the family, the savior, but you tried to trick me. When I was fourteen."

"I was trying to help you pay for school."

"By getting me to sign papers that I didn't understand."

Wilder opened his mouth to say something, but then fell silent. He stared at the bourbon in his glass, as if trying to see the past there.

"Let's not pretend that you did everything you did out of the goodness of your heart, okay?"

"That was a difficult time. Your mother was working against me. I needed to maintain control. Only then could I help you all. Save the family."

Liam barked a laugh. "You think you're the hero, but you did that all for yourself. For your greed."

"I always tried to help you—and your brothers," Wilder protested. "I helped Seth come out. When nobody else would."

Liam rolled his eyes. He'd been hearing about this all the time. As if Liam neglected Seth, as if Liam wasn't also pushing their parents to accept him when he came out. "You act like this big savior, helping Mom and Dad come to terms with their gay son, but don't you think Seth could've done that just fine by himself? I think you got in the middle because it suited you—politically."

"How on earth—"

"You never make a move unless it's to your advantage. I don't believe you do things out of the goodness of your heart, Wilder. That's what Seth and Stuart may think, but I know better."

"You always believed the worst of me," Wilder said.

"That's because you always showed me your worst side," Liam countered.

Wilder sighed, leaned back in his overstuffed leather chair, and took another drink. "So you won't tell me *why* you want to sell your seat. Will you tell me how much you want to sell it for?"

"Half a million," Liam said, keeping his gaze focused on Wilder's. He figured there was the surgery, and then there was time she'd need to heal, and travel and other expenses, and the fact he wouldn't be able to work when he was with her. Not to mention, he thought, he wanted to make sure he had plenty, in case the experimental treatment didn't work out.

"I offered you much more than that the first time around," Wilder said. "Why not ask for that?"

"I don't need it. This is what I need, and I'm asking you for it." Liam wrapped his fingers around the hard, wooden arms of his chair. He needed to hold on to something, so he didn't spring up and *make* Wilder give him the cash. "You owe me much more than that, and we both know it."

"But why do you need it?" Wilder's dark eyes met his. They were his own eyes, their father's eyes.

"It's none of your business."

"Doesn't have anything to do with the beautiful woman on your arm? Cecily?"

Liam tightened his grip on the arms of the chair. "I said it's none of your business."

Wilder leaned forward, pressing his palms together, almost as if in prayer. "If you don't tell me why, then I won't sell you the seat. It's really that simple."

Liam felt fury rise in him. This is what he hated about Wilder. His half brother was always trying to make the rules, control the outcome. It was why he loved running the family business so much. He could tell all the trained monkeys who worked for him to dance, and they would. But not him.

"And if you do know the reason, will you still say no?" Liam asked.

Wilder crossed his legs, looking every bit like a king on his throne, as he rested his glass on the arm of his chair. "I might. But I will definitely say no if you don't tell me the why."

Liam felt the war in him brewing: Cecily's surgery versus kowtowing to Wilder's whims. He hated the power struggle, hated that once again, Wilder held all the cards. That no matter what Liam tried to do, he never could get out from under Wilder's boot.

He struggled with a growing desire to punch Wilder in the face and leave. But that wouldn't help Cecily. He saw her innocent blue eyes, remembered the tears clouding them when she talked about her uncertain future.

"I need it to save Cecily," he admitted. "If I don't get that money, she's going to die."

CHAPTER THIRTEEN

CECILY FOLLOWED HARLEY onto the huge and beautiful sky patio on the rooftop of the penthouse, trying hard not to gape at the more than eight thousand–square foot space surrounded by a ten-foot privacy fence. It was divided into sections, too: the lounge area with a full couch and chairs and colorful potted plants, and then at the edge, a single lap pool and an adjacent Jacuzzi, lit in blue. Above them, the clear blue June sky stretched out for miles, dotted only with a few white fluffy clouds. She glanced up, feeling the warm sunshine on her bare arms, wondering how it must feel to live like this: both in the city and yet so far removed from it at the same time.

"It's all so beautiful," she said, unable to keep the awe from her voice. A butterfly flittered by to the potted flowers. It seemed like an oasis far above the city.

"Thank you. Wilder...doesn't believe in doing things by halves," Harley said. "When I first saw this place, I couldn't even believe this existed in New

York." She moved to the lounge area and took a seat in the chair. "Come. Sit. Let's talk."

Harley's tone was friendly and conversational, but Cecily wondered if she was about to be interrogated. There was already a pitcher of iced lemonade on the table, filled with slices of real lemon, mint leaves and crushed ice.

"Lemonade?" she asked, offering up a crystal glass with initials etched in the side, almost like a brand.

"Uh. Sure. Thanks." Harley poured a glass and handed it to Cecily. She took the cool glass, noting how heavy and thick the highball was.

"So." Harley inhaled. "How do you think the boys are doing?" She looked worried, and probably for good reason. Harley reached out and poured her own glass of lemonade.

"I'm just hoping they're not fighting," Cecily admitted.

Harley took a sip of her own lemonade, contemplating her next question. "How did you two meet?"

"A dive bar," Cecily said. "About a month ago."

Harley coughed, patting her chest, as if the lemonade had found its way down the wrong pipe. "You two haven't been dating long, then." Suspicion crowded the edges of her question.

"Right. We haven't."

"But you've already had sex." It wasn't a question. Cecily felt like that was out of bounds.

"That's right," Cecily said, feeling defensive. "I

was in his bed about an hour after I met him. So what?" She didn't add that normally she didn't fall into strange men's beds. That she didn't make a habit of one-night stands. There was the pesky little problem of cancer, and dying, and her trying to get in as much living as she could before her time was up.

"I'm sorry. I didn't mean to offend," Harley said, trying to backtrack. "It's just that…this is going to sound odd. I'm a sexologist. I have a PhD in human sexuality, so how and when people choose to become intimate. It's really a focus of my career."

"Wait a second." Cecily's mind turned. "Are you Harley *Vega* Lange? As in Dr. Harley?" Harley Vega, world-famous sex advice columnist that Cecily used to read on her daily commute to work on the train. Before she was laid off.

"That's right." Harley smiled sheepishly.

"I used to read your column all the time. You give great advice."

"Thank you." A blush crept up Harley's cheek. "So, again, my apologies for prying into your love life. It's none of my business. And, just so you know, there's no judgment from me."

"Okay. I mean, good." Cecily smiled, and still felt a little stunned. She was drinking lemonade with *Dr. Harley*. She couldn't believe it. This was the most famous celebrity she'd ever met, unless you included that insurance spokesperson she saw at a fast-food restaurant in downtown once.

"I was just noticing that you two seem very

close. For a casual relationship," Harley said, seamlessly pivoting back to her and Liam. Harley didn't mince words. Cecily was surprised by the bluntness, but also, a little reassured by it. She didn't have to worry about veiled threats. Harley was coming at her straight, and that was fine by Cecily. She met Harley's questioning gaze and didn't blink. Cecily reminded herself she really didn't have anything to hide.

"Yeah. Well, it was my intention to be casual, but Liam…he's doesn't seem to do things halfway, either. Maybe he's more like Wilder than he wants to admit."

"Maybe," Harley conceded. The silence between them grew. Harley waited, eyes sympathetic and friendly, as if waiting for Cecily to offer up the next bit of conversation. The silence deepened, and suddenly, Cecily felt the need to fill the dead air.

"I have cancer," she blurted. She didn't even know why she said that. Why had she gone there?

Harley raised her eyebrows in surprise. "Oh. I'm sorry to hear that." Her eyes filled with sympathy and warmth. "What kind?"

"Liver. It's rare for a person of my age."

"And the prognosis?" Harley asked.

Cecily fidgeted with her lemonade glass, wiping off a streak of condensation. She didn't want to admit she was dying. That all of this was useless. What was the point of getting into the nitty-gritty with Dr. Harley? It's not like they'd have time to be best friends.

Then again, there was little point in lying, either, for the same reason. "Not good," she admitted.

"Does Liam know?"

Cecily broke Harley's probing gaze. "Yes. And that's why he's here."

"Did you ask him to come?" Harley asked, voice carefully neutral.

"No," Cecily blurted, still a bit offended. "He insisted. There's an experimental surgery he wants me to do. But I don't know. I think it's all likely a waste of time."

"No, you don't." Harley cut straight through her defensive wall. Cecily put the lemonade on the table, her appetite for it lost. "Or you wouldn't be here."

"I'm just here to make sure Liam doesn't do something foolish," Cecily snapped. She suddenly felt like a bug under a microscope. And why did she get the impression that Harley was implying she had ulterior motives? She was just trying to do what was best for Liam.

"Of course." Harley said it neutrally.

"Look, I don't want his money. Or Wilder's. I just want…" She realized right in that moment that she just wanted Liam. For as long—or as little—as she could have him. "I love Liam."

"Love him? After just a month?" Harley's skepticism was palpable. Cecily felt a little as if she was on the defensive. But how to explain what she and Liam had? Lightning in a bottle. She knew in her gut that he was special, he was *the one*, whatever that meant, even though they hadn't known each other long.

"Look, I met him…well, I probably would never even have talked to him, but I guess my diagnosis gave me the courage."

"Of course." Harley frowned just a little.

"I look at the world in a whole new way, and that's why I approached him at the bar." She recounted quickly their meeting: the rude regular giving her trouble, Liam standing up for her, and then the fact that they'd been nearly inseparable since.

"Sounds like there was a lot of chemistry right at that first meeting."

"There sure was!" Cecily remembered just *how* much chemistry they'd shared that first night, and nearly every night since. "But it's also more than chemistry," she added, growing thoughtful. "Liam and I, we just click. I know it sounds crazy, but it's true. Haven't you ever just met someone and known?"

Harley shook her head slowly. "No."

"Not even Wilder?"

Harley tilted her head backward and laughed. "No. I hated him on first sight," she admitted. She twirled an end of her brunette hair around her finger, absently. "He had me fired."

"That doesn't seem like a good start to a romance," Cecily admitted.

"It wasn't. But… Wilder won me over. Eventually. It took a little longer than a month." Harley glanced at her lemonade glass. "And given your circumstances, there are a lot of pretty intense emotions around sickness, and couple that with a new love, and it can be pretty explosive."

"You say that like it's a bad thing." Why did Harley suddenly seem to be *not* on her side? What was her angle?

"I'm just saying that you two haven't known each other a long time, but this situation, it's like an added stress in a relationship. And sometimes, relationships born from that kind of stress feel very intense, but they don't last."

"You think we're not going to last?" She grit her teeth, wanting to tell her that she was right about that in a way. They wouldn't last. *Because she was dying.* But the real stickler, the real thing that annoyed her was the doubt in Harley's voice. Even if somehow, by a miracle, she did survive, why shouldn't they be together?

"I think that relationships begun in such stressful conditions often don't last. That's all I'm saying. It's why so many reality TV romances unravel once the cameras are off. The adrenaline fades, and then so does the passion."

"I don't have a reality TV relationship."

Harley looked at her with a little pity. "No, of course not. I just mean…" Harley glanced up at the clear blue sky. "I mean…just…be careful. That's all. Nobody intends for bad things to happen, but if you can't keep the urgency in the relationship, then it might be hard to maintain. That's all." Harley wiped some of the condensation off the side of her lemonade glass. "And the desire to be a white knight, it's strong in many men. But especially for Liam. He was very protective of his mother from a young age. He wanted to save her." Harley gave a shrug of her shoulder. "But all human beings want to feel needed, and so I can see why some are attracted to complicated situations."

"Like a woman with cancer," Cecily finished, putting the pieces together. Suddenly, Harley's claims didn't seem so far-fetched. Could Harley be right? What happened if suddenly Cecily did get well, and then the urgency was gone? Would Liam feel the same for her if he couldn't be the white knight anymore? If she didn't need saving?

Cecily wasn't sure what to do with all the new information swimming around her brain. She couldn't help feeling a little unsettled. A nagging thought popped into her brain then: Why should she worry? There was no guarantee she'd live, anyway. That dark, heavy truth still lingered over everything, like a storm cloud stuck stubbornly in the sky.

Harley leaned forward, looking pensive, as she placed her hand on Cecily's. "Look, I can see I've upset you. I'm sorry. It wasn't my intention. I am truly sorry about that."

"No, it's okay," Cecily said.

"Ignore me. Sometimes, I can't turn the sexual behavior PhD off. Forget what I said. More lemonade?" Harley asked, reaching for the pitcher. Cecily nodded, absently, the wheels in her mind turning. "Now, I know you don't want to talk about this, either, but…" Harley took a deep breath. "We should talk about Wilder and Liam. Do you know their history?"

"I know what Liam told me. That…" How did she put this nicely? "That Wilder took the company from him. Left him and his mom penniless."

"There are two sides to every story," Harley said. Cecily had suspected there might be, but she couldn't imagine how Wilder ended up coming out the hero on this one. "Things aren't so simple between those two."

"Like what?"

"Like there wasn't much left of the family fortune to steal," Harley said. "Liam's father had bankrupted the company, used it as his own personal bank account. When Wilder took over, it was near collapse." The sun hit Harley's dark, shiny hair then and her light brown eyes almost looked golden.

"Is that true?"

Harley shaded her face from the sun. "I'm afraid so. Look it up. There have been a few articles about it in the *Wall Street Journal* and *Financial Times*. Wilder saved the company, saved the family's wealth. Liam disagreed with *how* Wilder did it, sure, but he did it all the same."

"Does Liam know that the company was bankrupt?" Because it sure didn't seem like he did. Not from the way he acted.

"Sometimes, people believe what they want to believe," Harley said. "If you have a core belief, something that's fundamental to your outlook on the world, you have a hard time changing that belief. So, anytime a bit of information might come in that disagrees with you, you might just explain it away. It's called bias confirmation. It's why it's so hard to change someone's mind when they've dug in their heels about politics—or anything, really. Facts presented can be explained away or excused."

"You're saying Liam lied to himself?" Now Cecily was starting to get angry on Liam's behalf. Harley held up a hand defensively, shaking her head.

"No. Not on purpose, not maliciously," she explained. "Liam is a good man. He believes he's doing the right thing. In some ways, he's a white knight for his mom. He feels he's protecting her by remaining angry at Wilder."

"But you're saying that anger is misplaced."

"I'm saying that Liam was basically a kid when all this happened. He formed some pretty hardened beliefs around what happened, and he's had a hard time changing those beliefs. His brothers don't see it the same way, but then, Liam was a lot closer to his mother than they were. He took her side and stuck with her, even if she didn't deserve his support. Liam is very loyal that way."

"Yes," Cecily agreed. She remembered, too, him telling her he didn't do things by halves. That he was all in or all out. He was loyal. To a fault, given that he seemed committed to being with her, even though she was a lost cause. "He is loyal. Very loyal."

"That loyalty holds value. He's been protecting his mom, maybe even enabling her for a long time. Liam didn't lie to himself. He just wanted to protect what he thought was valuable in his life. That's why he continues to be there for his mother, but she's not always there for him."

"She's got a disease. She's an addict," Cecily said, already rising to her defense, though she'd never met the woman. She was doing it for Liam. "And he says that she started drinking heavily after they were dis-inherited."

"That's not quite right." Harley shook her head. "She'd had trouble long before her husband died. She always drank heavily and it had been a problem before Liam's father died. Of course, it could've gotten worse after, but I know for a fact she wasn't a great mother to the boys when they were little. Wilder told me stories. About how she'd punish them." Harley shuddered. "Once, she locked Wilder in a closet for days."

"That's awful." Cecily couldn't imagine someone doing that to a child.

"His father blamed it on her drinking, and maybe that was true, but still. She hasn't really made amends to the boys. Never really took responsibility. Wilder told me it fell to him to make sure Seth, Stuart and Liam got to school. That their clothes were washed. That they got fed. Their mother checked out, went on binges for long periods. Their father worked long hours, so Wilder was the one who put them to bed at night. Who made sure they ate their vegetables. He was barely older than they were, and he had to be their parent."

"So why is Liam so loyal to his mother?"

The sun went behind a cloud then, and the shade enveloped them both. Harley stared at her, eyes sad. "No one wants to believe their parents are bad. That they don't have their best interests at heart. Liam made excuses for his mother because he truly wanted to believe the best of her. We all do of our parents."

She set down her lemonade glass on the small outdoor table.

Now Cecily felt like she had a lot to process. She glanced at Harley. "Do you psychoanalyze everybody you meet?" She laughed a little, hoping to blunt the criticism.

"I can't help it." Harley sent her an apologetic smile. "It's hard to turn off that PhD. I'm sorry, really. I should mind my own business!" Harley beamed at her, and Cecily couldn't find it in herself to be annoyed. There was something genuine about Harley's manner, about her open, sunny disposition, that made her comments feel less pointed. Harley really seemed to want to help, and Cecily couldn't blame her for that. "I can see that you do love him, and that you are certainly in his loyalty circle. I think he'd do most anything for you."

"How can you tell that?" Cecily asked. She wasn't

sure if she should feel honored, or worried, that Liam's blind loyalty was now hers.

"Well, he's here now, isn't he? I would've bet he would never have come back here for anyone or anything. But you've proven me wrong."

CHAPTER FOURTEEN

WILDER BLINKED, LOOKING STOIC, as he sat in his leather armchair in this study inside the penthouse, and gripped his glass of bourbon a little tighter.

"Cecily is dying?" Wilder asked, straight-faced, his expression giving up almost nothing. Did he care? Was he concerned that another human being, and not just any human being, but beautiful, sweet Cecily who was dying?

Liam nodded once. He noticed his left knee bobbing. He willed it to be still. "Yes. Cancer."

Wilder said nothing. Liam wondered why he was surprised. He didn't even manage a "That's too bad," or "Sorry, brother." Nothing. The wheels in his older brother's mind seemed to whirl as he stood, placed his glass on a side table and wandered over to the large windows overlooking Manhattan, his view largely of the tops of the smaller buildings around him, and in the distance, the rectangle of green that was Central Park. He kept his back to Liam as he stared out on the city, the sharp angles of steel buildings jutting into the blue sky.

"Are you going to say something?" he asked his brother. Maybe condolences? Maybe something better, like, *Sure, I'll give you the money. Let's save the love of your life. Let me finally do something worthwhile. Prove that after everything, maybe I do have a heart.*

Liam hadn't wanted to tell him Cecily's secret, but he also realized there'd be no way he'd get the money without coming clean. He hated this game of cat and mouse. Hated trying to figure out which lever he needed to pull to get Wilder to cooperate. He'd never been any good at scheming, one of many reasons he'd walked away from this family. He'd been tired of the endless plotting, the conspiracies, the backstabbing. His mother would probably always want to fight Wilder, always want to scheme against him, and Liam didn't blame her. But it wasn't the life for him.

"She needs an experimental surgery if she has any hope of living. And the surgery is expensive." Liam kept his voice flat, but inside, his stomach churned. He hadn't realized how dire things were until he said them out loud, how much he needed this to work. He couldn't sit by while she wasted away, not while there was a chance he could save her.

Wilder glanced at Liam over his shoulder, but kept his arms crossed over his chest.

"I see."

Silence fell between the two brothers. Would Seth have to beg? Would Wilder make him? Did that even matter? He loved Cecily more than he'd ever loved anyone in his life. Her living was the only thing that mattered, wasn't it?

"I don't really need the seat. Maria was right when she told you that things have changed." Wilder turned now and stared at Liam, as he clasped his hands behind his back.

"I know you don't need it," Liam said, an anxious fear rising in him. If there wasn't an angle for Wilder, he'd never be interested. "But I'm asking you for this." He swallowed hard, as he stood. "Please," he added, his voice so low he almost didn't hear the word. Surprise crossed Wilder's face. "Cecily needs this. And I love her."

Wilder studied Liam. "I believe you do love her."

Well, that was something, Liam guessed.

"But how long have you two known each other?"

"What does that matter?" Liam's whole body bristled with indignation.

"I heard from your friend, Dr. Kelly."

Liam held his breath. "Why'd she contact you?"

"I reached out to several of your friends after… you wouldn't sign over your seat. I just asked them for the personal favor of letting me know when you resurfaced in their lives. Or if you did."

"You're spying on me." Liam wondered how many other "friends" might be reporting back to him.

"I'm keeping tabs on my baby brother. Making sure he's okay."

Liam sniffed. "Sure. If that's what you tell yourself." Liam glared. "What did Rebecca tell you?"

"She said you and Cecily had just recently met, and that Cecily didn't want to have her tests redone. That she preferred to use her old charts. Rebecca thought it was suspicious."

"Rebecca is just jealous," Liam said.

"Did Cecily make contact with you first, or did you approach her?" Wilder changed the subject, as he reached for his glass on the side table. He took a sip of his drink, but his eyes remained sharply focused on Liam.

"Why the hell does that even matter?" What was he getting at? Liam took a step closer. Wilder stood his ground by the window.

"I think you should be careful."

"What the hell are you trying to say, Wilder?" He hated the way Wilder danced around everything, how he leaned so heavily on innuendo. And he wasn't going to let him sit there and make insinuations about Cecily.

"I'm saying that it's all a little suspicious. Maybe she's playing you." Wilder set his cup down, now two-thirds empty.

Liam felt a boiling rage bubble up inside him. How dare *he* even think *she* was the bad guy? "She's not," Liam ground out, realizing a little late that he'd balled his right hand into a fist. What was he going to do? Hit his brother? Part of him wanted to, but he also knew that he was Cecily's last chance. "Are you going to give me the money or not?"

"I'm just saying what do you really know about this girl? What if it's all some scam? What if she knew exactly who you were when she met you?"

He thought about the dive bar, about how she made a beeline for him. But what did that matter? "Even if she did know who I was, even if she did target me, she'd know that I had none of the Lange fortune."

"But maybe she thought she could get you here, now, in front of me. Asking for some of it."

Liam didn't want to even consider the thought. Cecily loved him. And she wasn't a crook. "Cecily didn't even want me to ask you for this. She told me not to come. She isn't even sure she wants the surgery."

Wilder raised a suspicious eyebrow. "That's just what I would say if I'm playing someone."

Liam's blood, now on fire, pushed him forward a step closer to his brother. "You're wrong." They were nose to nose now.

"And you've got a history of being blindly loyal," Wilder said, without blinking. "To the wrong people."

Liam sucked in a breath trying to contain his fury. He thought of Cecily, of what this meant to her, and counted backward in his head from ten, trying to maintain his calm.

"You better be careful how you speak to me," Liam managed, uncurling his fists, deciding that hitting Wilder wasn't worth it.

"I'm just trying to help you," Wilder said.

"If you really cared about me, you'd just buy my seat. Give me what I'm asking for."

Wilder paused—too long. In that moment, Liam knew this whole ask had been a waste of time. Wilder was never going to help him. What was he thinking?

Liam turned away from Wilder, feeling a rush of emotion: anger, disappointment, but most of all, sadness—that his brother was the same. That he'd likely always be the same. That when he needed his help the most, Wilder always turned his back on him.

"I'm just trying to look after you," Wilder said.

"Like you give a shit about me," Liam managed. "Don't play big brother now, okay? It's too late."

"Liam. I'm not playing big brother. I am the head of this family." There it was, he thought, Wilder's signature move: reminding him exactly who had all the power.

"This was a waste of time," Liam said. "I'm going. You won't see me again." Liam headed to the door.

"Liam! Wait," Wilder called. Liam paused at the doorway. "I'll buy the seat, okay?"

Liam wanted to tell him to go to hell. That the deal was off. Except, he couldn't. Not with Cecily's life in the balance. "Fine," he ground out.

"I'll have Maria contact you with details."

Liam hesitated, glancing at Wilder. "What's the catch?"

"I want you to be a part of the family again."

Liam laughed bitterly. "What the hell do you mean? You want me to come home for Thanksgiving?"

"For a start."

Liam couldn't figure out the angle. Why did Wilder care whether or not he was in the family? He'd never much cared for him anyway. "Why?"

"Because we're your family."

Liam glanced at the magazine on Wilder's side table. He was gracing the cover of *Business Monthly*, and the headline promised big ideas and innovation from the country's wealthiest communications CEO, as he plots new mergers, including one with one of the biggest family entertainment companies in the world.

"No, this isn't about family. This is about business." Liam tapped the magazine. "You want to polish your image? Make sure you can merge with the world's biggest animation studio? Wouldn't look great if you were at the center of a family feud."

A frown line appeared between Wilder's eyebrows. "This doesn't have anything to do with business. I want you back in the family. That's the deal. Take it or leave it."

He wanted to tell Wilder to shove it. But he thought of Cecily. Of her need. "I'll come back to the family—when Cecily is well."

Wilder considered this. "Okay," he said after a moment.

Liam turned to go. Liam ran into Cecily in the foyer, Harley on her heels. The two were laughing about something. Great. Glad *they* got along.

"Cecily, we're leaving."

Cecily glanced up at him, blue eyes wary. "Everything okay?"

"Let's just go," Liam grumbled, as he took her by the hand.

"Leaving so soon, sir?" Jacob asked, appearing from seemingly nowhere.

"Yes, Jacob. We're going."

Jacob sent for the elevator, even as Cecily glanced back at Harley, sending her an apologetic smile.

"It was nice meeting you," Harley said.

"You, too!" Cecily managed, just as the elevator arrived. Wilder came out of his study, standing stoically in the hallway.

"Liam! Wait. Please stay for dinner," he called.

"No," Liam said, even as Liam tugged on Cecily's arm, pulling her into the open elevator. "We can't."

The elevator doors closed before Cecily could finish her goodbyes. "I take it, that didn't go so well?" she asked Liam. He didn't want to answer at first, didn't want to dash her hopes.

"No," he said after a while. "It actually went okay."

"But you're angry?"

Liam pulled her close. "He's going to give us the money."

"Wait? What?" Cecily pulled away, looking shocked. "But you said it didn't go well."

"It didn't, but he's going to buy the board seat, so we can have the surgery."

"It might not even work," she said.

"But it *might*."

Cecily looked worried. "What did he ask in return?"

Liam sighed. "He wants me to rejoin the family."

Cecily brightened. "That's a good thing, isn't it?"

Liam shook his head. How to explain that it had taken nearly all of his resolve to leave the toxic Langes behind? That going back just felt like the biggest defeat of his life.

"He doesn't want to do it out of the goodness of his heart. It's because it's all about appearances. For a new merger. For the business."

"Oh." Cecily considered this a bit. "We don't have to take the money."

He whirled. "Of course we do. It's your life we're talking about."

"You know, you don't have to be my white knight." Her eyes flashed with—what? Anger? Resentment? Why?

"Your what?" He didn't understand what she was saying.

"I mean, you don't have to save me."

"What are you saying? I love you. I want you to live."

"I'm not just a damsel in distress. I'm more than that. That's all I'm trying to say," Cecily countered, as the door opened. "I don't need saving."

Liam had no idea what this nonsense was or why they suddenly seemed like they were speaking two different languages. "Of course you need saving.

What are we even arguing about? I don't understand what you're saying."

Cecily stared up at the numbers in the elevator. She'd stopped talking. Wasn't explaining why she was upset. It was driving him mad.

"Cee, please." Liam reached out for her and pulled her close. "I don't want to fight."

"I don't, either." She leaned her head against his shoulder. "I'm sorry. That visit was stressful."

"Damn right it was." The elevators opened into the sleek, expansive lobby and they made their way out to the street. What he wanted to do was head to the nearest dive bar and order a PBR. But there wasn't any such thing as a dive bar in this neighborhood. Everything was craft cocktails and gastropubs. He didn't want to step foot in a place where a beer would run him fifteen dollars. They probably didn't even have PBR.

"What did Wilder say, anyway?"

"You don't want to know." Liam wasn't going to repeat those vile accusations.

"I do, though. Please." Cecily tugged on his arm. She stopped him in the middle of the sidewalk as folks bustled by. A man brushed past him, not bothering to apologize.

"He'll give me the money, but he wants me to re-join the family. But he's just doing that to make himself look good. To protect the company."

"That's not what Harley says."

So, Harley had filled Cecily head with stories of

how Wilder's a great guy? Just like Seth tried to do with him.

"Well, she doesn't know what she's talking about," Liam said, feeling uneasy. He didn't trust any member of the Lange family to shoot straight. He didn't want them twisting Cecily's mind.

"He's giving me the money, but he…" Liam trailed off. He didn't want to even voice Wilder's accusations.

"But what? Go on, what did he say? Please. Liam. We promised to be open and honest with one another, remember?"

Liam hesitated. Damn. She had him there. "He told me that he thought you were just with me for the money. That you were trying to con me."

Cecily went stock-still and quiet. "He did?" She pressed her hand to her chest.

"Yeah. He did. But he's an asshole who doesn't know what he's talking about."

"He's just trying to protect you," Cecily said softly. She seemed sad suddenly, and that made Liam want to march right back up to Wilder's penthouse and punch the man in the face. Cecily couldn't waste time being sad. Her time was running out. "Maybe he's not the bad guy you think he is."

"How can you even say that?" Liam felt taken aback. "After everything he's done?"

"Maybe there are two sides to this story," she offered.

"No. There's not." He felt anger building in him,

new grudges set atop old ones. But he didn't want to fight about it. Not with Cecily. Not now. "And don't try to protect him," Liam said. "He's not worth it."

"Okay." Cecily backed off, and he took her hand gently. He didn't mean to rant at her. She didn't deserve that.

"What are we going to do now?" Cecily asked.

Liam saw a nearby subway station. "We're going to take the train to Hoboken, and then we're going to hit the first dive bar we see."

Cecily brightened a little. "Just like old times."

He laughed. "Exactly right."

CHAPTER FIFTEEN

THEY NEVER MADE IT to the bar. On the way up from the subway, with the sunlight streaming down on their New Jersey stop, Cecily felt light-headed again as she clutched the steel railing. She pressed a hand against her forehead, even as Liam stopped beside her, worry knotting his brow.

"Are you okay?"

"Yeah," she said, even though she wasn't sure that she was. The light-headed spells were getting more frequent now, and it was harder to predict when they were coming. "Maybe I'm just hungry?"

Liam sent her a skeptical look as he steadied her with a hand across her lower back, helping her up the steps. "Just take it easy," he offered. "I've got you."

She was suddenly grateful for his presence, his strong arms, and those warm brown eyes, so full of love, so full of concern. What would she have done without him? Sit on the subway steps? Fear gripped her suddenly, a fear of her own decline. Of what would happen when things got really bad.

"Thank you," she said, holding on to him, clinging to him, really.

"You don't have to thank me. I'm here for you." On the street, Liam glanced right and then left. "My place isn't far from here. Maybe two blocks. Do you think you can make it?"

"That means we miss the dive bar," she said.

"I've got PBRs in the fridge, and I'll dim the lights. My place is half dive bar already," he joked.

She had to laugh at that. But she took two steps and then everything went black. She came to on the ground, being cradled by Liam, his face stricken with panic. Seeing her awake, his face brightened.

"There you are. Come back to me," he breathed. A small group of onlookers had gathered. One of them, an older woman with silver-gray hair, clucked her tongue.

"You okay, girl? We were going to call an ambulance." She held up her phone as if to prove it.

"I'm fine. I just…fainted." She sat up, still feeling woozy. The first doctor's words haunted her. Fainting spells were supposed to become more and more frequent.

"Are you okay to stand?" Liam asked.

"Yeah, I think so." Liam pulled her to her feet. Most of the onlookers dispersed now, and a few gave worried backward glances as they walked. She'd never felt more embarrassed. Or more helpless.

"How long was I out?" Cecily asked.

"Just a minute or so." Liam's voice sounded tight,

worried. She linked her arm in his, glad for the support. "I can call a rideshare," he offered.

"No. I can walk. I think." His place was so close. No more than two blocks.

"Have you blacked out like that before?" he asked her.

She shook her head. "This is the first time the light-headedness ended with me collapsing."

"It's getting worse," he said, voice low. She knew it was. The fainting was worrisome. What else would come before the end?

Her mind whirled with worry, as they walked past the dive bar where the two had met. She felt too weak now to go in, her knees like jelly. She wondered what would have happened that night last month if she'd decided to walk on by. She never would have met Liam. Never would have fallen in love. But, then again, she wouldn't be the burden she was to him now. Wouldn't be the reason he had to crawl back to his family. She felt a pang of guilt.

Would it have been better if they'd never met? She didn't even want to let that thought into her brain. She couldn't imagine what her life would be like without Liam. He was the one who'd attacked her bucket list with gusto. How many items would she have even bothered to do without his determination and enthusiasm? She certainly never would have ridden a horse. Or even thought seriously about doing it.

Her knees wobbled a bit as they rounded the corner to the door to his apartment. He buzzed in the code, and the door opened. Her head felt fuzzy again, and she leaned against him a little.

"Here, let me carry you," he said, whisking her off her feet before she could protest.

"I can walk up the steps."

"I'm sure you can, but why would you when you have a human elevator?"

She had to laugh at that, as she tucked her head under his chin. She clung to his neck, but he carried her as if she weighed nothing. Soon they were on his landing, and after he'd set her down, he unlocked the door, and nudged it open with his foot.

"I also offer threshold service," he said, opening his arms.

"I'm okay," she said, but as she took a step, she faltered. Once more, he swept her up, and then walked her straight to his couch. Molly mewed in protest as he laid her down a little too closely to where the calico sat curled in a ball.

"Molly, no complaints. Be good to our guest," he told his cat, who flicked her tail in annoyance and then hopped off the couch and onto the ground, stopping to lick her paw.

"I'm such a burden, I'm sorry," Cecily murmured, her head throbbing.

"You're no burden," Liam said. "Let me get you some water." He appeared again by her side with a cool glass. She took it and sipped. She handed him back the glass and he set it on the side table. Their eyes met, and suddenly, Cecily was very aware how close he was, how she wanted him this close, always.

"I love you," she said, reaching up to touch his dirty blond hair. He covered her hand with his, freezing its movement. His brown eyes lit up then, and she could see how much the words affected him.

"You do?"

"Yes. I do." It was no use fighting it anymore. She loved him, whether it was wise or not. Whether she'd live or not.

"I love you, too."

She pulled him close then and kissed him, the passion igniting almost the second their lips touched. Suddenly, it wasn't just a kiss, it was a promise, a hope, her hunger for him, her want to have a future, in every lash of her tongue. Suddenly, she didn't feel light-headed, or sick, or in any way held back. She was a woman in love with a man, and showing him just how much she did love him. She devoured him with her mouth, and wrapped her fingers in his shirt. She pulled him on top of her, but then he broke the kiss.

"Is this okay?" he asked her, eyes filled with concern. "You sure with—" She put her finger over his lips. She didn't want to hear about her blackout moment. She felt as if she now had something to prove. That she was still strong enough for this. That the cancer hadn't won. Not yet.

"It's more than okay," she said, and wrapped her arms around his neck as she felt his delicious weight on her body. She could feel the want in him growing through the thin fabric of her jumper, and she welcomed it. She reached up, hoping to wrap her arms around his neck, but found herself hemmed in by the cushions of the couch. Liam fought the constraints of the attached pillows, too. He pulled himself up.

"Maybe we should take this to the bed," he offered.

"Yes," she said, voice thick with want. "We should."

Liam walked her across his efficiency, up the single step to his bed, near the open windows. She attacked him almost before they'd made it to the bed's edge. She wanted to drink him in, wanted to drown in him. He peeled off her jumper, as she tugged at his shirt. Soon, their clothes were off. He'd reached for a condom at the bedside table, and rolled it on to himself, even as she waited in anticipation. When he moved on top of her, her legs parted, and he filled her deliberately, never breaking eye contact. She gasped at the sensation, sucking in a breath. As he began to move in her slowly, reverentially.

She felt like she was drowning in his eyes, as he gently moved inside her, building her want, the need, in her. He held most of his weight on his elbows. She'd never stared into a man's eyes like this before during sex, and she felt carried away, felt lost in his loving gaze. Time stopped then, their bodies coming together in a dance that she remembered was supposed to make life. And it did make life, inside her very core, the very act making her feel wildly alive, making her feel as if she was immortal.

"I love you, Cecily," he said, the words melting her from the inside.

"I love you, too." She stroked his face, as her body opened for him. She wanted this moment to last forever, wanted them to be entwined like this for all time.

The need in her grew, the want, the desire for him, for life, for all of it. She spread her legs further, letting him in deeper, to a place she didn't even know she had. And when she came, she never broke eye contact, kept her gaze fixed on his, and watched the wonder spread across his face as he watched her. She'd never felt more intimate with anyone, more vulnerable, more herself. He came then, too, and she saw the love for her in his eyes, how he was overcome with it in that moment. She laughed a little, giddy, feeling that despite everything, despite her horrible prognosis, that right in this moment, she was the luckiest woman in the world.

Liam fell against her, and they both panted. Where she'd gotten the energy for that, she didn't know, but she was glad she did. He rolled off her gently and discarded the condom in the trash nearby. He lay back on the bed and kissed her, and studied her face as if she were a ghost who might disappear at any moment.

"That's one cure for fainting," she managed, laughing at her weak joke.

"Are you okay?" he asked, voice suddenly full of concern.

"Better than okay," she assured him, rolling to her side, meeting his worried gaze. He relaxed a bit. And stroked her hair. They stared at each other for who knows how long. Time didn't seem to work normally when they were together. It both moved too fast and too slow, all at the same time.

He stroked her face, a gentle touch, a reverential touch.

"I want to marry you," Liam said.

The pronouncement took her by surprise, and she froze beneath him. She searched his eyes but found only shimmering honesty there. "I want you to be my wife."

"I want that, too," she told him, the truth coming out of her unbidden. She wanted to be his in all the ways that mattered, no matter how short a time.

"Good, because I want to have a dozen kids with you, all with your beautiful blue eyes," he said.

She couldn't help but laugh, thinking he was joking.

"I'm not kidding. After this surgery, after you're all healed, I want at least three kids. At *least*."

"You do?" She tried to keep her tone teasing and light, but something solemn and heavy was pulling at her heart.

"Yes. And I know you want to be a mother. I saw you looking at those kids at the zoo. I've always wanted to be a father, so let's do this. Let's just do it."

He made it sound so easy, as if they were a normal couple, as if the hard truth of the biology and the science didn't matter.

"But—" she tried, even as he put a single finger across her lips.

"No," he said, shaking his head. "No bad vibes. No doubts. Let's just focus on your recovery. I *know* it will happen."

She wanted to believe him, wanted more than anything to be his wife, have his children, live a long and happy life together, and yet, despite the hope in his brown eyes, all she felt inside was dread. She tried not to think about how she could make him a widow in a few short months. About how maybe she wouldn't even live long enough to exchange vows with this beautiful man. Because despite his shining hope, his brilliant optimism, she wasn't sure, deep down, that she shared it.

And then there was the nagging fear, the one planted by Harley. What if he lost interest when she was no longer a damsel in need of saving?

"What happens when the cancer is gone?"

"What do you mean?" Liam asked, sitting up a little. "Then, we celebrate."

"What if I'm not a damsel who needs saving anymore?"

"You'll always need saving. From jerks at dive bars, or anybody else," Liam teased, wrapping her up in his arms, and tickling her. She laughed, unable to help herself. And, yet, inside her, the nagging doubt persisted. She went into Liam's arms, anyway, the doubts growing louder in her head. "You won't grow bored with me."

"Never."

"And what about Wilder? He thinks I'm just after your money. Will he—or your family—really even accept me?" She thought about how they doubted her, about how Wilder thought she was a fraud.

"They can't tell you you're a fraud after the surgery. And besides, who cares what they think? I don't." Liam shook his head.

But Cecily did. That was the thing. How could she tell him that? It mattered to her.

"So, Wilder wants to parade me around to his investors, pretend we're all just one big happy family. That's fine. As long as he pays for the surgery. I don't care."

"Maybe they really love you. Maybe Wilder wants to make amends."

Liam snorted. "Doubtful."

"If you really don't want to return to the family, you don't have to. Not for my sake."

"I'd walk through fire for you, Cecily. I'd happily give up anything for you." His words buoyed her high up into the sky, but then the reality of what his loyalty meant sent her crashing down again.

She believed him, too. Believed that he'd do most anything for her. And that's what worried her. Would he sacrifice all his values in the process? Would he give away everything that he held dear? And what if the surgery didn't work? Would he have betrayed his heart, given up his freedom, and for what?

"We're going to grow old together, Cecily," he promised her, as he kissed her hair. "I know we will."

Suddenly, his bright outlook just seemed far-fetched, seemed impossible. But she stayed silent, not wanting to dim his hopes. He pulled her close, kissing her neck, as a single tear slid from her eye and down her cheek.

She'd spent a fitful and sleepless night in Liam's bed. He'd slept soundly the entire night, cocooned in his hope, cradled in his positivity and his dreams about the future. But she was weighed down by the present, by the hopelessness of it. Yes, the surgery might work, but what if it didn't? What if all she could offer Liam was pain and grief? And, yes, part of her was scared, too, scared of letting hope in. Hope was dangerous. Hope meant she had something to live for, something valuable she could lose.

Everything suddenly seemed so complicated. And dangerous.

That was why later that morning, she'd told Liam she needed to go to her place, shower and change and take care of her cat. That she'd meet him later for dinner, because she needed to run some errands on her own. He'd been surprised. After all, they'd been nearly inseparable for most of their short time together, the urgency of time on both of their minds. But he let her go. And as soon as she left, she headed straight to Wilder Lange's penthouse. She didn't even know if the man was home, didn't even know if this was a fool's errand, but she had to try.

Jacob let her in with a surprised smile. "We weren't expecting you, Miss Cecily," he said, and she was flattered he remembered her name. "I'm afraid Miss Harley is out at the moment."

"I'm here to see Wilder. If he'll see me." Jacob nodded, disappearing down the long corridor, and then reappearing again. "Right this way, Miss Cecily."

Inside Wilder's study, Liam's brother sat behind his big desk, laptop open. He stood when she entered, though he kept a carefully guarded expression fixed to his face. She expected it. Knew that he probably thought she was just here to ask for money. She almost laughed thinking how wrong he was.

"I'm sorry for barging in like this, but I needed to talk to you." Wilder's gaze seemed to grow darker, more resigned. She barreled on before she lost her nerve. "I think you shouldn't buy Liam's board seat."

Wilder's eyebrows raised in genuine surprise. "But your surgery? I thought it was the only treatment open to you."

"It is. But Liam's sacrificing too much for it. For me." She clasped her hands, twisting her fingers. "I tried to tell him that, but he won't listen. He wants to marry me."

Wilder's mouth parted in further shock. "Marry you?" he echoed.

She nodded. "I love him. There's nothing more I

would want than to be his wife. Except he's giving up too much. I don't want him to sacrifice everything, only to watch me die if this surgery doesn't work. After I'm gone, he'll just be left with the knowledge that he sold out to you, and it was all for naught. It's not fair to him."

Wilder swiped a hand through his dark hair, his eyes never leaving her. "You realize that if he does return to the family, that he will once again be eligible for his share of the company, and eventually, for a substantial inheritance. In the meantime, his company shares now are worth hundreds of millions."

She didn't know this. But it didn't change her mind. She knew Liam's thoughts about money. About how much pride he took in being on his own.

"And that if you marry him," Wilder continued, "you, too, would have half that share."

"I don't care about money," she said, lifting her chin. "I care about Liam. He's put too much hope on this surgery. He thinks it will all work out, but…"

"You don't," Wilder finished.

Tears choked her. She nodded. She struggled to regain control of her voice and found it. "If you care about Liam at all, you'll not do this. You'll tell him no."

Wilder leaned back, studying her. "Okay, then," he said after a beat. "I'll do what you ask."

CHAPTER SIXTEEN

LIAM WANTED TO KNOW what the hell was going on. All afternoon, Cecily ignored his texts and phone calls. Sure, she'd been distant and odd that morning, but now, as he stood on her porch, ringing her buzzer and finding no answer, he was beginning to think something was very, very wrong. He glanced up at her window, and saw her cat, Tripp, in the window, flicking his tail and looking serene. Though her cat wasn't likely to tell him if something was wrong. He had a flash of a million dire emergencies. Cecily fainting and hitting her head. Cecily getting hit by a car on her way home. All of them, somehow, with Cecily on the ground, unresponsive.

He tamped down the panic. She was probably fine. She was probably just mad at him. But why? He'd proposed. He thought she'd been happy about that. As he glanced at her door, wondering if he should try to get in somehow, check to make sure she wasn't sprawled on her apartment floor, his phone rang. He yanked it out of his back jean pocket but was disappointed to see Wilder calling. He thought about sending it to voice mail, but then thought this couldn't be a coincidence.

"Hello?" he answered, tentative.

"Cecily really loves you," Wilder said without preamble.

"Well, no shit," Liam grumbled, but he wasn't feeling the love right at this moment as he glanced at Tripp in her window. Where was she? Deliberately ignoring him? Or hurt and needing him in an ER somewhere?

"She came by today."

All the warning lights in Liam's brain clicked on at once. "And?"

"And she tried to convince me *not* to give you the money for her surgery."

"What?" What the hell? "Did you listen to her?"

"I did. I told her I'd do as she asked."

Liam felt a sliver of ice slice through his belly. "You can't do that."

"Well, I can," Wilder pointed out. And here it was, Liam thought. One more time Wilder would disappoint him, one more time Wilder would fail him when he needed him most. Wilder took a deep breath on the other end of the line. "But, I won't."

"Wait. I don't understand."

"If you come back to the family, you'll be eligible for your inheritance."

"What inheritance? I thought you stole it."

"I'm the trustee. Your money is still there, Liam.

I tried to tell you before. You didn't want to listen because you hated that I was in charge."

"Maybe that was true. Or maybe I just hated what money did to this family." Liam had never wanted to listen to anything Wilder had to say. Liam also knew he'd spent years punishing his brother for a crime that maybe his brother hadn't committed.

"I get it. I do. Money can corrupt people. I told Cecily you'd be a millionaire, if you came back to the family."

"And?" Liam felt his stomach twist a little. Even now part of him worried she'd change her mind. Like so many other women he knew, that the money would make a difference.

"And she told me she wasn't interested. She just wanted to make sure that you didn't sacrifice your principles because of her. That's why she doesn't want the money."

"That's ridiculous," Liam sputtered. But then again, it did sound like Cecily. "I'd do anything so she could get this surgery."

"About that," Wilder said, voice turning somber. "She's really worried it might not work. She's worried that she's going to die and break your heart. She doesn't want to do that to you."

"She doesn't get to decide what I risk," Liam said.

"You might want to tell her that." For the first time in a very long time, Liam felt like Wilder was the older brother he always hoped he would be. That maybe he'd been wrong. Maybe there was more to

Wilder than just greed. "Oh, and Cecily is a good woman. A very good woman. You've done well there." He paused. "And just so you know, I'm proud of you, brother."

He stood stock-still on the sidewalk outside Cecily's apartment, processing what he just heard. His half brother was proud of him. He'd never known until right at that moment that his half brother's approval had even been something he'd wanted. But, he realized he did. Somewhere, deep inside him, Wilder's approval still mattered. Even though he'd spent years trying to convince himself it didn't.

"You are?"

"Yes. You struck out. Made something of yourself. Supported yourself on your own terms. I'm proud of you. Dad would be, too."

He felt emotion well up in his throat. "Thanks," he said, meaning it. Maybe there was hope after all that they could be true brothers again. Or, short of that, not enemies.

"Listen, I've been thinking," Wilder said. "Why don't I just give you your shares of the company, to do with what you will?"

Liam's guard went up. "What's the catch?"

"None," Wilder said. "You don't have to come to Thanksgiving. You don't have to be a part of the family if you don't want to. Hell, you can give the entire sum to your mother if you'd like. I won't stop you."

Liam couldn't have been more shocked. Wilder

had spent years scheming to keep money out of his mother's hands.

"I've been talking to Harley, and..." Wilder paused. "She's made me see that the tough love act I've been doing with you was all wrong. All I ever wanted was for you to come back to the family. I thought this was the way to do it, by being strict with your inheritance, by giving you ultimatums. But I was wrong. I'm sorry."

Liam checked the sky, half expecting to see pigs fly. Wilder was apologizing? Really?

"Why are you doing this?"

"Look, Harley has taught me a lot. And I know the kind of love I have with Harley is the kind of love you have with Cecily. I'm not going to stand in the way of that."

Liam suddenly felt full of gratitude, and felt, for the first time, he might actually really be understood, really seen by his brother.

"What do you think I should do? About Cecily?" he asked, the question surprising even himself. Was Liam truly asking Wilder for advice?

Wilder paused, seeming to be surprised himself.

"Cecily is just scared," Wilder said after recovering. "I would be, too. She's worried none of it will work out, so she's deciding that it's safer not to try. She doesn't want to face the possibility of death and the possibility that she's made you give up too much."

"That's crazy," Liam said.

"I know. But it's just human. Right?"

"I guess."

"She thinks she's doing the right thing by leaving. But if I were you, though, I'd not let her go."

"I don't plan on it," Liam said.

Liam decided to camp out on Cecily's stoop. There was nothing else to do. Eventually, she'd have to come home, or leave, if she was hidden inside. During that time, waiting, he thought of all the million things he was going to say to convince her she shouldn't be scared. That risking the surgery was the right thing to do, regardless of how it turned out. Eventually, she did come walking down the sidewalk, grocery bag in hand. She froze as she saw him, slowing her steps to her stoop.

"What are you doing here?" she asked, eyes darting around as if he'd materialized from nowhere.

"Looking for you," he said. "You're not returning my calls."

"I know. I—" She hesitated, lowering her long lashes.

"You told Wilder not to give me the money for the surgery. Why?" He took a step closer. She grasped her grocery bag a little tighter.

"Because I can't let you risk everything for me. This surgery is a long shot. It probably won't even work."

"We don't know that."

"You're too optimistic," she said, hurt in her eyes. "None of this could work, and then what? You're indebted to Wilder for the rest of your life? You have no independence and you're dragged right back into the family you swore would never own you?" She set down her bag on the sidewalk. "I can't let you do that. Not for me."

"You don't get to decide that," he said. "Besides, I think I might have been wrong about Wilder."

"Really?" Now he had her attention.

"Yeah. I mean, I'm still not sure I trust him, but he told me about your meeting. And seemed to really be rooting for us. And I don't think that has anything to do with the company or profits. He told me he'd give me shares of the company with no strings. I could do what I want with them."

Cecily gaped. "What are you going to do?"

"Take the money. To help you."

"No. I don't want you to sacrifice for me. Not like this."

"It's not a sacrifice. If anything, I realize that maybe I do want some contact with the family. Maybe I was wrong. Maybe spending some holidays with them wouldn't be the end of the world."

Cecily blinked fast, processing the information. "Really?"

"Yes. And I know you're scared." Liam pulled Cecily into his arms and she went, her mind still whirling. "I know this is terrifying. But I want you to have this surgery. I want you to try. For me." He hugged her tight. "I know it's scary. I know it might not work out, but isn't our love worth risking this for?"

"Yes, but—" Cecily pulled back a little.

"I want all the time I can get with you," Liam said. "And if that's just a few months, then that's okay. I'd rather spend a few months with you than never having known you at all."

"But what if it shortens our time together?"

"Then we'll just take advantage of the time we *do* have," he said.

Tears sprung to Cecily's eyes. "I love you so very much," she said, voice breaking.

"And I love you," Liam said. "So, please tell me this means you'll do this surgery."

"Yes," she said, sniffling and wiping her eyes. "Yes, I will."

"Good," he said. "Now, let's figure out how we're going to get to Tokyo."

"Traveling is on my bucket list," she said, grinning. "Any chance we could go through London and Paris on the way?"

"Considering they're in the *exact* opposite direction of Tokyo?" Liam pretended to think. Cecily gave him a playful punch. He laughed. "That could be arranged. If…"

"If what?"

"If you marry me," Liam said. Liam kneeled in front of her, and Cecily dropped her grocery bag.

Cecily felt all the air leave her lungs. Could she do this? Could she take this risk? She felt fear rising in her and knew she feared losing him. But she also realized in that moment that if she walked away now, she was giving up too soon.

"Yes. I will," she said, not even quite believing her own answer. Yet, in her heart, she knew it was the only one that made any sense in a world that too often didn't.

"Then Paris and London it is," Liam said. "Anything my *fiancée* wants, my *fiancée* will get." And he rose then to his full height, pulled her into his arms and covered her lips with his.

EPILOGUE

Two years later

CECILY SAT IN the waiting room of the fancy doctor's office on the Upper East Side, clasping Liam's hand. The overhead lights shone on her large diamond engagement ring and wedding band, flashing bright white. She'd worn it to Paris and to London, and then eventually to Tokyo. She still couldn't believe all the things they'd managed to do in so short a time. Her head was bursting with memories, her heart filled with love for her husband, and for all that they'd done together. This was more time than she'd ever thought she'd have, and every new day that dawned, brought her more gratitude.

"Mrs. Lange?" the medical technician, a woman with short dark hair wearing blue scrubs, called from the door, and Cecily started. Even now, she was still getting used to her new name. Liam squeezed her hand and they both stood, following the medical technician to the exam room.

"Nervous?" the woman asked her. She read her name tag: Aliyah Jennings.

"A little," Cecily admitted.

"A lot," Liam added, and they both laughed.

"My husband is always brutally honest, Ms. Jennings," Cecily explained.

"Call me Aliyah, and I don't mind at all. But y'all have nothing to worry about. This is the easy part." She indicated the gurney in the room. "If you would, just take off your top and put on this." She held up a short hospital gown. "With the ties in the front."

Cecily glanced at the blue cloth shirt with the white ties and remembered all the times she'd been in hospital gowns over the last two years. The surgery in Tokyo, the recovery, and, then, the second surgery. Aliyah left the room and Liam shut the door. She tugged off her sweater, aware of the scar along her torso. Small, but there. The doctors had managed to get the cancer. She'd been cancer-free for more than a year. So far, that is. She'd have to have regular medical checkups maybe for the rest of her life to make sure the cancer didn't come back.

"Need help?" Liam asked, moving toward her as she unlatched the back of her bra.

"Not your kind of help," she teased, and he flashed her a wolfish grin. If he had his way, they'd be naked and doing it on the exam table in five seconds flat. Not exactly what the medical technician would expect, she thought.

"I can restrain myself," Liam said, taking her lacy

demi-cup bra as she slid into the gown, tying it at the front.

"Can you?" she asked, skeptical.

"Maybe," he said, sliding a hand around her back and tugging her to him, laying a long, slow kiss on her lips.

A hard knock came at the door then. "Ready?" Aliyah called.

Reluctantly, Cecily broke the embrace. "Unfortunately, too ready," Liam complained, rubbing the fly of his jeans. Cecily giggled, and gave him a playful slap on the arm.

"Ready," Cecily said. The medical technician bustled in, smiling at them both.

"If you would, just go ahead and lie down on the gurney here," Aliyah said. Cecily obeyed, and the technician undid the lower half of her gown, so that her belly was exposed. Cecily wondered about the white scar of her surgery, wondered if Aliyah noticed it. If she did, she didn't say anything. Liam moved to her side, to hold her hand.

"Now, I'm just going to put some gel here on your belly," Aliyah said as she spread the gel around Cecily's torso. Then, she grabbed a wand and held it against Cecily's belly. The medical technician flipped the ultrasound machine on and studied the monitor.

"What do you see?" Cecily asked, inwardly sending up a prayer.

"Well, this is unexpected," Aliyah said, squinting

at the monitor. Cecily grasped Liam's hand tighter. Liam moved toward the screen.

"Is something wrong?" Bad news was what neither one of them wanted. Not after more than a year of being cancer-free. They desperately wanted good news. But, Cecily worried, had their good luck run out?

"Not wrong," the medical tech said. She turned the screen toward both Liam and Cecily. "But did you know you were having twins?"

"What?" Cecily arched her neck and glanced at the screen. There, on the fuzzy ultrasound monitor, she saw two distinct babies, not one. They were small still, but she saw tiny hands and the shape of two distinct bodies.

"We are?" Liam's joy came through in his voice.

"Looks like a boy and a girl," Aliyah said, glancing at the fuzzy images. "So, congratulations, Mom and Dad, you've got a set, one of each."

Cecily laughed. A boy and a girl. Liam beamed at her, and she grinned back.

"You wanted an instant family," she told him.

"I did." He almost seemed to be reeling from the news. "And now we've got one."

"You okay with that?" Cecily asked, studying his face.

"More than okay with that," Liam said, grinning at her. She saw the pure joy on his face, and his happiness was contagious. "I told you everything would work out. And you doubted me."

"Is he always so cocky?" Aliyah joked.

"Always." Cecily grinned at him, tears of joy in her eyes. "You were right, and I was wrong."

"Can I have that put in writing?"

Aliyah shook her head. "You are pushing your luck, mister," she warned him. "This lovely lady is carrying *two* of your babies."

"And I couldn't be happier about it," Liam said.

"Then you'd better get over here and kiss me," Cecily said, feeling one happy tear slip down her cheek. Liam wiped it away.

"You don't have to ask me twice," Liam said, and bent down to give her a kiss filled with love, promise and, most of all, hope for the future they'd share together—with their new family.

* * * * *

COMING SOON!

We really hope you enjoyed reading this book.
If you're looking for more romance, be sure to
head to the shops when new books are
available on

Thursday 18th March

To see which titles are coming soon, please visit

millsandboon.co.uk/nextmonth

MILLS & BOON
A ROMANCE FOR EVERY READER

- **FREE** delivery direct to your door
- **EXCLUSIVE** offers every month
- **SAVE** up to 25% on pre-paid subscriptions

SUBSCRIBE AND SAVE

millsandboon.co.uk/Subscribe